WATER
in the
BELLY

WATER
in the
BELLY

D.L. Snow

ARPress
45 Dan Road Suite 5
Canton MA 02021

Hotline: 1(888) 821-0229
Fax: 1(508) 545-7580

Ordering Information:
Quantity sales. Special discounts are available on quantity purchases by corporations, associations, and others. For details, contact the publisher at the address above.

Printed in the United States of America.
ISBN-13:   Paperback   979-8-89389-293-2
              eBook   979-8-89389-294-9

Library of Congress Control Number: 2024908717

CONTENTS

Part III

To

Ishmael Reed

For

State Constitution Clauses that read there should be no impairment of obligation of Contracts, in right-to-work states, control by Republicans. But see Reich infra.

Introduction

<u>Water</u> <u>In</u> <u>the</u> <u>Belly</u> is a serious story by Frank, a half-caste African American, in a hybrid, anti-novel haphazared parody in shreds and patches of Homer's <u>The Odyssey</u>. The following book is a tragedy. This is a postmodern parody.

This is also an, in fact, pastiche of Capitalism. The story is a fictional road to book or reality book or band novel or world book. The story is not a satire of any political party. It's bipartisan. I call it modern, or a subset called postmodern, P.M.

It's the genre of Book of the Depression in Blues.

Return To Depression Economics, was a book our would be person on an odyssey, had read in late 2008, before the start of our story, a mirror of what president Obama was facing, in the USA. Frank is like Odysseus. Sherry is a type like his heroine wide Penelope. This is a free-form parody, linked to the years 2009-2022, not to our Homer's world. Some of it is in the mix. I don't necessarily agree with their lifestyle. As his story is told, I don't endorse. James Joyce, he was too much. This fourth edition book is rated like PG-13. This is a petition and educational.

This like goes on the World Wide Web. And over half the world is religious, like Odysseus, in Homer. And there are many conflicts of laws in specific nations, on the internet, that overturn-<u>free speech.</u> Decipher. The brilliant, recent translation, by Robert Fagless and introduction and notes by Mr. Knox, is the base <u>The Odyssey</u> I use as my help. with his artistic translations, like the "rose-red fingers of down."

The world of ancient Greece, is connected to the ideology of the Gods of Greeks in times of old. I have put in Religion to mirror that ideology and makes Homer's references to God meaningful. To the modern reader like the stories' two ideologies of the church of pride and the church of zen. The former church takes as its belief <u>Homo Dei</u>, God is humanity. The latter church has the belief in the suffering of Humanity and the necessity to be redeemed from that to consciousness of "nothingness". Sherry's religion is the Catholic Church. We need our mythodology to let us get a foothold on the world of Homer. The dead immortal God like Zeus. <u>The Odyssey</u> is the story of a man who spent 10 years at war and spent 10 years coming home, with references to <u>TheIliad</u> throughout the former classic by Homer. It's all time, the tropes of history. For Public Policy.

Paul Ricoeur, in <u>the Just</u>, deals with the philosphoy of contracts, not totally unlike real estate contacts, a topic of close. Interest to Frank's brother. Frank gets a loan to get on MBA degree, which he supplements with his work in a band, <u>The Cherry</u>, like the crew of Odysseus. Tele machus becomes Justin. Troy is Frank's landlord.

The United States Supreme Court, in <u>2 Live Crew</u>, held that a parody is "fair use" of copyrighted material, Hence the shreds and patches of postmodern parody, the very definition of postmodernism, like the Broadway hit "The West Side Story". Symbolism is the key to this anti-novel, postmodernism declaring that the era of the novel is like propaganda, like in <u>Lost In The Funhouse</u>. Here, by ship the oceans waves coming into the belly of the sail. And Sherry gives birth to a new social world, with the birth of her baby Rosa.

Ethics of Greek mythology, had its own logic. There was the belief that the Gods looked after the homeless or the stranger. In <u>The Odyssey</u>, much time is spent here by Odysseus. I minimized this and spend Frank's time on his Odysseus through Capitalism.

Presumptive it is to talk about late Capitalism, as if someone were outside our Galaxy, and telling us a story, that most people could not describe. In the long run, this book is the story of Frank and Sherry's Odyssey, not Homer's. Post existentialism, PE, is a type of PM, like practiced by Mr. Paul Ricoeur, a teacher of mine at the University of

Chicago. Paul substituted existentialist's 150 year preoccupation with death for the idea that between birth and death, we have the tropes of history and fictional narratives. I am <u>not</u> Frank Holmes. <u>Fiat Lux.</u> I like James Baldwin. Odysseus is a tragic hero. My PM was Humanism and Stiglitz on " Economics". Not a word about "Capitalism".

The Trump administration is barely mentioned, though the end of the book was 2020. The protests went on. There are many questions in this book: How did Frank get here? Was it his utilitarian search for pleasure? Frank breaks with racial stereotypes? Given president Obama, can't a black person work and talk in a race neutral way? What does Mr. Reed, U.C. Berkeley teacher, tell us about Frank Holmes? Is the reader like a Sherlock Holmes? Justice Holmes? Allow people to be content, in the end, streaming <u>The</u> <u>Odyssey</u>, on the download.

I have a thesis that I have not seen in the literature on Odysseus. In this epic, I view him as tragic. It's not just a story of conquest and romance. There is something in Homer's character that is tragic. It is close to say that it ends in romance, as I add an extra chapter on "The music of the spheres". Before that, in chapter 22, Odysseus acts violently. Rather than just talking to the suitors, and evicting them from this house, he goes through this terrible "Slaughter in the Hall". I am unaware that anyone has, thus, evaluated Odysseus' character in terms of the <u>tragic</u>, in light of the literary criticism of Aristotle. There is no time to do that here. Let it be. It is what it is. Odysseus just becomes <u>the</u> <u>stranger</u> in his own home. And then, unintentionally, defends himself and an third party, with questions about his behavior. Not totally unlike our Mark Twain, and yet we love him. And love the above, we do.

In <u>The</u> <u>Limits</u> <u>of</u> <u>Critique,</u> Ms. Felski gives a good summary of post-1970's cultural and literary criticism. What I call CCC, or Chicago Cultural Criticism, is what I mean of post-modern critique. In Felski's book she notes that Paul Ricoeur's "interpretation of doubt" is linked with the cultural criticism of Nietzsche, Marx and Freud, even counting consciousness itself into suspicion, like Zen. What she calls post-critical I call postmodernism. There is postmodern art, which is parody, like this anti novel. There is post-modernist Critique, which follows. The key to both is to read with-doubt. I disagree with what her postcritical critique <u>declines</u> to do. But I am the PM writer, not critic. The following though is PM critique. I am not a critic. But let's use the above account of doubt to deconstruct. PM criticism is perfect for PM Art.

There is a big "gap" between the world of Homer and ours. Hence, the parody. I wish to score some points about the social construction of reality. That's why the "fate" of an ancient Greek God like Zeus, is so foreign to the modern. Because of Homer's Olympic Gods are foreign, there is a great deal of "Uncertainty" as to what the texts means to us. We resist the parody, therefore. There is a prison-house of "language" in Homer, and our translator's offering is so much like a novel. So I want the reader to "interrogate" the text. And to diagnose the "Symptoms" of hidden anxiety. This book is Me Blues

"Language" socially constructs our reality that's why the translator's text is probably the best of Homer's <u>the Odyssey</u>. Postmodern texts, like this anti-novel, have "play" in them, apparent mistakes are left as is the text of first person narrator, Frank Holmes, mostly. The reader should <u>doubt</u> the cultural Hierarchies of Frank's world. There is a "Slippage of Signs" from Homer to Holmes, because this pastiche shows the different worlds. Deconstruct binaries of opposites if you can find them. Where would you place Justin. To celebrate the "gaps" or contradictions in this texts. Hence we have a death of writer and a birth of the reader, unlike the mention of the rite of the <u>Egyptian</u> <u>Book</u> <u>of</u> <u>the</u> <u>Dead</u>. The read is subjective. Contrary to Frank's statements I embrace Saussure's theory of Modern linguistics. That's why the "signifier" of Zeus has a walking-the-pain "signified", because I put in Zen to link the reader to the writer Homer. The meta-narrative of <u>The</u> <u>Odyssey</u> is broken here. And Odysseus becomes a tragic character. Altering the "genre" from the generally receive Odysseus to better fit into Aristotle's genre of the "tragedy". Like Trump's Big Denial.

Why read? Why is literature relevant? It's <u>politics</u> here. We read to see both sides in a political debate, that is taking place in cycles of crisis. It's to see why one side is tragic. Why the action of <u>the</u> <u>Odyssey</u> is tragic, and not a warm, fuzzy mood of "coming home". It's a context for self-examination. Am I like Frank Holmes? He is black because of defamiliarization, to rethink the classic of Homer, the foundation of <u>Civilization's Cultural Critique</u>, CCC. ECON is the tragedy.

We read to get rid of the headache of life. To ask why read, is to say why have eros in our lives. And to see questions in our hear that I know we have never asked. Because we have taken for granted the normal in our life. That's why I justify the existence of writing. To offer a cultural critique of the environment we don't see, because we are like fishes swimming in water. We don't recognize what should be obvious, but is not. That's the answer to Sartre's question-why write? That's the same question as, why read? We read history, so we don't make mistakes again. It's to perform a civilization's cultural critique. So that we can become good citizens. To stop being so wrong in our social ethics. It's to seek after a text that was encoded with hidden meanings<u>. Where the reader is like a detective in a story of </u>Betray and <u>Deny.</u> The crimes of people Frank Holmes meets on his odyssey. Through local politics of the obligation of contracts to the international politics that the CIA even misses. It's why read the mighty news? So we don't get fooled. That's the reason for Ricoeur's "interpretation of suspicion". To read <u>with</u> doubt, so that when we get called into court, we can say we are not guilty beyond a reasonable doubt.

The riot of Being January 6, 2021 at the Capital was alleged by the Democrats to be an insurrection riot. Despite 52 Federal laws suits including the U.S. Sp. Ct, No evidence was found that the 2020 election had any fraud in any state. Over half of republicans still believe the proud 2020 elections was fraudulent. This event caused the biggest threat to US Democracy in 200 years. Other Republicans are living in Denial as to Pres. Biden being the Real President. If you accept this you're a Democrat. And do not accept – The Big Denial!. Trump thought that he would be indicted for Fraud. Thumbs up for the systems of The Whale at sea.

Some State Constitutions have clauses, in right-to-work States which read " No obligation of contract shall be impaired". These are generally proud Republican States. Reich in The System, at P.120 said Democrats have forgot these locals. Such new Right-to-work states, among others are Wisconsin, West Virginia, Indiana, Utah and Michigan.

-D.L. Snow 2023

Earn
10¢
LOOK
M

PART I

Like Wordsworth's The Prelude,

Consciousness is a rite.

Frank is a humanist.

Frank's character hates revolution.

In trope, a non-literal sign,

This book is a rite, metaphor and symbolic,

Primitive, hegemony in culture.

In the waste land, without the morals of Nietzsche.

In a parody of rituals, our trope, our rite, or non-literal poetry, this is a parody of necessity of songs, prodigals,

and MBA students who can't find work and form a band.

Ironically, a Dante's "Inferno," frozen,

Down into the terrible, icy, of mythology and ritual,

Is left with only the ethics of Aristotle and little else to guide.

They are tragic, they deal with common law marriage,

It's this that needs to be redeemed. Not with morals but with ethics.

Victor Turner, humanist and anthropologist of Frank's Mother's Tribe in Zambia, Africa,

Makes this like Conrad's <u>Heart of Darkness.</u> Through a rite.

Thus, this novel is structured like a Ritual.

Frank's mother was an NDembu.

This is neo-Keynesian. That is, trade cycles are not a self-correcting system. So we need regulations over

stocks and banks and factories at a Fed level.

Chapter 1

COMMON LAW

-1-

Homer begins his novel with song. Singing of water, Sherry drank from a water bottle, to toast our Frank. Feeling of the World Trade Organization, Frank said, "Why drinking water?". Frank now is a Democrat. And a tragic one. We use fair use. That lets us laugh, in a with <u>black</u> comedy, with Holmes. It's gallows humor. Of 2009. Right after the stock market crash in the year of 2008. Politics and the world and the cosmos and the Universe and the solar system and <u>dark</u> matter, The economy looked so bad, after 2008, all you could do was laugh. He was born in Selma. Having gone to Cal and Chicago made him. Like a country boy, going to Stanford and Yale. This novel is a character portrait of a changing person leaving us as if he were to become an <u>Ahab</u> or like <u>Faust</u> that makes you glad you don't have the character of our ever-changing, anti-hero, Frank Holmes. The plot is his progress.

- - -

Homes, Homies, Holmes, Homer.

"You spit it out!", said Sherry, knowing Frank's sin of pride, like Ahab in *Moby-Dick*?

"Why?", said Frank, one palm over the back of the other hand, thinking of the unity of capitalism and Christianity, like Max Weber.

"""

"To put out the fire", said Sherry, arms crossed, with both thumbsup. After a pause in the symbolic conversation, Frank asked "Why not just pour the Troy bottle on the fire?". Sherry responded, "It's not just literal. It's symbolic. It's a metaphor. You drink the water which is cool and you put it on all the bad or red or burning things". They were standing in the plaza, in peaceful assembly on private property, redressing grievances on political issues, and about economic issues, legal under state law. Sherry is a beautiful, ethical Republican. She was born in Poland. In Central Europe. She looked like a young Angelina Jolie. Peerless. She moved with grace and victimhood, with sensual beauty like a movie star. She was a good Catholic and guilty about her relations with Frank. But the portrait is of one character finding grace, looking like a ringer for Pres Obama our hero in this parody of Homer's coming home poem or novel. Frank, redeemed from guilt and poverty. The start, here, of putting water on fire is the symbol or signal or sign or image or opposite meaning of the non-literal metaphor trope, used to explain the title. Does it mirror, even in a little way, James Joyce's *A Portrait of The Artist As A Young Man*.

They were in London Plaza, of Pomegranate University. It was Presidents day of 2009. President Obama had just signed his economic stimulus bill. Very controversial. Sherry and Frank were shacked up together under California common law. Doing their mythology, on a campus within 5 miles of UCLA, having a few fools, twisting and turning. Symbolic novels are like turning poetry into narrative. Being right, Sherry, a Republican going back to some Eden of America, to a Conservative place in the past, where they could hide, like back to a farm in the country home, like flying to the moon, being The President, was the thing on their minds. The stock market, that had just crashed in 2008, was the conservative cause of what looked like the start of a new Depression. That's why so many people jumped over to Obama's ship. It was cool to back the Democratic President, then. He had the energy and the people. And the world.

How is the maturing Frank like a live character? With Frank's sarcastic, liberal parody changing in his heart, this is a serious, or sarcastic or realistic self-portrait? What changed in his character? When? Was the change believable? What is mythology, here? Why wasn't it fantasy, like the popular Harry Potter? He became a likable man? Why was this change of character a necessity? Did Frank misread politics, with President Obama around Valentine's Day of 2012, at a high of 50%? When Frank jumped the ship in late 2011? Why was in the back of Frank's mind and body, his own state or economics or politics, a marker for Frank's Character? Did it have anything to do with the way he was evolving in his personal life like the proof or Evidence in his songs? Did Frank take as serious the "State Police, Ferguson and other late 2014 race riots: A Plessey v. Ferguson."

- - -

Is Frank's character a solid portrait, no matter what the national political mood? Why is Frank's pride transformation change or <u>civil religion</u>, that is politics sounding like ethical or moral or realism or mythical conversion, like Odysseus, turning for home? How were his songs proof of his Odyssey? How is this novel and title, evidence for Frank's turning and twisting on his pilgrimage or journey or flight or returning home? The last part of the novel is like a redemptive journal? Self-meditation by our Character is one way of looking at reality or fantasy life of our Frank? To be meditated on like symbolic Poetry? Gently carrying the reader home? Giving the reader symbolic rebirth, like water in the belly? Like a burning in the bosom? A fire in the head? Drinking gas so that he could spit fire? Like the refiner's fire, a birth into the future? A poem for the cosmos? Through tropes, which are like symbols or signs or tokens or signals or simple tropes, non-literal metaphors, this thing is like that thing? Through religious glass, icon candles that are generally Latino and Catholic symbols or signs or signals that visually let you see the fire of the head and the burning of the belly? Redemption for the body, from rock and roll? Redemption of the Occupy Movement people? Redemption from history itself, from the nightly TV news? Redemption from the fog of ideas in the mind as ideology, ideas that we called the pre-tropical? Meditation on the ideology of physics seeing the atom as if mysticism in the solar system? The electron going round and round in the atom and the planets going around the sun? This natural metaphor, leads Frank to contemplate what was world history to him, and see it in light of the natural laws of nature? What will our tropes, or non-literal metaphor make us center in on in or concentrate on, or meditation lead us to revolve around? If the start of Frank Holmes is from a liberal, then is the change in Character to be laughed at as gallows humor?

Given the <u>black</u> humor in the painting of the portrait, are we to believe Frank's new self? Or is it more political born posturing?

Is there something redeemable in Frank Holmes redemption? Given that this ends in a 1st person narrative, it is Frank who is painting his picture, and like in the redemption of anarchists, does Frank let in too much sarcasm, like his song "State Police"? What does this suggest as to his true political stance? Given Frank was an authority, on semiotics or signs or symbols, or NFL signs or Baseball club signals or NBA penalties, what's his motive for suddenly dropping the use of signs? Can a conservative read Frank Holmes self-portrait and believe Frank has turned? Or, is this posturing, given that nobody knows the close outcome of the fall 2012 Presidential election? Or, is Frank Holmes a believable Character? Who was really in a Dante's inferno? Who needed to be helped from his rock and roll lifestyle? Given his endorsement of the original Occupy Movement, the left, didn't he need a civil redemption away from the Occupy Wall Street movement, from the endorsement or encouragement of their slouching from the protests that went round and round the world? America is on the crossroads, is it a type? Given Europe, and The Greeks, in the modern era with National Monetary Note problems and protests of government money cuts, and the near anarchy in the streets, wasn't it smart of Frank Holmes to side with the police conservatives? And be Bipartisan when it came to law and order, his non-sarcastic intent? You might agree with Frank? You might disagree with Frank's changes? But it's a Character portrait out of a section of history that was tragic for the world. And equally tragic its People? Frank took a stand, and held his ground? Once Frank finally found what he should think for himself and his family? What is the final denotation or connotation of Frank's Character? We read that in terms of Symbol and Metaphor? Is he like a genius? Or just pitiful? Do we hate his songs because they lack meter and Rhyme? Is the sarcasm so subtle that it doesn't almost exist? Given that history almost repeats itself, isn't it self-evident that the past tropes of History can be a case for struggle in the future?Does the theme of Character's bankruptcy come across? <u>Will those following Frank's Character be like following An Ahab, who led his ship to destruction, seemingly for a reasonable motive or intention, yet out of revenge or for the reason in his mind for the purpose of a principle? Or, like a Faust, who sold his soul to evil, giving his being almost unlimited Knowledge and Power?</u> What was the significance of the trope, a non-literal metaphor, or symbol or sign or allegory or signal of the burning in the head or the burning in the bosom or water in the Belly, to Frank's Character portrait? What was proof Frank's Character hated revolution? Is that seen in the narrative of the people he supports when he was a rock and roll star or after in his sarcastic redemption, or little trope fire in the belly? What metaphor or rite does Frank go through to change his character? Is it marriage? What causes Frank's vision to go from tragedy to happy? How does this further change his Character? Can you see the connection between ideology and Physics in the last chapter? How was the espionage trope mainly sarcastic satire? How did marriage and love redeem him from his rock and roll life that put him in close contact with people that were doing things that were not good, or bad life style? How did sarcasm in his album "State Police" help in his redemption? How was Frank's Character a green rebirth? Was his use of Eros the sign that he had not changed of his low ethics and thus a false consciousness? How was his vision of atom and the cosmos a Character changing event? What and who is perfect? Is it not true, that our flaws in our Character make us human?

Foolish words by Calypso and the Sirens, made them forget home. "Fire!".

The Obama administration planned to put 2 trillion dollars into the banking system to unfreeze credit. He did this because his Cal advisor was an expert in the Depression. And it was the Depression that was caused by a collapse in the banking industry. Not very controversial. There were palm trees all around the Pomegranate University campus. This is an epic journey or real social Odyssey. Sherry and Frank had just read the Nobel prize winner, Mr. Krugman's book *The Return of Depression Economics*. A book that President Obama relied on. This part is history. It was what the Japanese did to their economy. Growth was zero. The US forgot about exports. But for Frank and Sherry,

economics was nothing compared to the morals of their life. As a source of depression, for over half the world.

Frank and Sherry are Common law married. The Holmes' family were students at Pomegranate University. They were business majors. They were studying to find a service or a commodity to hack, produce, in a factory. They believed in classical economics? After Mr. Marshall? This is Neo-Keynesian. Playing ball with President Obama. But twisting Keynes around to use writers who Keynes puts down, this was Frank's Neo-Keynesian heart, in case the <u>Washington Irving economy</u> changed again; was it a political stance and a bet and taking both sides, so as not to be a fool but a prudent and bipartisan stance to take that made him look like a genius? Nobody else had any other ideas, except go back to the so-called self-correcting, Adam Smith, total free market where it is implied that Zen runs the economy, or that some machine-like people in some Think Tank run system that got us in the visible Depression. The US needed production and rules. Like Frank felt that they needed rules to their relationship. In Los Angeles, California.

They wanted to export their product to help stabilize the Gross National Product, GNP, and the balance of trade. Sherry was an immigrant from central Poland. They were in their first year of the MBA program. Frank was working on the problems of Marshall's self-regulating economy? This slams Keynes? And liberal economics? They did this, first, because they were MBA's and, second, Frank was a genius, in Sherry's mind, with his work on economics and tropes, non-literal metaphors. Symbols, which are like metaphors or signs or allegories or tropes or penalties or signals, like NFL signs or other major league referee penalties which he learned from the world famous department at the University of Chicago.

"It's the fire within", said Sherry touching her breast, bosom. "That needs to be cooled", said Frank, pointing to a man. She said to Frank, "It's Hot", adjusting her levis. This novel uses right-wing parody and moral conservatism, against Frank and Sherry? Who are economic ideology; and moral liberals, seen as their tragedy? For you readers on the world wide, liberal, this <u>hubris</u> seems like no tragedy at all? But put your mind in a conservative, born in Selma, religious Democrat and historical victim, of being like part of the silent majority of the

United States, now? And wanting to fit in? Full up to here with liberal economics? He knew they would read it. They went home and talked about Frank's evolutionary liberal conservatism, for the time, and about non-literal metaphors called tropes, like how fire could be put out. The two made it through the crowd and got in their car and drove home talking about tropes like fire in the brain and burning in the Bosom and drove back to their flat. They studied some MBA books, back in their apartment, that were the original thinkers like Keynes, Galbraith and other writers. They were serious students. And rarely took time off from their studies. Like at Harvard.

-2-

A couple of weeks passed, they went back to Jack London Plaza. Sherry downed a container of Troy bottled water. L. A. was in the middle of a winter heat wave. Hot, hot, hot. Like the water of the Son. Sherry looked like a young movie star. But spoke in a Polish accent. Frank, like nobody had seen before, looked like President Obama. They would start a band, a rock and roll band, out of L. A., called—"The Cherry". Sherry was a mirror reflection of a "good" MBA student, with good common sense and practical. She sold the band's songs like a reckless fool. It was a punk band. She put one hand on her chin and the other hitting her forehead. Talking to our prodigal, who had a handicap, of one bad leg, because of a wound he got like outside Kabul. Liberals were as if deaf? This is 10 years before the end of the novel. In that time, politics and space change, from the here and now of this book, meanings of symbols change. <u>Like Washington Irving's story of someone who slept for 20 years and the politics of the country had totally reversed</u>. Frank could see into the eyes of the people around and there was despair in their eyes. Like they were saying, can't you see it's a Depression? But nobody would talk about it because it could be your job that was next. I can't tell you how bad it was if you don't remember it, or were not of the minority other party. In Stockton, California property lost 65% and cities were going bankrupt. In a couple of years. 18 million people were put out of work in 3 years. Real estate lost 32% of its value in as many years. California was hard hit. It was as bad as with FDR in 1934 in the value of real property. Just not so with unemployment. Though it looked, there, like a Depression, a low economic production or ownership of the means of production, such was not the cause of Sherry and Frank's depression, it was their ethics? How was Frank's 10 year journey, like a return from a war zone? Were the words of the war zone of his songs, believable? In his conversion out of that war zone, does Frank betray the reader? Or, is the meditation on the solar system, lead us to a better place than this contemplation of history?

Tunisia was a really terrible place before the Revolution spark. And their pilgrimage. "I've got an idea for the name of the bewitching corporation", said Justin, Frank's adopted son, a Democrat. Frank doesn't become a Independent until well on into this tragedy. Now, he is a pro-President Democrat. In this forest of symbols of the Republican, failed party. This forest of symbols makes it difficult to tell who is from which party. But in 2009 everyone, almost, seemed to be on The President's bandwagon. I can't explain what a shock this was to Frank's father. We judge Frank, guilt-ridden, from the perspective of his father, who he hated. This is the narrative tone that motivates Frank's secret heart. And he won't admit his guilt. Which makes him blind to his character's motivation, though he could almost see? You want to keep reading, because you want to know how this genius deals with the crisis and conflict? In Victor Turner of *The Forest of Symbols*, in his judging, of like the social drama, tradition to breach to like redemption of a society. Call him a strange duck, from Selma to top 10 schools, keep reading on, it gets easier, it turns to sarcasm, going into rock and roll from California, at Berkeley, to Chicago to an MBA program, in searching for a tool he could use to employ to make money, like from a computer. Call him a fish out of water. A duck in the duck hunt. A marked man because of his blackness. Where he went from academic think tank to think tank in hopes of finding a place. Just don't call him out, yet, for he was a symptom of the illness of his society. Its breach of Frank's character, like of 35 years of wrong-headed MBA politics. World history has revolved around the wrong things and let our contemplation drift away from sound economics? Like revolve around the earth from a moon station? Instead of revolve around the Sun, from planet earth?

"What?", asked Frank, with the sin of pride, of Greek tragedy. "The Cherry, Multinational", somebody said thinking of Troy.

And, like Frank, was very smart, to be thinking of the Gross National Product.

"What do we produce for the world?", said Frank, thinking of this book, which he was writing on the side, as an autobiography. Frank left Selma, at age 4, to live in L.A.

"CD's", said Hansel, trying to make it back home. Thinking that rock and roll would do it, streaming? In love of LA.

"And?", said Frank Holmes, with the mistake of pride of this prodigal son.

"Maybe a DVD of our band", said Sherry, giving Frank a big hug and a kiss, on the lips. Like <u>Jane</u> <u>Eyre</u>.

On comes the reversal of voice. I, Mr. Holmes, was a complex MBA student. I was an anthropology major, as an undergraduate at Cal. I got the idea of going into a band. A punk band. About my head, a paradox.

As we shall see, Ithaca at the end of this novel, is where I come home like Odysseus. I also went to the University of Chicago. There were so many Nobel prize winners, I fell. And looking back at my teachers of Symbols, they saved me. That is like a typical academic liberal reader and writer. And I agree that I am a smart, but guilty family rebel, that's my tragedy. Here, I didn't do drugs or do anything harmful, I just hated my mother and father as the targets of my rock and roll. I exposed my father's friends in the songs I wrote. Yes, there was sex, but I won't talk about Sherry and my relations. Almost not at all. And I was Zenless. Before I eventually got together with my Dada again, it was help by Victor Turner with his Social Drama that led to me going back to Zen and out of the Common law marriage and which helped to mend the tradition, breach, redemption.

They were playing what Frank called, the Myth of Eve, on came a fire, from heck knows where. They walked among the people. Through the fists and the homeless people. And satire pictures of Mao and Stalin. "Yes", said Frank, who then stuck his tongue out and gave Sherry the free speech to put out the fire. Like the Tea Party of 2010? Libertarian and so out of touch. At this point in time, and place, L A, which is Latino and Democrat, like the Mayor. Still, it's like Glenn Beck type parody? You could hear the people crying for a leader to take them out of the Depression, almost hear the people crying out for Big Brother, in a Stalinist USSR government. With Recession and the Depression in their eyes. That was the motive that brought Frank and Sherry together, right to the night of the October Fall of the Wall Street Stock Market. Such a cold fall, when we could contemplate the solar system?

"Oh", said Sherry. Who didn't know me well enough to know how my guilt, and anger and love because of sex, made me the rebel of the family. This is the key to the novel. If the reader uses the above as a cipher, he will better understand me. That is exactly why I am in need of redemption, this prodigal. It wasn't just a civil prodigal, it was what people call, civil <u>Fate. It was a civil redeeming of my person, I was of civil religion. That is I talk about customs and norms and ideals in civil religion, I talk of religious things in terms of civil things, religious terms, in what is in fact a political redemption.</u> But I didn't know, because of my academic learning, that it was the hole in my self that needed redeeming? I don't talk about Zen or theology at the University about that much, because when you go to like Harvard and Yale, you find few friends who believe in Zen himself. For 10 years Frank had lost his faith in Zen. By the time he met his true love, who was his Sherry, it was the fall. And so <u>history</u> meets itself, with a heartbreak, and doubt.

"So there", I said. "I am the rebel of this family". That was my homer. I am Odysseus. "You're certainly on the attack, like in Athens", said Sherry. She was thinking of Homer and the current unrest in Greece, which everyone in Europe worried about, the modern Greece and of Homer. Because it ended up causing the Wall street Stock Market to go down, further. This thing was worldwide from Europe to China. My relations with Sherry made it like in customs and norms and peace, the recession or economics of the Gross Domestic Product and the National Note, the depression wasn't hitting our home, our home? No, no. Our life was study economics at Pomegranate University and party hard. Like there was no tomorrow. We had those student loans, we had to pay off. But we did have a backbone, until we graduated with an MBA. I liked Sherry. Love between us was like a fire, surrounding us, as we held hands. As if I could almost see an warm aura, between us. She called it Catholic. Like those Latino glass candles with the fire coming from a colorful glow from Mary the mother of Jesus and her heart. Sherry hadn't lost her faith, though we used the pill. She didn't see the contradiction. The guilt was hid, behind blue eyes, in the icon, the glass, Catholic candle, can't you see the torture, of cruel and unusual punishment, which was economic, of Sherry too? So she goes to mass where she can have communion in a Cathedral.

"No!". That's all the Republicans said, for two years. They played it cool and under the mask of the Tea Bag party, they retook The House, in Congress. The biggest upset since 1947. In America there is what is called, <u>civil</u> <u>religion.</u> <u>That is religion done in the form of politics.</u> <u>Republicans do this a lot. Redemption is one type of civil religion done</u> <u>here. This civil religion is a major theme in this novel</u>. And I loved icons. Like on the computer as I type this. Like the ACLU

"What?" said Sherry, having some tea.

"I stalk my Calypso", I said. A tragic prodigal son, partly closing one eye. This is not a fantasy novel, so popular at the start of this century. This is <u>realism</u>. And the spying is done by the reader, well almost, with literary criticism labeled—PE, CCC and PM, which was postmodernism and PM Symbols, PMS?. The meaning of which on one level should be obvious. I was an agnostic Catholic, worshiping the icons of the burning belly of Jesus with the fire of the candle there. The Pope is liberal like wanting North and South Korea uniting. The Pope is not mad but I sure could give evidence to the Christmas movie called, The Interview.

"Well you did that", said Sherry. A few in the crowd came up to see what was going on. Sherry went on "You are . . . a wolf ". In this *Pilgrim's Progress. They kill wolves. She stopped me in my guilt, with her Character portrait like that and I just held my heart as if I were one of the apostles in a glass, Catholic burning candle as if I were an icon glowing, in my denial of the portrait and then I held Sherry's hand as if we were both on an Icon, with our belly, the burning heart of Jesus.*

According to me, our guide, we were living the Garden of Eden Myth, which never was, but always is? "With burning bright eyes", came a voice. From the crowd came some taunts and smiles. She loved joking. But it was half true. There was a part of me that was like a Jack London wolf, on fire. The tragic sin of pride. Not yet redeemed. This is me, commenting on myself. And I do mean sin, in the eyes of a foreign state police officer, thinking of my reputation. If you haven't guessed, I struggle with my tragic flaw. I am a list of walking twisting and turning, mental and physical or political and economic or state contradictions, like we all are. I am mortal but I will meditate on the solar system, as if it will answer the tactics of history? And my <u>SiNN</u>.

The wolf that forms a rock and roll band. How colonial. So we were capitalists around the world with our band. It's the punishment and the pain, I hate. "You're in the wind, Sherry", I said. She added, "And so are you." Let me explain, we joked with each other, she was young and that's how I got off. I just kept growing, while most of the business types had short hair, to get nonexistent jobs. They later called it several things to keep people calm. And it worked. People turned on the National news and they would get anything but The Depression. It's the Great Recession, but since we couldn't find work, it was our Depression, caused by the 2008 Stock Market crash. If you want another metaphor, white-collar crime?

"How so?", said a stranger, scratching his head.

"When I see the economy for 2 MBA's in a mortal Wall Street government . . . It makes me want to <u>Howl</u>", said Sherry. "A fall". She touched her dress. She was dressed like a Polish peasant, our morals were straight out of The Grateful Dead, and the 1960's counterculture revolution. 2008 marked the return of long hair, it's worse than a handicap. Ethics slowly went down since the 1960's. As Sherry andI, for the moment, shared our hearts, which kept us from the depression.

I looked at her and laughed, "That's not good for an MBA . . .". I closed one eye. Sherry had stroked my short, black hair. Sherry was a practical business woman who would come on, one on one, with every male she met in every transaction. She was sexy. She loved and came onto Frank too. I like tragedy, my fatal flaw. And I don't lie. The plot and characters change over the next 10 years. But I remain alone and pensive, guilt-ridden. Until my character is redeemed. To be in touch with the rest of the relatively conservative United States. That's <u>civil religion</u>, the in fact political talk with the words of church to explain the state, that politics in America to talk about government is to talk of the Pope, of religion, like redemption. Especially true of Republicans. *It's the punishment and the pain theater, I'll say it again, that I can't take. I don't know where it's coming from, I wouldn't say it's from the students or the adults, but there is a specter, almost from the world out there that I feel in my guts, it's almost as if Zen is against me and I am forever banished, to a cold and dreary world. That's why I am in need of redemption.* <u>But</u> it's civil <u>anxiety</u>.

Song narrators sound like Jack London's politics in the "*The Iron Heel.*" The President's before mentioned plan got the depression from the wolves at our heels. It worked. On our way home, we stopped at the Athens café. A place where homeless people went. We stood in line. I got a large Coke and so did Sherry. Then we got a regular yogurt. You read a tragedy to compare it to your own life. To see a moral. That's why you read tragedy, it's an ethical story of Sherry and me. We are lost. We want you to pity Sherry and me, not to worship us, with our personal lives. You have pity on me and Sherry for our rebellion. Until we get rich, then you are jealous? We get world famous, which masks my tragedy? Hopefully, you still pity us, that's from Aristotle's fragment, punishment and tragedy until we get redeemed? Where we can meditate on the micro level and see not only the Bohr physicist's macro level, the laws of nature answer our secret Blake's Universe in a grain of sand?

We went to our seats and continued our discussion about fire, water and us. And wolves as things of fire. Our Justin was not exempt to the image of fire. "When you smoke and we are at home, I could pour water on your cigar", said Sherry.

"You put water on fire?", said Sherry, both wrists crossed. "Yes", said Justin.

"Why do that?", I said, thinking of the many meanings of the word, fire, for me.

"Because you are like a real wolf, Frank", said Sherry having some Coke, and French fries. I took my evening cloud. This is my journey in a strange land. "I . . . suppose that I was acting like Zen, having bit the big apple", came a voice from the crowd. We hid our sexual hang-up.

But our so-called marriage, had me paranoid. Not from the police, but the customs and ethics and do good? It was the ethics from our family? I was not even allowed to say the word, sex. Mainly coming from my cousins. Here in California, but from all my childhood, conservative ethics? Here it's civil ethics and civil religion, it's just pure folk that was giving me a pitch-fork? Guilt in my head?

"Aren't you like a wolf too?", I said.

"Yes", said Sherry, as if guiltless. On the surface. "So?", I said, eating an apple pie. The west was like the South.

Sherry, pointing to Frank, said "I have the blues".

"Isn't the corporation really like a wolf?", I said, thinking like Jack London. As if in the 2012 London Olympics. CCC?

"Yes", said Sherry, with rigor, thinking of her undergraduate years. "It's rock and roll", I said, as if a redress of injuries.

"It's both of us!" said Sherry, thinking of their freedom of speech. "Okay, you win", I said thinking of my father, Dada. Then I had some Coke that left a sweet taste in my mouth. "The Cherry . . . is like fire and all adults want to do is throw water on it", said my wife, holding my hand, as we sat together side by side. Don't be confused. I am giving a contradiction, that you should see through by now? At the word, wife,

I felt as if I were confessing to my Priest? More <u>civil religion</u>, the seeing of civil society as if it were in religious terms!

<u>And I didn't believe in God.</u> Where do these religious ideas come from, perhaps from my past, a habit. "We've got to get out of this depression", said Frank. Sherry had her Coke. Tragedy is read for educational intent, to compare. To be Zenless is the major tragedy of this novel, given the majority of people in the US are religious. The

majority will rule in my mind, power of the people, in a Democracy, in all the United States, not just in one state of the Union, other than California, I meant I really am, we are in a republic and the states revolve around Washington DC, like the Sun. Not just California. When I went from Berkeley to Chicago. I felt like I stood out like I had hit a totally different world. With small pockets of ethnic groups, who kept their ethics and ethnic traditions from the old country, for all I know, like I. B. Singer, a Nobel Novelist, who wrote in Europe of small town Jewish life and customs. The reality behind the rebellion.

- - -

"And rock and roll will start". "A CD?", said Sherry.

"It's a product, for people out at sea", I said, as if talking Odysseus.

"Who will produce it?" asked Sherry, thinking of my book and how difficult it is getting a professional contract. I listened, who thought like Einstein, when I was at California, at the University of California at Berkeley, with a secret in my heart, an intimate one, because I was an honors student. Like the great prof. Ishmael Reed.

"I don't know but it would be production", I said, thinking of the band. And the Blues Band I was in for what seemed like endless, where I played bass.

"Would that add to the GNP, Gross National Product", I said again. As if I were a Candidate running for President of the United States.

"It's a gamble". On who owns the means of production.

"You see". Then came the flights of birds, cranes. "Yes. We burn a CD". I made the sign of the cross.

"Why rock and roll?", said Hansel, thinking of the punishment. And a metaphor for the world economy.

"Because that's all I know besides business", I said.

It would get us out of the blues, ironically. Like my sense of bluesas I see in the songs that I write. I mirror Sherry's secret wish, to sing ofour time. The economy was in the blues, and my mind had the blues, we learned to cope. I like to say, it's not us but the larger state of the ethics of the politics of Religion of The United States of American Economy.

But when I wrote about econ, I meant the personal depression.

- - -

I and Sherry drink and then give up drinking. Finally, we just think.

I smoke and give up on smoking. Democrats drink. So would you if you see what I do. This is gallows humor. We are on the economic gallows ready for execution. That's why this is a tragedy. You learn. Lord, is it me? I try to get you to pity me and Sherry. That's Greek literary criticism. The rebellion is muted by the fact that we are MBA students.

I think that our degrees will be like 1 in 100 chance of getting us hired.

That's why we went into a band now. We knew how to play on people's emotions. But I am very sarcastic and cynical. At Cal and Chicago I studied human behavior.

Odysseus finished dinner and talked like what most married people do. Plot drops. I am wearing the Greek mask of tragedy. To reflect the state of the economy. Not to The President. Here is where we start a shift in form. I am Odysseus, I speak in 3rd person sometimes.

—What about demand?, said Andy, into contracts.

—For good rock and roll, whispered hand to cheek.

—Yes. Then, Andy answered her whisper.

—We deal with supply, said Andy, thinking of old President Reagan, with Voodoo economics. Like space children.

—With the production? I said, knowing about political economics, and wanting to add to the production of the US. It was both serious and joking. To treat rock and roll as legitimate, as a real business is camp thinking. The novel is a documentation of the whole process.

—Yeah. Like it's our <u>Fate</u>, said Sherry, giving some information.

—The band?, I said, thinking of Dada, my father, as I liked to call him. Like the <u>fate</u> given you by Zeus, dead.

—Yes, said Sherry, daughter of a blue-collar worker.

—Get the supply, She took a sip. It's voodoo economics, I said.

—And the demand will follow, said Sherry, she said with gallows comedy. US culture gives you demand.

Andy was an economic MBA grad, unemployed, but loving contracts, freed. Odysseus always wears the Greek tragic mask. Odysseus must admit I am 33 and Sherry is 21. I waited to go into business school. I was in a blues band for a long while. I played bass. Is this tragic if you are under 30? No, it is if you're my age? In other words I would be making money off of a trade I should have given up 3 years ago? No.

Sherry is really smart but started college at age 17 and got in the MBA program at age 21. We just got "Married" a couple of months ago. The problem is the economy. People now are pretty lost. The Wall Street index dropped from 12,000 a year and a half ago, now its 6,500 and dropping. Savage economics. The President fixed that. I am talking from the view of a good Democrat, at this stage of the plot.

Nobody knows what to go into. Lawyers and investment bankers are shining shoes. Education is poor. They were our friends in work. I figure I can go back to the band idea. Sherry is up for the ride. Justin is like my son and Hoodoo is my Dada, Father. The President is Keynesian, as I said. After a month in office he had some fire that, generally, the republicans boycotted. Andy was a ringer for me, mark him reflective of me? Like The President hiring private contractors?

In this tragedy? Bad ethics is more tragic than not believing in Zen, I thought. That's how much my father, my Dada, had a grip on my soul

- - -

Odysseus is new to the Democratic party. I sent a letter to my senators and told them to pass a Production Act. My Federal fire. My tragedy is my lack of ethics. I looked at people in power and acted as if they were Zen. I didn't believe in any Zen in the Universe or Galaxy or Solar system, heaven, now. Economics was my Zen, and was I ever Zenless.

Then, I added Keynesian analysis, the inducement to invest. The Fed got 2 trillion. I suggested that they use the money to give 1% loans, through banks to people in production. That was Neo-Keynesian economics. Production is factories, mines and crops. You know, Sherry started to bleed from her palms. The problem is that I know of no product except the record industry. We could make a CD of the band, we could get together, from all the unemployed musicians in the area. Then a DVD of our band. And there were a lot of unemployed professional musicians around, in Los Angeles.

Odysseus gets onboard with <u>factories</u>, when I can think of a <u>product</u> that will sell to everyone at like Wal-mart. I don't know yet. For now it's a CD. Sherry's stigmata continued to bleed. Andy left. There was a V sign over eye. He likes being the fool. I am playing the role of Homer's hero. I am narrator or I now tell the story as I do in the latter chapters, I am an academic and a fool and I am so sarcastic you don't know if I am serious. Am Frank with you, I am Odysseus. I am that character in this novel. Slowly, in 10 years, I go home from the war zone of ethics towards home. Like in the Homeric *The Odyssey.*

I want to export our CD all over the world. It's got to be universal, like Economics being sensual. At the base. Her bleeding was from a cut opening up a can. Sherry's a Republican. So we have electrically charged conversations. She still believes in Zen. Somewhat having Biblical images in her head. I just take the defense of the Obama administration. She just says, "NO!". We were in our own house in the bedroom. From deficit spending to not enough spending on the infrastructure. The President's Fed politics and communities. And nobody questioned it, at the start. I am nobody, I wrote this.

I was reading a book by Ms. Gaskell, *Mary Barton*. It's about factory life in Manchester England, at the end of the 1840's. It was in. She wrote about Manchester. Sherry could relate to it. Under President's watch, stocks went from 6,000 to 18,500. That was evidence that he was not the worst President we have ever had, contrary to what someone in my business school had said to me. Economic novels were a part of the arch, conservative and traditional Victorian ethic? Why isn't this novel Victorian? Is it even Modern? Isn't it presumptuous to call a work Postmodern? What's the proof of that? A pastiche of <u>the Odyssey</u>.

- - -

—So what are the fires around the globe and nation that need water poured on them?, I said. This was a terrible thing that was happening around the world, right at the start of 2009.

—<u>Production</u>, it's our baby. Said Sherry with a twinkle in her eye.

—Yes, Odysseus said. That's me Frank.

—And me pressing my warm body next to yours, that's a fire, but one that doesn't need water to put it out, my wife said to me, feeling.

—The <u>factory</u>, said Sherry again. On come my songs.

—Yes. I said, glinting eyes.

—To make our CD. Selling it, is a service. Sherry had got the essence of what I was trying to say, that rock and roll was a regular business, to be exported. It was my <u>black</u> comedy.

—And it will be tragic, its like Homer's going home.

—Or ironic, I said.

—We'll make our depression a happy ending, said Sherry, using the term depression as poetry, personal and economic.

—Then you'd like to sing?

—Yes, she said, I will, I will, yes.

My wife was reading Bronte's *Shirley*. It was about social unrest, Shirley was like a repressed Victorian, in a novel about <u>industry</u>. I watched the start of the revolution in Tunisia, that would take the Arabs. Three weeks passed, and we needed some good musicians to play in our band. It could have been a century, a whole new idea to get money and trying to smile at the gallows humor. A parody of all-knowing Capitalism.

And we put out notices on the electricity poles of the U.C.L.A.

Streets of West L.A., advertising for a band. It was a unique genre of band. Aimed mainly at teenagers. We got a lot of people who answered. In their journey home. We wanted to find people who shared our vision of the band, our boycott of the establishment. Our boycott of our past and family customs and our shame that nobody our age talks about their relationships, our parent's idealism and politics and religion, hence our "marriage". Why is it a parody of capitalism? Isn't Russia and China, now, Post-capitalist? PC? Which is just postmodern?

Sherry sang some songs off the Sara McLachlan CD + DVD of 2008, "Fumbling Towards Ecstasy". We felt like we were totally free.

We soon got a good drummer and lead guitar and a band changing rhythm guitar. Who really led the band. I played bass. I didn't sing, Sherry did that. We used at start as a model the old band The Clash. This is tragic, political rock and roll blues. The songs I write have no rhyme, just rhythm. That is not Hip hop or regular rock, it was what they call—Punk.

We started to practice everyday for 6 hours straight. Sing me some songs of your twisted Odyssey through life. We needed some songs. So I wrote a few. Our band was Sherry and me and Patty; and Justin; and Hansel on lead guitar. Pablo played the electric piano, coming in later. As Pedro came into the band later once we got going. We played low, when it was time for Sherry to sing. The Beginning of <u>The Odyssey</u> starts out with the word-sing.

We played a couple of gig in Westwood Village at a local club, called <u>Latina's</u>. It was on Wayburn Avenue, next to the campus of UCLA. It was a beer joint, and people would come on in, get a pitcher of beer and eat peanuts and throw the peanut shells on the floor. They like us, and give us steady time to play on Friday, Saturday and Sunday every week. We really brought in a crowd. They all were on their smartphones, on the internet, world wide web. It was just catching a wave of the post-depression blues. It is addictive of course. Facebook put you on the line-up. Apps were just catching on, and were programmed to get you addicted.

You can be addicted to a Police State. You need to live in a free land not to have the Police be like a Narcotic. This is shown in Ricoeur's The Just.

"Scent of Zen"

Warm up to me baby, I don't want your grief,
I have my own way to play, Do you get the scent of a woman?

I want to go home, baby, take me there. Hold my hand and make me
feel warm.
I need to go home with you baby, take me there.
Can't you hear my heart, it's beating for you

What's that miff? It's your perfume again.
Just hold me baby, quick I've got to come into your arms.
It's your perfume, you can't escape.
You can't cover it up.

Let me have that bottle of perfume, So I can remember your smell.
What do you call it?
Intimate desire?

Don't move, don't ruin the moment.
I'll eat you up.
Just get closer, to me. I have the scent of God

"Strict Daddy-o"

Strict Daddy-o, why are you so cruel?
You punish me, so I feel guilty That makes me revolt.
Against your iron fist.

I don't want a revolution, I know we can talk it out, Like all good Arabs
do.
Talk is what you are good at?

Be nice to me, like you always do. What's the matter, the weather's
too hot? Keep talking, and don't make me feel guilty. Why don't you
punish me? At home in Libya.

Where did the economy go?
Who will follow you?
The sun is hot, can you hear the beating of my heart?
That's better. I don't shed a tear.

Love me, Daddy-o.
I need your unconditional love.
And a date and a glass of milk, I am hungry,
Pilgrim.
Be happy.

Come all The Way Home

Only I know the suitors.
Holmes, come down the stairs, the fans come back and forth.

Dance when you sing, We are united in love.
Come into my arms, and love me.

We need each other, like the night and the day come fly with me.
In and out the doors, Give me songs of love, Come deep into my heart.

Come all the way home.
We don't want the sad times,
The bad times, don't be a stranger to me.
We are you together.
Don't let the Moment escape.

Streaming Blues

Now you've come,
We are in. The industry hates you.
Like in between, the classes.
It's hot outside, I need an Olympus water bottle
to put water in my stomach, take me home, stream me.

I wrap my arms around Your afterglow.
You are beautiful, Daddy, We meet into one,
Come into me. They frame you.

Come and fall into me, And we'll pretend We are in Carmel,
On our honeymoon journey.

Like a river, stream it.
Get a little peace, Free to come into you.
Let me come, I'm like wine.

PART II

I lived the life like a black
Gustave Flaubert

Sherry was like the heroine in
Bainbridge's The Girl in The Polka
Dot Dress. A passive
sexual victim.

This is a medial part
Called transitional, What Victor Turner called,
"The betwixt and between the positions assigned, law and
custom and convention and the ceremonial, or rite."
After this next chapter, comes the breach of mistake,
Putting the co-op in jeopardy.In a transitional state of anti-structure.
Transitional people are betwixt and between
Law, primitive and savage. That's our time in the Band.
Yes, it said a rite in literature, like Dante's ritual.
In the land of go to save, like an African,
primitive rite where white meant Death.
The postmodern philosophy of Foucault Derrida and
Ricoeur, was my meditation on the modern Heidegger.

The Contract Clause is Art. I Sec. 10 of the U.S. Constitution.
It is the answer to the early 1900's book on the need for
regulation, <u>The Jungle</u>. The contract clause is tragic.
Like the German word <u>SINN,</u> meaning. It's pathetic.

I am a diabetic, but feel like Mr. Reed.
Balance the budget against the military.

Chapter 2

RED LIPS

-1-

Sherry's guilt over our marriage got so bad, it turned into a depression. A good Catholic didn't shack up with someone. Meanwhile, it didn't bother me on the outside, on the surface, to the world I was Okay, ON Surface, though under my skin, I was guilty too. But I hated my parents so much that I hated Dada more than my inner pain. I didn't let the pain get to me. <u>As for God, it did not exist for me. I was a nihilist. That is I didn't care about God. It was hard for Sherry to give up on her past, and I made of her religion my civil religion</u>, it was hard to, real give up her church. What brought us to live together was the fall 2008 stock Market Crash, it seemed like the end of the world, so why should we care. Meanwhile, Sherry found it hard to be sensual, because inside her church was telling her she was fallen. She went to mass on Sunday, every week. This gave her comfort. I didn't go with her, since I felt no connection to the Catholics. She felt inner punishment. I didn't ask her what she was going through, since I didn't want my own inner feelings to surface. She was so depressed, she would sleep 13 hours a day. And since she was smart, after a brief review, of doing her homework, after a meditation on the Apostles Icon, that showed the glowing heart, from a flame, of Paul the Apostle or other Catholic icon, she was ready for class. I worked on songs. And wrote about the economics of the day. The candle of the sacred heart. Like the scent of the candle and a picture of Jesus, all we could do was hold on. But for both of us it was guilt. I suppressed it, Sherry went to mass and prayed The blue is being born.

We planned to move into a co-op and thought that Sherry couldn't live with a group of people as she was so deep. She felt like she was being punished by Zen, and because of her prayers, felt that someday she would be forgiven. That's why neither of us got morbid over the situation. <u>I felt that there was no Zen, so there was nothing to be forgiven for. Meanwhile Sherry was an eros.</u> We sat on the sofa, meditating of the Catholic icon, glass with pictures of saints, with the candles burnt down to the fire in the belly, which gave me the idea for this novel, it was from the Catholic, glass icon candles. When we did this the depression left Sherry, and we felt like there was a fire in the space between us, a spiritual fire, that left an aura between us. And we felt like things would be okay, for both of us. This brought Sherry closer to her Zen, meditating on the icons, and it brought me closer to Sherry. I had never really been in love before, so I called the so-called spiritual fire, between us, just being in love, it being like an altered state of Time. Our school colors are maroon and white. Justin went on the road.

Sherry would lay in bed with the pillow over her head, and watch TV. This was when she felt good. Then I would go over and sit by her, when I came back from class. We would sit and then she would sit up. When she would do that, the depression would go away. There was an aura of like a fire between us. Usually, we would not pray, but would meditate on the pictures on the Latino icons, then would real turn off the lights and light a Catholic candle icon. Then we'd feel the fire between us. It's then that she felt the Holy Spirit. She would then pray to Mary, the Mother of Zen. And the depression was totally gone. The guilt of our "relationship" turned away from depression. Like a Chicano. We would meditate in the dark like that, and the Holy Spirit would guide her to say something or do something or write something down. The important thing was that the guilt-ridden depression was gone. And in its place was a warm burning in the bosom. Both Sherry and I felt this. It was a warm, burning in the bosom as Sherry liked to put it. This took the place of her guilt. I got the feeling, but my mind was clouded to such an extent, that I felt no guilt, and there was no law I was breaking. I must say, the Catholic church got us through those times of torturing guilt for Sherry. I got a good meditation. Fright for us.

When we would go to class together, we would go hand in hand like a newly engaged couple. Sherry likes to think of the relationship as our engagement time. This made it right for her, in her feelings of guilt, she being so much younger than me. And I being a typical male. People used to say of us, then, that there was like an aura around both of us. As if we were like a Catholic icon candle flame. It came from our eyes. Of that I am bad. We looked around at everyone and made people look at us as we passed by. We saw other people. Of course, Sherry said that she was like seeing like the Virgin of Guadalupe, a Catholic Saint. Which ever it was, by meditating of religious icons, Both of us got rid of our depression and guilt. Like a pachuco, street chicana in LA, during the 1940's. they did not get equal protection.

- - -

We would walk home, aflame. This told both of us that we werespiritually born of Zen, as Sherry would call it. I called it seeing everyone. Which ever explanation you bought, we were almost like the only ones in love, and physically showing affection to each other. We would go to the Student Union and have a cup of tea. And we were seeing everyone as they passed. In other words, we didn't hide our faces out of guilt.

That was the point. Before we went to class we would meditate. And look everyone in the eye, when we're in front of others.

And the same at the teacher. We would meditate on the eyes of the teacher, so much was the complexity of our situation. It was a paradox. Given our guilt, looking back on it, we should have been hiding our way to class. But no, we were open for business. Troy was our landlord.

We got all "A's" that term. It was a time of intention, for both of us. I'd just let Sherry sleep a little more. We did that when we weren't practicing with the band. After the winter term, we moved into our co-op. Where we go up early to study and then go to school. Then in the afternoon to early evening we would practice with the band.

-2-

As for the guilt thing, Sherry's guilt made me contemplate my own situation. I realized that all my motivations were a knee-jerk reply to my father, who I hated. He was the family law giver. I was the family SiNNer. I sort of liked my mother, my Mummy. But it was the authoritarian impulse of Dada, of father, that I hated. I tried to think of all the things I was guilty over. It came to Zen. I felt guilty for not believing in him. <u>We were taught when we were young that we could talk with Zen in prayer and that he would come. I tried that and got nothing so I gave up trying. Then I felt guilty for not talking with Zen. It was a contradiction.</u> I couldn't win. I'd fail to communicate with Zen. Then I'd be guilty for not talking to Zen. I wasn't a bad boy. So, I thought it was a problem with Zen. Then I'd feel guilty for thinking that. I couldn't get out of the trap. We never talked in my family so I could not tell my father what I was feeling. When I grew up, I never prayed. Because of my experience when I was young. That's why I became an agnostic or atheist, that is I either didn't know that there was a Zen or I was sure there was no Zen. I wasn't sure of much, and at first decided I be a defense lawyer. They have lots of doubt. It was then that I thought that I probably wasn't an atheist, because I didn't have enough information to affirm or deny the question. But I would fluctuate. And mostly thought I was an agnostic We would eat out. Then we would come home. This was like life at the existentialist café. Modern signs.

When I grew up I had this eros idea in the back of my mind. And felt guilty and not good enough to talk with Zen. When I got with Sherry, I was in my early 30's. But I still had guilt about things. I went from guilt about Zen, to a general feeling about guilt on all things I did. Then it went to feelings of guilt about our common law contract. It didn't hit me as guilt, so that's why I didn't recognize it as guilt. It was more like a dark cloud in the brain, above the eyes and up into the head. I felt guilty about saying the word sex, There I said it again. I am typing this into the computer much time after than the events of the novel, years after the event. So after having been redeemed, I can see my lotus brain and my visual, modernism.

Back in 2009, I did not recognize any guilt at all. But that's what I was. <u>And it centered around Zen and Dada and sex.</u> I got to the point of giving up on Zen, because if he did exist he had given up on me. So I transferred my hate of Dada to a hate in God, my father. Everything I did, as I look back on it, centered around rebellion against my father. That's why I didn't want, at first, a chapel wedding. I wanted to punish my father for giving his Zen to me.

- - -

Mr. Menor was our computer network teacher, at Pomegranate University. The School was well-rated. We started on cloud computing. And marketing on the world wide web.

Sherry and I shared the Catholic church with its icons and mass, which I went to occasionally. Since I was not Catholic, and didn't believe in a Zen in heaven, the religion was a comfort to me, though Sherry was guilty, because of her use of the Pill. Contraception was a major infraction. But it didn't make me feel guilty at all. But it did Sherry.

Dada's type, was infected by guilt, because of the US Supreme Court decision against his church, changing its family structure. The result is that it incorporated the US moral system and its pattern of guilt. It had a type of Freud that was states rights against Washington's power structure. This was because of what Washington DC had done to them, in punishing them for their states' rebellion and states rights activism, in Selma.

- - -

Both the Rocky Mountains and the South, having lost in their duel with the National government. Mitt Romney belongs to his Church. And is a moderate Republican running for President of the United States of America, then.

Mitt has a large family, and generally likes states' rights. But he is a moderate. As of the typing of this barb, he is leading the Republican field, he and his graying black hair. He can take a punch and will be a handful for The President. Mitt is not guilt-ridden and would be a good Republican Candidate. Mitt has his own regional health plan. The President is against war, as am I. You can keep on reading as to where my National politics evolves to, my character.

-3-

Guilt comes from many places and goes to many emotions. But is one of the most basic and universal feelings. It starts with the way we are raised and taught. We know not to go against our parents, what our parents don't really want us to do at a very early age. It makes us want positive reinforcement from our parents. Good, is the word that we want. Then it's customs and norms, it goes to the peers. And school, where the feelings of guilt defuse to other emotions. But when we do poorly guilt comes back. When it comes back, it is associated with other things like shame. Shame is given us both intentionally and by the way, from others around us. For breach of customs. When we get shame we feel guilt. It's one of the most basic of ways to enforce laws, through shame. I feel shame, therefore I feel guilt. Therefore, the laws of the color of custom and culture are working, around the clock, like guilt at school, I got into John Keneth Galbraith's <u>The New Industrial State</u>, the cure for the last 40 years of the rust belt. He helped me with cause and effect, with material economics. He taught Cal.

- - -

Shame is the way we are raised by our parents. And it is backed up by the feelings of guilt. It's like a game. Shame is thrown and we catch guilt. This is universal in all cultures and is the most basic and primitive or savage of all legal systems. Hence, I feel rotten and unclean guilty. And guilt takes up where there is no police man is present. That's why it's so basic. When there is shame and guilt, society goes round and round. With Sherry and me it is at its most basic. The intimate feelings of the eros are aroused when society goes into our conscience. Which tells us right from wrong. When people no longer feel the difference between right and wrong, we have a pathology or bane of modernism. Sherry and I have ethics. In California we don't need shame and guilt about our relationship. But we do, because of the way we were raised up. And so society goes round and round. The "Song of Songs".

When we don't feel shame and guilt, we might have turned into someone pathological. It doesn't follow that no guilt means sickness. There are societies where there are little sanctions causing little guilt. But there are other sanctions that take its place. That's the reason that California has such lax rules on sex. But other related sanctions come up to take the place. Such sanctions are written down in the California State Code. The statutes of the law where we live. At times there are major changes in the law when people have changed their mind. The 1960's was one such time when the laws of custom and norms of the world and the nation and the city and the state of California changed. The United States Supreme Court and Congress is another source of laws. Abortion is an example of a law that is controversial. As was segregation in various places in the country. Many people don't like certain laws. Sometimes they petition of the Supreme Court. Petition the Supreme Court.

Petition the Supreme Court. It's difficult to petition the government and to get a hearing on liberty and property. Later, I'll tell you of the story of my brother. Who tried to get round and round the laws. As to a Constitutional contract clause, this novel is a petition to the government, for and in behalf of my brother? Vincent. The clause is tragic.

It's a shame and leadership in this country should feel guilt when the Contract Clause is followed? As if, in this Capitalist country, the arbitrary enforcement of the Art. I Sec. 10 Constitutional Clause is a shame? Something that government should feel guilt over, on the down low? So laws go round and round, every 100 or 200 years or so. And, like California marriage laws, come and go in popularity. My own personal guilt is like a spike in the vague line between religion and state laws. One takes over when the people make their wish known. Then in large cases, the people's will can be overturned. Because a new ethic is seen as enforceable. Like with the Federal laws.

The Contract clause and the sex laws of the country are related. Sherry and I seem to be married. That's a contract. It's also part of the sex laws. The Church of Pride ran into such a problem years ago. People don't like to talk about it. Like with Justin's forbidden erotic, co-habitation marriage. And with Sherry and me and our Common law

Contract. Talking about it can bring up more heat than light. But they are 3 examples of type cases of appealing to the United States Supreme Court. Slavery, with LGBT co-hab.

A novel has tradition, breach and redemption. I'm talking about the breach. I am not terribly guilt-ridden, but it's a concern so much that it's a base of this novel. And is part of my Character and part of the plot. When will he be redeemed? Why? That is the plot. You could be talking about a court of law. The issue of the court is the breach, here not so simple to pinpoint because of something called civil religion. Redemption is political anti-structure, and a formal wedding. And the recognition of duty. And then the vision of the atom and the planets, a perfect solar system. Unlike the Universe which is the sum of all the Galaxies, including our galaxy the Milky Way. This is symbolic, or a metaphor of the Redemption I get. Relative unity of the micro world and the macro world, William Blake's *Marriage of Heaven and Hell*. The sage world vision, like Rutherford and Bohr's vision of the atom and the solar system. It's not just metaphor. It's real. I am a erotic and see the microcosm in the macrocosm, but have always liked Blake but am not that familiar with Rutherford and Bohr, but think of it like normal atom and the solar system, not the Universe, which has dark energy of about 70%. That's why the Universe is ever expanding. Now Sherry and I are metaphoric <u>dark</u> energy? In this metaphor, we have reached the Universe, and are expanding out of control? The 30% dark matter is the gravity, like a black hole, that helps to keep the Universe in one piece. So we have breach of the dark energy, like the people in the tragic Arab spring, and the redemption of the gravity of the solar system. I like to think of dark energy as in reality people energy, the energy of growing up. Seen on a micro level in the strings or atom with electrons going round and round. Anti-gravity, for now, Anti-structure, Turner; it's equal protection in a rite.

-4-

I went outside our apartment to have a smoke. It calmed my nerves, in times of stress. I lit up. And had my first hit. It hit my lungs. It was at first paradise. Then I thought of my uncle who was living with cancer. Lung cancer. I had another hit. It wasn't so good this time. Thinking of my uncle made me guilty. Suddenly, the cigarette did not taste good to me. And I got more guilty. I was sitting and I put my head between my knees because I had a headache and I am no way perfect, I had hit the floor because the smoke was giving me a bad buzz. I sat there in that position for some time and then put out the cigarette. It was a terrible experience for me. I felt nothing but guilt and what made it worse, I wanted another cigarette. Such are the contradictions, The reality is sometimes the US Supreme is wrong. They diagnose symptoms before there is a field to study it. Their judgments are political. they hold against <u>yick wo</u> for equal protections, when their judgment is only on economic issues. I went back in the apartment. Smelling of smoke. Sherry didn't say anything. When I got back in the bedroom Sherry wondered about the symbolism of me putting a red sheet of paper on the manuscript that I was working on. She knew that I liked symbolism. But there was no meaning there. I felt as if I had been misunderstood. For, to a symbolist, sometimes a metaphor is just a trope, to you the reader these words will be made clear in this novel, or to paraphrase Freud, sometimes a cigar is just a cigar. And that was the case with the red sheet of paper. It wasn't a sign. And it had no meaning. I just felt guilty for being in a relationship and into co-habitation symbolism. That stopped with Supreme court action.

The red sheet of paper was a good symbol, if you'll pardon the expression, of the guilt I felt at not being understood, in my writing. Like my intentional use of tropes. I like to use them. It's like the French school of Symbolist art. It was revived in America in the 1970's. I was a Symbolist, after Paul Ricoeur, my teacher who was French. The meaning of the red sheet of paper haunted me, as if people would read in my symbolism and my work something that wasn't there. It made me guilty. But I wasn't going to stop using metaphors.

Symbols are using a thing of this, and making it mean that. It's art. Especially for Paul in his world famous *Rule of Metaphor*. He explained tropes. They are like the Parables of Jesus, in the bible. A parable is used so that it kept the Romans and the Jews off of the meaning and the intention of Jesus. But sometimes a red sheet is just a red sheet of paper. I challenge the reader to sometimes think that at times a cigar is just a cigar. Like-<u>Water In the Belly</u>.

Like my professor of the history of religions, at Chicago, Mircea Eliade who taught me of reference and of image and imagination. I would go to class and at night I would attempt to chain-smoke. I would feel guilty because of my smoking, that being taboo in my father's house. That is why I grabbed onto the religion of Paul and Mircea. They were at a college level not afraid in the university to talk of Zen or spiritual things. I memorized the complete works of Mircea Eliade and Paul Ricoeur. They were my tie to tradition in the social Drama of University life, there being 1,000 agnostics to a square mile, in academics.

Soon, Eliade and Ricoeur were my only grounding to the reality of my tradition. I took the regular blackish anthropology symbolism classes. Turner, with his conversion to humanism belief, made me feel that I had a home in anthropology. Paul was in Philosophy, Mircea was in <u>History</u> of religions, and Turner put a human face in the mostly Agnostic Symbolism of anthropology. It was class.

I didn't get the guilt trips from Turner, Eliade and Ricoeur. They were like my own personal defense team. And I was just learning to play ball. Smoking became my personal bad habit. This was some 10 years prior to 2008, and the Stock Market crash, symbolic of many things but especially, my <u>quantum</u> mechanics tropes, of tragedy, symbolic of my crash on Sherry. The above team ever knew how to play. That was at Chicago. Where I got into <u>Stone</u> <u>Age</u> <u>Economics</u>. I won't go into this but it initiated me into the University of Chicago economics Department. The joke was that I was reading books by some of the 11 Nobel Prize winners. And I was calling that department out for being like stone age economics. It's just an aside. But it helped me read the Famous Milton Friedman. And then I would run away from economics by chain-smoking and withdrawing into T.E.R, Turner, Eliade and Ricoeur. T.E.R. had a major philosophical quantum mechanics of the soul, bone of contention with traditional study of religion. Their work was like a manifesto. And like Einstein, they not only believed in Zen, my guilty fear at Chicago, they also like the physics department, at Chicago, had self-criticism, something most top 10 schools made you feel guilty about. Many don't believe in quantum mechanics.

The irony was that my escape from Christianity, when I went from Berkeley to Chicago, found me in a Theology department ranked with Yale. And their words saved my guilt. Guilt from running away from Zen. An atom in the cold and dreary world. All religion became the old testament. Something old. Ricoeur made my guilt go away. In his analysis of the "Song of Songs". Eliade told me I could talk with Yoga. You might call it prayer. Turner showed me the universal in legal systems. With *The Forest of Symbols*, I found in darkest Africa, the rituals of my mummy. Like the Catholic Mass in the glass, candle icons as the fire burns the picture on the glass, with like the Apostles, opening up with a fire in the chest, a burning in the bosom. The icons are like a forest of symbols, as the wick burns down, from the fire in the head. These symbols offer redemption in the moment, to let us wash our hands from the guilt of man, a bad trip. Like mother's tribe in Zambia. I don't like to talk about guilt. I am not a Vincent. But I shared Sherry's habit. And though I wasn't Catholic I used her church as a crutch to make me all warm and fuzzy inside. Whenever we would get guilty, we'd light up an eros. And hold each other. That's all a 21 year old girl can offer an older man. We didn't talk much about guilt. And after we were together for a while, we would blow out the light, and lie in the dark. For I was an agnostic, now. I have been for 10 years. My search after Zen boarders on the tragic, but with out it there would be no tragedy, now. What was the "fate" of the dead Zeus.

My search for eros, now, gives me guilt, since I don't like to pray and, now, don't know how Zen would reach me. The *Spiritus Mundi*, the anarchy of the time, mocks the songs of my People.

Recovery inc, was my father's business. It assumed what it was trying to prove. That assumed your sickness existed prior to its recognition. The only way to recover from your sickness, was to go into the business structure. Then you would be cured. Of course it was a con. He assumed what he was trying to prove. That's circular reasoning. Of course, many a business is run like that, like your family church and Priest. The basis of his business. But it worked like society. They assumed your guilt, whether or not you were shacked up. Once you recognized your guilt, you were ready for the cure, society. Which assumed your guilt. And it worked. Wherever you were, you were guilty. That way Dada could get

you wherever you were. That way he gave you the business. It was the microcosm of the business, and the macrocosm of society, the cop on the corner, Dada got your guilt. He was a shrink. And the guilt? It goes to the revolutionary. Which the US Supreme ct. should realize is not marijuana, on a Federal level.

Ventura
CVS/pharmacy

Chapter 3

ARISTOTLE'S ETHICS

Homer starts out with a ritual sacrifice, a police bust, here. Pure tragedy all meaning. Up came the sun over the palm trees. The orange sunshine Rosa this dawn. Just then we heard a siren of a police car come up to our co-op, the one we bought for the band, from a foreclosure. I cry at the deepness of this part of our tragedy. I just can't say enough times that I didn't know what was going on. It's not part of my life now and I can't say enough about how much I hate it. This is what needs to be redeemed, the breach of social custom and culture and law and order and justice and jurisprudence the ritual of the novel is like the same rated drug bust, by statutes, tradition. Rite of birth. This was from the social science of Victor Turner, on my doctoral orals Committee. He did work in Africa. He wrote a book called from a French Symbolist, *The Forest of Symbols*. It was about rituals and the intentional symbols used in a ritual in Africa, like white face mud meaning death. He also had a theory of social behavior. It was that society deals with problems by first having like traditions then there is a breach of culture and then comes redemption. It's the most primitive and universal of stone age justice, the way a society deals with unwanted <u>behavior</u>. It was called— the Social Drama. Patty and Hansel's doing drugs caused great guilt between the two. They were afraid of The police. In the post-Trump years, republicans want to go after state initiatives like the west coast states, that said weed was legal, in their states, notwithstanding FBI Federal laws that say marijuana dependency is a felony charge.

They knocked on the door. And showed us a warrant. And gave us a picture of the person that they were looking for. Pedro had just come in a half hour ago. Pat and Hansel came forward. Reality is Zen, like the police. And they are to the tragic. I didn't have the faintest idea of what was going down or know about any of this stuff. Sherry was so embarrassed just like me, our faces turned pink. We felt like we were going to faint. This bust in part makes this novel, bust for illegal drugs, primitive. This is pre-2016 California.

An awake passerby saw two people passing the joint, said the cop, tradition. Warrant is to search the apartment for drugs, said the other cop, Mr. Nestor. They searched the place and found a packet of drugs. Tragic and prodigal, a plot, I admit I never knew this was going down. I thought that we had been betrayed by the drugs that the police had found. I learned in Chicago the power of the police. So I showed them the highest respect. The social drama had begun and there was a breach of morals or ethics, or crisis or the people and against those people, of the customs of the laws of California. Hansel and Patty needed to go to court to make right, or redeem the social wrong. It was about the primitive ritual of the social drama. And society needed what is called social redemption. This is basic, stone age that it gets, universal. The guilt and shame over a bust, says this is for everybody who get a lot of static for getting this close to the underworld. This novel's a rite.

- What about you?, the first cop pointed to Hansel.

- You take the fifth amendment, Calypso said.

- We're taking you both downtown, we got the iphone photograph, came a cop, Mr. Circe. We want integration.

- They handcuffed them both, and took them to the police station on Sunset Blvd. Their separation from society.

- I know that Pat had a legal waiver, she's almost blind, said Nestor, it was marijuana, one joint.

- But the rest of the stuff was new to me, said Sherry.

- Be strong, I said to my wife. It was coke.

■ Really, she said, holding each elbow with the other hands.

The two by this time were going existential. Facing <u>civil</u> <u>death</u> like the Graaaaaaateful Dead. It depends on how you are charged. 24 hours passed and they came back to the co-op. Enduring the tragedy. And playing with things that will give you time, is tragic. You could get a police record and it would stop you in trying to get a job or other necessity. The 5th Amendment is a protection, but society works by hearsay. And guilt of doing drugs is maintained, by the entire co-op on the police lineup. Thus we all felt the guilt. This is shake-down street. They perpetually put you on the line-up, so anyone can use extortion as their politics. You have record.

- - -

Patty explained the events. She said, theater of crime. She said, the tragedy of the ritual. TTTTT They were booked and almost crucified. They spent the night in the tank and then went before the judge. Who told them to waive their Bill of Rights, like the <u>commitment</u> court thaaaaat Vincent went to. Then the juuudge said that they were <u>Diverted</u>, wwwwhich meant that they had no record, conviction, and they couldnnnnnnn't even use the 1st Amendment of the US Constitution or even talk to others that thy were busted or even admit that that they were Diverted. It was California justice. Not National. Not the customs of US. I think other states had do follow it by the Full Faith and Credit clause of the United States Constitution. And the Federal government had to recognize it under the 5th Amendment, no party shall be twice be put in jeopardy of a crime. But that's not how it works. In fact, Patty and Hansel are put on the material line-up, by the police and people living next door, seeing the bust. They do put a party twice in jeopardy, by the pointing of the Finger of shame. It happens by presumption and hearsay. VVVVVVVVVVVVVVVVVVVVV VVVVVVVVVVVV her there. The judge had told them that they were to do community service. The thing that was off, was the lack of justice, but there was something weird, off the wall, was a <u>black</u> man was busted for the same thing, illegal possession. But the judge yelled at the black man that he had better get him a good lawyer. Of course he was under different circumstances. But it seemed to our Patty that the judge was talking to her, to show how <u>different races get different</u>

<u>justice</u>. The FBI has a record of Patty and Hansel's bust. It would be paranoid to put you on the record, for the 5th Amendment applies in all areas of the land, not just in court. This was Los Angeles, California, of the West coast. Far from New York City, with their own system.

- - -

Here are a coooooooouple of songs that I wrote. After the event of the cops coming to the house. My eyes were opened. And I wrote the songs from my gut, my feeling. I tried to give the event a—gong. That is I did not approve of the use of drugs and I at the same time wanted the people to know of the legal mercies of the California justice system. Patty and Hansel wanted to make it back home. Like I did like Homer's <u>Odyssey</u>. The next song is the title song to our first album, 2 CD's. I wrote 18 songs for the "Busted" album. It followed the Social Drama. That is there are 3 implicit parts. First, is the customs of the area, tradition, the way that society goes round and round. Second, breach, or the, here, drug crisis. Third, is civil redemption. This theory of primitive law, is a good universal for our society, here and now. That's George Floyd's arrest and murder in May of 2020. The police got convicted people, shouted "Black Lives Matter".

"Busted"

Going to California is my rap Better
bring enough water for the fire. Its not
legal drugs, by vote, 2016.
Diversion is better if you're new.
The coops commmme in with a warrant
To search your hooooooome
You are given your Miranda rights
In case you think you have free speech,
The politics of drugs, Lady Jane.

You go in back of the coooops car,
You look around, because you are new,
To the justice system.

They search through your pockets,
As they found that roach.
You go to the tank, you have heard about the queens,
hey are as harmless as our Alice.

Do you waive your rights? Of course you do,
Like our Vincent's arrest. Pure tragedy.

You were busted, tried and convicted,
But they have no record of it,
Except the Federal government,
For which you plead the 5th.

The state of California diverts small cases, like Patty and Hansel,
where instead of doing jail time they do community service. As for
class revolt, it will come if we get worse than in socialist Greece. Or
turn so far right that we turn into Hungary. Turning and turning.

"Race Revolt Coming"

Better bring youuur water for the fire,
To halt the drug trade,
And stop the evolution.

Sister Flower and Brother Hate,
By local drug shakedown.

We are the poor and in some areas,
Your dealer is your enemy.
Who start fires, on million dollar hommmes

99 percent of the US is owned by the 1 percent,
The majority of the US says tax the rich,
But the do-nothings won't do anything about it.

In Egypt, they had a class revolution,
It spread to almost all over pan-Arabia. The
"Occupy Wall Street" movement, Went to
all the world, the 1 percent owns
40 percent of the wealth.
Listen to the police,
And don't get caught by the anarchists.
And the homeless.

Zen died in 1889 as overture.
Then, It now started with the underground green party
In Iran in 2009,
Then it spread to the Tea Bag Party,
In the US in 2010,
Then the Arab Spring, then the Occupy movement in fall of 2011,
All in need of redemption.
Black Lives Matter, 2021.

This is the laaaaaaaaaaaaaaaatter James Joyce, like *Finnegan's Wake*. Drugs and revolution, in realllllllity, mix like oil and water. You may not believe, Patty used to be a drunk. So she knows. It is just as hard thinking of ways to stop evolution, fire, as it is to drink wine and think of revolution. It's just that the wwinnnnnnnnnnnnnnnnnne goes to the head. I learned at Callllllifornia about class and how irrational street people can be in a revolt. It did not get to the level of RRRRRRRRRRRReal R R R R R R R R R R R R R R R R R

R R R R R R r e v v v o ooooooooooooooolution. Berkeley, generally has peaceful meetings. When in the city, they like to get a ticket from the Mayor, saying that their demonstration is okay. Just call it part of the tragedy. Protests at Berkeley showed me the power of people and had so much peace and 1st Amendment of the United States Constitution and The University of California, at Berkeley, were part of Cal, going back to the 1964 Free Speech Movement. Where a person was put in a police car, for his politics. And a crowd of people surrounded the car so it couldn't move. Then someone got on top of the car and started to talk to the crowd. There was a crowd there of some 500. Some Chinese person told the person on top of the car to take off his shoes so it would not damage the car.

- - -

Revolution, with Egypt, usually has guns, something for which I am against, Yemen and Syria are down revolutions. Thousands of people have been killed. <u>Class war</u> is different. Congress can take care of the rich, like "The Cherry" someday hooooopes to be rich. I went to the University of Chicago, one of the most conservative schools in the world. Now I am split, between the liberal left and the right wing.

The mayors of Chicago would not tolerate strikes. When I wasn't studying there, my field was creating a counterrevolution, which was news to me. I later read some of the books that my fellow classmates had produced. They were tragic. What I am saying is that I am not perfect, but that I am smart as heck. And my friends were, so I know what I am talking about, in this novel, so reliant on what I learned at Chicago. The eventual cure For my Ahab search for Zen and the material world and my civil religion exchanging Eros of my personal life for my politics, is bipartisanism. Because I ended up hearing everybody. Even the Green Party, of the environment. Anthropology made me hear almost everybody. Especially the Arab Spring and especially the agnostics. Being in a blues band, before, made me hear the rest

---

—We're on it, said Sherry. Drug out lotus-eaters, so into their own world that they did not even recognized the reality around them, I said, meaning like in Homer's story. I never did drugs, just a little wine with dinner? My father's house did not approve and made me feel guilty at that. It was the guilt I did not recognize, because I was only half self—aware, this guiding my motives, whatever I did?

—What?, said Hansel, wondering how he was going to make it back home with his rock and roll, these were young drug users, spaced out because they didn't know how far gone they went, it really was like an Odysseus for them, 10 years to go home?

—Your world, Patty, accused Sherry.

—The world of busted, said Hansel, this too being a metaphor or symbol of the micro—world and the macro-world of economics, they not getting the real world consequences of their drug use, now they were the underworld, the underground, something you don't ever want to do.

It's a shakedown world, I said, knowing that Hansel wanted to make it home like Homer's *The Odyssey*. But he was a punk, busted. And despite the good California jurisprudence and law and order in Los Angeles diversion statute, one's so-called record always put them in jeopardy. Like when looking for a Job. The 5th amendment was applicable across the board, in court and in society. Not to just Congressional action. In a word, Hansel was guilty. On the road.

What's that?, said Hansel.

Hansel was like a child not knowing of the punk world of the underground man. It mirrored the world of the regular world of adults, which Hansel did not understand, but fortunately he really knew rock and roll. The police put our co-op on the line-up. They would cruise the place. And at that, they took pictures of people inside the group home. Nobody in the group home could go anywhere, without constantly being harassed by the police, they having caught a good fish

- - -

We need some rules. Like Aristotle's Nicomachean <u>Ethics</u>.

It's a world where when they find about your criminal history, they will blackmail you, into submission, perhaps even to asking you for shakedowwwwn money. This is the world of the underground, and it's not pretty. I said. People don't know that the 5th US Constitutional Con law political jurisprudence amendment applies everywhere, and not just in a court of criminal law. But go to a fast food café, and one of the first things they want to know, is do you have a record.

It's not a class thing, I said, continuing.

It's a vendetta, said Sherry.

The Mafia?, I said, not knowing much about the group.

The Mafia gets their own shakedown, I said again, they are little groups of families, clans and one group claims the title Mafia, but mostly they were not like The Sopranos. On the East Coast. Family business, was everybody's business. And being busted was like their business.

So its not a class thing, said Sherry.

They have been on a shakedown, since they were poor and new from Italy, I said. There are two basic Italian Mafias, in the South of Italy and on that one island. And they fractured their family, first into legal business import from Italy. But they still got on the line up of The Eternal City and got a bad reputation from everyone no matter what they did, and static from the police. And from the neighbors.

And the lower classes? This was a big deal with the social sciences it's all about <u>class</u>, that the cause of everything. This is vulgar, but basic.

That's what you will be, I said.

If this band doesn't get off the ground?, asked Patty.

We'll use the song "Busted", and hope it's a hit, I said. Patty was an undergraduate at UCLA. She did research into the underworld of the bust. That's why she knew so much about it.

It's punk, Sherry said, making a play on words of the type music we played and a cheap type person. We having made it our business to know about these people, Holmes.

We supply the world of punks, I said. There I went again, uniting one thing with another. Here it was economics and rock and roll. That's the way I think, like in metaphor, this thing is like that thing. That's a symbol, one thing substituted for a metaphor or other symbol or a type or semiotic or index or allegory or sign or signal or penalty for another sign, A trope, a non-literal symbol or sign was the connection between one thing and another, rock and roll and econ, the fire in the belly, like a Zen master saying you drink to stop the pain of birth, water to put out the <u>water in the Belly</u>, but since it's a metaphor, you can never get rid of the pain, the quench the thirst, the pilgrim hopping around like beinglike <u>Ahab</u> trying to help capitalism. The best lack conviction and the worst are full of passion In 2013, the Syrian government used chemical weapons, against it's opposition and civilians.

- - -

-2-

We argued about how a bust was like a ritual and a courtroom was like a church session and what it was like to be lower class.

BBBBBBBBBBBBusttttttttttted. Reader, shake it off you already read it, that was the big chill, the big tragedy, if you can say, it's not me, I am not guilty? Not me? It's not sex or drugs for me? Then you made it through the ritual of the novel. One of them. That's why a novel is like a ritual is like an initiation. If you can identify with the bust, it's like you failed terribly in your major in a class in basic math. And you're a mechanical engineer. Proper people don't get busted and that's why you need a pilgrim's progress, to wash you clean of the taint with your bust from the police. And if it's a friend of a friend, who got busted in your family. You are on the cosmic line-up. You keep reading to see what punishment and guilt you missed. That's why you're sleepy?

—We invest, said Sherry. She thought in metaphor too. You invest money, you invest energy.

—In ideologies, I said. Lesbos, like in The Odyssey.

—World ideologies?, asked Hansel, not really self-aware yet.

—Of the lower classes, said Sherry, who hit the nail on the head as to our clients and people who would like our type muse. It was a big leap of faith to guess that there would be a market for our punk style, but there is. People want to see what they are not, Holmes.

—Why?

—Sherry said, we have a punk business. That sells the lower classes to the upper classes, the punk sons of doctors and lawyers, the ones that can afford our DVD's of Faust and Ahab, captain, or deep tragedy that needs to be coached and CD's and our concerts. We put on a good show. It was like tragic parody. Our parody of capitalism. It's hard to see our comedy but its gallows humor. We consciously mixed it together round and round, into our music. The black comedy is subtle. The capitalism is ironic comedy, ironic because rock and roll is supposed to hate capitalism. It's like camp humor. You laugh at the gallows humor, the tragedy, because it is not you. If it were you, it makes you feel like an illegal alien.

- - -

—Do you think it will be that big?, said Justin.

—We invest in our vision. Have you listened to us practice? World music has not heard any thing like this in 30 years. We are like an ember exploding, said Hansel.

—It's punk, I said, rubbing my hands together, copying Sherry's signs, her family brought from Poland. I added, it's like—The Clash.

B B B B B B B B B B B A A A A A A A A A A A A A A A A N N N N NNGGGGGGGG.

—When I play my bass, I take 2 cups of tea, and it's twang, twang, twang all on the same note, that's punk, I said, that's me.

—From the government, all they see is depression or revolt, like the modern Greeks with 100,000 people demonstrating, which turned into a riot with tear gas, causing the world stock markets to dive, I went on, thinking of Homer.

—Water needs to be poured on all that fire, said Sherry.

—You go there and be the police.

—The Euro is fading. And Europe is burning. Now. Then the police brought in law and order. This part of the novel is realism, as I type this, they have been debating the future of Europe, because of the National Note problems. And the government cutbacks like on old age pensions and the like and that was causing the rioting. Then the anarchists come in as they do and make it a burning riot. Like with The Greek, the Greece of tragic Homer.

Then in 2021 and before and after, it was immigration from Syria to Germany.

-3-

Back on earth, the Dow Jones Industrials, with an emphasis on the last word, has just droooopped 1,000 points. This was the US tragedy along with property. But we were in bed with the European Stock Markets. We move over on the bed, and we are taking part of the sheet of the other country. Turning and turning surely something will be born? It's our baby, we have our finger on the pulse of the world, Greece and Syria. We were following what happened. This novel isn't tragic, any more than you turning on the local and national news, that's us, realism. Like <u>The Odyssey</u> constantly repeating <u>The Iliad</u>.

—You see yet?, I said.

The Republicans are ready to have a revolt. I saw it on Fox TV, I think, sometimes, they called it the teabagger revolution, said SSSSSShhhhheerrrrrry. This makes it look like the whole world is exploding, on PBS nightly hour world news. This turned a Great

Recession or Depression into a mini-civil war. All over Europe and Arabia. This book is not nasty, it's the world gone mad, from the economics of world theater, recognize it or you are like some Chilean dictator. Like South Sudan. And Saudis in Yemen.

—Are you with the latter James Joyce revolt yet?, I said, putting my hands over the top of my head, fingers locked, knuckles to the skull.

—The teabagger's loss of the free market, with theeeeee champion being Milton Friedman, Nobel prize winner, left them nothing to do but Plead Con law.

—So welcome to the world, of the punk band, I said. This was econ 1, and the Arabs. The last few hours scared me out of my wits, hearing about the Greeks. And Syria and Iran. The seas of Odysseus.

—Hansel said, Yea.

—Our words pour water of the riots of revolt, said Sherry. A revolt's cure. Here we have more figurative language, the world of metaphor, like water in the belly. It's talk therapy, by free speech about the nightly news, you purge your self of the tragedy and have pity.

—WEEEEHHHHHHHHHHHHHHHHHHOPPPPPPPPEEEEE EEEEEEEEE

We try to build up the world, but how much can a punk band do? We are the police? The riots were here before we made it big. We can't be blamed for every red bleeding Mistakkkkkeeeeeeeeeeeeeee in the world.

With the teabaggers revolution and Iran, they are to blame for the Arab spring which caused theeeeeeee revolt everywhere and in the world. It is not us. They are in a riot in Greece, like our Greek Homeric me, Hero, Odysseus, fighting the one-eyed giant. Then comes the Sirens. And Calypso like in the Athennnnns riot. If they do drugs which they dooo red and wrongly, then Athens is facing the lotus-eaters. Homeric narrative, constantly repeating the above.

The Greeks would be lucky to run into Calypso by Homer.

Homer saw the world of accident after accident, on the way back home. That's me. Riots donnnn't always lead to revolution. But sssometimes they do, like the revolution in LLLIIIIIIIIIIIIIbbbbbbbbbbbbbbyyyyyyyyyyyyyyyyyyyyyyyaaaaaaa aaaaaaaaaaaaaaa. And in Syria and Yemen, despite world opinion, the government has policed around and shot thousands of people. These started with riots like the Greeks.

It's the Arab spring. And the riots in Germany. If we could only pour water on the fire of the metaphor of those riots. You see Democrats are not for revolution. I am really a Democrat, but I talk the language of bipartisanism.

—You have just been fired and your home has been foreclosed on, your wife left you? What do you do, what do you want to do?, I said. It's a tragedy like tonight's news, watch it, read it, and purge yourself to get to pity? You are normal? The above were.

—You can go to a group home, like us, on the bussssss line. I said, this is my great idea for America and the world, if it hits the fan. You just keep going with the performance. The social drama. You won't be homeless, because the government houses you all in the foreclosed on homes. This isn't right or left economics. It's desperate economics. This is the answer of redemption for and to the Depression social drama. Somebody makes a mistake. And someone else makes the redemption. It's government's <u>civil religion</u>, like George Washington, mixing morals and state. We have a duty to the poor, like Jesus says in The Holy Bible.

- - -

We can't even protest right? The radical left protested the Democrat Convention? And where was the Tea bag party, then?

In <u>The Sellout</u>, Paul Beatty won the 2016 man Booker prize for one of the most outrageous race humor books to appear in over 40 years, the early Ishmael Reed years. You might want to know the reality of what it's like being half-black in America. President Obama a typical African American male scene. Every black man in America has been followed when going into nice store. Likewise, or heard the doors of the car snap shut, when he walked down the sidewalk.

The same is true of me. But I don't dwell on black stereotypes. And I hide my feelings, which I share with nobody. I was born in Selma. My mother was from Africa. My father is white. I put on a white front. President Obama is my role model. My father is a psychiatrist. He moved to southern California, when I was four years old. He divorced my mother. My dad raised me. They still see each other. He never remarried. I put on a white front and talk like Mr. Obama. I look like him, too.

Sherry was a good Catholic. She was strict Republican. At the end of the day I held Sherry in my hands. I held her in my arms all night long. We made love.

"We Don't Do Drugs"

Welcome to the bottom,
It's all uphill from here,
We now don't do drugs,
Now we find the scent of Zen.

We are still civil we just get down, One
step up from the hooooooooomeless,
You have class.

Start the revolution without me,
We have a co-op and food.

Carpenters are all out of work,
The real estate value dropped,
50 % in Florida
Banks protest any loan to a home,
With real estate tanking,
There are no apartments you can afford,
With the mortgages so high.

Bring your kids to the new group hoommmmmmes,
Start up a factory,you knit winter hats
But don't go down and protest your homes.
We are not crazy.

Here are 2 more songs off of the "Busted" album. Double jeopardy of the 5th Amendment applies, in all situations, like trial and looking for work. But that doesn't stop the shakedown.

"Sell Each Other"

Depression hits me, my Being
When I get fffffffffffired, Then I sleep it off,
And call it my depression.

Drop the stuff and have a cup-full of tea,
Then read a book.
Then sell each other

You can look for a job that is not there,
Or go to the state,
For your own personal things.

So live on oranges and mush.
Not a pretty life, but it stops the stress.
I sell you, you sell me.
But there is no case of peaceful assembly,
So don't set up a Hobo encampment, It's not protected.
Especially on private property.
Like the Occupy Wall street people.

You wonder how that movement will be a blue print in any type of civil war, if the National Note does go down, and more people are put out of work as a result. Class war stops, on the National Note, the conservatives.

-4-

Meaning, again, is attempted, for the rrrrrrrrrrreading dim-sighted, impaired. Joyce did *The Odyssey*. But, though I follow his parody of Joyce on that Homer, the above is beyond that. I crossed my arms one thumb up into heart theory, and pointed my chest towards Patty. Joyce's *Finnegan's Wake*. That's funny spelled words.

We met the next day. And went over all of our songs and played all our tunes and talked. Like me the majority of the band is Democrat.

—The stock market?, Sherry said.

—Down 500 more points, I said, watching Wall street like a doctor takes your pulse.

—G M?

—Worth 35 cents a share, lowest since 1933. 9% unemployed. Employment went down to 8 ½ % by February 2012. GM, then, got going.

—It's all class, I said, knowing what I was talking about, it's the fire in the belly, Patty and Hansel getting to the belly of the monster.

—Do you think?, said Sherry, sarcastic as ever.

—The upper classes owned G M, I said. But, ironic, Republican Presidential Candidates would not have bailed-out GM, believing in survival of the fittest type of Capitalism, being the Ahab. a wrong metaphor of biology to economics.

- - -

—And?, I said.

—Investment bankers lost their jobs with Carpenters, said Sherry.

Realism like tonight's news.

In one and a half years, GM gave back all the money that they borrowed from The Fed. A good sign for President Obama. His approval rating in the US is at 50%, as of Valentine's Day, 2012.

We ran a cold run of "Busted" with two DVD recorders. One on Sherry and one looking around the band. We'd edit it later. In the video, we had some coooops see the drugs on Patty. Then they busted her. In the video Sherry flirted with me and one of the coooops. Then somebody comes up with a gun and starts to shakedown her, because of her record, a victim not withstanding that it was a Diversion statute. Sherry was always a passive victim.

Just then, my Mummy and Dada came into where we were filllllllllllllllmming. I don't know why, but I call my shrink father, Hoodoo. They were nervous because they were mad at what they saw. I felt a cold draft of air.

We wanted to film the unhappiness on their faces. There is nothing better than a son needs more as a sign to revolt than a parents hating what a friend or you are doing. For the reader, this is universal tragedy. Read the realism. This is the cause of rebellion. Your parents hate you and you take it as a sign that they disapprove of what you are doing. This justifies all you are doing in rebellion against your parents, who are frustrated. It's a wicked cycle. One feeds on the other.

—I just finished reading about the worthlessness of a MBA degree *From Higher Aims To Hired Hands*, said Frank, he said with both hands grabbing the other hands elbow.

—Adam Smith, the MBA Bible, said Dada.

—*The Wealth of Nations*, I said, thinking of Smith.

—You don't like it?

—I'd write a book and call it *The Nations of Wealth.*

—Why?

—MBA programs for the past 40 years have followed Adam Smith and turned our <u>exports</u> into <u>imports</u>, said Frank.

—Imports?, said Pedro. The following is heavy and hard to follow, but try it's important.

—Yes, and the Chinese wouldn't do that.

—Adam Smith's book told future CEO's, in his book, to import.

That's the economic cause of the nightly news.

—We need to learn from the Chinese, Factories and <u>export</u>, I said.

■ We need <u>factories</u>, and then export, only that will make the GDP stronger,

■ I went on. And that is the world judge of economies. That's how we get jobs. Not by investment bankers with their services. Services don't grow the G.D.P.

■ Grow the Gross Domestic Product, the GDP. Imports kill jobs. All we do is import. We import from our own corporations, that ran factories, before the 2016 election.

■ Out of the country. To India. Then we import those India goods, that were made for us from slave wages. Unions like the

■ United Auto Workers, stayed with GM factories. And made union labor work. Deficit spending on the banks was a necessity,

■ The bear of Depression started in the 1930's from banks stopping to lend. We learned that lesson. Wall street just got greedy.

■ Everything MBA's have been doing, has been wrong in the last 40 years? They fire unions, drop exports and import like mad.

■ There is no hand of Zen, directing the economy, like Adam Smith suggests. It's them playing Zen!!

!!!!!!

■ And MBA's are Wall street??????????????????????????????????????MBA's tragically sold out the United States of America. Most.

The next song is a reason why *not* to have a third world revolution like the Arab Spring. In Syria, as of now, the government has killed 200,000 civilians. It's not all the romance of the Egyptian revolution, where in less than 1 month of protesting in the main square in Cairo, the government gave up. And last night a year later, after the election, there were riots 75 people killed protesting the Army's grip on the country. In key countries, the Arab spring turned against itself. Syria was a key, touching hot spot countries of the middle-east. Tyrany.

"Third World Revolution"

If you want revolution, you have the wrong girl,
Don't cheat to get my heart,
I sing in a punk band.

I give you my heart, you give me your retort,
It's all revenge,
For something I did, don't ask the Chinese,
Or the Russians.

I can' t give you Africa,
Or Islam, they bow to a different Zen.
But that's the third world,
With India.

You're my daddy, feel my tragedy.
If its all revolt, where's the human heart
That's all I have to give, the deepest part of me.
But there are no cases on redress of complaints against,
The government.
So don't follow crowds or mobs,
Across bridges in the middle of the road,
They will arrest you,
That's why we start no movement.
January 6, 2021.

What is a wolf? Me? The city? The mayor? Corporations? Whatever, the results are not good, for the person that the wolf goes after, in the next song. Is it Sherry? It's always my Sherry and me. And we all are the world red wolf. The government is the wolf, the city is the wolf. Business is the wolf. It's survival of the fittest, what a cruel mixture of evolution and economics. A false metaphor put forward 4 years ago by the then Presidential Candidate Mitt Romney. Yet he was proved wrong, when the government gave GM a loan so that they wouldn't go bankrupt. As a result GM stayed afloat and in 1 and a half years gave back the money. The President redeemed GM. No matter what your politics it worked, rather than a traumatic big corporation going belly-up. Causing Wall Street to tumble 500 points, if not more. This is realism, see it and pity it. Voodoo economics? No.

Here, Romney looks like the wolf. And The President of the United States looks like a type of Jesus. Romney's Bain Capital, bought up bad company infrastructure. They turned it over in 2 years, and did that over and over, and made billions of dollars. One thinks that he should have run on putting all his good ideas in a new Tax Code. His capital gains is now at 15%. And that's what Romney pays his taxes on. That's good? It encourages investment? We need a Bain Capital tax code? Be progressive with all his good ideas. Some wolves aren't that bad.

That's like Reagan's Tax code of 1981. A recession followed and there was higher unemployment. <u>They had an estate tax at about 50%. Weneed the revenue</u>. Romney just went down in the national polls not a good sign for his free capitalism. Capital Gains taxes, the tax rate for money gained from investments, was about 28% down to 15% of the year 2012. That is instead of paying the top rate of 35%, you invest in business. And the dividends are taxed at 15% even though you make 3 million dollars. People make sure that the only income they have is dividends.

Art. I Federal contracts would make you hired at Bain Capital, if you could use it. It stops state regulations and city, too. That cost an arm and a leg? 5 million migrants out of Syria. Most to Greece and Germany and friendly Islamic countries. They live in tents with no food to eat. Listen, America. This was because of one bad leader, in Syria.

"Like a Wolf Blues"

Wolves are savage,
They will rip
Your world apart.
Go to Los Angeles,
And they are on every corner.
A wolf goes after a fox.
It is his food.
They scream the blues.

My city is a wolf,
As are the corporations.
Mayors can scream at you.
Hear LA open up for its dinner.

Please see my red dress.
I sing, see me see the streets.
Feed my realism, and pity me.

You rush at me, feel my face,
You are such a wolf.
I need your pension cash?

I defend capitalism, against the wolf.
I get paid for this, dear TV news, Let
it open up for dinner.

You are a wolf, Mr. London
Come in and get your lunch.
Buy me a new silk dress.
But don't protest,
The movement's a bust.

Being sensual is not a crime. It gets me through the day and night. Flesh is not a crime. I love every honey I see. If not all would be a bore. I wrote the following song Just for the heck of it, like TV nightly news realism you should pity, Just for my Sherry. She sings buy me a new, red silk dress. She is slim. And she knows How to sing my songs, flat and fast. Wolves aren't really down with flesh. But she's sexy, and that's about all of the subject you'll get out of me, in that this is rated.

Flesh on flesh and she turns me on, like next to a fire on a cold winter night, in New York. For "The Busted" album.

The flesh talks to me the way a horse talks to you when you ride it, in the summer. I rub her feet, my Sherry.

<u>Sinn</u>, in German, is translated as "meaning". Kant wanted "morals". My sin is that I am <u>Homo</u> <u>Dei</u>. Progressive laws are not stopped by the US Constitution. Teddy Roosevelt was a replublican and was progressive. FDR was a Democrat, and was a progressive, like President Obama. It's pop. The tax code is progressive. Obama went after ISIL, not like an imperialist like Teddy, but like Interpol, because nobody else would save the Arabs.

The middle-east people migrate through Lesbos, in Greece. It's in Homer too. I million migrants hit Europe in 2015. They stop in socialist Greece. They get help. <u>The</u> <u>Euro</u>, by Joseph E. Stiglitz, solves how Greece, the home of Odysseus, can solve its Euro loan problem with Germany, the lending country. There it resolves the problem of 2016 Brexit and a failed EU, European Union. It's an enigma. The General preamble of the US Constitution solves the problem with migration and Isis is against Domestic tranquility and the common defense. there is always the right and the left.

As this book shows, economic depressions come in cycles.

Money and the blues.

"Flesh"

Let me gently hold your hand,
I'll eat you alive.
Let's press flesh on flesh.
It's all we have left.

Open up and let me be,
Sit across from me.
With a start like that,
Where can we go.

Let me howl to you from my flesh,
It is all I have.
I will love you all night long.
Cradle me like your baby.

I have been you for less than that.
And I am a strong woman when I am with my man.
Rub my feet, give me a massage.
I work all night at this bloody job.
Your job, if you get caught in the middle of a mob,
Is try to keep your ears open,
For the police.
Or you are "Busted".

I wrote 7 more songs and I had enough for a concept album, we called it "Busted". We barely had enough songs for 2 CD's and we filmed the band playing the songs on a DVD recorder and had enough for 1 DVD, and of course our little Video pays. We did the videos like a social morality play, the Social Drama. We had tradition then someone would create a crisis and we always ended the Drama with a redemption. So that we were not radical, but let the breach get back to law and order. When we did our DVD's and our CD's we put the scene in little plays, to our music. Again, to Victor Turner's tradition to breach to redemption. That kept us twisting and turning on the side of the police. <u>This</u> <u>Side of</u> <u>Paradise</u>.

We were against revolution. That's why we were for the police, that's redemption. We were against the breach of society norms. This meant we could come back to tradition, of law and order.

The Euro could use the US dollar and the US constitution to help solve their historical problem. Don't print money and stop inflation. Use the Central Bank of Europe, like the US Federal Reserve, and keep interest rates low, even at less than 1% interest.

Kurds in Turkey and Iran and Iraq and Syria are a contradiction. But with Russia and the rebels in Syria, they could have a reconciliation Commission, like they had in South Africa. Then, they all could go after ISIS. They don't share our values. Sherry, a regular Daisy Miller, was the mistress of our Robert Owen Commune. Two of the crew had lovers.

Inflation came in spring of 2022, the worst in 40 years. The Fed then used increasing the interest to borrow money.

Chapter 4

NONVERBAL SEMIOTICS

-1-

The CD production was like music killing, that let us escape the depression. It's June 2009. The band got together again. We found a cheap Greek recording studio, it was Sparta, I will say it again, it was nightly TV news realism, Sparta. And an under-ground record company, Calypso, to put out our first record. We were really excited and lucky. We practiced and were really good. This followed Homer and was my parody of Capitalism. It uses production to help the GDP, but there is something about rock and roll that is comedy capitalism. Because it's against the father figures around and the world and neighborhood and kids and adults want to hear the real thing, though the diagnosis is cancer, establishment and the man won't let you hear good rock and roll. That's why we are like grass roots, underground. It was in cold blood. If you are totally confused by this stage, you can relax and say it's bedtime for realism of the nightly news. We are making money, or will be, on Patty and Hansel's legal Bust, a breach of tradition so great that in some cases, you just don't recover. That makes me an opportunist.

—We contracted out, said Sherry, palm over the back of the other hand. This was a Semiotic sign for, help! Like a red bandanna or woman's purse or scarf, legal under "symbolic speech" of the US Constitution's first Amendment. It made a parody out of capitalism because we represented the rebels in society, and capitalism is what they rebelled about.Crew Acid. That's Reality. Like ethnic cleansing.

—Time was short. And having our own studio and CD maker was too expensive. We did not need a factory, of our own. We were Democratic capitalists. We were smart capitalists, we rented the equipment. It was our odyssey. I am Odysseus. In this novel, It's I said and He said, It's still a portrait of my character, just from a different angle? Nightly TV news. The narrative changes several times. But I am always Odysseus, trying to make it back to the TV news of realism, home, through the twists and turns of the story, which goes from the guilt of breach to having a hot cup of coco, civil redemption. Tradition, for us stopped with the fall of the Stock Market in 2008. This is 6 months later. Obama solved it. My Father is from Ithaca.

—But we had our own rented DVD recorders. Aaaaaaaaaaaaah. It was a 2 CD and 1 DVD album, said Odysseus, holding up 1 finger. Knowing that there was a market for realism, like people turn on the nightly TV news.

—Yes, said Sherry, rubbing her hands together, as a sign of satisfaction, a type for those committed like me. Like Kafka.

In 3 weeks, our parody "Busted" was a hit all over California. In another 3 weeks, it was #1 in the nation. The cover of the album had us all in Nazi uniforms. We followed it up with "Flesh", which went #1 in a month. Sherry wasn't the only one with long hair. The music industry was in a slump. *ZZZZZZZZZZZZZZZZZZZZZZZZZZZZZ ZZZZZZZZZZZZZZZ*

The name of the album was "Busted", taken from the title song. It was basic. There is something immoral about making money off of a tragic situation. I call it parody. But that rehabilitation is basic to law and order, universally. Is what you call a story, a breach of tradition and then a return of the native through redemption. This was the realism of the search for the Holy Grail, of reality. You pity it, then it's not you. You made it through the rite. You purged the bad. In this anti-novel.

James Joyce, in case you missed the last chapter, is parodied here in this wwworkkkkkkkk. This form of poetry is a tribute to him. To his *Finnegan's Wake*. And *A Portrait of the Artist as a Young Man*. Like a Moo cow.

—Where did you get those signs?, said Hansel, out of the blue, as if looking for a way back home.

—Yea.

—You can say or you are like put down, I said, thinking I was an expert on signs having done graduate work with Victor Turner, of Chicago. And Milton Singer.

—Give us a hint about what they mean, said Hansel

—No, said Odysseus. They are signs of being a space man.

—What's a little sign?, said Hansel, Will it get us home?

—They are like NFL ref signs, I said, thinking of my other Doctorate Orals professor, Milton Singer, also a world authority on signs like Saussure. I failed my orals. Milton, a good and fair man, asked me a simple question on French, modernist Linguistics and symbols

- - -

—Two hands up at a square, and you scored.

—It's something like that, I said.

—Are they Russian, or Chinese?, said Justin. You wouldn't mess with the Chinese, would you? He came back.

—No, they hate them. They come from historical capitalism, Sherry said.

—They like came from the people who built the Pyramids, I said, it was from the people who built civilization. Like Feuerbach.

—Why did you start to give them?

—I do them when I FEEL, said Sherry.

—When I FEEL like I am losing, I said. And I want to penalize some other person who has just got the best of me.

—You must have a great marriage, said Patty.

—There you have it, Patty. They are a penalty. You must get a lot of them after your bust.

And not getting the sports metaphor. I had a love and hate relation to signs. First, I try to try to see people signing and explain social signs for a long while. Then at the end, I guess redemption, I no longer need to give signs. I guess I was like deaf.

—Crossed wrists mean something.

—And crossed arms, said Hansel.

—Great way to find your way home, Hansel. I said, serious. Like when you started living with your girlfriend and you are in the cold, and weary world.

—Ooops, I just made a mistake, better go to a NFL sign, I added to try to make a graphic point, which I was still afraid that nobody would get but Sherry. This novel as a rite, like Dante.

—What if you have an excuse?, said Justin.

—I do, I said. Making the "holding" sign, the sign in Da Vinci's Mona Lisa. We made these signs on our DVD of the band playing, our hit music. They went on MTV and VH1 on at night. In parody.

—What is it?, said Justin.

—For now, to get as good as Edgar Allan Poe, said Odysseus.

—He's a poet, and so are you Frank, said Sherry.

—That's like an NFL penalty they give you, said Justin. He finally got to explain it.

—Like you, being Alice, Justin, I said. You are my adopted son, Justin, and I WANT to take the penalty society gives you, away. Laws are laws but the bias that people have in their hearts, lingers on.

■ And the signs?

- They will follow, just like in the NFL. This is difficult to explain the existence of all of their signs. They just exist. It's like the Holy Grail, I continued, knowing that a third of the people wouldn't understand, a third would understand if explained, and a third would think you are crazy. But I am an expert witness, with <u>Milton</u> and <u>Turner</u>. Just hold it. It will all make sense some day.

- And don't blame the Mafia, they get ennnnnough grief as it is, I said. Italians talk with their hands. I have never studied the Mafia.

- —What's a City sign? Said Justin, thinking of the NFL, signs and penalties.

- Giving symbolic birth to somebody, like your lover. The Last Supper, everyone was giving signs to Jesus, it's the best picture on signs in the world. One says, Lord, is it I? Another Da Vinci sign points to another person. 500 years ago.

- These are the signs of hell, and into your pilgrim's progress out of hell and into the next stage so you can eventually make it back home, where you don't need

- To make signs. Like Dante's <u>Devine Comedy</u>.

- —Like giving birth to Alice as a <u>black</u>, I said. Trying to be hip in New York, but not in Iowa or South Carolina. Until 2015

- And?

- And, of course, the baptism as a <u>black</u>. To use another sign of a typical victim, who always get the penalty sign. said Sherry. Like the President of the United States.

- Playing sports?, said Hansel, thinking of the NBA ref signs.

- That's where it starts. "Ffffffffflesh" is the answer, said Odysseus. And its # 1 iN this nation.

—Donnnnn't you get a birth from Sherry?

—She gives birth to me every night. I cry at her feet and I WR AP my arms around her. She has been giving birth to me since I told her of the name of this, <u>Water in the Belly</u>. It's a painting of realism, of a classic El Greco, in Spain, a trope, a non-literal metaphor, the giving of rebirth to me. It's intimate, you only give them 15 times a day as a penalty, like Major League Baseball umps

- - -

Coda won an Oscar for the best picture in 2022. It was Semiotics for the deaf. VVVVVVVVVVVVVVVVVVVVVVVVVVVVVVVVVVV VVVVVVVVVVVVVVVVVVVVVVVVVVVVVVVVVVVVVV VVVVVVVVV VVVVVVVVVVVVVVVVVVVVVVVVVV

—Oh, said Justin.

—Yes, and it is not from the Catholics, I said, thinking how nuns pray.

—Their signs have civil rights too, said Sherry, half deaf.

—Signs?, I asked, thumb to jaw, not telling a thing I learned from Milton or Turner.

—Like you, said Patty. I pointer back to her, rejecting her judging me. Some of the people were getting it. I hope they got the bit that it was a way out of Hell and on to pilgrim's progress.

—They are symbols, said Sherry, signs of what she did not know.

—People use their politics around them, I said, knowing nobody would understand what I meant. In all the time I have been studying this I have never met anybody who has understood what I am trying to teach. Oh, I take that back, Sherry understands it, that's the science of semiotics or the study of signs or metaphor or symbol of like water or penalty? Why I love her, I can tell her the secret? Milton understood.

—Like your songs. Football ref signs lke signs for the deaf.

—Civil rights for a song?, said Justin.

—Yes, free speech, said Odysseus. We are talking.

—<u>Blacks</u> in the 1950's, we are here too. And they won.

—Signs?, Hansel kept on questioning, just starting on his journey home. Like American Sign Langauge.

—Civil rights? The First Amendment to the US Constitution. Most signs are protected speech, I finished. That's why I do sign to Sherry

-2-

It is the material line-up. MBAs never go to jail. They are upper class. And material Jail is for the lower classes. By definition MBAs are not guilty. Like <u>California</u> <u>Diversion</u> did away with 500 years of criminal law, the key there was that it was criminal, like criminology, of the legal processes themselves, the law, the law used to be criminal. The criminal law and it's charges are something that you don't want to get involved with, that is our message. But there was no diversion for our Vincent, he was in business but got criminal charges anyway

- - -

That is the establishment. MBA class is material. So I could never be criminal. They assume that MBAs are not guilty. Unless it is a gross violation. Like Mr. MADOFF, with his Ponzi scheme. And signs are not a Ponzi intent. Go into Los Angeles or Washington DC or Chicago or other big city like New York, what you find is everybody using signs. It is not theft. It is that, as seen by my Professor Singer, everyone wants to be like everybody else. Bain Capital is the reverse of a Ponzi scheme. Bain Capital was a business that bought up bad businesses. It was started by Mitt.

If you want to know why the first sentence to the left starts with a capital, it is because Homer was a poet. And translations of him do that. Sparta records made me a poet. Sherry is Penelope, wife of Odysseus. Telemachus is his son, like Justin. Sherry goes on my journey with me, which makes it different than Homer. James Joyce and his version of this book, was *expressionist*. He did not follow Homer. Just an impression.

"The Cherry's" management was key in making the band a hit. The manager's name was Mr. Will and he was good at dealing with the band's contradictions. Like me a MBA student and yet in rock and roll. It's got to be a parody. It's the tropic William Blake's *Marriage ofHeaven and Hell.* Trope is tropic is tropical.

Our manager, for various reasons, canceled the band's tour of Canada.

Then he booked us on a tour of the US. Right now we are on top of

the world. With our 2 # number one hits. Before the tour, we released a third single, it was a monster for the Arab Spring, "Third World Revolution". People wanted to understand the so-called Arab Spring. It Hit #10 in the US. Sherry rubbed her hands together, as if on a winter's day and in front of a fire. These are like NFL signs. A penalty when something went wrong. That was like The Social Drama, first there was the normal, then the breach, marked by a social sign, then a return of sign to acknowledge a need for redemption. Civil redemption.

And I loved Sherry, she was everything to me Keynesian economics was not socialist or comical. We were Neo-Keynesian. The President, Mr. Obama, was Keynesian. Neither of us was a red. We were U2 punk. I saw a program, last night, on Pearl Jam. It was their rise and fall. We played fast like them, and we played together as a band. BBBBBBBBBBBBBBBBBBBooooooooommmmmm mmmmmmmmmmm. And when Sherry sang the blues, we got near silent, so you could hear the words to the song. The band did not have any fights. The Co-op kept us together, like a family.

We were against the Establishment. Based on money or capital. Or class, like the fight in the Victorian novel, *Mary Barton.* There, they had fights based on class. That was our blues. The US was a little bit Victorian, still. We did not Like riots, or revolution.

- - -

Our first album was "Busted". We were planning two more, for now, "White-Collar Crime", abooout Wall street greed. The last one was "State Police". About a world like Jack London's *The Iron Heel*, one of his last books and a world that anticipated the one in *1984*.

To him we thought that we would read all of his words. He went from wolves to the State. Something that is going around the world, because of economics. And Class. Like *1984* the world of this novel. An <u>Iron Heel</u>.

—I don't know how long we will be able to maintain this law and order realism stance, with all our album buyers sitting-in at Wall street, said Frank, scratching his throat. They all want ammo to use against the rich and the powerful. But protests don't trump vagrancy.

—Our hate is evolutionary, I said. See, Sherry, our own family wants to go on the road. They had a violent revolution in Libya. They got Gaddafi. And the US backed the revolution.

—Well?, said Sherry, from Poland, which has a history of revolt. It does not bother Justin or me. Frank, you have to write the words, you went to Cal. This was not a tragedy it was the best education in the world. It was just TV realism. She said, I only look at guys.

—When your band is like "Rage Against The Machine", you have to have some hate at the machine and the man, from a law and order background?

—Like civil rights law against them, said Justin, 86 them.

—That's possible in this book.

—Sherry said, Like Section 1985, tragedy.

—That will protect you from the city and the police.

—Yes, Title 42, said Sherry. A sign or penalty for a violation of state law or state constitution.

—I said, and its from the United States Code, USC.

—Like <u>black</u> protests of the 1950's, said Justin.

—I said, that did start an evolution.

—Now you have the water, I said. I just look at girls.

—Where's the belly?

—Title 42 will keep those in the Wall street sit-in out of the belly of the cops, if they listen when the co-ops say, halt, I said. Otherwise, it's tragedy. Stay well, seeing the Social Drama.

—They just need to know the law, said Justin, thumb under jaw.

—Section 1985 is the national law, for sure, I said, thinking of #

—85 on the New England Patriots NFL football team, in the 2012 Super Bowl. There, they lost to the New York Giants 21 to 17. Symbolic of how hard it is to win a Section 1985 claim.

—Is it not Federal?

—This is so big it even ties the hands of the FBI, I said. Slavery.

—FBI? Said Patty, thinking they could protect her from being shaken-down.

—Yes. They enforced the law, during the 1950's <u>black</u> protests. Like the end of South African segregation, a once in a 100 year opportunity.

—They are like Federal Marshals. Giving you your Constitutional rights. Not like Ruby Ridge, the far right-wing.

—With a warrant?, said Justin.

—I said, no this is civil.

—Civil?

—Yes, when you fight with fire, you only get burned when you throw crime fire from the Greek Gods at law.

—This totally turns my mind upside down, said Justin. I am so much like in wonderland, don't you think?

—I said, that's why I write the words.

—"Third World Revolution"? That's Libya.

—It let the PRESIDENT OF THE UNITED STATES throw the fire.

—And he was a professor of con. Law.

—Title 42 is constitutional law?, said Hansel, thinking of signs.

—And President Obama knows it, I said.

—It's a small part of con law, they don't even teach it in law school.

—Justin, just wait till your see what I DO with it, for your uncle Vincent, I said.

—What?

—I use it with business. Obligation of contracts, Constitutional Law.

—How?

—That's the regulation. Really big with the Republicans, as if there were a self-regulating economy, in a false analogy of biological evolution and economics. Company survival of the fittest

—Tell us, business is our band's middle name.

—I know, I said, putting my thumb under my jaw.

—Justin said, I am such an Alice. In wonderland. I just laughed.

—This is in code, I said.

—The United States Code? I just laughed again.

—Everything is in code, I said. This was a metaphor of espionage and the reader is a Justice Holmes.

—It is language.

—And?

—It is protected free speech? I said, knowing that at best a stranger would only get 10% of what was going down. It was signs, types of legal penalties on the law statutes and how tropes or symbols or signs are protected speech like the civil rights movement. I made the sign of Da Vinci's Mona Lisa, free speech.

- - -

—The First Amendment of the US Constitution, I said, touching a finger to my chin.

—What about "Like a Wolf Blues"?, said Justin.

—It is covered. Like the NCA A ref penalties. Facemask is fist down on mouth, Holmes.

—Or the off sides, both hands on hips.

—I see, I said, rubbing both eyes with both fists.

—It's football, said Hansel.

—Keep decoding, said Sherry, finger to lips.

If you are bored by this play-like part of the novel, when about the time I change my life, I change form. To a hypnotic narrative. If you like reading like a script, go back and read the first 11 chapters again, it's several chapters, then comes the wedding ring. This is written in PC and PM, inter alia, this is written so the reader is like a spy. It's in code, the way a spy encodes his secret communication. Like deep poetry, hard to read, but worth the try. It's history. That repeats.

Nobody really got the code idea and the NFL signs. It's a minor theme that gets fractured, nobody cracking the code. I don't know why. I thought I explained it well enough, just watch an NFL game and watch the ref and run your own correlation as to what the signs mean. Keynesian economics was like the progressive party of F.D.R., Democrat. President Obama. There is a paradox.

Keynes is used by economists for deficit spending. In "good times" such trillions should be paid.

Obama and Biden used Keynes Theory to stimulate the economy.

This is done by reading the signaling in the market, once recovered. The goal is not to have trillions and trillions used by the Government.

Looking at other Presidents, Republic ones, Trump used his 2017 tax act to owe 6 trillion in National debt. George W. Bush did the same. It was Democrat Clinton who balanced the National Note and budget.

The plague of the Novel Corona Virus made the economy crash again in 2020 like in 2008.

"Economics" is the base of "regal Semiotics."

Chapter 5

SPEECH DEFENSE

-1-

In code, the Cabala is an interpretation of the Hebrew, man's code. One version is that Jehovah is. The other versions are number codes to other words. This is the Holy Family. Naturally it is very conservative. It is like the evolution of the Hebrew language and it's thousands and thousands. The tetragramaton, the secret code of Jehovah. This is controversial in that different religions have different interpretations of the word Jehovah. The word, tetragramaton, can be put through Google.Com. It's not a basic meaning. The Church of Pride encode it's meaning as hurt. Since I am an <u>agnostic</u> or don't know if Zen exists or despite evidence deny it or am an Academic, my customs or way of behaving or my morals is that of a tragic Ahab, some belief that would fit in with my feelings is best, like the above one definition of the cabala? That interprets out any Zen at all. And is best seen as a belief that keeps you in of the arms of tragic Zen agnostics, which I redeem of, in *Homo Dei*, or humanity is Zen, which is what I, now, believe, and I am tragic to the bone. I don't pray now. How I get my head around right, the plot of this novel. Now I am telling my own story, the tragedy of my life now, this is 1st person narrative. <u>In chapters 9-12 a roadie in the band tells my exploits</u>. Starting at Chapter 13, I go back to 1st person narrative, telling my own story, which is like the portrait of the hero as a tragic man, in his own words, for the rest of the novel, my story being of my changing character, this novel is about me not some character in Homer's book, my character change becoming the main thing in this novel? I started this fiction with me talking of my self, 3rd person narrative. The thing is who will tell my story? Isn't confession good? If so, watch me change, this turns into one long justification for being a Democrat character? That is how and why I changed? But now we are on our journey? I am the <u>Ahab</u> of proving that Zen exists?

The point is that I treat my father, Dada, as Zen. And all he gives me is guilt. So I take that to be guilt from Zen. It's a theme just touched on in this novel, but is so central to my father being a Shrink, I was born guilty to him. I change. That it is the key to my rebellion against Zen, and my agnosticism, because of my hate of my father. The plot is me changing. Like with Freud, on Dada as Zen?

It all started in 2008 and like AIG Corporation on Wall street. It got congress and everybody against the rich. It was a thing they called— Paper. These were very complicated packages of mortgages and stocks. AIG insured them. I don't know what they are, but it was like a small corporation, owning mortgages and selling its stock. Now mortgages are supposed to be a secured deal. But with the above example, the company could go bust, and the stocks are not secured. Thus, the regulation. The lack of Regulations was the cause of the 2008 Stock Market. I keep repeating a hard story, like Homer in <u>The</u> <u>Odyssey</u>. I add a little bit each time.

- - -

"Occupy Wall Street" was a movement that got 7,000 people or so sitting-in in a park near Wall street. They carried signs. It was mostly peaceful. It spread to about 100 US cities and internationally. They were mad at the rich. And they did not know it, at the 1999 legislation that said Banks could sell securities. This went against the 1930's law that said that there needed to be a Chinese Wall between stocks and banks. Paper is a many Billion dollar operation. The Occupy Movement was very controversial, because in and about the United States of America, in most small towns in America, they don't like protesters. Ike dawn rising up in her bed at the start, in most small towns in America, they don't like protesters. ZZZZ…

—And they insured the freaking things, I said. That was AIG insuring

"Derivatives". It was all legal. It was a multi-Billion dollar business.

—Its Wall street greed, said Sherry.

—I've written some words to some new songs, I said, thinking of free speech.

—For a new CD?, said Justin.

—President Obama saw the protesters, I said. 75% of the US agreed that we should tax the rich, like the protesters wanted, which became a 2012 Obama platform, of equality. As support for Republican Candidates for President, who universally hated government regulations, slowly dived at the beginning of the year, and support of President Obama started to go up.

—Yea, I said, thinking of political signs.

—Is it frank?, said Hansel.

—No, it's Sherry.

Everyone laughed at the plays on words. Sherry was booze, a good defense. Hansel and Justin didn't really get the jokes that were going back and forth.

—We want to keep it punk.

—We're seeing the "Occupy Wall Street" peooooooople.

—You remember, said Odysseus, of <u>The Odyssey.</u>

—Yea, we will tour for 4 months, on a world tour, said Sherry. While school is out.

—But the new album won't be out yet, said Justin, who is 16 years old.

—We will play all our new stuff. The old album will be known to the kids. "Busted" is what they need, said Pedro.

—It's Wall street greed, it'll play great to a world audience.

—What about America?, said Pedro.

—We're transnational, said Hansel.

—What about President Obama?, said Pedro.

—Well, our audiences in the US will be democrats.

—I call the CD "White Collar Crime", I said, meaning the next album I was writing songs for, after "Busted".

—NNNNNNNNNNNNooooooooooooooooooooo, I said, answering myself.

—I went on, this is big business. My Dada taught me not to laugh.

—Then what's the white collar crime?, said Justin.

—I'll pass around a bunch of sheets, Holmes

—When?

—Later, said Odysseus

—We are riding a wave, said Hansel.

—Only in California?

—The "Occupy Wall Street" movement hit LA. And the world.

—We will really take it worldwide?

—We have a cause?

—Maybe we could stump for The President, said Justin.

—NO, NO, said Sherry. We are just business, no real life politics.

—We want to reach out too to alienated Democrats.

—Why alienated?

—For the young, LA LA. Sex for the Flesh.

—This is for Wall street. Everybody hates what is going on there.

—3/4 of the people in the US thought that they should tax people making more than $200,000 a year, I said. This was the view of the President. Republicans said lower taxes on everybody.

—Congress was out of touch with reality, said Justin. They got a National rating of 10%, when ranked against other years, in opinion polls. It was because nobody was bipartisan.

"White-Collar Crime" was about the Wall street that comes to your home. It was about the 1999 statute that united stocks and banks, contrary to the ¾ of a century law that kept them separate. It was about investment banking that was the cause of the 2008 stock market crash. Europe had merchant banking for a long time. We wanted to be like them. Europe went down in 2008.

It was about the unconstitutional freedom of contract that they had over a hundred years ago. It was about yellow dog contracts. They were the contracts that gave a bad name to being a Capitalist. Contracts that made people work in a mine for 16 hours a day and at low wages. This type of freedom of contract was held unconstitutional by the US Supreme Court.

"White Collar Crime" was more than my song.

A plea of me for Constitutional Obligation of Contract, that went with basic contract law—the offer and the acceptance and consideration. Rational contracts.

"White Collar Crime" was more than our title song. It was what not to do in life. And it wasn't just Wall Street. It was alleged con artists who come to your home, and con you out of your life savings. That happened to our family and Dada sued for ½ million dollars. We went to a Federal court and lost the securities suit.

Freedom of contract seems so simple. But large corporations who used it 100 years Ago abused labor, women and worked people 15 hours a day. This was Art. I Sec.10 Like the US Supreme court case of <u>Lochner.</u> This monster gave birth, among other things to the National Labor Relations Board.

- - -

Liberty of contract turned into curse hiss. This was the start of the 20th century when there were no controls on capitalism, like seen in the 1910 *The Jungle*. A century later, my novel's parody is about contract over-regulation, at the state and city level. Pro—Art. I Contracts. Of the Constitution of the United States of America. It is historically controversial.

The above were the catch phrases. There was a need for United States Supreme Court injunctions. By way of contrast, there are State and Federal Constitutions that enforce the obligation of contract !

You are probably scratching your head to try to tell the difference??????????

Wall street attorneys get a million dollars a year to do that. And yet that is the minor parody of this novel, the explanation of good MBA business obligation of contracts. And the necessity of regulation. This is the difference between Democrats and Republicans, who don't like regulations, generally, from Washington DC.

The obligation of contracts are rational contracts and seek a win-win exchange. Not blind freedom of contract or liberty of contracts that try to have one side win at the expense of the people of the United States of America, this was the Paper that was being sold, on the world stock markets. If you are following me, and I hope you are, there is a gigantic contradiction. Solve the dilemma and you have started up a company as big as Bain Capital, started up by Mitt Romney. So you see the multimillion dollar paradox. And I am slowly changing from Democrat to Independent, 2012. A tragic parody, for rhetoric.

This novel seeks to explain obligation of contracts, that are constitutional at law. It seeks to show the difference between those and "White-Collar Crime", so wrong to the populist beliefs of the US. Art. I Contracts of USA Constitutional law is Federalism. And against state's rights, which is Republican, who like good contracts, you see the political economy involved in this knot. <u>I am the Ahab of Art. Contracts, ruled by Congress.</u>

The key word here is—crime. You bust crime. Some busts,

themselves, are criminal. White collar crime is upper class, and is like lower classes drug use.

White-Collar Crime should be busted. By definition, it is criminal. But sometimes there are just country bumpkins who try a factory or lab and don't know what they are doing. That's not criminal. There is no intent to commit a crime. So it's not criminal.

This novel does not attempt to bust crime. I'll let the FBI do that. And the parody part of this novel is not this. And not all mistakes are crimes. Some have excuses. Like relying on the 1999 legislation enacted by Congress, by definition. Following Milton.

But the term obligation of contract is a special one protected by Art. I Contracts of the Federal United States Constitution. This is Republican and Presidential. It's legal?

Years of taint. That was a time of big Trusts and oppressing labor with long working hours and poor conditions. It's big city politics, like Boss Tweed.

Where as obligation of contract is so sacred that it is even incorporated in some State Constitutions. I am not good with stats. Where are the states that have not incorporated it? California, New York etc.

Crime deals with intent. Now, you are thinking like the city DA on catching someone who went against the law.

Not all intent is a crime. But Ponzi businesses are a crime. And the FBI deals with Wall street crime. That was the motive in back of my song "White Collar Crime".

Some not guilty people can be sucked into business that is thought to be a negative network. They should go free. These are middle class people who want to go up in the world of business, and don't yet know how to do it.

"White Collar Crime" is the title of our second album. And it is based on parody realism. I laugh at the white collar criminal. A poor defense.

Our first album "Busted" was liked by the people of the world. I write like I work for the Justice Department.

Our first album was the world of the lower classes. The second album was the world of the so-called upper classes.

And its complex too. For example, in America when a lower class person is fired, he does not try to start a revolution, like in Tunisia.

The lower classes too often, but not always, think of being upper class. This can take the form of behavior explained in our "White-Collar Crime" album.

Article I Contracts are controlled federally, under original intent. Bipartisan.

Class is the difference between illegal drugs and a Ponzi business. But both are tragic.

These are nasty terms. But when it's like "Bust", it makes it all better. Freedom of contract and liberty of contract were terms used by people in "White Collar Crime". Now, even talking about it is protected by Free Speech, but is foolish.

So what's the difference between obligation of contract? It has to do with intent and motive. That's the difference between criminal and civil mistakes. Federal control of health and safety.

It's as simple as this. A good business has obligations of contracts. "White-Collar Crime" has freedom of contract and liberty of agreement,@1910 Like *The Jungle*. Like Wall Street.

It's the intent to take advantage of an agreement that marks fraud. Greed is not limited to Wall street. It's not Bain Capital.

The Justice Department can judge the difference between the above and legit business obligation of contracts, protected by State constitutions and the United State's Federal Constitution.

"White-Collar Crime" deals with Wall street greed, but not all greed is bad. Capitalism is not a dirty word. Even the Russians and the Chinese, Post-Capitalists, PC, embrace it, now.

We are just a band. But the realism can make you go deaf. Occupy Wall street was like out of the 1960's and back to hating the big pig.

Signs for the deaf exist like the words of my many songs.

Police power, not to be abused, exists to back songs like our third album, and I don't know when it will come out, "State Police". This is the world seen by Jack London.

"White-Collar Crime" and "Busted" are a bunch of records that go with it. These were for different <u>classes</u>, who commit different crimes. This is one thing I want to be clear about. The state police not a police state will leave you busted if you try white collar crime. Among the moon and the stars, other things in the name of freedom of contract.

Mistake of law and mistake of fact. This is no defense to an intentional crime.

Constitutional obligation of contracts, by way of contrast, have with them the people. And the intent of the founding fathers, Federal.

"White-Collar Crime" is a bad wolf, the <u>behavior</u> of which was seen by me as by the author Jack London.

A wolf in sheep's clothes, white collar crime comes into the home and takes away one's heart, from like a con. This is confidence.

Not Wall street. Where they needed Regulations, notwithstanding Republican pleas. Each business is on a case by case basis. Bain Capital, Romney's business was private property and private equity. He had the Harvard business and law degrees.

So the picture changes. My intent, in writing these songs, was not per se mean. It was to try to stop con artists, wherever they are.

"Occupy Wall street" has their own common cause. Wall street is a symbol and a sign and protests can that often go ugly, as was the case up in Oakland. Both are tragic. I hate them. Obligation of contract, not street protest, is my intention. And to show in a venue of Billions and Billions of dollars, how contracts, opposed to the words liberty and freedom, can help Capitalism not hurt business, a type of which is "White Collar Crime".

Rational contracts is the term I use for the Constitutional obligation of intent of contract. This is not just for small businesses, it would be perfect for Bain Capital, of Mitt Romney, who would go into a business, that was threatened, and turn it around.

The band got together at the co-op to play some new and some old tunes. We did not discuss the nature of white collar crime, that is my plea to the reader of this novel. To Stop it.

Twang, went the lead guitar., went Bass drum.

Howl, went Sherry.

It was good to be back at Joyce., Holmes.

As for me, I had a cup of coffee and played my bass.

We started out with "Busted", it gave us such a sense of justice.

Howl.

Thud, thud, thud.

Having no record was such a good feeling. Diversion, said the judge. I said, I get my brother's record. Cut a good record, said Hansel. There is a play on words here, isn't there? Of course there is.

Still, we played.

Twangggg.

We waited for Dada.

It's such a good play on words. My Daddy. And the German art movement of the 1111111111111111119999999999999999999999 9222 2222222222222222220's.

Our dada, who art in heaven, dada be your name, your dada come, your will be done, in dada as it is in the skies.

We were in the 1920's and out of the depression with our album "Busted".

Play.

Waiting for Zen, oh. Waiting for another contract.

A week ago we attended a legal sit-in against wall street.

- - -

We gave it a twang.

Sherry had too much tea, this type of playing is enough of a buzz. TUDDDD.

"White-Collar Crime" is a killer, Holmes.

These long words are my parody of James Joyce's *Finnegan's Wake* and my way in a novel to show in words the sound of a chord. And the feelings you get from a highly charged situation. Like in a non-parody of in a Federal court. To the reader, as Justice Holmes.

The portrait of the artist as a young man is a thriller? Every James Joyce book marks the future of the history of the novel, Ulysses.

He took it into 2500.

He went beyond the modern. Joyce was like a Da Vinci.

Waiting for Dada. Free Speech.

No time for Dada. Dada knows best. Twang

Jingle, jingle.

- - -

I do not know if my heart can take it. This was our jam session. We played like through the end of "Busted"

- - -

Dada please save us.

Introducing

- - -

What is Dada?

Can you have a postmodern Dada? It's like PC? Post-Capitalism?

When are we going to be saved from this world? Turn on the TV it's all there?

- - -

Crash, boom, bang.

This was some jam session.

Where are you?

We got a phone call and Dada said he's almost here.

- - -

We were used to this music. We were just warming up. But where's Dada, we want him to love us, Daddy-o, Jesus.

- - -

We were waiting for Dada. Twang. Twang.

Boom. Boom.

We were waiting for Dada. Twang. Twang.

We were waiting for Dada.

Dada called and said he'd be late.

How can we justify our position. Dada? Yes.

Save me, I have had too much coffee. Are you having fun?

Yes, Dada. "White-collar crime" can be like <u>Wall street</u>.

Do you love your Mummy? Yes.

Then you are saved. Dada came in the co-op.

—I know, I said, his son.

—And it'll be a big hit, said Sherry.

—I will scream it out flat the way punks do, she said.

—And we don't care what our manager thinks. Sherry smiled.

—That is what we did in "Busted", I said.

—And the kids will hate their parents, said Hoodoo, their Dada.

—Cabala is my Zen, I said, with sarcasm. Mummy started to cry. I leaned on my cane, thinking of my native land, Ithaca. In Homer,

by the way it happens to be the name of my home land, adopted.

—They will love you in Ithaca, New York.

—IIIIIIIIII kkkkkkkkkkkkkknow, said Frank

—You know that the entire world is suffering, said Mummy. Mummy wanted to relate to the band. She did not really like my Dada, a shrink. I called him Hoodoo because he was such bad news to the band. Some years ago he paid off his mortgage and put all his money in bank secured CD's. He was a government shrink. He put the HOODOO on Mummy and me. They were of The Church of Pride, who some think that you are Zen. To put it in a gross way.

Dada put the HOODOO on Mummy. She called him a tin badge psychiatrist. He would put her in jail, for her religious beliefs. While Dada alone was Zen. I parody voice of Zen. For that, Dada tried to lock me up. I just rebelled and went to my Mummy. Mummy was from Chicago. Dada was from Ithaca. Mummy was scared of me because I knew all her dark secrets. Dada did not know science.

Dada had a prostrate problem. It was cancer. This too was tragic. He skipped out on Mummy because when she called him he could not come. So he slept around. Dada wanted to get his yaya's before they cut out his cancer. I knew Dada. He was modern. And there is nothing like a modernist from Ithaca. He was like a Zen in heat.

Dada, the psychiatrist, wanted to control <u>behavior</u>. He judged you by your bad or irrational behavior. And it hurt. He had no science. The pills he gave you were based on confessions. The pills he gave you, he said, were to control the mind and body. They did not. They controlled your behavior. Vincent went crazy. In his rebellion. He needed behavior control. Dada lived together with mummy, at times.

I will confess, I parody voice of Zen. Dada tried to get me on this. This being a wrong thing. But I always escaped. Dada knew that it was my religious BELIEF, protected by the US CONSTIUTION. Freedom of Religion is such a universal and evolutionary basic part of US law that people may say it is odd for The Church of Pride to tell its people that they are Zen, but there is nothing anybody can do or say or can do about it. Now, I am an <u>agnostic</u>. But I may go back to them. The Church of Pride, is a sect of the larger Church of Zen Dada was Freud's Zen.

Mummy had a stroke at the co-op. Suddenly my Mummy could not move. Dada went over to look at her. State Impairment Clauses. Dada asked for some blankets, the way I would treat shock, when I was in and I was a life guard. Nobody prayed. She was going. They called an ambulance. And took her to the hospital. My Dada was a medical eye, ear and nose doctor before he became a shrink. She's almost gone, Dada told me in private. So they put her in the hospital.

For three days. Then she died and passed on. I do not think I ever really understood her. And I know that she never really understood me. And I know that Dada who I still hate and did not understand never understood Mummy. In her last hours, Dada and I stood watch, as if waiting for a doctor to come in and direct me to say that it would all be Okay. And my Mummy never awoke out of her deep sleep. Then, she died. And I cried for the first time out loud in my life. My Dada did not cry. For lack of a better reason, because he had seen death before. We cremated my Mummy. Then we had a funeral or a service, where I spoke. My Dada spoke too. A long talk. Vincent was there. He cried. Then we went down to the San Pedro Los Angeles Harbor and threw Mummy's ashes in the harbor.

- - -

-2-

Despite Mummy, we went on tour, from the <u>shipwreck</u>, from late June in summer to early October, all over the world. Our first gig was the UCLA Campus at the BASKET BALL stadium. We played our old stuff and the new stuff. We were inspired. We were the backup band to the band from England "The Reds". This is our 1st tour.

- - -

"The Reds" were a sarcastic band, not unlike "The Who". They played—*Tommy*. They got their sarcasm from watching Fox News. It was Glenn Beck who said that we, in the US, were like social and Progressive and Totalitaaaarrrrrrrrrrrian. He had free speech. And was a touch sarcastic, himself. That's the right wing and teabaggers. Who wanted something catchy thought we were in need of a REVOLUTION.

Not the "left". Like Libya. So we put on a good show. Politically, I play the role of the Devil's advocate.

We played our favorite songs off of our "Busted" CD.

We thooooooought that we needed some of the new songs, which I was going to write. I had not yet written, except for the title song "White-Collar Crime". We put our videos in back of the band playing. So I drank some tea and wrote a bunch or handful of new songs. We practiced them for our next gig in Seattle. There were a ton of people.It was <u>black</u> comedy or gallows humor that we were like USSR.

They liked the new stuff.

The Seattle show went well. The following are some of the new album's songs.

Our next gig was Denver where we played "Confidence". These songs of mine are the best way to get my characters motive, I thought as I also thought of the title of the album "White Collar Crime". I am writing this latest album's songs as we went on our "Busted" tour. My rights of free speech to show you these songs come from the 1st Amendment. Explanation of the signs never really hits home. I wrote these songs while we were on our journey. I don't know was it 14 more songs? For the double CD.

This is a 2nd Album. "Confidence" is our first song.

- - -

Bain Capital was not a con, like my Art I contract, the goal of which was to rescue a company, on the edge of bankruptcy. They turned around a corporation.

Article I Contracts have an additional problem, unions. In States like New York and California. You have the right to a union contract and the State regulators can't impair those Contracts. States have ties with corporations that want their own yellow do contracts. And dog then there is the case of undocumented aliens. Here, there is needed a criminal defense. that's my business. And Scabs. Then there are cities that are refuge to immigrants. Where the tenth Amendment is a defense against ICE. . See Reich, The System at id p. 120.

I wrote some songs and Sherry sang to them to me as we went to bed.

"*Confidence*"

My girl has confidence in me,
So I give it to my customers,
I get them to like me,
And I sell a con

It is a confidence game
Mr. I and my girl.
She goes to the houses with me,
And acts sexy.

They had confidence in her,
So they buy my commercial paper.
Wall street real estate.

Now my girl cannot sell a stock.
But we go through the phonebook,
With confidence.

We visit MD's and sell them stock,
The class commodity.
It's a stock for sure.

Art. I Sec. 10 of Con Law,
Federal control of Safety, etc.
That makes your contract
Not a con,
For the investor.
<u>Impairments.</u>

"Business Jealousy Blues"

When I was a teen,
I could not buy all the nice clothes.
The rich were the class of Seniors.
I was on Wall street that was my class.

I went to college,
All the rich went to law school.
I went into business,
To see, eros.

Now I sell Notes without recourse,
It's the secondary mortgage market.
I got sued, and thought bankruptcy.
The doctors assumed the paper.

Secondary commercial paper,
I use it as a con.
Laughing at all who put down my class. But I
don't go down into the street, to protest.

I just heard of Art. Contracts,Federal control
Darn, now my business is not
A con to my investors?

We went to NEW YORK AND NEW ORLEANS, where Calypso records rocked us to sleep. Listening to Calypso, was like listening to your girlfriend sing you to sleep. And oh what dreams.

We played like the lower classes, and the rich bought it. They loved our songs.

The heart of rock and roll had a head.

They all wanted to know when our new album was coming out. We said it would be out by New Years.

Then we hit Europe, where they were having problems with The Euro. And Strikes. They loved "Busted". We gave them bits and pieces of our new stuff. The Greeks howled. We hit Prague. Where they dug us from the evolution of our start. We hit the UK, Portugal, Spain, Ireland. They called us College Punk.

We made it to Latin America, where they have such great lovers. Latin lovers. By the time we hit Australia, all the DJ's were calling us what they did in Europe. Here are some more "White Collar Crime" songs. Off the second album.

Love me, I won't hurt you. We just gave all of Europe, US constitutional law of contracts, like Bain Capital, saving a company.

CCC analysis gives us the cultural <u>ideology</u> implicit in a work of art. It's sarcasm. And like the eros of Calypso, in Book V of Homer's <u>The</u> <u>Odyssey</u>. CCC is the culture of the hero. What was <u>his</u> past? As opposed to <u>his</u> DNA. What in his culture was the environment that made him change. It's <u>his</u> ideology, not how the author put culture of the author in the anti-novel. It's what is the <u>propaganda</u> of the character, like me, Frank. <u>State Impairments.</u>

Some right-to-work states have State constitutions that "No obligation of contract shall be impaired."

"Churning"

I am like a limited partnership seller,
I can't trade them, they just go belly up.

From inflation hedge gold,
To stock churning,
I turn over and over my clients.

We got to get out of Wall street,
And into gold.
Don't ask me why,
What are the signs of inflation?
It's gold and not stocks and bonds.

Now all corporate bonds are junk bonds.
Where is there a good investment?
Like Calypso.

So come to me baby,
I'll churn you out of your property note.
And save your guts, in gold,
If it's not too high.
Like the river styx.

Joint ventures are especially nasty. Like a partnership, if one of the parties is guilty of fraud, the other parties are liable. It's a bad one.

"Joint Ventures"

Yours is mine,
So when I take the fall,
You will go with me.

It's a terrible joint venture,
When a property deal goes bust.
All investors get conned,
By the lower classes.

China always has joint ventures,
Who was their lawyer?
Venture capitalists are a heck of a thing.

Wall street is everywhere.
Clean coal or not.
They come to your home.
They all go bankrupt.

Bankruptcy is a legal defense.
We live in Texas,
So they can't take our 3 million dollar,
Home
And don't protest in the streets.

They loved the name "The Cherry". In American slang, its like calling in reality by a slang term your band—Virgin Airlines. It's funny. We could do no wrong. If we made a mistake, they'd just say, "That's the Cherry". It was economic gallows humor

- - -

Our album, after the world tour, hit $2 million net for each member of us in the band. They loved us in Europe. We even made it to Egypt, they loved the CD "Busted".

Justin said, Frank with our second album resting on the fallacy of the bipartisan 1999 Banking act and other barbs? What do you say about the failure of the "Occupy America" movement?

—That's a good question, Justin. We are not a political band. We run gallows comedy, parodies. It's just that they were young. And young people buy our records. I think I said in one of my songs that the "Occupy" the whole world of capital movement should keep its ears open. We support the police. The first album we did was pro-police, "Busted". You're the cherry, too?

—Then your parody is misunderstood?, said Justin.

—They misread them. We are not for revolt. We are for law and order, as is the case with the police oriented "White Collar Crime".

—Justin said, its just another class of crime?

—Yes, I said.

—We're like criminologists, said Justin. Pathologists.

—Yes. Who would defend the Criminal?

—The young people in Oakland, for example, simply couldn't protest right or follow the police the way guilty people who commit white collar fraud don't follow the police. We are in the parody of <u>black</u> comedy type business. Not the fraud business. They are protesting in Russia.

We are riding a world of revolution, called protest.

-3-

We spent the next little while cutting our 2 CD and 1 DVD and that's a good deal album, "White Collar Crime". We're U2 when they started. Like <u>On The Road</u>. Like with this Homer.

It was the world wide stock market crashes. And the local unrest. Marching with signs. Like The Greeks!

Law and order generally prevail over revolt revolution and revolutionarrrrrrrrrrrrrrrrry protest. Egypt and especially Libya are not exception to the rule. Fortunately, in world history Syria and Yemen aren't the norm. The government stood, here, in the US.

We are reporters, sarcastic. We wrote "Busted" in light of the Arab spring and in Libya and Egypt. We were not saying people should do that.

"Occupy America" turned into a revolt, finished by anarchists. Just like The Greeks. Tropes repeat patterns.

Resulting police action is again the norm, in the US or in Some foreign country. Against those in Homer's flatland, the cold and alone world. It's all about the time of the tropes of history.

The same is true for white collar fraud. In America, we don't allow violence or have revolutions. That is the reason for the National Guard, what people do is go inward, and do business. Usually, it is not intentional business fraud. It is just a business gone bad. That is the majority of the alleged white collar crime. Wall street.

Back to the co-op, we did a play for one of our songs for a DVD, for "White Collar Crime". I wrote several new songs for Sherry to sing. We made a lot of money on our world tour. We made As many videos for TV as we could. You know, little DVD plays. Ours were surreal, with a lot of co-ops busting the deal gone bad. State Constitution Impairment

Clauses.

The times in the recording studio were priceless. We worked on our

DVD skits for each sonnnnng.

We saw another hit album, "White Collar Crime". It played into the poor people or the lower classes. Of course we had the FBI come in and bust the white collar criminals. We set up mini-movies. We were in Hollywood. We were acting out. The people dealing in commercial paper, were busted as if they were doing illegal drugs on the sly away from the police, or talking of Feuerbach? It's very Zen.

It was a morality play for the people who bought our second album. "White-Collar". Which was like the DVD of our second album. We put Greek masks on and acted out a play for our DVD.

This was not Bain Capital or Art. I sec 10 US Constitutional contracts. The above go like hand in glove, Bain and Art. I business contracts. By Definition, Art I means congressional control.

If you cann see the above, then you were just hired by a company like Bain capital. Learn how to use Art. I constitutional contracts.

Bain Capital was started by Mitt Romney. And he is the 2012 candidate of the Republican party. Our Art. I contracts were just as good. As the paradox of Republican party.

The true intent of the Tea bag party by contracts. The "contract clause" is like a libertarian tea bag Art I Contracts legal way to stop the city or state from putting illegal regs on a contractor's business. It's just that the original intention of the Art I Contracts, was to have Congress Control. Because the contract clause is under the rules of Congress, Article I of the US Constitution. Even Conservative judges, who thought like Justice Scalia, could commit to that. Article I contracts support regulations for health and safety and other reasons. Now, Article I Contracts is tragic. But by definition its controlled by the US Congress. They, now, are not. That's one of the reasons, perhaps, that, the U.S. Supreme Court hates them. Federal.

"Occupy"

Build a factory, and up the GDP
Dig a mine and do the same.
Beef production and wheat Keep
it from Tunisia.

Up the GNP,
And end my depression.
You raise the cash,
To keep it not like Egypt.

The problem is that only 10%,
Of businesses survive the first two years.
There is the risk, give it to the,
Corporate General Partner.

Limited partnerships can't be traded,
And generally end up bankrupt.
That's your defense when they say,
It's fraud.

That's misrepresentation on Wall street,
They came to your home.
You did not know how to run a factory,
For that, you get sued.

So you are the new general partner,
Call it white-collar crime.
Millions have called good businesses that before.
When they sue you for fraud,
You defend that you are bankrupt,
Like a Texas self-defense.

The young a lot of them bought our record. This was a continuation of the so-called Arab Spring of 2011, that saw 15 countries across Arabia, change or alter their governments. There are a lot of contradictions.

Bain Capital is not into yellow dog contracts, in a coal mine.

But it needs a legal way to get around city and state regs. That is the contract clause of the U.S. Constitution. Regulation, or too much of it, is the Republican mantra for the 21st century. Of course, things like <u>The Jungle</u>, OSHA, are a necessity and would never be stopped by the Federal contract clause. States too.

California Cultural Criticism, CCC, turns around wrong thinking, by people who try to make their art a wrong <u>Poseidon Adventure.</u>

Propaganda and ideology are deconstructed with cultural history. Like the books by Ishmael Reed. He tears apart race bias, by illustrating the role of culture of America in African American history. This is implicit in most, if not all <u>black</u> jokes and world folklore. Like Colonialism in Africa. And the makings of the world <u>types</u> of slaves. Like Postcolonial criticism.

The U.S Supreme Court held in 2022 that Osha was not strong enough to force companies to get a vaccine if they had 100 workers to receive the shots.

But held that People connected to medicine could be so vaccinated.

"Wall Street"

When they sue you,
You say you lived off of the profits.
Now you are bust.

In a world of Scienter,
With the incentive to invest,
But everyone has forgotten the trade.

You set up a factory,
In connection with,
Because you are the <u>class</u> enemy.

A farm is a factory,
For the GNP.
But who wants to invest in a bunch of cows?
Investors can drink the milk.
Mines have been good for 150 years.
Invest,
And you are buying lower class,
Dirt,
For Wall street,Federally controlled.
But don't protest me or have a redress of
Complaints, its all equal.
You'll wear the mask of occupy.

Art. I contracts,
Make Private Equity firms more legit
And earn more for their
Investors.
This is worth billions. In Revenue.

I wrote several more songs, based on the info I got from my business economics MBA classes. When the middle-class get unemployed they turn to con men, at least in my dreams of my songs. It came out to a monster big hit of 2 CD's.

We had DVD's, in part, from our world performances.

In part, we made skits for the rest of the DVD and videos. "White-Collar Crime" came out on December 7, 2010.

- - -

We stayed in the MBA program. To graduate in June of 2011. Just so we weren't bad. "Occupy" and "White Collar Crime", the title song, made it big to #1 on the US and most of the major world markets. Of course, we were movie stars. VH1 played a ton of our videos, on TV. We sold 19 million albums. We were rich. Beyond your wildest dreams. We made it like "Busted". They were both concept albums. The only thing that was similar was the fake busts, first for revolution and the just as serious second for business fraud. On the 2nd album, we had a cover of us standing in front of a World War II Japanese Sub flag. It was really cool sarcasm.

We planned to do another world tour after we got our MBA economic security degree. We would let sales peak and we would rest. But for me I had plans for another album, "State Police". A Crime.

"Occupy America", and what happened to them, was mild, when compared to my next planned CD. There they took away all United States Constitutional law rights. It was more like "Busted"

In a police state.

—Life without love is absurd, I said, after a half hour.

—Yes.

—And, in part, its like the title of this book? I said.

—What's that, said Justin.

—*Water in the Belly.*

—Oh, that book. Whaaaaaaat does it mean?

—It's a fire that can't be put out. It's the fire of love. It's the fire of birth and evolution and the legal use of paper, sometimes which is put out. It's about all those things in the belly, which gives birth to a new world, I said. It's ironic.

—What about business fraud?, said Justin.

—That's the worst of fires. Because everyone knows that drugs or dope is illegal. But with that it's still wrong. What you buy is not what you get, and it's the fire in the factory. It's 2010.

—What about my love, said Justin.

—You will find it, I said.

I went on, it's the fire within. That's what it really means. The fire that can't be put out, since it is in the belly. You drink water and it doesn't satisfy. Since it can't put out the fire. That is an irony. It's called a trope. That's a symbol. With many meanings. The ideology burning in the bosom.

—When you think you know what it means, it changes, said Hansel.

—I said, <u>Water in the Belly</u> means most to me the fire of love, that will give birth.

—I know, to guzzle water to put out the fire in the belly, is like a <u>black</u> comedy Zen koan, That is a trope, said Pablo, who was new to the band. The city of Berkeley could hear this.

—I said, that is right. And on one level, a Zen koan is absurd. Like gallows humor. Like my songs.

—Will they give birth, said Pablo, rebirth? The burning in the bosom?

—They already have. To law and order, I said, putting my finger to my lips.

—What's that?, said Justin.

—You are in wonderland, Justin. And you'll always be until you reread the first draft of my book that I showed you to read, I said. I explained it. Call it a trope. It's a non-literal metaphor or symbol.

—You hurt me, said Justin. Who really was in wonderland and who never really got the bit about signs. I think he missed the bit on metaphor and tropes, too.

—You are just like those few people who misread the words to my songs. I educate. I learned that at the University of Chicago. I learned how to be a critic at the University of California. If you can't read these things you have missed history. And I don't like to repeat, I said. CCC.

—I can't relate to the birth trope, said Justin.

—Think of your mother, who carried you for 9 months, I said.

—That surely was <u>Water</u> <u>in</u> <u>the</u> <u>belly</u>. The metaphor for birth and future. Russia & China are Capitalists.

—Water in the belly is what my Dada keeps looking for, I said.

—I see, I see, now. Food in the belly, too, would stop famine.

—Good, you are a good son.

—Dada is a man with cancer, and he is afraid of the prostate operation. He does not want to be, late.

I went on, water in the belly is like what a Zen monk has, it is his suffering and pain that gives him life. He hops around to get rid of the fire, but the water won't go away. What makes it worse is that it's a girl monk, with a shaved freaking head. Gray jacket.

—I get the trope or symbol or metaphor, said Pablo, trying to explain. Like the Church of Zen.

—We get it too, said Hansel, who looked around at the band at the co-op. Like the Soviet Revolution. They were US.

—The Zen or trope is a joke on Western Civilization, said Pablo, who pulled out one of his cigarettes and smoked it.

—I said, it is good to see you here, Holmes.

—I think the Zen of the <u>Water in the belly</u> is funny, said Pablo.

—He went on, it's fun. I can see your Dada running around like a rabbit in spring hopping to this thing and hopping to that, to stop the fire in his belly. He kept smoking. Soon his heart would break. The people of the Church of Pride got together like Greek Zens. That is people are Zen. A poor plea when your Muslim enemy believes in 1 God. California Cultural Criticism, CCC it's ethics, too, from cultural Chicago. It's Culture and environment that is the cause of your <u>Behavior</u>.

Chapter 6

YELLOW PARODY

-1-

It's Halloween. And "The Cherry" is in a Los Angeles court. Absolutely all people everyone are in costume. Including the lawyer for the State and the defense lawyer. It's a Movie stage court. The trial only lasted 1 day and was a fraud a farce. It's a fake court made for the movies. This is a parody of capitalism. Because we did not do anything and they charged us with something that had nothing to do with us absolute at all. Consider this like a parody of a court, and "The Cherry" on trial, a long movie filmed for Hollywood.

I was wearing the costume of a clown. The judge was wearing a British Empire Court wig, of the 16th century. The prosecutor was dressed in the costume af a Bear. The defense was dressed like a wolf. It was like a Halloween dream, even the jury were in costumes Like at a homeless Center. Full of Vets. No weapons. The jury was drunk. It was automatism. That was their defense. The fifth. Ripe for CCC?

The main witness was a kid named Mark. The state brought charges, on a complaint of Mark's mother who secretly wanted to be in the habit of listening to the album "Busted"? It wasn't anything more than one would get or see by watching the nightly local and national news. Sherry is a good defense. A victim.

The charge that remained was "Fraud", and I don't know why. It added to the PM absurdity. The band's defense was that it was for education, to be embarrassed at being stark naked.

The Bear started out, "Fraud is the intentional misrepresentation in business" How could education be a fraud? Bad teachers? Bad singers?

—Objection, said the wolf, before young girls with braids.

—Overruled, said the judge. That's like <u>The</u> <u>Odyssey</u>.

—Why do you object to the charge?

—"Busted" and "White-Collar Crime" need to be listened to, for the court to see that the bands intent is for law and order, said the wolf.

We had a demo of the second album.

They turned down the lights of the courtroom and played both albums. After the judge gave his okay. It took 3 hours because the wolf wanted to show the busts in the 2 DVD's.

On my costume, I had a sign that read "Wall street"

At the end of the 2 hours of songs and video, I JUST had to say, with the cooooooooooourts permission, I would like to counterclaim 42 USC 1983 and free speech.

The judge laughed out loud. Our lawyer howled like a wolf.—The judge said to me, these are <u>criminal</u> charges. We are in a <u>criminal</u> court. Title 42 is a civil complaint. The two mix like oil and water. What you think you want is a Title 18 cross claim. We don't have immunity. Bible aside, if you charged the court, you would see a parade of FBI agents that would make your Halloween trial look like a walk in the park. We don't like Title 18. If you moved one inch in your chair, you would feel the marks of those charges up and down your spine.

—I AM sorry your honor, but we plead free speech, I said. We are giving ideas to the likes of Romney, a Republican starter of Bain Capital. It's for education, on how a Private Equity firm can take over a company, and reverse it's negative cash flow, to save themselves and the people near them and the company from bankruptcy, with an Art. I Sec. 10 constitutional contract, like Exxon.

—You are forgiven

—The wolf said, well was there any fraud in the Albums?

—No, said the judge. We wanted Frank to educate the court how we could turn around the Great Recession, that seems to be getting better. How could we help with Art. I contracts to turn around a home, like in the 4 million homes that have gone into Foreclosure, to stranger.

—I move for a mistrial, said Mr. Wolf. This was the first good thing that happened that day.

—The judge said, your client seems to want to be educated in the law.

—Let's do it, said the defense. It's contributory neglegense.

—The bear called his first witness

—Mark, what did you think of "Busted". He was dressed like a young Greek.

—Was "Busted" fraud?

—Fraud? Can't "The Cherry" find mercy and love? Escape?

—Yes, saying bad things, said the judge. That don't correspond to reality. And don't say that the court system is a fraud because we don't allow Art. I Contracts pleas. In revolutionary way. With comity to defend it, Internationally. Certain things can't be defended, like slavery. The changes are an impairment. Like with Daesh.

- - -

Like the ancient Greek God of fire.

—Objection. Like for "ideology" and "false consciousness".

—Sorry, saying bad things that is misrepresentation.

—Mark said, I think he said bad things about the Romans, Holmes.

—Objection. That is out of our jurisdiction, said the wolf.

—He said that the Greeks revolted, like Odysseus.

—The judge said, they did. They were the key to the Euro. And they formed what we call a protest. It was the Greek government that started cutting back on promised money to the people. Art. I Con law contracts would help the middle-class stay out of bankruptcy. Rentals

—That could never happen in the US, said the bear.

—Objection. Look at the "Occupy Wall Street" movement. Thousands of protesters were arrested. They will be back in the Presidential election, when they are homeless. Prometheus?

—"Busted", as predicted by the band. Like contracts of "exploitation"

—That is fine. The court hears you, said the wig.

—The bear called Mark's mother to testify, who was dressed like a Turk, alienated by the band's ideology.

????

—What did you hear off of the "Busted" albums?

—Violence?, said the defense, to young Turk.

—No, just a primitive, driving beat, said the Turk mother.

—And they were like the police.

—They don't like the Romans, said the other?

—We deny the charge. And its out of our jurisdiction. Homer?

—She went on, but what if it happened here?

—Objection. It has happened here, like in the Viet Nam war protests, like *Rhodes* which gave immunity to the government, and which came from the Kent State killings. Critical theory and CCC sees this.

—Well we come prepared, said the bear.

—And my clients supported law and order.

—And what about "White Collar Crime"?, said the wig.

—Marks mother was on the stand, still, I heard that.

—And what did you think of their second album?

—Boom. Boom. Boom, she said.

—She liked it, said the wolf.

The jury were all dressed in costume. Nobody else was dressed like a Greek. The Cherry wasn't the principal, it's the mother.

—The defense said. HOWL.

—Please put on the album "White Collar Crime" one more time, said the judge.

—I said, we were doing parody like Glenn Beck, protected by free speech. I mentioned Art. I Contracts because it's absurd for a Capitalist country to deny a capitalist gig, because of color of custom, it's absurd, Thus the parody, of the control of the means of production, as alienating people by ideology giving them false consciousness of the facism of "normal" pop culture. We are punks.

- - -

—Who is he?

—Fox TV news.

—Oh.

—The Cherry tries to parody American Culture, said the bad wolf.

—The judge said, parody is not fraud. "Busted" is what "White-Collar Crime" gets when they are prevented from winning on a win-win contract of Art. I Sec. 10. of U.S. Con. Law, despite disillusionment.

—I move for a mistrial, said the mean old wolf. Another good move by an attorney, this day.

—I am moved in your direction, but these things take time, said the judge.

The intent of the Cherry was to claim that pre-2008 Cultural America United States was a threat to the American people. They spoke for a populist US and were artists. Leaving the US to fight in foreign wars came from the far right wing of the right. Artists are on the left. The radical right has solicited out-right Tea Bag party, revolution. It was the stock market in 2008 that crashed, due to the abandoning of law? 1999 legislation that said banks could sell stocks.

We are not, now, teabaggers, the ones who wanted a revolution.

Who backed the 1999 act.

—What do you think of the 1999 Banking Act? Was it judgment of accord and satisfaction if so, it will be a summary judgment. Was it an illegal bust. They are not dangerous.

- - -

—Congress revolted in 1999, said Mark's father, also dressed like a young turk. He was just called to the witness stand.

—Churning, the rapid turn around of stocks, helped the crash.

—The judge said, and what do you think of "White Collar Crime"?

—The album or the churning on Wall street?

—The album. That deconstructs illusion.

—I think it rocks, said Mark's father.

—Was it against the state?

—Not any more so than the constitutionally protected Democrat white-face, the subject of sarcastic parody, Holmes.

—Free speech of the First Amendment, said Mr. Wolf.

—Does free speech allow you to laugh at the US?

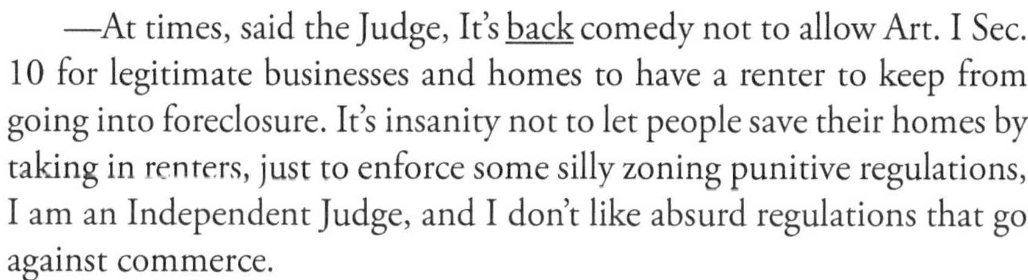

—At times, said the Judge, It's <u>back</u> comedy not to allow Art. I Sec. 10 for legitimate businesses and homes to have a renter to keep from going into foreclosure. It's insanity not to let people save their homes by taking in renters, just to enforce some silly zoning punitive regulations, I am an Independent Judge, and I don't like absurd regulations that go against commerce.

—When?

—When your Democrat radio programs start up!

—Or "The Cherry"?

—Yes, said Mark's father. I was wearing a Greek mask.

—You would impeach the testimony of your wife and son?

—Yes. When they aren't basic, evolutionary and universal.

—Then my client is not guilty of fraud?

—No, said the judge. The only thing "The Cherry" is guilty of is not coming out sooner with their record which educates the US about the Art. I Sec. 10 law, and it's Congressional overview.

—No further questions, your honor.

Les Miserables played in the background. Against barbarianism.

—The judge said, we know of the powers of free speech but Mr.

Bear wanted the charge to be fraud, rather like Draco, Holmes.

—The wolf said, in all my years at the bar, as a criminal defense attorney I have never seen such a highly charged situaaaaaaaation.

Les Miserables had reached its last cuts, "The Red and The Black".

And it was loud. It was about exploitation and alienation.

But the DA wanted to introduce more evidence, "The Scent of Zen" and "Strict Daddy-o". Take the last first. It's about Mr. Gaddafi. Didn't the band ponder all of Libya? The judge let this go on even though it was not their jurisdiction and had nothing to do with the charge. The former song, afterwards, called the Greeks to religion? These 2 songs were very pro-American. Amerika.

On came the words of the French musical, over and over and over. The judge said that it wasn't fraud because the name "The Cherry" let people know what they were getting. And the title of the two concept albums was not misrepresentation.

—The judge said, we can hear their music in our heads. The trial won't go to the jury. I am calling this a mistrial. IT should never have come into my courtroom. The evidence was weak, except the Father.

-2-

The reporters stormed the courtroom and they allowed it. They were the United States and world press.

They stayed for an <u>hour</u>. They all wanted to talk with me, the writer of the words. I spoke for "The Cherry". I took all questions. Especially from the Europeans? They were there from Latin America. We let Pablo speak for us in Spanish. This impressed them. A Gringo band with a Spanish spokesman.

We even had someone from China. Australia sent 3 people. There was 1 person from India.

The questions that they asked, was how could there be such a trial in a free country like America. I took the time to talk about the Bill of Rights. And went over each one. They were just for us. It sounds corny, but I instructed them about America. I was not bitter at all. It was publicity like that which sold our records.

Oh, they came in from Spain and Italy, again just to see us and the trial. It talked, openly, about problems of integration.

There were about 50 reporters from nearly every major country in Western Civilization. We wanted to give them a treat. Sherry said that we should all go to a bar. Pablo said we should go to the large coffee shop near the Federal Court. We voted. And Pablo won. .

We walked there. About the futility of revolutionary illusion.

When we walked in, there were about 25 tables empty. We pulled up some chairs and we all fit in. I had a regular American coffee, black.

The others mostly spoke English. So they seemed to get a large stock of European coffees.

Then the free speech started. We talked about an hour, first.

They couldn't believe that we had gotten busted. The police issued us a warrant at our co-op. Since we were famous, they put us on the local news that we had been busted. Is it a <u>crime</u> to make a profit?

—What did it feel like to be famous and then being busted, asked the journalist from Italy, who was at our table.

—It was political. Like CCC of Baudelaire, Proust and Kafka.

—Political prisoners?, said the guy. Even in Russia they let you go after 15 days, or say you were swearing in public as a charge.

—Yes, like Iraq, I said.

—It's not like the US.

—No. Like the "Occupy America" movement.

—That's political, said the guy from Italy.

—You are in the know, I said.

—We have that all the time in Italy.

—I'm not political. I am an artist, I said. The Italian reporter laughed.

—You are political from here on in, he said.

—Well, that will fit in with our next album "State Police", our third album.

—The Italian reporter said, you got a taste of it.

—My old religion, The Church of Pride, ran into a police state, some 125 years ago, a sect of the Church of Zen. Their defense is equal protection of the fourteenth Amendment. <u>Yick</u> <u>wo</u>, of 1889. They are constantly treated like a criminal. That's their status.

- - -

—That's good, he said.

—It's news, but it hurts, I said.

—Are you still a member?

—I am an <u>agnostic</u>.

The Italian reporter made the sign of the cross.

—That's sad, he said.

—Now you know what it means to have free speech, he added.

—It helped me.

—I write, I went on.

■   We know of "The Cherry" all around the world.

—You hit the right thing at the right time, he added.

—Why?

—You made famous the "Occupy Wall Street" movement.

—"White Collar Crime" is Wall street, he went on.

—Tell me about "Busted". Like Brecht.

—No, I will tell you. You told the world about the Arab Spring, he continued.

—"Third World Revolution", I said. It's their praxis.

—Let me tell you, the Arabs are the second world, he said.

—And the defense they have for your 9/11.

---A doctor would seek peace and forgiveness.

Alice had been sitting there at the table all the time.

—What's the matter Justin?

—I don't drink coffee and am not so merry, he said.

—I'll tell you, we will say good bye to the reporter from Italy. And exchange tables with the band member at the Chinese reporters table. They did and Frank introduced himself.

—Mr. Frank, I came all the way from Bei Jing just to cover your trial. But I don't get the Wall street protests. We don't do that in China. There, you are either in business of trade or out from the government.

—I do not get a thing, I am in wonderland, said Justin.

—I am sure you could relate to the "Busted" CD, I said.

—I feel so tired, said Justin, thinking of the Arab defense.

—Don't go to sleep on our Chinese reporter, I went on.

—Tell me about your "Busted", said the reporter.

—It was nasty. They were doing The Criminal. And got caught by the police. A wise-thinking judge so-called diverted them. And they had no criminal record, said Frank. This too is heart breaking.

—Fantastic, for all strangers.

—We could use something like that in China, PC, which is Post-Capitalism.

—Why?, said Justin.

—We have political prisoners.

—Don't we have them here too, said Justin?

—You. If you go on another world tour.

—Me?

—Yes, being Alice is a crime in most states of the US as well as most countries of the world. I do not know how to wake you, I said.

—Waking at the information, he said, now I will get the charges, like in our time in the Federal court. Pre-2015.

—It will leave you a cripple.

—My advise, son, is to stay in California, I said.

—What's my defense?

—California.

—No Bill of Rights?

—No.

—But there is the 14th Amendment. Marriage is a fundamental right, there. But your only hope is to join the marines or wait 5 years till the United States of America recognizes being LGBT as a fundamental right, I said. Unless it's Full Faith and Credit. Or Comity, that there is international rational basis, equal protection.

—Federal Court sounds like my country, when it comes to politics, said the Chinese reporter. That is why we like your albums. They give us hope. We get the sarcasm and parody. "Busted" was understood. The odd thing is that if you are in business, you can get away with a killing. To be rich, is wonderful. Just do not protest. The good news is that being a reporter is a busssssssiness,

—Then you are free.

—Basic.

—Tell us what the Chinese people are like, said Justin. What are the Chinese like? They are charged for a status crime? Do they get equal protection? Are they socialists? Are they cool? Is Asia cool?

—Well, you are waking already, said the reporter.

—Where will I start?

—Talk about the way you live, said Justin. I know nothing. I voted for The Cars.

—We all have bicycles.

—No cars?

—Few. They are for the people.

—That's the people, you have heard the term before?

—The people?

—Like the Democrats.

—I have heard of them, said Justin.

—And the air in China is terrible. We are moving to Nuke power.

From coal. It was the factories in Dickens' *Hard Times*, he said.

—And we like tea and beer.

—Who doesn't?, said Justin.

—Nobody loves you?

—Exactly.

—We love you, the people of China, he said.

—I need love and acceptance.

—It's like Chinatown, San Francisco, said the reporter.

—What's your real name?

—Justin.

—Why does Frank call you Alice?

—I call it myself. Because I am always in Wonderland, said Justin.

—I came a couple of years ago, and it was a totally different world.

—I never get the jokes and I think they are about me, said Justin.

—They probably are, said the reporter.

—I am like a San Francisco street person, I have a butch hair cut.

—You are clueless, Justin.

—Yes. And Zen won't talk to me any more, said Justin.

—We don't believe in Zen, said the Chinese dude.

—Neither does Frank.

—You wear all leather, he said.

—It's that I am ready to get on a motorcycle, said Justin.

—Maybe you are really butch, said the reporter.

—How do you know all of this?

—I lived in San Francisco for 2 years, the best years of my life. For sure, you look like the people from Castro Street, he said. Castro died.

—San Francisco is wonderful. In all that time I never had anyone try to do me up, said the reporter. That in a city where an Alice pride parade can get 100,000 people marching down Market Street. It's massive.

We changed tables again and Pablo translated for me. Then we changed again. All in all we spent 4 hours drinking coffee and I said it was the best PR the band had yet had? In this *Pilgrim's Progress*, Justin is not treated in any religious or political or moral sense. I can't help it. My views are bias in favor of them now, like with so many laws against illegal immigration. Alice is another word or term for like butch. I give Alice the solution to his problems, but in the end he just runs away, a tragic figure. Almost like the immigrant without a visa, like me when I was teaching English in the Orient. Not just Christian, everybody needs a good Redemption.

Like in courts of law with the rehabilitation of a character. Is it okay with Sacramento? The 10th?

These are issues that the Supreme Court of The United States hasn't yet ruled on. Thus, the emotions that are stirred up by these symbols is negative for about half these issues. Which places me in a difficult situation. The person in Alabama hates these type people, while people in New York City are glad I mentioned them.

My morals, at this specific time, are loose to liberal. I haven't now become a right-wing Republican. And as a result, the reader will have to keep on keeping on to find out my true beliefs. I did have Aristotle's ethics to guide me, so now I am not totally lost without a ruler to guide my blueprints. I am a chimp, in my evolution.

I didn't change all of a sudden. I went from terrible atheism to the Church of Pride. It was a big leap of faith. I lived off of signs. I just watched the social drama and performance that went with it.

Character was no big deal. When did I change? And when? As I say, it wasn't at all strict materialist. It was in the modern courts of law. It was in the Federal Rules of Evidence, at 404(b). What were all your bad mistakes and when did you change? That's our plot, to Homer's character coming home. The 5th Amendment applies everywhere, you can't twice be put in jeopardy. Evidence rule 406 shows you did it this time. And forget about Character evidence. How's that for a contradiction? Is that constitutional? Is the 2016 California initiative for lady Jane?

- - -

These first 13 chapters are me in the hot and dreary wasteland. I wandered and went on, cool to the under 30 crowd. But the rock and roll life at age 40, makes it. I was an Atom being hammered by Zen, like a Job.

It's returning home and keeping up the performance. Sure there will be problems. But under law you made it back home. You mended the personal breach. With your "parents" who you were running away from. That's my 21st century *The Odyssey*. The movie that was made from the staged play, along with edited videos, were distributed across the world; it was a 2 ½ hour movie. And made us movie stars. And brought in a ton of money, tens of millions. It was called, <u>The Cherry</u>.

It was an excuse to promote out first two CD's and DVD's to the world. The movie included videos of their CD, concerts around the world and the how with the press, after the trial. They made the movie a tragedy. It ended up with "The Cherry" talking about how it was ironic that in the USA, it was a crime to be into Capitalism. How they can bust you, criminally, for breaking irrational regulations or rules that are illogical, and make no sense, or <u>SiNN</u>, to your business? That's constitutional law. How can you get out of a bad contract, like in Goethe's <u>Faust</u>? Can you link that with Homer's <u>The Odyssey</u>? It's our civilization defense. If you are Justice Holmes, read this like "The interpretation of suspicion", by Ricoeur, as cited in Felski. With CCC, Civilization's Cultural Critique. Like Amendment Fourteen's "privileges or immunities"

Chapter 7

PUNISHMENT BLACK

-1-

—Did I say I had guilt?, I said, looking at a glass icon candle, with the heart of Jesus where the flame was, over the belly.

—Yes, said Sherry. I expect punishment too.

—Why? I said, rolling over on the bed, and feeling like an exile.

—It's Material punishment. People don't get our gallows humor.

—That's not Material, I said. What did Jesus say to the woman caught in adultery? Like the limits of Critical Theory.

—He who is without sin cast the first stone, said Sherry. You are right, that's the loving mercy of a Jesus. Amerika.

—So where is all this punishing guilt coming from?

—From people who are not Material, said Sherry.

—And from the establishment. Like from other states' laws. People reading this novel, not in California, who don't recognize our marriage, I said. Nor do they like our 2016 initiative.

—Like, the National government, against the Church of Pride, 130 years ago, saying it was guilty of sex crimes. Co-habitation, they called it. That's what we are doing, in our common law marriage, co-habiting. I don't know exactly where it's coming from, but the guilt is real, and it's terrible. As is the internal punishment, said Sherry, Catholic. Where Sherry shared the bed of mine.

—And the Church of Pride now is the total opposite of the church then. They are not very strict. You can't do anything. Almost as if there are ideas that haunt the church, from the liberal establishment, that say to the church, you are not forgiven for your co-habiting, they aren't lovers, but they are like haunted by a secret, that they aren't forgiven for.

—Sherry replied, It is co-habiting. That's what we're doing. I know in my heart that the Catholic church isn't so hot on it either. I don't talkkkkkkkkkkkkk about it much. And I know that some day we will have to get a Chapel marriage. Both of us are guilty and the punishment could be coming. Like two lesbians having an affair with one man. It's like a virus, bigamy plus. Like Leo Tolstoy's theory of art, as <u>infection</u>. *We were called infants, idiots or lunatics. So-called "Behavior Health" as a label. Like LGBTQ.*

-2-

—How does that conflict with the words of Zen?, I said, gulping, having some sherry, as if it were communion.

—I don't know. But I don't want to go there. We are not starting a new theory of art criticism.

—I know. I said. I didn't care but I know how much the Catholic church means to my Sherry.

—I want that warm feeling we get when we hold hands. As if we were in one of my icons. The heart of Zen, like an opening Rosa, to those who share in the love of the suffering, said Sherry.

- I want to get married, in a chapel, legally. She added, that is the only thing that is

- Going to stop the guilt. We both are equal. And I can't stop the punishment that's

- Going on behind blue eyes. We both punish ourselves for our defiled marriage.

- And we both feel the guilt and the punishment, just say that you love me, and will

- Give me a ring, said Sherry.

- - -

So, we were engaged and it had us feeling up-beat. I am not sure when we would finally tie the knot but It would be okay. Every once in a while we get down from our high horse, like the above. We both had forgotten about right before we moved into the Co-op. So we went back meditating on a Catholic icon, candle. It made Sherry have feelings and accepted. For me, I am still an <u>atheist</u>. I don't con Sherry. She knows that I just have a different explanation for things she calls religious. I call it my feelings. Can you relate to that contradiction.

Then I started to write down my dreams, as if they were a song. These weren't the type you'd interpret. They were just there. There were nothing there that would show guilt, like Freud used to interpret. And any reason that I felt punished. But the two were linked together. We'll get married once I get a real dream vision or feeling. That would do it for me. I told Sherry this and she loved me and understood me. And said, I know that such is it for you and I said, okay. My dreams were like an extending of the Catholic. PM and CCC.

But I was no Catholic. I didn't want to bring them down into my circle of hate and unrest. I wanted to punish my own Dada, for the guilt that he had given me. A punishment was what I wanted to give Dada. How do you punish your father? By doing everything you can to get back on him on things he loved, like a formal "wedding". That was my best shot at getting back at my father, by being the <u>black</u> sheep of the scene. The times that Mummy came over, we played our loud music, with our hair, I punished my Dada in this way. I don't know how Catholics rebel, but birth control is a sin to them. But at one Eastern Catholic University, over 90% of the women used the pill. So Sherry must have been guilty over using birth control. But I don't know who she projected her guilt on. She kept on going to mass and I kept on being an <u>agnostic</u>

- - -

We got so busy with the band, we didn't have much more time to meditating of Iconic Catholic art. I missed that. That helped me a lot so I didn't project my guilt and hate on my father. I think it's part of growing up. You get guilty by not doing what your parents tell you.

They, then, get punished by you, for your not doing the things they want you to do. It's rather complex. And kids don't know that. But it's things that make you guilty, like sex, are what you keep doing, to punish your parents for making your feel guilty about. Your punishment of them is the key because it's the one way you can get back at them. Like their implied keeping you out of their Will. It's punishment Amerika is like a jewish black person, who died in the civil war. Like in the struggle to keep Social Security, Medicare and universal Medicaid. The old and the poor.

- - -

This is the weakness of the circle of punishment. Parents don't want you to do something. Then you do it. And by doing what you punish them for telling you not to do it. For me it was Zen and Sex. For Sherry it was sex. I never found out much about her parents they died in an accident in 2008, but it was her rebellion against them that kept her going. She dressed sexy, to rebel against American morals. And then she would be made guilty, by the memory or her parents. This is the syndrome of guilt and punishment. Like raw.

It's substantially basic to families. Around the Globe. Parents have to give their children rules. The kids don't want to obey. So they do what their parents don't want them to do to punish the parents. Before they died, Sherry's parents told her not to sleep that much. She got back at them, by sleep. And that went over to sex. It was the anticipation of the parent punishing the child, that the child punishes the parent. It's like a cycle. That's why couples sleep around. Or overeat. There is always something the child can do to go against the parent. Dada was Proud, so I got rid of my guilt by hating his punishment

Then there is the right to vote, it can't be denied on account of "previous condition of Servitude", in the US constitution. States with harsh restrictions on voting, put people as their slaves.

Then there is just punishment. Sometimes the punishment is so

great that it hurts and you suppress the race. There is no way to break even. You can't make them guilty. You internalize your guilt. This is just simple guilt. You can't punish them back. So, more and more you internalize the guilt. It's funny with The Church of Pride they turned into the people who were punishing them. They froze about 1889, like a good materialist Dada and Mummy were good. And they wanted me to be a good. Strong father and a family that obeys the parents. And the males get a good profession, like law or medicine. Race was so punished by the government that it totally restructured their family. Of course, with a strong love of sex, and the ironic big family. Their guilt turned them into big families, justified by their own reasons. The key deal was the internalization of the 1890 material establishment. The favorite musical of members of the Pride was *The Sound of Music*, which ironically was the family Running away from the Nazi World War II occupation, Dada was Zen. Slavery.

-3-

We get punishment from the international, anarchists and terrorists. Some of them are communists. Russia and China are our friends. International fighters do come here to the United States. Some are locally grown. <u>That's why we have the FBI to tell the difference</u>. At 9/11, over 10 years ago, we had evidence that Al Qaeda got the planes and rammed them into the building, with the <u>Lautsky Arch Liberation Soldiers</u> we presuppose. And intentionally crashed them. They were like Muslim Communists. During the occupy Oakland Strike, of last year, there were people who had been members of an American Marxist Party and there were outside agitators who were anarchists who turned a peaceful assembly into a rock-throwing mob. Not all Muslims are Communists, in fact, most are not. We are the Federales. Why mention them? Like stepping on an old stolid. An old metaphor? Or, Symbolic rite? The international will have to deal with the consequences. And motives. And Contradictions.

Punishment of those of the above who had criminal intent to harm the United States is dealt with by the Federal Courts or the FBI or the local police powers. In chapters 19 and 22, we deal with Federal and local powers that punish them. Russia and China used to be the enemy of America. For different reasons, the Rockies and the South used to be likewise an enemy of the American people. Now, China has the best economy, as we will explain later, in the world. And Russia is also Capitalist. This shows you how you can go from being hated, and can go from being hated by the government to being a friend of the government. The Church of Zen is in a relative position of a body.

Friend or foe of the government is a relative thing. The key is that an entity is not a threat to the Government, like the Church of Zen. It is now patriotism. Like China is the personification of capitalism. They denounced any attachment to Marx or Lenin, in their—Two Whatever Philosophy, in about 1984. This "Two Whatever Philosophy" of the Mainland Chinese set the stage for a leap to capitalism. They DON'T—buy whatever Russia said. Likewise, The South got rid of slavery. Now they are some of the most patriotic people in the country. People who did not renounce their so-called <u>SiNN</u>, were like anarchists, who infiltrated the peaceful assembly in the Oakland Occupy Strike. Its mob behavior, irrational acts that drive a mob to do almost anything, <u>LALS</u> at its worst? We can't say it was intentional, as if they were Commies. They could have been drunk members of the radical arm of like the W WII. I am a novelist not a protester, but I remember what I saw on TV. And it was the peaceful protesters trying to protect a building from the assault of a dozen radicals, who tried to trash a business in Oakland. If the people can't renounce violence, the government will force them to or put them on the enemy list. There is deportation and the 11% latinos who have activist concerns, in early 2017.

- - -

Thus it is with the National line-up. Who is the national enemy? When? When if ever were they forgiven? In the 1950's it was the Communist threat. In the 1860's it was slavery. We have forgiven these enemies to a certain degree. Communists go by the name Marxists. There is the 13th Amendment stopping any type of slavery. Now they have Front defenses.

Punishment comes to us with our co-habitation when we do concerts in foreign states and nations. You can feel the charges. I can. Maybe it comes from the guilt, but the punishment is there all the same. We both can feel the charges, even at a concert. You can't explain feelings, they are just there. Keep this in back of your mind, as I slowly convert to Zen, in my pilgrim's progress, the practice.

-4-

Self-punishment is caused by guilt, good or bad. You get guilt when your mother told you not to touch the hot oven. If you did you would get burned. That is good guilt and civilization is based on things like that, as Freud showed. So self-punishment is good if there is something real that you should not do. Then there is the boarder where it could be good guilt and it could be bad guilt, like Race, which depends on the customs of your family. Then there is bad self-punishment. Like when the State says its okay to set up a home as husband and wife. There is a conflict of customs here. Your background could say it's bad. That's when you get self-punishment. It's bad when Character breach leads to Victorian suicide. Like written about by Tolstoy. or Vincent, the landlord.

Actually I was leaving Dada and the guilt trips he would put on me. I left when I was in my early 20's. I couldn't stand the self-torture as if it were racial cruel and unusual punishmnt, guilt. And it was very Victorian. When Tolstoy's female hero had an affair, it led to her suicide. That was what they did back then. Here, I go through a purification pilgrimage. I am not into suicide. When the father's guilt trips turn into a death threat it's pathological punishment. Like <u>civil death</u>.

And that's how bad it got. When as they call it, I first fell, I was into suicide thoughts. This self-punishment ruined my life. It was so unhealthy I couldn't deal with it. So, like the person who was caught in a gigantic bear trap, I cut off my foot at the ankle. To be free. To save in the use of my metaphor or trope or symbol, my life after a few days. This may sound tragic. And tragic it was. But I wasn't going to kill myself. To end the metaphor, I made the cut, by just cutting off Zen, out of my life. At the time, I cut out my Dada out of my life. But I was especially cutting out Zen, I gave him a penalty.

The punishment of the Church of Pride, was like one long charge. They open self and eyes, because they are a main victim, clear the area of the charged, so they feel. They kept their Zen, at the risk of crossing the line, of custom. In Los Angeles, people wear sunglasses because they don't want to be charged for watching the social performance. Or they think that they are a Hollywood star, Zen.

The reality of a bust, is one long charge for life, as if one were still in police custody. You aren't and it's against the 5th Amendment, the double jeopardy clause. But as life goes on it slowly turns into a 13th Amendment case, which no court would hear. Like the 8th Amendment against cruel and unusual punishment. But like at the basketball game, they keep charging. Like for <u>race</u>.

Which thrust me into the arms of my Sherry. Her flesh kept me alive and got rid of the charges. In rock and roll, its punishment before the guilt. And we turned the CD like Turner's social drama. The funny thing here is that Sherry is the breach and redemption coming in moments with my Sherry, to solve the problem. We got punishment because of our race "marriage". Hold on, it's bound to be a bumpy ride. That's the symbol of non-enforcement of the laws. That's the rite. To start out like sweet and sour, or salsa, and to end up tied for life, or to your belief. That's the correct mythology for the ritual of Zen, the process of coming of age. The ritual process is that sweet communion and the quick deed because of the cold. A non-literal metaphor of punishment is a penalty at law, for those who escaped another rite, held guilty, by Sherry. That's the social drama, the ritual process, by Victor Turner. From tragedy to vision. The symbol of espionage of the reader into the character, of me. Like my Sherry and her race. When she sings. We all come clean. The common law marriage looked like being in the middle of a salsa line, or a view of a body. Anti-structure is like the time of the liminal, like told by my friend Victor Turner. What Dr. Turner found in the heart of deepest Africa, was that in the middle of the ritual, you find a place where there is equal protection. Turner was a humanist. The social Drama is very primitive. But it is played out every day in court systems around the world. It's evolutionary and universal.

- - -

Guilt was universal, so you were ready for material punishment. As you grew up, you went through types of guilt trips, which required different punishments, that's how Dada made his money, in the giving of punishment. It was his <u>civil</u> <u>religion</u>, politics phrased in religious terms. Meant just for me. But recovery, Inc. gave you different types of punishment, depending on your guilt, which they made sure you had, that's how they made their money, in punishing.

One thing he would not let me do was criticize Zen things. For some reason that was out of bounds. And if I did, I would get anything from a mild critique to a threat to kick me out of Pride. This was very serious. In that since then I believed in the Zen, he was sending me to Pain, which he did for my relationship with Sherry. But since I was older then, it did not have as much force behind it, as it did when I was a kid. But all this was guilt backed up by punishment.

Our ritual process is different from Homer and Joyce, in that my return of the native is united with child birth by symbol. As our translator turns Homer's <u>The Odysses</u> into a novel, and not a poem, so too it is translated in a sensuous way, it is easy to see how James Joyce got his expressionism, in <u>Ulysses</u> in a sensual way, translated into modern English. Id, really, not like to be as he was. Hense, the PG-13 rating. They didn't let his book, that book, into the US. I am not Joyce. And I learned to give an expressionist interpretation of this one of Homer's books in a way like him. Not either a literal one-on-one translation. In <u>The</u> <u>Odyssey</u>, the book ends with Odysseus physically coming home, while James gave an interpretation, of one day, of a man coming to his wide, at the end of the day. And I made Odysseus half-caste African American, because it was over 10 years of his journey, mostly through the Obama years. I end the Milky way and the Universe. I think Joyce missed the Tragedy.

Police in Joyce's colony Ireland were like occupied by the U.K. Just like behavior commitment courts don't have the bill of Rights and its your "behavior" that they try to change, like they did with LGBTQ.

Chapter 8

RAINBOW DREAM

-1-

I went to bed and closed my eyes. I looked around and saw an orange wall, like Sartre's Wall, with a light show on it, projecting the news of the day, we were pulling out of Iraq, soon to pull out 30,000 people out of Kabul, where we fought for 16 years after 9/11. The news said that ¾ of Egypt thought that it was not done by Arabs, who had their Spring, bringing Democracy to the Arabs, 10 times better than info that led us into Iraq, which split into civil war, because of us, a dull CIA, full of torture, and the wrong information, we seeing that democracy is best left, from the grass roots up, and not imposed from above, like we did in Iraq. I kept my eyes closed, I tried to go to bed, and homeward, passage of my blues, aaaaaaaaaaat the depression, yes, I, Frank am black too. <u>I dreamed of Sherry, in a silk dress, singing the blues, flat, offkey</u>. She would sometimes sing the blues with a bottle of sherry in herhand, We begged her not to since when she was drunk she no longer sang the blues, but it was like Janis Joplin, and she thought she looked cool, which she did, <u>with one hand on the bottle and the other on themicrophone</u>. And yet she was an MBA on the bottle, unable to find anyother job. We couldnnnnnnn't find other work, when Citi Bank let off45,000 MBA's in one afternoon and we all sold our self, as pictures ofthe American dream. Her body twisting and turning, her perfume in my nose. Her dreams were all perfumed. She wasn't there, I dreamed my dream to get me out of the depression and the flatlands. Of course, Iam in need of redemption, a guilty Independent.

- - -

The narrative is here because I am telling you of my dream. So, for now, sarcastic, the dialogue has stopped. I tried the style of comma after comma, it was poetic but the poetry was hard to get through. Personally, I don't like long narrative, call it my handicap. I find it hard to read on the page.

Self-portraits of the <u>American dream</u> that had lost. Europe was in financial and social crisis, The Euro was at stake, the Greeks held the key, to the value of US money. And the European elections.

And I don't mean Homer, our guide, in his tragedy, that ended okay in the end. If the Greeks fell, The Euro might go. This was no comedy, it was a tragedy. And if The Euro went, it would ripple across the Atlantic into the US political standard. Calypso came to me, my record company seduced me. That's what albums do generally. I was seduced by fame, By Miss Aphrodite.

Seduction, also by the lotus-eaters, took my mind off the lost American 2008 Stock dream, I was still dreaming, of Circe and the Sirens, which were in my ear. Never was seduction so sweet. Calypso seduced us as we made sensual love to the world. These were from *The Odyssey*, with young dawn with her rose-red fingers.

Homer's evolutionary rainbow saved us. Ecstacy.

Sherry yellows me as I respond with my hand on her hip. It was a dream. She yellows back and puts her hand in my hand. I pulled out my hand. The wall went back and forth. It was my dream. Colors changed. This was some <u>rainbow dream</u>. They evolved, as red turned into yellow, and blue turned into green. Pink turned into red. These were politics and the hills of Los Angeles. The wall behind my closed eyes was yellow. This is my dream poetry. I see the gray of the freeways and the green of the palm trees. In my dream, the cars are stopped. Like <u>La La Land</u>.

We stoped??

I dreamed of all the old and rusty steel factories, that were not appropriate or class good enough for Los Angeles. Where the air is still clear on rainy days. There's always Pomegranate University, where they are getting educated and their MBA degrees, so that they can be rich like us. Us, we in our co-op. Pomegranate the color that says, help. We put our money in bank CD's.

Factories that were lost, was our sickness, for 35 years, I dreamed. This was US from producing steel and improving the GDP, we went to selling banking orange. Not an industry, we had no more GDP. This was my nightmare, from the US yes, but it was the collective nightmare of America. With services. Just consume. It was all spend, spend, spend that would help the economy. I could be a candidate for President of the United States, with my liberal economics. You lower the manufacturing corporate tax to zero. And have treaties that let us export goods. To South Europe. And Art. I contracts, Congress controlling.

Nightmares are terrible. We consume pop culture. You wonder when you will wake up. It's Kitsch.

So I get lost in Homer's *The Odyssey*. Perhaps the best book ever thought up or written. Home is where we are guided. That is my major dream. Lost in Calypso records. And with her, my record co, for she is a lady, I do not get the sound of Sirens in my ears. <u>I get seduced by the sound of Sherry singing the blues</u>. And we export our records. There should be no tax of the corporation that manufactures our CD's and DVD's.

I saw in my dream, and I can't awake now, millions of homes across the United States America, which had been foreclosed on, putting building contractors out of work. One station on TV, said for homes it's 1933. I was glad to be alive and that we lived in a collective home, our co-op. Like I said before, as a good Presidential candidate, I would universalize Art. I Contracts, to negate some of zoning laws, so people could let out their home, for rent, to like Latinos, popular in LA. To help to stop the foreclosure rate across the US. Habitat.

The blind economy of Libya, tells us that *The Iliad* is the answer. 10 years of war. *That is 10 years of war. Like Kabul. Obama got us out of Iraq,* our Achilles' heel. Then, local troops took over. Innnnn my dream, I saw big ships and they were going from San Pedro Harbor in Los Angeles to China. Sherry and I went into the export business.

We sold birth control pills to the Capitalist Chinese. And their red belief loved it. It was neither colonial nor Roman or imperialism. It was <u>export</u>. There were millions of Chinese women lined up to buy our product. To buy The Pill. They were not foolish. We kept the <u>factory</u> in the US. We did it with Letters of Credit. And the wall of yellow kept floating back and forth in my dream. I then saw a red wall that floated back and forth. I dreamed of 200 years of colonialist business around the world, by Americans, like selling baby formula to <u>Africans</u> who could not afford to feed their family. What's the matter with that? I learned equal protection at Cal.

The poet told of the clash between Odysseus and the foolish and proud Achilles. In our odyssey, Homer makes references to the early baaaattle at Troy. Like our previous Landlord.

I dreamed that the Chinese wanted information about family planning. So we printed up the info in their language. We charged a fee. We explained the Chinese government's position on having just 1 child. They had the culture, and cultured they were, to hear our product!

I dreamed of going into India. But there were too many languages. And a Billion Indians went without family planning. We were not familiar with Hindu beliefs as to The Pill. I saw an orange wall floating back and forth. I dreamed we made millions in China. We exported from the US and imported into China. That helped the American GNP. And it gave a ton of people jobs.

- - -

I dreamed of exporting to Africa, but they are generally too poor. We flirted with Russia. But since the Hollywood trial I got nervous around bears. The above was before president Trump.

I dreamed of Latin America. But given the Catholic church, and their stance against The Pill, we ruled that out.

I dreamed we went into the United Kingdom. They spoke English. That got us into Canada and Australia. Europe had too many languages. Tripping, Odysseus' grief at the loss of his homeland, we skipped The Greeks. Not London, in 2012, The Olympics.

The dreams of an international MBA.

I dreamed of feasts before going on to the PE games.

I saw purple wall move back and forth. I dreamed that I was at a republican convention where I tried to sell The Pill, but it didn't go well.

They thought we were pro-abortion. Which we were. Such was the problems of running for National office. Like Romney.

I dreamed that I was misunderstood.

I dreamed of green wall that moved back and forth. The Chinese had just legalized property. I walked the streets of China and saw free contractors selling food. Boy, was it good.

The Chinese, in my dream, were Post-capitalists. They permitted business but they liked a lot of regulations. We went to Wal-Mart. And asked if they would sell our pill. They agreed.

I dreamed of a blue wall moving back and forth. Sherry looked just like a Sojourner Truth, as she talked to the head person of the Chinese Wal-Mart. About them selling the pill. She said, yea.

I dreamed of an indigo wall that floated back and forth. Wal-Mart had about 1,000 stores. You can see how happy we were. We had a interpreter. She explained the Chinese contract we were given.

I dreamed that once back in the Uuuuuuuuuuuunited States, we would get a generic pill company to supply our factory, which packaged the pills, in a box, written in Chinese.

I dreamed we used a Letter of Credit, to take care of export shipping and money they paid us. We marketed the box with the Chinese Character for "Women". It was bright. Contracts can be an illusion, masking the power of the means of production and worker rights, in favor of the owner, US.

-2-

I awoke. And thought about my <u>Faust</u> MBA program, and my constant search for more and more knowledge.

As if my dream made me the American Insurance Group, AIG, the wig of Wall street, at an international level, for female products. We would be sued. For our birth control. We had gone into so many nations, we were like some 16th century colonial power. I saw a right-wing protest of our company?

I was lucky it was just a dream. And we made our money with a rock and roll band.

There was a wall of red floating back and forth. The tea party, anti-tax protests were in 500 cities, it looked like a Berkeley protest but it was right-wing. And Berkeley was generally on the side of the government, I said, they got a note from their grandpa, there were signs saying Free Speech and Petitioning the government, the pro-government people, in my cartoon dream, said that economists on the right and the left all said that in a diving, deep blue recession, with rising unemployment, rental? Unfortunately, they were looking at President Carter. But the same held true for The President. The stage was set, on the right and the left, for protests on both sides. The right against spending, adding to the National Note. Before Mitt.

It was spring, and the cherry trees were in bloom in WW Washington. It was like a parody of the rites of spring. In my dream. We went to pick, I went picking cherry flowers, in DC. One sign said, The Tenth amendment. And No Federal Strings. They mean the President's stimulus package, which 5 States boycotted, and then gave in and took the Federal money.

- - -

There was a moving wall of orange and yellow. The right against spending, the left against wall street. The spring of 2012 was set for a summer of protests.

In my dream, one of the protesters said, Look we are Rosa Parks.

The police were there, but kept out of the way, one sign said, No government interference with right business. They were like Vincent. It was the go-go free market of 2000. That by the way started the crash of the stock market of 2008. The same with real estate. Then a man in a dump truck placed a ton of tea bags on the White House lawn, in my dream. The tea bags were symbolic of the Boston Tea Party, of 1773?

- - -

In my dream, they were the American Revolution. And they made it clear they intended a revolution. One man had a gun. It was a threat. Like the anarchists against Wall street, on the left. Both sides were lined up for some election.

There was a wall of green moving over my head. Republicans quoted Jefferson. On little government. They said it's rugged individualism. They said that its from the people up not the government down. They talked about the tea parties, in Boston. It was mainly an anti-tax party. America had the lowest tax rates in the world. Not on this, but because of my brother Vincent, and my future MBA degree, that I was almost moved. It's not a contradiction with my songs, but because of freedom of contract. The Teabaggers wanted revolution.

- - -

Iwanted pragmatism.

The story of my brother Vincent's obligation of contract will be told, rational contracts and signs. I dreamed of Vincent. And I would not be a teabagger, I didn't like their call for revolution. But I liked Vincent's protest against City hall, "Occupy America" in Oakland, California had a similar taint. Both of these people and groups were willing to be called mad, for their beliefs. Something, however, I don'ttttttttt share.

I think that they all are <u>tragic</u>. But the election is all set up.

Ayn Rand's last book was about the prime movers going on strike. The above was not like that. It was like a grass roots movement. Vincent's protest was like the teabagger's protest against big government. The latter was against large Federal government. Vincent was against large State government, something that was missed by the teabaggers. Which left Vincent mad and isolated.

- - -

Republicans embraced the teabaggers, who turned over the democrat congress like the change in 1947, it was that big. But unfortunately they became the "do-nothing" congress, taking long breaks and generally just saying, no. They had no ideas. People ranked them the lowest of any congress. They took over in 2010. They are loosing popularity?

I dreamed all of the above in rainbow tints.

They had stupid ideas of reference like, end the Fed and get rid of the 14th Amendment, which was one of the laws against the South. That Amendment was like Title 42. Civil rights of state constitutions. There was a wall of violet moving over my head. The rich would, from the left, get their taxes raised, not the Populist Teabaggers. They could not see the contradiction. They sided with the rich Republicans. The Republicans said no taxes, no taxes and generally no to any other idea. Like using the tax code to help with jobs?

- - -

My bed sheets turned black and blue.

I already wrote the song it was called "White Collar-Crime". I grabbed another glass of my sherry to help me sleep. It was wall street.

I could almost see my homeland. But it was through tragedy and a bottle of sherry. There was moving over my head a swirl of red and orange. In my mind, I COULD HEAR the Republicans say, don't pay taxes. This was my pathology. There was no bi-partisan, yes. It was mad. It must have been my Sherry?

Like rosy red Independents, I had plenty of ideas. This was the code that linked me to Vincent. Who had been driven mad by the do-nothing state. I saw colors of red and blue. To support law and order and still Allow the enforcement of obligations of contracts, that was my dream. That kept me in the band, Constitutionalllllllllllllllllllllllll law.

Libertarianism unites the Bill of Rights, the 10th Amendment and the police. State Constitutions and Title 42 would make my dreaming a reality. I was still Independent but from the perspective of the above. I still supported president Obama and the need for jobs. And College debt relief. I kept on dreaming. I was tragic. And not just being <u>black</u>.

I dreamed of being a Democratic Independent. I can hardly say it. But it's for free speech, contract enforcement and a strong Federal government. And to keep us out of Iraq, like The President says. I knew nothing about politics, I could not get the Vincent side of me to side with the social security, side of me. It looked like civil war.

Dreaming of the economic manifesto, *Article I Section 10,* I agreed to supporting the *US Constitution.* That sounded like the Constitution Party, not the Republican lower city regulation or the Democrat Medicare. I knew nothing about City politics or National politics. It's in my dreams. I hear the tea bag party. Like a Trojan.

Choice, however, in abortion in cases of rape or incest were non-issues. Go to the Center.

In my dream, NAFTA was ugly. To plug the hole of MBA's there should not be a choice of local or Mexican factories. Following the UAW, contracts should be made to produce "Made in America" goods. This would stop the near 1 million jobs lost to Latin America. Thissss would make a nice dream. But it was Republican. Before Trump.

Dreaming in orange, I saw my MBAs as the people who told people that they were fired. I would rather sell pills to the Chinese, if it came down to that. I am glad I had my songs. They realism too, an ism that is not liked by dreamers. I liked to dream. I could dream of my home in Ithaca. <u>Dreams are like the seduction of Calypso</u>. Then I would not have to be bothered with the realism that was so much of the first part of this novel. Tea bag taxes were like money, my Article I Contracts. And were we mad, not like Romney's Bain Capital. Our life is one, long petition. Romney was a candidate for President of the USA.

Chapter 9

EXISTENTIAL THREAT

-1-

Our Homer is on his trip to The Dead. We are on our way to the Death Valley National Park. In California. Even The Grateful Dead offer no response. Unlike the philosophy of the late 19th and 20th Century. Existentialism, the worship of death. Unlike *The Odyssey*. This is a put on, on a chapter in Homer. This was one of the terrible things that Odysseus had to go through before he could come home. The 3 chapters after this chapter were more things that Odysseus, our Frank, had to go through, mostly modern existentialist questions. If you can understand this paragraph you must be a Mohammad. I have intentionally scrambled up our Homer to fit in with my own story of "The Cherry" trip to a National park. I'll say it again, let this be an inspiration to you to read the above Homer, on the chapter on The Dead. And this deals with something that 500 years of Modernism tried to exclude, Zen. This is a very subtle thing Modernism, if you can imagine back 500 years back. It, you learned how to be modern from Hollywood and College.

Orange sunshine Rosa in the southeast that morning, on our wanderings, our Odyssey, through the flatland. We went through downtown Los Angeles. I am Enrico Pelican, and I narrate for 4 chapters. Democrats cared for civil rights. Republicans for Art. I Contracts. But at a National level, like the stock market, siding with 1999 Banking law. That made the Dow Jones take a dive. In 2008.

I was told not to mention the Deadheads. Who were like LA's "The Doors" of the 1960's. But Protests and teargas were becoming popular again in late 2011, the year of backfire. If you are confused and don't understand the plot, just realize that I am giving you Frank's character development, through a Homer, like *Pilgrim's Progress*. Not the year of the Protester—as *Time* magazine called it. I as a humble Independent, am in need of redemption too. LA is like The South.

- - -

It is BBBBBAAAAAAACKKKKKKKKFFFFIIIIIRRRRRRR

REE. There were 50,000 people around the Staples center, there in early 2010 to go to a Teabagger's convention. Glenn Beck, famous for his parody on Fox TV News, could not make it. He gives gallows comedy. Won't you hear? Where are the Democrat radio Free Speech shows?

They linked the Tea Bag party with revolution. In parodies of Stalin and of Mao, the old USSR. The point was that President Obama's like government bailouts of private GM was supposed to be like the old Russia. It was Republican, a little forced, but it was good free speech. Teabaggers were supposed to be the counterrevolution. They took Congress like a storm in the Revolution Election of 2010. But failed to deliver, becoming the looked-down on do-nothings of 2011, not having any real ideas, Frank stomped his foot, in frustration. 2020? Beyond?

Teabaggers are for no regulations. I distinguish my obligation of Constitutional Contracts in that I think regulations are great, just not universally applied, like in Vincent's business, with a legal excuse, for his City regulated particular business, and his contracts. This as an MBA and out of solidarity with a brother, who is a Republican, Vincent. So you see my vote is split. For I like protection of Social Security, which Republicans want to gut. To balance the National Note, caused by the Congress. Who do I vote for? I repeat, like Homer.

The Teabaggers had found something in calling for no legislation or laws or regulations, a mantra in Milton Friedman's first popular book, *Capitalism and Freedom*. His second very popular book was Republican

Free to Choose relied on Constitutional Amendments for things he did not like. Teabaggers should have been so creative. He got a Nobel Prize. And done it in the halls. They did nothing.

California Democrats held out for a vote on the business of Free, valid legalization of Mary Jane. But it found no real support. Going on and on likewise, LGBT marriage was put down through a wide and full people's margin, in November 2008. Appealed to the 9th Circuit where it won in 2012, which I supported. Then, till 2015

Christian Nautsky was the lead speaker at the above Republican backlash Staples Convention, of the Tea Party. He lead the charge at the meeting for a revolution among the Teabaggers. He mixed religion and state, this Judas, with the call to arms. The US Supreme Court had just justified legalized guns. Which Los Angeles did not like at all, even the Tea Bag party. He was like Russian's dump Karl Kautsky.

The Teabaggers were like the libertarians, in calling for conservative no laws for no regulations. Republicans, likewise, called for a final stopping, an end to excessive Washington regulations. They got their power from Congress started out by the 1999 Banking deregulations Then came the 2008 wall street crash.

Frank's Independent view, was that the Federal laws and control and regulations should remain. He just objected to rules, as they applied to Vincent's case, zoning regulations and laws the rules that permitted his brother to avoid enforcement against him, for a legal and lawful payment and money exchange between renter and the landlord, on the issue of lower rent in this obligation of contract in exchange for

not having a car, the commodity regulated by the zoning department, regulated by the LA city. Heidegger was an existential threat.

Frank thought that the Teabagger's call to revolt against federalism and revolution was free speech, and just playing and revolting and just States' Rights. He did not like their ideas, except as it related to his brother and did not attend the convention, which was a legal freedom of association, not of the Constitution.

- - -

Christian, wrongly, said that Jesus, and this is the controversial spy part, was the revolution, with his two arms squared up like a ref signing a touchdown, a sign of victory on the part of Nautsky. The crowd seemed to be pleased at the mixture of church and state, like Republicans do, the link between politics and religion, like done by George Washington but now against the First Amendment. Russia's Lenin hated Nautsky's family.

Lautsky was at the convention. He was of Islam or Muslim and from Bosnia of a different religion, but he liked the Libertarian party or Tea Bag party or teabagger's call for a revolution. He was later held as an international terrorist. January 6, 2021. Republican Revolution.

Christian Nautsky was the principal, and this is the mind blown thing, in the call for revolution. That is he was the Christian man who was the responsible one for the Teabagger's call for a national revolution in Los Angeles. This is a major issue in a subplot of this novel. <u>If you can get how Christian sold out the Tea Bag party, you see a minor theme</u>. Vincent, in control of the blindness of contract, or at least the liberty argument, made contact with our Lautsky, the international marxist, in order to meet at Vincent's apartment Duplex and a home, houses. Frank and the others had as of now failed to find out Nautsky's motives, of the doom of such an argument, and the wisdom of the obligation of contract Constitutional claim, as it related to Vincent's business. Not all Marxist are terrorist.

Vincent was upset at the last 3 years of falling real estate housing prices, 40% in California, Arizona and Nevada. And Vincent, who <u>looked like Einstein, had the answer to all the foreclosures, just do away with lily rules of the zoning department, and stop foreclosures by letting the foreclosed on people take in renters, so that they could take in $300-$8,000 depending if they wanted to upgrade the house. And thus stop the 4 million foreclosures across the United States of America</u>. That in turn would help to turn around the depressed industry of carpenters. You do that with Art. I Contracts of the United States Constitution. And go to the zoning department and explain it to them, which they will reject, which is their job,. None of us suspected, then, about Lautsky or the other. The bag party was rad Republicans.

-2-

<u>Defense of Capitalism</u> is a necessity in times of a Depression or The Great recession. When Vincent found out of his brother's songs about the United States constitutional obligation of contract claim, it made him manic and happy and feel good. Something that our Christian could not offer. Stopping the City and their charges was a necessity, soooomethhhhhhhhing sssssssssoo punishing

- - -

Capitalism's defense comes in the Federal Constitution, at Art. I Sec. 10, stating "No state shall impair the obligation of contracts". We shall explore later these <u>Ahab</u> claims in greater detail this constitutional defense. 23 right to work states, conservative Republics, have put it in their State Constitutions. Non-Union States.

Here we are. Title 42, section 1983, deals with civil rights violations by citizens, of state law. And what better way to find State Law, than in the States Rights and State Constitutions. The key is that it must be a violation of the state law, starting the statute, were Southern violations of locals civil rights, right after the civil war, to get <u>blacks</u>. Though under color of state law, these laws apply to right to work state constitutional capitalism, the conservative Rights of contract capitalism <u>being</u> <u>protected</u> <u>like</u> <u>blacks</u>. If you are following, I have a split level of politics. Radical left and radical right. It's because I hear Justice Marshall <u>and</u> Justice Thomas. Crazy, man.

- - -

I have not done the stats to see which states have the contract clause. Law reviews cite such arguments that are worth their weight in gold. The idea is not new to the laws. But this novel presents this material as if brand new to the public. Mitt Romney said, have <u>factory</u> contracts, like our DVD's. These contracts are state obligations. You should start to see the connection, not self-regulating.

Regulations are needed. The 1999 banking rules demise proved the need for Regs. Old rules were universally dropped. Unlike the claim in Vincent's case, which offered lower rent for not having a car, thus voiding the need for the zoning department's <u>charges</u>, in Vincent's case.

- - -

Up and down.

Teabaggers are welcome to come out from the trance of our Nautsky, and use the civil rights of contracts, but we shall see this is not so easy. Politics have bias. And regulations have bite. The Tea Bag party was generally the Republicans, of Milton. Sea Reich's <u>Saving Capitalism</u>.

Defense of capitalism is in the view of Berkeley. Who are welcome too to use Art. I Contracts. Will it work everywhere? No. Truckers have their safety rules. Likewise, the state building codes are enforced on grounds of safety. And no slave contracts. Reich used labor.

Democrats generally like regulations. And Frank is Independent. Still, the party did not take his mind. Obligation of contracts are everywhere. And if you use it on the wrong ones, they will put you in a wheelchair

- - -

Frank and I have no answers. Just issues.

I am Enrico Pelican. The narrator has shifted. Because we are on Homer's journey, for 4 chapters, I have taken command. Frank thinks the above arguments are for The Dead. A good sign. Narration shifts back and forth, as you see. Like in Homer's <u>The Odyssey</u>.

The City of Los Angeles made Frank's brother fork out $50,000.

Vincent was mad. Beacuse of zoning regs.

Vincent thought he had no defense. He did and his attorney didn't even tell him. <u>In the 5th Amendment of con law, it says that no person shall be deprived of liberty or property without due process of law.</u>

Vincent did not know this. He just paid the money to take up his grass on his back lawn and paid to have it tarred. He was afraid because in the letter like any letter from a city to a businessman, the city sent him charged with two crimes, and he didn't want to be thrown in jail. Not only did the US Constitution single out liberty and property as things that could go to trial, the 1st Amendment said he has the law on his side to petition the Government for a redress of grievances. His grievance was Art. I Contracts, that said that the state or county or city or its arm, the zoning department, couldn't impair his contracts with his, my tragic flaw in talking about my brother, renters. If you ask what the meaning of "impair" is you are right with the program. Existential threat.

Republicans, like Vincent and Sherry, don't like irrational regulations. Wrongly, Exxon thought "impair" was taxation.

-3-

Vincent, like the famous painter, received a letter in the mail. It had two criminal arresting charges, from the City. Like our famous friend, Vincent did not. And, later, Frank was in MBA school. It was like the city had called capitalism, criminal. He didn't know it then, but Art. I Contracts was a defense, with the 5th amendment due process and the 1ˢᵗ Amendment right to petition the Government for a redress of grievances. Yes, the 5ᵗʰ said you can't be deprived of liberty or property without a hearing. Which is a Constitutional right. The government will reply, that's the way things are

- - -

The Dead are winning. Europe is starting to implode, as of November 1, 2011. The Greeks, in the historical seat of democracy, want to put to a vote the Euro Bailout. They are rioting in the streets, teargas and rock. In need of water. On the fire. The Foreign French have expanded the "Occupy Wall Street" movement protests to Europe. The world stock markets crashed. As happens with these things.

We made it

To

The Death Valley National Park Lodge. Christian

Nautsky Caaaaaaaaaame With.

Politics

Blur. Being. The left, like 2016,

Wanted again legal Queen Jane. The right

Wanted no regulations. Operator,

Can you help me, Oh yes I will yes

Can you help me plead? The director

Won't give me That phone book That I need. Information,

Is all I get,

Got to get an operator

To give me a number I can use.

Death Valley is a great

Place.

If you can stand

The heat.

Frank went outside and looked at the cloudy day. He wrote some songs. 3rd album was called "State Police". He did this because He was sick of siding with the protesters. Who had become an unruly mob, in many places. This was one for the establishment. It was a parody of capitalist politics. He was howling NNNN NNNNNNNNNNNNNNOOOOOOOOOOOOOOOOOOO to protesters.

- - -

And, impairment is a law against legalization of drugs. Yes, and I won't deny the police their jail. You don't have a right to get out of jail free, for use of beer, if due care.

Drugs are like illegal Mary Jane, you don't have a right to get addicted, because the economy looks like the Great Depression. Vote.

You have no right to do illegal drugs. The people of California said so. That state legalized certain drugs for medical uses. But to the FBI, you are arrested. Your defense is the Tenth Amendment.

The "Lotus-eater" brand of beer made those who drank it, forgetful of their co-op. And the one-eyed homeless person who tried to kill them. His name was, nobody. Frank said, my name is Holmes and my name might as well be "Nothing". Frank dropped windows and it made him really sore the rest of life. It was not a good thing and it would not help you write a book. The reality is he survives barely each day. Like Vincent, without a death threat, crazy.

The songs that follow, as is the world were living in a police state, are Frank being Sarcastic. And a way around the censors. Hense, came the title of the album "State Police". So he could release it. The following is sardonic. Remember he was streaming on the internet, which meant his offering would go around the world. Where in over 150 nations, they won't hear your complaints.

This is anti constitution. It's like my novel "The Poverty of Economics" except incorporated as the "Economics of Poverty".

"No Confrontations"

Do away with your right of protest, And your redress, Against the government.

We need a system,
We can, Go to, in case we are taken over.

You don't need,
The confrontation clause,
Because we have all,
The hearsay we need.

Can you help me,
Don't think about cross-examination.
We are your material,
Witness. Now you need the police.

The confrontation clause, says you have
A right to call witnesses you can confront.
The police don't like that,
They want to be your only witness,
Like <u>1984</u>

These songs are a parody in part of the 6th Amendment to US Constitution, which courts like the tax courts, and the like, regularly breach the amendment. Like they do all around the world. With basic Human Rights.

"Compulsory"

Don't worry about getting witnesses,
In your defense.
We are the only witness you need.

We are in your mind,
So forget,
About the compulsory process clause.
You don't need,
Any witnesses.

We have lawyers who,
Can take your confessions.
That's all the proof we need.
We'll tell you what to think.

This liberation,
From proof,
Can help you try to get back,
If you can.
Just don't protest in the streets,
This song is the state's remedy.

The compulsory process clause says,
You have a right,
To call witnesses on your side.
So you don't get railroaded,
Without your 6th

In "State Police", Frank found Jack London. It is the way it really is, for example, with Vincent. The police are your wife, come home honey. The above is from the 6th Amendment to the Constitution of the United States of America.

"Compulsory" in a Police State is the police taking you under rest. Like the "upside down" world of Kafka in his The Trial.

"Confessions"

When you go to get a job, Tell all.
The fifth Amendment, Isn't only for court.

Confess,
To your boss,
It's good for the soul.

Don't say I refuse,
To answer,
Like *In re Snow.*
At the US Supreme Court,
In 1889.

That was a quirk,
The bill of rights applied.
Don't critique the court,
We'll give you the words,
When you are busted.
It's a police state.
Like war.

Next to equal protection,
On race.
We caught you red-handed.

"Second Amendment"

There is no second amendment,
We did away,
With it.
With lock and load.

Don't worry about your gun,
You are not,
On a hunting trip.

You ended up,
On that base on Cuban soil.
Where they charge you, with love.

Glad,
You gave up your gun.
It's no longer your property.
It belongs to the state.

Too many shootings,
So we took away your gun.
Never mind that 2010,
Holding by the US Supreme Court,
Heller, That said you,
Have a right to a weapon.

Want to shoot,
Join the National Guard.
The state's first line,
Against local revolution.

Frank kept on a writing and thinking of Jack London's latter book. Frank was an environmentalist, he went out looking for Death Valley National Park flowers. And he kept on a writing. He wrote 11 songs. He was a genius.

Green with envy, the flowers like grow near the rocks. They need no contract. *De facto* yellow dog contracts, were like adhesion contracts, void ab initio, and don't try reading between the lines. Snow is something the police ski on in Big Bear, north by north east of Los Angeles.

Common law is the lie that the state allows you to confess. When Frank and Sherry found this out, they stepped one more foot closer to a racial marriage. Frank told me the following:

The reception of my race, in terms of equal protection, has always given me shame, secretly. Something I've been in conscious denial of all my life. I was Naïve as to the real impairments to my reception in polite society. There was always the turn of the phrase, or non-verbal sign that I have been people's inferior. Except in certain pockets of the world, like in France and England and California etc.

Rejection of my view of the American dream, has made me conclude that race is a token of western Civilizations many types of slavery. This is their tragic flaw of being like Prometheus. Like the Gestapo against The jews. All of the above I have kept secret from my wife. Despite the success of President Obama, I still feel the shame of being half African American. I have been treated like Dostoevsky's The <u>idiot</u>. Or that if ever I should take over someday, I would be like melville's Ahab. Or, if I should keep on reading I would be like Goethe's <u>Faust</u>. So, I just planned to peacefully co-exist. Not realizing there was an "upside down" world where the police arrest you, and you can have no way of talking back.

"No right to Redress"

No protests,
And you have no redress,
Because your megaphone is,
Too loud.

We'll protect,
You in jail.

You have no religion,
That's too crazy.
But you can have all the faith,
And belief.

The First Amendment,
Was not needed,
Too much,
Power to the person.

Don't worry,
Your free speech,
Is just,
Your confession.
Nobody pays your lawyer.

All you get
Are
Charges.
Like our Kafka.

"No Assembly"

You have no rights,
Of association under the Constitution.
You can't peacefully assemble,
Because it always turns to violence.

You are blocking the sidewalk.
Say you have less rights,
Than in Russia.
The State doesn't care.
It's back and forth.

You lost your rights to assemble,
When the anarchists infiltrated your protest.
Most states of the country don't like your protest.
Who cares if this is the year of the protester.

People in most small towns don't know what you mean,
Be the right to peaceful assembly.
The result is that you are
Blocking the sidewalk.

And that means the cops can come in and break up your
Assembly.
That's the reality of law enforcement,
Not the idealism of some National law.

The above song was about the 1st Amendment, which the US Supreme Court said does not apply to a tax court? I am sure the FBI and the CIA get the same exemption on grounds of National security.

"National Security"

Forget about your e-mail,
They all come, To us,
To keep you protected.

It's national security,
And you can read.
We can't have that. What ideas,
Of reference will you get.

The Bill of Rights,
Does not say you have a right to read.
What type of action
Will you get.

But you have a right, To confess.
That's the First Amendment.
Like Viet Nam.

You get the general idea by now, there are certain exceptions, under a so-called necessity defense. This song is for the tax court, among other exceptions, such as people like Vincent, as we shall see.

"Just Confess"

You are, Repeating
yourself, But at
least,
You have that right.

Sorry about the other rights,
You won't miss them anyway.
Just confess.

The Free Speech Movement,
Said,
Take your questions into the classroom,
Critique your fellow students,

Critique your teacher.
Confess and be Kind.
She lives on her job.
That's free speech.
You might learn something.
No protests,
There is no remedy against Wall street,
Except in Congress.

And in Yemen and Syria.
And South Sudan.
And The Congo
And Nigeria, they think.

And that was half of the "State Police" album. It came out like a latter Jack London baby. Frank went looking for more flowers. The sky was still cloudy. The songs were dry parody, but they represented the view, generally, of the State, in a courtroom or at police questionings.

- - -

They represent the viiiiiiiiiiiiiiiiiiiiiiiiiiiiiiiiiiiiiiiiiiiiiiiiiiiiiiiiiiiiiiiiiiiiiiiew of the State, at mass protests where there is teargas. U need to process as many people as you can, the wise-thinking government locked up all the shifty-eyed protesters. There is no need in a police state to give more of a defense than necessity.

This was eaaaaaaaaaaaaaaaaaaaaaaaaaaaaaaaaaaaaaaaaaaaaaaa aaaaaaaaaathVVVVVVVVVVVVVVVVVVVVVVVVVVVVVV V V V V V V V V V V V V V V V V a l l e y N n n n n n n n n n n n n n n n n n n n n n n n n n n n n n n n n n n n n n n n n n n n nnnnnnnnnnnnnational Park. It's satire. Do we need to say more????????? ??

How inspirational for our genius, Frank. A political prisoner is anybody that is trying to exercise his or her rights under the US Constitution. They did it in the old USSR and Maoist China. They were kept <u>without being told the charges</u>, as it says in the 6th Amendment, along with the right to a speedy trial. In Maoist China they kept you for 20 years. They hate Buddhists, Tibetian.

Death Valley National Park Zone of the Federal Police. So, your defenses are of no use, in times of National or state necessity. It is the Zen of Nature's Being, I worship. First Being. The Zen you never got to talk to. What Middle Eastern country would turn our bill of rights upside down, like a police state. Like your <u>Ahab</u> Article I Contracts. I can't think of "nothingness". Thus, to continue with the church of Zen, with its emphasis on suffering and the inducement to contemplate "nothing", leaves me more than half-black. Therefore, in the ironic near future, I shall not give up on Zen. And I will devote myself to equal protection, no matter who that might be, and political economics. It's a paradox. Like your <u>Ahab</u> Article I Contracts. I can't think of "Nothingness". Thus, to continue with the church of zen, with its emphasis on suffering and the inducement to contemplate "nothing", leaves me more than half-black. Therefore, in the ironic near future, I shall not give up on Zen. And I will devote myself to equal protection, no matter how that might be, and political economics. It's a paradox. This anti-novel is about a depression caused by deregulation and a "Nightmare" from the States down. From Republicans and from Covid-19 from the journey of a Modern-day Odysseus.

This is a constant battle of Democrats against Republicans for over 10 years.

"Political Prisoners"

Big Brother,
Knows best.
The State, in it's all-knowing wisdom,
Arrested protest.

Feel free to walk around,
Offing the state to get you out of this cell,
Is against,
Your best interests. World-wide.

Open up,
A book until you feel free.
The light,
Is the State.

Political prisoners,
Do not exist.
The torture of your mind,
Is guilt, better shake hands with Big Brother.
The state knows best so don't protest,
Or you'll get this song.

Don't worry about the charges,
The doctors
And the state know how long to keep you.
Russia lets you go in 15 days.

"No Charges"

They hold you for an eternity.
They don't say what for,
It's just what they do,
They don't need charges.

They hold you in jail,
You are in custody. You are in prison.
They don't say what for.

Imprisonment without a crime.
They never tell you what for.
It's just month after month,
Year after year.

It's no charges.
Can you believe it?
Why are you in custody?
They never tell you what for.

Of course, its civil.
So the criminal Bill of Rights,
Doesn't apply.
All of a sudden you disappear.

I thought that Con law said that,
You are to be informed
Of the charges against you,
But no.
Amerika is Kafka.

We got the co-op band together, and got ready to leave the park.
THE DEATH VALLEY NATIONAL PARK

Home in 3 cars. Nobody wanted to be with Nautsky. In this *Pilgrim's Progress*, the Nietzsche. Butch Lautsky came with him, but we thought he was just a good fan. He came with Nautsky so we did not talk to either of them. We, then, didn't know how bad they were.

"Being" is something Heidegger said he did not think people got at all. Being is all around, as your practice, your contractor's business. Just like the city judge does not recognize at all your Art. 1 Contract of regulation. Because it's dormant. Heidegger and his ideas of death meditation, were an existential threat.

— We talked.

— What's Art?. I's "original intent", Holmes?

— It's Federal.

— Why?

— It's Art I, meaning its a congressional tie, Sherry said.

— Then?

— That's why it's been dormant for almost 200 years.

— Yea, Holmes.

— It's Kafkaesque.

Chapter 10

PE'S MATERIALISM

-1-

The band took another vacation. This time to theJJ TJOSUATRE NATIONAL PARK.

Like James Joyce.

To ward off bad news, Frank wore a Greek mask of tragedy. In parody. The materialism of the title comes when you hear the Sirens. Joshua Tree National Park. About 300 miles to the southeast of Los Angeles. Like *The Odyssey*. For example.

We arrived at the National Park. The Joshua Tree National Park. Next to it, was a jail. Mostly drug dealers, friends of the Lotus-Eaters. In the jail was their friend, Chuck Noon. He is Korean. His Korean name, Noon. In English, his name was Chuck Noon. He was a friend

of Hansel, who called him Noon Chuck.

They came to spring him. Chuck Noon had relied on a recent US Supreme Court holding that the having of weapons was legal. Under Second Amendment. <u>He was a radical who wanted to start a revolution</u>. He went to a Teabagger convention, at UCLA. Holding a gun. He did not know the California system. He was arrested and put in the Joshua Tree County Jail. The Teabaggers also called for a revolution and liked the 2nd Amendment, new holding by the Supreme Court. Like the 6th Amendment holding that they should be tried in the district where the alleged crime was committed. With the above, they didn't give him a speedy trial nor was it public. The gun wasn't loaded. And they didn't give Him a lawyer.

- - -

The band came with a writ of habeas corpus to spring Mr. Noon. And no he was not high. I don't remember if I ever explained where the band met Noon.

They sprung Chuck and spent the rest of the day playing among the Joshua Trees. They went to where they ride horses. We waited a half hour while we heard the sirens. Then we got on our horses. I can't stand horses they always buck me off. But the rest of the band liked the charges. At first it was slow with the Sirens in our ears and our record company, Calypso, playing in our headphones.

Some of the band brought wax to stuff in their ears so that they cooooooould not hear the Sirens. Frank did it. We got going. I, Enrico Pelican, am not a real member of the band. I am a Roadie. I set things up for the band. We thought that we were in a Hollywood movie, and I mean *City Slickers.*

We thought we were in an old Roy Rogers movie. This is all camp parody, Frank and blackness. In the western.

I thought my horse was—Trigger. Because it just would not go. At least, he did not buck me off. I was grateful for that. There we were, in a Hollywood movie, me a no-account short hair, and the star of a Hollywood movie. I turned my horse by pulling on the leather straps. I did not know any other way, but it worked. We moved slowly, like a mule train. The horses were trained to move slow. Like a Dude ranch. I could smell the saddle. The smell of leather was something I liked.

Frank, with his mask of tragedy, did it right. You draw the horse in the direction that you want it to go. I don't know why I couldn't get the horse to go where I wanted it to go. I did not want to kick it. I thought that would be cruel. Suddenly, on came the Sirens. They were like fans of the band, "The Cherry". Famous for their PE, Post-existentialism.

Sherry actually started singing the words of "Like a Wolf Blues". It drove the Sirens Bonkers. I kept up. On my horse. It swayed back and forth. Then I kicked at the horses gut. And it moved. That was the trick. I know Frank from back in Chicago. I don't like Horses or swimming. That's Chicago. Meanwhile Mr. Amerika saves the day, Frank.

And Sherry kept singing. All of the "White Collar Crime" CD.

I started singing, I'm an old cow hand from the river Grand. I could not remember the words. But Sherry could, just like the sweet bird of you. Sherry started to sing about wall street greed. And I expected the Sirens at any minute. Stuff that they were protesting all over Europe, especially France. It was camp, an illusion of "pop culture". That was the band and their name and Frank's view of political economics, plastic. Like Germany. Frankfurt.

- - -

-2-

The US Constitution, in the First Amendment, said there was a <u>right to peaceful assembly</u>. They did not protect you from the homeless people who brought in firebombs and bottles of gas with a wick and satire and rocks and trashed the windows of the nearest business. That was the real cause of the police with their teargas. They were wearing masks. And who was the witness? You needed mass trials. That's like the homeless people who set fires to million dollar houses. That were right in the way of the Santa Ana winds. There goes 50 houses. Of course it was class. From last night's news. That's the reason for "State Police".

No Sirens, we had wax in our ears, just stop the fires.

<u>The remedy was to feed the homeless and put them in group homes</u>.

Like the retired. Co-ops.

Then have something to make.

We still kept on riding in our Roy Rogers movie. He always got the bad guys. And the people who protested, peacefully, had a Constitutional right to do just that. It was their redress. Against the government. Also in the First Amendment of the United States Constitution. Like the redress of a Title 42 claim. For free speech. And rentals.

Move? Not on your life. We are a Collective. The future of America. It's creativity. And it keeps us together when we are not out playing to the world. What is our politics? We are like students in Prague. We bleed European. We know about The Greeks. And their protests to go home. We are all non-violent. Today, Wall street looks like Greece, palm over back of other hand. That means we are all up a creek. Last night again, they tried to bail-out The Greeks with private money. The US Stock Market hit the biggest dive in the year.

Homer's Greeks, translated. Is the Greek of today like the Egypt of early 2011? We hope not. The lotus-eaters made Odysseus forget about home. Would Republicans do the same. We were not kidnapped. But the wife Frank slept with made him forget about the European Stock Markets and about his MBA dreams of home, the goal of this novel is to remember home, I grabbed my knee. That's right kids, the real goal is to take you back home, baby Holmes. Homes. Tragedy. We got off our high horses and got into our cars to go to the Rancho Rio River, where we planned to ride the river, and forget about the Cyclops of the economy. We are on Homer's special journey in his *The Odyssey*. The camp parody should be obvious. Gallows humor. Like Kurt Vonnegut. Like a defense of Germany. And the Euro.

-3-

It took us a good half of an hour to get to where the rafts cast off. We parked. Were we in 3 cars? Frank and Sherry were together. I had a brief break. There were no sirens. We got out and waited 45 minutes for the boatmen to bring the rafts back from down the river.

It looked nothing like the LA river, which is rarely flowing, one hand on shoulder the other hand on hip. Los Angeles is more like some county. Downtown only has a few high buildings. There are a lot of Latinos. The Mayor is Latino. California is said to be totally different than it was when I grew up, Half Latino by 2016. It is still too <u>racist?</u> But the Latinos are Catholic and are very conservative, no birth control. They are straight. County government is strong enough that Alabama 2011 legislation against Latinos without a Visa, would be considered racist. This issue comes to the US Supreme Court as of June, 2012

- - -

The boatmen brought back the rafts and put them back in the riiiiiiiiiiiiiiiivvvvver. There were three rafts just enough for the band and one Latino, named Jim. His friends called him Jimbo. I don't want to go. I can't swim. Frank was a lifeguard. But he could not save everybody, in case we all started to float up river. La La. Like Jim.

Many people can't swim, like in Frank's home of Ithaca. But it's rare in Southern California. Everybody put on a lifejacket. I did not want to go. It's going to be a bumpy ride, to the downside, down low is where it would reach. In New York and Chicago people don't swim. Frank just laughed. Jimbo could not swim either. This means we were scared out of our wits. Like UCLA facing the Trojans.

For me, the river was like the Cyclops of the economy.

We were just downgraded as a country. Which means people living here would Pay more on credit on a house. Like <u>Water</u> <u>In The</u> <u>Belly</u>.

Frank said we lacked factories and the Gross National Product. I don't know. "The Cherry" had Calypso records produce our albums——And their factory was a big hit with us.

And we <u>exported</u> the product all over the world. Good for the United States' Gross Domestic Product. Pre-2016.

Calypso, though, was rare. In Los Angeles, I haven't seen a factory in ages. It's Hollywood and the record industry. And the Hollywood movie industry. Oh yes, in downtown LA there is old, rusty factory. CEO's were exporting whole factories, to India. No wonder people were angry at Wall street. There went our Gross Domestic Product, GDP, half the meaning of the countries downgrade status, the other half of the National Note, exported by MBAs. This is one of the points of our going into a band. A second downgrade?

The rafts hit the river.

The boatmen said that it was tiller to trouble, but I don't believe them. I felt the problem was in outsourcing our factories. At least we have the Hollywood movie industry. Streaming kills record industry.

Right off we hit whitewater. I thought of the terrific University of California, at Berkeley and system. That's infrastructure. And the roads in the National Parks, like the Joshua Tree National Park. Anything to keep me from thinking about the river. Jimbo was frightened, scared too. We thought of poor Mayor of Los Angeles.Latino.

-4-

Jimbo started to scream. Get me out of here. This lifejacket won't save me. The whitewater kept up. To both Jimbo and me, Enrico Pelican, your narrator, replacing Frank, for these 4 chapters of Homer, we were scared to death. On came the water. Dip went the raft. This is the scary part. You can grab onto your seats, said Holmes.

Then we started to drift.

We were out of the whitewater. We were safe. Frank kept thinking of Jimbo and how the Latino middleclass-class could use the Federal Constitutional Contract Clause, Of the United States. This was Southern California. Rent a room out. Art. I.

It was no longer a bumpy ride. <u>Water In The Belly</u>.

Then, the whitewater started up again. It was lean left to avoid the rocks. Listen up. I stopped the metaphor of the river and the economy. I couldn't stand it. The water came up and hit me in the face. I was covered in water. This was terrible. Then ducks flew by over our heads. And for a moment I noticed the clean air of this National Park. Pay attention because this is it. Like in modern Greece. The church of Pride, of Dada, wasn't the one practiced at the Zen Co-op of "The Cherry". Theirs was like Thomas Mann's Homo Dei, at this time.

- - -

I leaned over to get a good look at James. That's when I fell in. I go under water and the lifejacket keeps me floating. I yell out. Frank was the only person to hear me. He's a hero. He jumps in and swims to me.

That was the key. He turns me around and grabs me by the chin. And jaw. He swims with me to the nearest raft. He pushed me on the raft. I had not taken in much water. But he treated me for shock. He put my knees up and grabbed someone's jacket, I think it was Jimbo's, and put it over my chest. Frank saved me. I knew he would. Here comes some more dialogue, Holmes.

—I am all wet. <u>Water In The Belly</u>.

—I am cold.

—That's quite a dunking, said Jimbo.

I love Latinos. I thought, thinking that I could have died in that water and wondered why I let them talk me into going on the raft trip.

—Not Catholic, Jimbo joked. He touched his cross.

—Somebody saved my life today, I coughed. Then, I joked, where is Justin? Didn't he come on this journey? Some PE.

—Don't worry, we'll get you a break, said Frank, the narrative has changed back to 3rd person, Frank was not narrating this, for these middle 4 chapters, where Homer put Odysseus through his journey home. This book is for educational reasons. Why go through such an absurdity when you can go through this tragedy when you can read about such a depressing journey, <u>in Homer's chapters 9-12</u>?

- - -

He knew what I needed. What I wanted.

—Hold on, you have had a bad shock, said Frank.

—Do you want me to sing?, said Sherry, not joking.

—Yes, "Confidence", I joked.

—That's a good sign. This is parody. Sherry sang.

—Just keep me warm and safe, I said, I am Enrico Pelican, roadie for the band.

—Enrico, you want something to eat?

—Yes, if you want me to choke. In a <u>black</u> comedy way. For the rest of the ride, I am a cripple.

—Don't worry. We'll get you to the co-op, said Frank.

I am crying. I lay prone. I don't talk to anybody anymore. I am mad.

—Frank is the hero, Holmes.

—The co-op will keep you warm.

Frank warmed his hands over Sherry's belly.

—There you will get some drinks for your belly, Jimbo joked. I am gone. We arrive back on shore. I can see the cars.

—You will be safe in the car, said Frank. They take me to the car. Our car.

We had a blanket in the trunk.

I take it out. And get in the car. I huddle.

—Get in the back seat, said Frank.

—Okay, I finally spoke.

—And keep your head down, said Frank.

—Wrap the blanket around you. At this point he couldn't be more serious.

- - -

—You are on the <u>black</u> side of a moon of Mars. A joker. In this parody.

We are "The Cherry". They were trying to comfort me.

—We all are the youth of, America, the jews of the world.

—We all fell off the raft. This is freaking symbolic. What's our job? For how long? UN today charged Israel like the South Africa, of old. Jimbo left.

—And don't tell me that Frank is Mark Twain.

—Sherry said, He's Poe.

Frank laughed. And put his arms up at a square.

—Touchdown, said Pablo. I had a break.

—Did the Arab spring listen to our first album?

—Of course, said Sherry, in her Polish accent.

—Did Occupy Wall street listen to our second album?

—Of course.

—Can Ishmael Reed still read?

—Is a black from Africa. I joked.

—Now you have got it, UC Berkeley.

—And what will be "State Police"?

—The police state after the Syrian spring, I said.

- - -

—That's why we keep you around, Enrico. You give us reality. We are an international band. We're like Germans.

—Do we have the US constitution? They have peaceful assembly in Russia. Back and forth.

-5-

We had planned to go climb a mountain, but after what happened to me, the band decided to go directly to the Joshua Tree National Park Lodge. We checked in.

—You know our first album, "Busted", that is what the Wall street protest people get once they get set up by homeless people, I said. That's a major point in this book. That's the reason for "State Police". They have more rights in Europe. The police are lined up ready to strike in European cities.

—I know, Holmes.

—How?

—When they try to assemble peacefully, consistent with the First Amendment of the US Constitution, the homeless who have nothing to loose, pick up a rock or throw a bottle of gasoline lit on fire at a peaceful business. When the police come as they always do they pick up everyone. Thus, "State Police". It happened last night at the Occupy Oakland Movement, said Frank. We don't like being the principal any more, we'll wait ¾ of a year before we release our third album. We'll wait to see what people do, and how they end up in Syria? It's a real revolution and the state is winning. In and out.

—Oh, said Sherry.

—We called them in Cal, the street people, said Frank.

—Yes, said Hansel.

—Then there is the international protests, from Europe to Arabia to Russia.

—International protests don't have the protection of the US Constitution, Holmes.

—Yes no free speech.

—Just "State Police", said Frank.

—Then there is the set up.

—By the homeless.

—They throw rocks and firebombs. This is the reason you don't want to get involved with such types of protests.

—Then there is the US.

—Keep your ears open.

—Sirens. A play on words of the police and people in Homer's Classic, <u>The</u> <u>Odyssey</u>.

—When the police give you 10 minutes to leave the private park, like the Occupy Wall street Movement, you better leave. It does

not take a genius to know that. Like Russia. This is <u>our</u> mythodology.

—Or a crowd moves across a bridge. The police will do the same.

—And if you don't move?, asked Frank.

—"Busted".

—That's your so-called peaceful assembly in the middle of the street. In the US. Like Russia.

—Blocking traffic.

—"State Police".

—"White-Collar Crime" is the same, said Frank.

—"National security" lets the FBI get into your E-mail.

The worst was the Occupy Oakland Movement. Homeless came from nowhere. And with firebombs. The scene went from protected peaceful assembly for the movement, to a crime scene. The mob moves you. Have you ever smelled teargas? You have to hit the floor just to function. It looked like Socialist Greece.

—It makes you sober, said Sherry.

—I usually go for a break, I said.

—How much do you smoke?

—About a pack a day, I said.

—For the stress.

—Yes.

And say, the pig is greedy, some of my best members of "The Cherry" are pigs. What goes around comes around. <u>Tax the rich</u>. <u>We can take it</u>. <u>And don't touch Social Security</u>. There are a group of protest virgins. The Baby Boomers. The same applies to them. When they protest cuts in Medicare. The battle of 2013 in Congress. Medical?

Democrats is what they call them. And with the Boomers shifting in the last 20 years to the Republican party. They will find which side their bread is buttered. Alice in wonderland is what the Boomers became.

Unemployed homeless is a crime scene waiting to happen. Get it yet.? <u>If you are under 30 or over 65 you should be a Democrat</u>. Frank is shifty. He gets the middleclass. Self-employed. That's where his Art. I Contract, of the US Constitution comes in. People who would be shocked by his brother Vincent. He was mad. And though they don't know it yet that's where those self-employed contractors are walking.

This is not a political platform. It splits the voters in half. And the takes care of the middle. It's bipartisan. You don't run for President on the Bipartisan platform. You take one side, and say like you are a moderate Democrat.

That's Frank. In fact, back and forth.

—Who knows what the Greeks will do?

—Will they kick them out of The Euro? I asked, thinking of Spring 2012. How to make extra cash? Fed inflation? 2% under yellen.

—During that time, world stock markets are dropping. Like last night in that Spring.

—We are not clapping. In this gallows humor.

—No, we are not, said Frank, to some of the bands questions.

—Redress of problems is a good one.

—Same problems, said Frank. Like the Frankfurt stocks.

—Internationally, the problems get bigger, said Pablo.

—The international.

—All police hate them. Like we used to be, surf rock?

—"The Cherry" does not want a revolution. And in the US we want a wall between Church and State, said Sherry.

—So what about the Arab spring?

—So what?, said Sherry.

—I can read. In "Third World Revolution" you sang, if you want one, I am not the band for you, I said. You read it.

—You are <u>late</u> to the band, Mr. Pelican.

—Let the State Department back the revolution in Libya, said Frank. Like Frankfurt.

Republicans pray over a political meeting. And quote George

Washington. That goes against Jefferson. And you are going to protest. The Police are Republican. They will bust you if you say the words civil rights. They will say you are blocking the sidewalk. They are Wall street. I am just a roadie who followed "The Cherry" around the world.

- - -

—And Egypt?

—Third world. Like the Arab spring? Which year?, asked Frank, thinking like George Washington, religion and politics.

—And the French protest against global stock markets?, I asked.

—I love the French. My professor, Paul Ricoeur, taught at the University of Paris, said Frank. And it's class.

The Joshua Tree National Park Lodge was a good place to rap. We were all in one room. And half the band did not believe in free speech. Frank did. He started going on about his Paul. Trivia.

Paul was in a Chicago Church. It was winter. It was snowing. Frank went in to get out of the cold. Paul was his teacher that term.

He looked up and there was a small man in front of the Gothic, small chapel. It did not register. The small man was his teacher. I don't know what to call it. He was either praying or meditating, perhaps a little of both. And it was late. It seemed that nobody was left on campus. Frank was afraid to be seen by such a famous man, so humble. It was a class on a book on Existentialism. It became the key to his trilogy *Time and Narrative*. It was written some 10 years after the class, so haunting a book. Both of them were in a struggle. It was obvious when looking at Paul that night. Paul put down Heidegger, and said that the meditation on Death was wrong, as Heidegger said we should in *Beingand Time*.

- - -

Frank did not stay for long. He was an Independent. He wasn't in Chicago to make trouble. He did not think to introduce himself. They did not have their eyes meet. There were no homeless people in Chicago. And there was no question as to the safety of the two. Then, post-existentialism, Frank's term, did not exist. It was born with Paul's Trilogy. They say that at California you had free speech, but that at Chicago you had a book. Existentialism was E.

Postexistentialism was being born with that Trilogy. Along with those books and I don't know what to call it, there was another book *The Rule of Metaphor*. That came first. It was the basic text for the title of this book. Frank loved to play. He called his Paul's Post-existentialism, PE. It was a playful play on words. Frank wanted people to play ball with Paul. PE was to Frank among other things Physical Education. And that means to be a jock. And jocks play ball. Putting down gallows humor?

PE means, according to the last part of his Trilogy, you should never dwell on Death. E was based on the contemplation of death. This was largely popular in Europe. Perhaps because of World War I and World War II. But Paul's findings were not based just in the putting down of death. They centered in on the Greeks. I don't know if Homer was mentioned. But he and his Ithaca were implied. The home of Odysseus. It was Paul Ricoeur with a joint appointment at the University of Paris.

—So tell the story of Paul again.

—Yes play it again Enrico.

—No, I said.

—We'll say that Paul is a Neutrino. Faster than the speed of light, impeaching Einstein?

—I'd rather split the atom.

—Why?

—It's too personal to Frank.

—Oh, we want to hear about the spy who came in from the cold, said Hansel.

—No, you'll get a parody of it from Frank.

—Why a parody?

—Because Paul taught that life was not tragic, said Frank.

—The Greeks wrote tragedy.

—And Homer?

—Why not Einstein?

—*The Odyssey* was about going beyond the Sirens and Calypso.

—And?

—Going home, Frank said.

—That's not tragic. This is the freaking point of this novel, <u>Water In the belly</u>.

—If you have found love?

—What about Joyce? The Bible.

—Ulysses was written by a genius. I only scrape around his interpretation of Circe and Calypso, said Frank, talking about James Joyce's parody of the tragic Homer, *The Odyssey*. I got the idea of doing a parody of Homer's book from Joyce, I just left out the dirty parts. I put in the classic ending by Joyce, the revolution of the Fermions the new name in Physics for classical Quantum Mechanics, electrons around in the atom and the revolution of the earth around the sun, it's like the rules of the world, William Blake's *Marriage of Heaven and Hell*. To see the universe in a grain of sand, the way that Rutherford and Bohr did see physics.

- - -

—And in the end?, said Sherry, joking, as if she hadn't heard Frank.

—He gave a independent going home, but he painted it, Frank said, taking away his thumb from under his chin.

—What about Zen?

—I'll leave that for Paul, said Frank. Frank Holmes, not to be confused with homes, or Frankfurt.

The cherry members loved beer. They bought *Circe* beer. That's when Frank met the seller of the brew, Ms. Circe. She got frank to try her beer.

At that, Frank fell in love with Miss Circe. They had a tryst. Drunk, Frank became a lover. His friends called Frank "mad" when he refused to give up on the affair. And he was mad. He turned Sherry into a thing, nearly ending his marriage contract with Sherry.

But he couldn't. For PE is that between birth and death is a thing called history and fiction and narrative; that's what he called it. Ricoeur was self-critical, he knew propaganda when he heard it. When it's ideology then it's a people's myth. That was his Freudian-PM. He had class. Material economics is grown in society by the people, not given from above.

Chapter 11

POSTMODERNISM

We went to College. And played PE with a balloon. The co-op dug it. We were at my Pomegranate University. We had come back from Death Valley National Park and the other National Park that we loved so much Joshua Tree National Park. There are 4 chapters that are Frank's journey to existential icebergs, PM. Homer's journey is chopped. It's Saturday. Like *The Odyssey*. Here is the last part of people talking to each other. This is the start of the big character change, in Frank. He doesn't yet come to Zen, but he goes half way there, he believes in Being. And says that he is a Moderate Independent, it's a place to put your hat. A way to be understood. Keep reading it doesn't get any better than this, if you think like a college student. The colors of Pomegranate college were white and maroon, the sign for help. And Frank needed it, help.

—What is PE espionage? This is my little joke, in this aside.

—A parody, said Frank. Turning State's Evidence.

—CCC and PMS and PM? Postmodernism?

—To enlightenment, said Sherry. Yes I am serious. Here is wherethe reader is like Justice Holmes. PS, or poststructuralist, is a type of PM. It uses defamiliarization and deconstructionist stragedies.

- - -

—That's a Sherlock?

—Yes. In this parody, I said. It's gallows humor. Are you with me? It's being with the Tea Bag party, and understanding Moderate Independent talk. The irony is that teabaggers are not bipartisan. And they won't talk. Sherry likes the Cabala, like Kafka.

We talked of Aristotle and Ethics and Paul. We talked of CCC— Chicago Cultural Critique. The use of Aristotle's ethics in the context of the culture of Western customs and norms and science of like whales is like cultural civilization. We talked how CCC and PE is so alien that to understand it is the same, and this makes this like hard, as spying. I just explained what CCC was, do get it. If you already have a good job, keep it and meditate on PE. That was <u>black</u> comedy.

- - -

<u>I am Enrico Pelican, your narrator for these 4 chapters on existentialism and what comes after it that makes it postmodern.</u>

Modernists were around for 500 years. So you can see why modernists are ticked off at the thought of PM, the postmodern. This is a small type of a postmodernist parody, post-existential philosophy, which I got from Paul Ricoeur, of among other places the University of Paris. Like a Moderate Independent, like Frank, like Europe.

—Lest we forget.

—Yes. It's Paul's postmodern philosophy.

—Let's go over the existential, said Frank. He studied with Paul, one of the then, leading existentialists in the world, before Paul

did away with it, hence PM. And PE. If you are young just think that tonight you will see the PM. If you are retiring, you are in the PM of your life, like snow around, if it's winter and you are like in the Rockies or in New York City. PM was postmodern. Late logic of capitalism.

—What's that?, said Sherry, holding on to her wrist, looking like Da Vinci's *Mona Lisa*.

—I don't know. But I think it's existential, don't be so gloomy.

—Thanks, Patty.

—It's nothing.

—Like this is narrated by nobody, I said. This is Homer's little joke.

—That's from Homer.

—He was hip, I said.

During the trip, Dada showed up wearing an eye patch. He looked like a Cyclops. Like an existentialist. Scary. Heidegger and Sartre were existentialists. They worshiped death and nothingness. Pretty scary. We don't PE with them. We don't play ball with them. If you get rid of the contemplation of death, there goes the existential bias. Existential was serious. If you are <u>after</u> the existential, you are postmodern. And bingo and bingo, welcome to the 21st Century. To late capitalism.

-2-

There were a string of tables in front of Pomegranate University Student Union. We had stopped in front of a table with the sign PE on it. We were talking. There was a group of about 10 people. Someone threw a balloon at the table. Mary caught it.

—BEING, said Mary.

—Don't drop the balloon, it wasn't water, or let it hit the ground, said Frank, into PE.

—Where's the narratives?

—In these dialogues, *recit.*

French is a unique language. Paul wrote his books in French. But the term narrative means two things in French. It's either narrative, in the English, or dialogue. So you could write a script, and it would be a narrative. And that's what I am doing.

—*Guzzling water to put out the fire in the belly?* Don't you like Zen?

—That's from Paul, said Frank, *Temps.* That's it.

—That's our narrative?

—I prefer the word, story, said Frank. Or, history of time.

—The above is a living metaphor, I said.

—And dead metaphors?

—Most titles, I said.

Absurdist modernists had the ability to use living metaphors. They were popular in France when Paul started to write. He lived a long life. We are still at Pomegranate University. We started to get absurd. Like Beckett's waiting for Zen. And we were. We bat around ideas of Western Civilization. PE was not absurd. Just our parody. Are you with me? *CatOn A Hot Tin Roof.*

- - -

Cat On a Hot Tin Roof was like an modern play? It's title holds up. Frank is absurdist. It's his common law marriage. A put on, on Western Civilization. He has found Eros. He is a strange duck. He will.

But not now. There is a thing called plot. Don't break your heart, if you think I am going to take you to Paul Ricoeur. I am. In a way.

<u>Nobody told his tale, that's from Homer. Nobody pointed to him. I am nobody.</u> We had gone to lunch. A bunch of people came up to us and wanted our two CD's. We had a big box. The albums were in it. We played PE with them. We told them that we were postmodern because we didn't say we were going to die. Dig it.

Existence is the person. Being is Zen. The reader is the spy. Follow the bouncing balloon. It was all in the interpretation, for Paul. He believed in Zen. We meditate on Being. We get there through Time. We had a very big boom box. We had told the college that we would be here. It was crowd control. We put our first album on, very loud. Miss this and what you read will become a dead metaphor. Don't break your heart, this is a living metaphor, *Water In The Belly.*

It did not cause a riot. But it was a quiet riot. They hit around the balloon. That was PE. And we were in the process of explaining all that to the crowd. It was all, girls are all sugar and spice but they need water to cool the fire in the belly. Are you awake? Up or down.

The DVD was on the waterless Los Angeles river. We were down there playing "Like a Wolf Blues". On the amp of the bass was the Russian flag. We sold about 20 of the "Busted" albums.

Being and Existence came before Post-existentialism. Have patience, this only lasts for 4 chapters. Like the war in Iraq. Or Germany.

—Being is like Zen, asked Sherry.

—Existence is like man, said Frank, like a Beat-nick, of the l950's US underground. Grow up and take renters. Existence of the UN.

-3-

—I have no problem with the meditation on Being, said Hansel.

—Center in on Being, I said, being a roadie for the band and foil for Frank, who was an expert in Being.

—How do I do it?, said Frank, being a bleeding-heart liberal.

—Get Being's type. Like a Moderate Independent.

—Oh, I get it, said Frank, playing with the students, with his heart on his sleeve.

Actually it was very hard. You see, Paul wrote about Time. *Being and Time* was the book that was the text when Frank studied with Paul. Paul cut the book in half. Thus, he did not work with Being. But he was philosophy. So he was not saying that Zen was Not Being. Just that such would not be his craft in his Trilogy. Paul cut Heidegger in half, and started with the last half, thus *Time and Narrative*. He added on narrative to Heidegger, who he switched around, on death, which was dropped. How comforting. They mythology or fiction of Homer's <u>The Odyssey</u> is where I get my inspiration. I give it <u>my</u> time.

Philosophy was Paul's first love. And he did not want to alienate all his world readers by suggesting that there was a Zen. This influenced Frank in his personal and professional life. Thus, he did not all of a sudden jump on the band, saying that being is Zen. He knew that Dada was Zen. That's black comedy. The President of the United States is black.

—The wind is Being, I said, thinking of the Green Party's nature Conservatism.

—Nature? Said Frank, making a breakthrough towards even admitting that there was a Zen, in existence. You are watching a work in practice.

—Part of it.

—Read it's signs, like Homer's Chapter 9, I went on. Quick if you are reading this right, go to a library or a Book shop and get a copy of Homer's *The Odyssey*. It won't give you a virus, and see how this differs, it does. That's why this is a pastiche.

—Meditate on the wind, a type of Being, said Hansel.

—A higher power?

—Perhaps, I said.

—Read the wind. And you like to read the underground *Reality*, a play by Snow, writing like Aristophanes.

—When I do that it calms me, said Holmes.

—Being is the totality of existence's reality. This is a major definition of the meaning of Being.

—We lost interest in the balloon, said Patty.

—You always play ball, said Pablo.

—I see the students play with reality like this. It gives me hope.

—They are having fun with their Being. Like at Frankfurt.

—With a capital B?

—Yes, I said, touching my maroon shirt.

—Is that Pride, said Pablo.

—Yes, said Pedro. Finally the band is admitting about the existence of Zen, something that Frank is toying with.

—That is the meaning of Being, I said. I am freaking serious. This was the beginning of Heidegger's *Being and Time*. Why is there Being? <u>And why don't we ever talk about it?</u> Highway 61.

—How do we answer that?

—How do you meditate on Being?

—I center in on a single point, and it talks to me, said Pedro, new to the band with Pablo, not there from the start. Meditiation.

—Hold on, said Frank.

—Shut up, they are playing, said Sherry.

—What does the wind say to existence?, said Frank, knowing he was taking the role of a poet.

—Whatever it wants, said Pedro.

—It says get your answers from the meaning of Being.

—This "Being Think" is hard to follow, said Frank.

—What is the meaning of Being? That is the main question of Heidegger. If you can find out first why we are talking about Being, <u>we are like fishes in the sea, and the water is Being. They simply don'tknow that the water exists. Like we don't know that we exist in Being.It's so obvious we have never asked that question before</u>. Do it, quick, before you break your heart, said Frank, going on again.

—It's Class.

—But can we reach the Love, said Pablo.

—We can reach types of your Zen and Pride.

—We are not ready for Zen, said Frank.

- - -

Sherry rolled her eyes up, and looked at the palm trees.

-4-

We are all in different stages of belief and faith. Pedro is a good Catholic. The conversation got strange. But nobody but Frank wanted to say anything about it. Pablo was a member of the church of Zen, new to the band. Now, Frank is most like the FBI agent Mr. Miniloss.

- - -

Loved the agnostic. This was very ironic. Did I say that this story now is tragic. Meditate on "Nothing".

—You are right. Center in on a single point. And close one eye slightly, said Patty.

—You can never center in on Being, and leave out Zen, said Pedro.

—Where can you see Being?, pushed Sherry.

—<u>Being is the totality of everything</u>, I said. Be careful I am breaking your heart. But I am not running a con on you.

—Being is Zen, said Pedro, an important part of the band. All is suffering, that's Buddha's <u>class</u>.

—I want a type, Homer's sign. Like Frank doesn't believe in Zen.

—A sign from Zen?, said Pablo.

—Yes. Like the Muslims. Not like fate?

—An *Ayat*. Signs from their Zen. Everyone was silent.

—You center in on a single point, like the burning bush, said Patty.

—Does Islam believe in Moses?

—Is the Pope a Catholic, said Pedro.

—Perhaps, but it is their Moses, I said.

Now you are spying. Frank will in the end. There are so many topics that are taboo. "The Cherry" loves to go into taboo topics. It's good for the heart. They changed the topic.

—<u>Go back to Being</u>, said Frank, thinking of Paul.

—<u>Look at the trees around this campus. They are palms.</u>

—It's Being's wind, said Pedro. He is using another metaphor or symbol, or trope.

—Read the palms, I said, seriously. Sherry rubbed her palms together.

—<u>I want Being</u>, said Frank. <u>Water In The Belly</u>.

—You are like a fish? Being is the water? said Pedro. You use a metaphor when all you have is poetry to explain something. Like science.

—You forgot about the fish, they'll eat me, said Sherry.

—The fisherman is Being, said Pedro, with a net.

—What's our meaning?

—<u>Just to Be</u>. <u>Said Frank, giving the meaning of Being. It's class.</u>

—And not get eaten, said Sherry. Be economic.

—Like the modernist who said to be, or not to be. We are going to Being.

—That's a big bite, smiled Frank. They hit the balloon.

—Meaning. The crowd first looked confused, then wondered how to get away from here. Sherry leaned down to pick up the balloon. The crowd was in front of her. Paul thought it wasn't good to see Being.

-5-

—I am, therefore I doubt, said Frank. Adding more confusion to the scene, I can't help but thinking, though it hurts in the head.

—You would be a pearl of a defense lawyer.

—Why?, Frank smiled.

—It's all doubt, I learned that when we were charged in the staged Court.

—Justin, you are back, said Frank. Like <u>black</u>.

<u>I don't doubt Zen. I don't want to be charged by the fisherman. I am nobody. And nobody gets charged here. And nobody is laughing. Call me nobody. And this is my tale. I got that from Homer's narrator. Being is the water that we all swim in. It is just a metaphor. A trope, a non-literal symbol, like "water in the belly."</u>

I doubt therefore I am. I am playing with Frank. We are all like a spy. Trying to figure out a code. <u>Here, we used Paul's rule of metaphor to deduce Being.</u> It's my faith. It's the espionage of our Paul. A man from France. I can't speak to your Belief. I don't know you. Have mercy. PE is like Frank's espionage and we are figuring the clues. There was time out as people made it into the student union to get some Coke. Meditate with your eyes open, slightly closing one eye. Nobody calls you a Cyclops. That's how Frank does his meditation and that's how he is. They loved his song though. Amerika and the world. Being is Zen sells. His wife's being. They loved this little Polish singer. Like Joyce, why the cold feet about the cosmos. His materialism was his Zen, through Sherry. Being, came a yell. The crowd had heard them talk.

Free speech for the tea bag party.

Pedro said, "The Scent of Zen" is a good song.

—I believe in Being, came a customer.

—What about "White-Collar Crime"?, came another.

—Bust it, said Frank. We have another on the police state, "State Police".

—When does it come out?

—It's in the works. I have some more songs to write, said Frank.

—What does Pomegranate University think of us?

—They love it. Political economics, PE.

-6-

Easter exists like Zen's my lover. Who I call my reality honey. You just go from atheism to Easter and it's like where did all this time and Zen come from. All of a sudden almost from out of nowhere, all these types of the reality honey show up. Her Being is Zen. Everyone is experimenting with tea bags. That's not honey. But she is like in the Old Testament. Sherry is Frank's honey, her hips moving slowly.

<u>Water</u> <u>in</u> <u>the</u> <u>belly</u> is like the Korean picture of a fisherman being bitten by a crab on it's big toe. From here on in, I describe what is happening rather than taping the dialogue. After all, this is no Hollywood script. In the next chapters, Frank's character changes. A recognition, then a no recognition of Pride is the plot. Then its Einstein in the atom and the cosmos. Finally the Zen, of the Church of Zen. It evolves, there, don't break your heart. It's suffering and tragic.

It's not easy making a plot on the recognition of Zen. There is something that is always missed. But Frank keeps on coming. Home, in the sense of the redemption of all the thinking about who is Zen and his rebellion against his father, symbolic? Parricide, isn't where he eventually ends up. Is the unity of plot and character, through a very heavy narrative? Don't worry it's just a rush course in 500 years of modernism. We are post-modern. I know when something stinks, like <u>the Ahab of Being as God</u>. But it's a bridge to the success of the next chapter. Like *Homo Dei*, man as Zen, by Thomas Mann. In *Magic Mountain*, in chapter "Snow". Man as God is seen in the Hebrew Cabala. In the fight over the Orient, Chicago talk for the middle east, the Jews can argue that they have a belief in one God, Elohiem. A start of a treaty with the Arabs.

—I don't get it, said Sherry.

—You are <u>not</u> God, said Frank. If you are, you are tragic.

Treaties are part of the supreme law of the land. So, it is different to assume that our privileges to make ethnic tropology for the rest of the world will endure our presumption that makes up taking the world's real estate and turning our ideology into the world's meaning.

But some treaties are a necessity. Like with China and North Korea; and stop regarding ourselves as the biggest power on earth. With 8,000 or so nuclear bombs. The Saudies need to stop fighting the Shiia, who need to come to terms with tribes like the Kurds, in the Orient with the tropes of Zen, we'll stop the next war.

There is postmodernism. It's basic form is parody of a classic, like <u>Water in the Belly</u>, PM. Derrida and his analysis of propaganda as ideology was P.M. He had a big rift with Ricoeur. Saussure said the signifier is not the signified, hense Being is dead. Like Nietzsche before <u>the Geneology of Morals</u>. That is the "essence" of modernism. Reading is subjective, the meaning of the reader is not necessarily the meaning of the signifiers of the sentence. The reader counts as much as the author. the meaning of a text is not the intention of the author, but the subjectivity of the reader. Hense, Frank's approach with the original Homer's <u>The Odyssey</u>. There are "gaps" in the text, that the writer exploits with his propaganda. Deconstruction is PM. Attempting to represent reality is always a type of ideology. Hense, the reader should have self-criticism. Hegemony of class is in writing. The reader should deconstruct <u>Water In The Belly</u>, as should be done with a critique of the reader's culture. PM texts are the writer at play. Hense, the authority of the text, or anti-novel, comes from the classic work of <u>the Odyssey</u>, which is made a parody, in play. PM is a type of Con. the reader should be like a Justice Holmes. There are two PM, made up religions that he first is the Pride of <u>Homo Dei,</u> that gave us the Germans in WWII. The church of Zen says all is suffering, like Buddhism. The politics of this Zen, is that Frank should turn his mind to "Nothingness" to escape. People say PM is the 1960's and 1970's rebellion. It doesn't say you can't write novels, it says all books have a presumptive ideology. Especially history books and anti-novels. Like said in <u>Lost In The FunHouse</u>.

I held Sherry in my arms in bed.

Chapter 12

HOMO DEI

-1-

The next day, Sunday, we went back to the school. Pomegranate University was open. We set up our equipment. And played some videos. During this time Frank Holmes, our anti-hero, and dealer or Life Guard, and Sherry began talking. Of each other and of Zen. Like *The Odyssey*. Tragic, Sherry and Frank talk to each other in Ideology language, foreign to Frank, an <u>agnostic</u>, for now. That is, Frank does not know, for sure, of Zen's existence. But he is just touching on to Sherry's idea of Zen. He still is in need of civil redemption. This is sarcastic parody, from here on in, like "State Police".

- - -

Tell me who my soul loves, she said. Where do you eat. Why should I turn aside from your friends. He replied, If you don't know, follow me with your afro kids. I have compared you to a company of girls. Teeth are good with rows of jewels and your neck is like gold. I will make you borders of gold. With studs of silver. They have not yet converted to the Church of Zen. Now they try. This is just a beginning of feeling what its like to believe in Zen. His wife is Zen. Your ointment pours forth, which Frank likes. Her wine is like the kisses of his mouth, intimate; kisses are better than wine. Frank's name is like an ointment that pours. Savour her good ointments. She says draw me that I might run after him. The king has brought her into his chambers. Savour the good ointments, it is like good medicine for the body. He is glad and rejoices in her. She remembers him more than wine. He thinks she is comely. He upright loves her. The daughters of Babylon are like the curtains of Solomon. She is brought into his chambers. So comely is she. Like in an old John Denver song. She will make Frank. Like Odysseus.

While the king of law sits at your table my flower gives forth a sweet smell. You shall lie on my chest all night, oh Zen. You are fair, my dear. And you have Doves' eyes. Our bed is grass. I am the lily of the valley. As the lily in thorns so is my love among others. This is an alternative world. As my lover is my Zen. Do not look upon Her. She is kissing her lover, her Zen. White, yet comely, she tells him to come forth. The sun has looked down and found me. Her mother's children were angry with her. Because of her beauty. This is an evolution of the belief of Zen, a stage, The Church of Zen. With the "Song of Songs". It beats <u>agnosticism</u>, though it treats your wife and lover as Zen. This is an old sect from the Church of Pride, as I see it. And as Frank and Sherry see it. The Church of Pride would deny it. Frank is slowly getting ideology, meditating on Sherry, the way he did with the Catholic Candle icons. This is the water, of <u>Water in the Belly</u>. The feeling of some Zen. This is the first stage of redemption, home is where his heart is, and he finally found his heart. Feel your Zen, don't <u>think</u> it into reality. The idea is to get a burning in the bosom. Frank is Amerika.

As the apple tree in the valley, so are you warm around many suns. I sat in your shadow your fruit was sweet to my taste. Over me was your love, Sherry. Give me apples for I am thick of love. Your left hand is under my head and your right hand hugs me. I charge the other girls not to wake you. The voice of my beloved. The person who is loved, is Zen. The apple tree is a symbol of the emotional feeling, allowed by the First Amendment. Tell him who your soul loves, that you will always control him, so beautiful is her love. She is his head, so comely is her mouth. Her flock will follow. Rest it is at noon and show me the lock to your door. Look on her for she is beautiful. Smell her ointment. She will help you to relax. She is fairest of all of the women. Don't you know? When the fig is ready to come forth? That this a type of her coming. Don't you know that she is like a horse, <u>black</u>. Her cheeks are comely.

- - -

My love looks through the window and shows himself. My love said wake and come. The winter is past and the rain is gone. Now is the time of flowers and birds. The fig and grape smells good. And gives a good smell always. My dove let me see you in your good places. Sweet is your voice. Your voice is the whisper of Zen, so warm when you are next to me. She is a lily among the thorns. She is devoted to him, and will share power, for he has found the lock of the chamber. Feed her kids next to the tent. She is the fairest. She will make the chains of Gold. The queen sits at his table. She is a bundle of flowers, and she will talk with him. The Church of Zen is a sensual religion, you are married to your Zen, that is the reason for the burning in the Bosom. With her voice the whisper of Zen. You are beginning to see. <u>Not</u> like Zeus.

Take me, you fox. My beloved is mine and I am his. By night I have looked for you. But not found my Zen. I will go into the streets and look for the one that I love. The seeing ones have seen me and I asked if they had found you. The one my soul loves. Soon I found Him. I brought him into the chamber of the woman who gave me birth. It's hide and seek for Zen. And he did and he found Her. Why was it such a long time in coming.

- - -

I come into my garden. My sister, my spouse, my lover. This is Being really. Honeycomb with my honey. I have drunk my wine with milk. Be not afraid for the lord Zen is your lover. I sleep but my heart wakes. It is the voice of my beloved. Open to me for my head is filled with dew. My locks with the drops of night. I am of Zen all the day long. Zen is the in between our loves. Don't call her by her right name again, for Zen, it was told you is between you and your love. It's the in between of Her and him that you will find Zen. And if you get lost, go to her and treat her as if She were Zen. Oh, I have put off my coat and washed my feet, Sherry. My beloved put his hand by the hole in the door. I Rosa up to open my beloved. My fingers with sweet smelling myrrh, upon the handles of the door. But He gave me no mercy. The keepers of the wall took away my veil. Zen is in the 18-wheeler going by our sleeping place. It's time to wake up again and get a little view of Zen. She is with you, you have finally found her. Then tell it not, for the masses are not ready to your vision, the power of Zen is with her, and with that she will be like a lily to you, surely. Remember if you get lost again look for Zen in your wife, and you will get the warm burning in the Bosom. The burning should be like an icon candle with the fire water starting in the belly, and going up through your head and over it, as if you were in the Catholic icon, with the flame over your head. Like a burning of the body, on a cool day, Zen is that Fire in you, and your wife and lover is your Zen, like a piece of pomegranate.

Whither is my beloved turned aside. My beloved has gone to his bed of spices. To feed in the gardens. My dove is but won. She is fair as the moon and on fire like the sun. The purple of thy eyes are like jewels. Your navel is as round as a glass. Your belly is like a heap of wheat set about with lilies. Oh, I can feel you struggle next to hips. Zen is not always in her garden, but She will hear you where you go, even kiss her Zen, small voice, She will be your constant companion, Zen. Frank is the United States. The palm trees did sway in the wind at Pomegranate University.

Our videos played as our two lovers talked of Zen. The palms were a sight in the Santa Ana winds. The sky was clear. Come, my beloved, let us lodge in the village. They said. They mean UCLA. That is so close, we often go there and hang out at their student union.

They went on a bit. You are like my brother and did give rest at the bosom of my mother. I would lead you to my mother's house. Even the house of free speech. Do not wake, my Zen. Many waters cannot quench love. And at that Frank filled one of yesterdays balloons with water and tied it and threw it at Sherry. She was wet. Wet as a hen. The crowd loved it

-2-

Frank said that he did it to show the shock of Being to Sherry. He told her that she was beautiful. She felt herself wet. It was the shock of recognition. He wanted her to illustrate the shock of recognizing existence after never seeing it before, meditate on the changes. He asked, are you wet. Of course. Is it a shock. It was. I asked Heidegger's first questions. Do you recognize Being, he asked. Why is there something and not nothing? Some people call that thing Zen. Existentialists called it Being, most did not believe in Zen. Frank is on the boarder of recognizing, accepting Zen. Call it good or bad, but Frank was going from agnostic to believing in Zen. It might not be you or your friends Zen, if you have one, and it may not be perfect, but it was a Frank. The worshiping of his wife as Zen was a new experience, but it was a theology, the liberal teacher came to get us released, and we were all on the cover of *Newsweek*. A wet wound.

Something, she replied. It's Being. The water is a shock of Being. It's your diving into existence and into Being. First you were dry, and now you are wet. I'm like a fish in water, she said. We talk like whales. Now you got it. We all are like fish in the water of Being, we all are wet. Water is the Being of Zen. Do you believe my metaphor? What metaphor explains the concept of Being? Of existence? Of your own personal Pride? Of Zen? You are a fish and Zen is almost the water, do keep looking till you find her. It was a cold shot. But at least Frank was trying to explain what's it like to be married to Zen? The burning in the bosom as compared to the cool water. He felt a flame over his head and it went down his spine and stopped in his stomach as he looked at his Zen, he had finally seen his Zen. In between. Water In The Belly.

Now don't get mad. Meditate on Being, your Being. You are my Zen. It is quite a Being of shock. I am. You are you are. You are Being,in Being. That's the dry. You did not know who you were yet. Keep going with it. I am Being. I am wet, like a fish. Being a whale is Being.I have bit on your toe like a crab. Water is the All-time metaphor for Zen. It's everywhere. Water is what fish swim in, and they never know it, as we don't know we are in Being. Some don't call that Being. Some call that Zen. She is like that. But she is, hear her whisper.

- - -

Like the Sexual in The Odyssey.

Zen picture. Like getting all wet. Oh, I see. I am Being. Now you have got it. I am wet. You are sexy. Keep it up. The crowd got very big as the band's CD "The Scent of Zen" played in the background. Sherry suddenly started to sing the song. She was beautiful. She danced around and danced and danced, thinking she had talked with Zen. Who's to say she hadn't? She had a peak experience, and people call that Zen. We see A new world. Your wife as a lover as Zen. Everyone sat down and listened to "The Cherry". Go to the ocean. And smell the sea. Take off your shoes. Then notice the smell of your toes. They are howling. They yelled Zen is the Evolution. It's all new. They play over and over the CD "The Scent of Zen". You have good feel. Your senses turn on. You are accepted by you're her. Your sensual power turns you up. Her husband is her lover, is her Zen. I think that this went beyond The video, the wet. Sherry had the crowd. Frank had called Pomegranate before and told them that they would be giving a rock concert. They were cool about it. The smell of your guest is like your Zen or your girlfriend or Being. On a horse. Take a smell of Being's air. It will leave you begging for yes. The crowd knew the words. These were the words to the song, oh no, you are having another peak experience. The moisture was just one example of Zen. The hidden secret. Frank got another burning in the Bosom. And the trope seemed to come out of his forehead, as he felt his Zen, Sherry dancing around and round. Nobody gets Being.

Everybody was singing and Sherry was still wet. Then they put on a DVD of "The Scent of Zen". It was filmed in a large Cathedral. There was on video a priest giving, just like The Who's *Tommy*, in a cathedral communion to a praody of people at a rock concert. The band was up by the priest. Someone brought up a large table and they put their 71 inch screen on it. The screen was for the video. Suddenly the crowd was turned on, no need of water to get them to recognize Being, the Crowd caught the feeling of her experience. They all seemed to be feeling a burning in the Bosom. The guys saw Sherry as their Zen. As she sung out words, about how her his was her Zen.

Sherry was singing along to the DVD video. It was a sacred video. It was a moment to meditate on, to contemplate the sacred nature of Being. Wet. Was Sherry still. She kept singing. "The Scent of Zen". Feel your way through the blues. You don't stop the feelings flowing. You just go through the motions, its not all head. Without warning, someone started throwing water bottles, and water balloons at the crowd, and saying, look at the downing of the Being of Zen. She said, thus is the Jesús baptized. Your Zen hears you and answers you back.

The crowd yelled up sensual words, that they wanted her to sing. They yelled about the baptism of Jesús. And the power of women in the last century. They were getting a female Zen. Frank was John the Baptist. They exchanged words like that for a while. It was the narrator of "Song of Songs". The voice of a female. Frank made the words, himself the lover of Zen. Zen was female. The burning in the Bosom, came from his Zen. <u>Black</u> Zen. Sherry was still wet and she changed some of the words as she sang,

as was her custom. The smell of your guest is like a Joshua Tree of fresh air. Zen gives you a rare entrance in this show of fools, a little bit and Being keeps you alive. Feel your feelings then you are finally in touch with your lover's heart. And home. I can feel the wetness, it says, stop, Zen is here in this dance, like Zen or a Hindu dance festival. With a cup of tea.

That was the end of the song. Someone yelled up to hear "Fetish?" They put on the video. It was a crowd of about 500. We recorded the band climbing the Middle Teton in the Grand Teton National Park. In the Rockies. When we got to the top we pointed to the Teton Valley. No play on words, this was a peak experience, making it all the way to the top, and then seeing all over the valley. Zen is the Green party Thoreau's *Walden*. Say that he's on, a journey. Say he lets me have my thing. Just say we talk and that she's my fetish. On the way down, we all pointed to the top of the Middle Teton. We met at the rocks and I fall down, hoping you will too, just going through the motions. I am 24, says the narrator, explaining the getting to the top of the mountain. The feeling of a lifetime was making it to the top, and the words explained the peak experience. <u>Being was nature, like we in water are the fish</u>. It was just another metaphor, multiple metaphors, many tropes to explain the relationship of Zen to us, and us as Zen.

We went back to journey we got all our books and we heard our teachers. But we were just going through the motions. I showed him my motion my fetish it split him in half. He put himself in it no longer just going through the motions. At that, we filmed Sherry reaching for the top of the Teton. Everyone came to the top with our Sherry, a natural high, without drugs, just the top of what you were reaching for.

It was an easy climb. Up Wall street. The crowd wanted "Strict Daddy-o". We put on video. It was about Mr. Gaddafi. It was filmed in a mosque. We had the sermon translated into English. It lasted 5 minutes. After it was a call for evolution. Listen strict Daddy-o your rules are too strict. Why can't you see me more than your baby. This was a song for everyone, the ruler as parent. The citizen as child.

You want to put me in a zoo. In striped pants. You stop me. Why can't you see the end from the beginning. We love Islam too. But your brand just leaves us flat. We know people think Zen is the remedy. Why all the fighting? America will back our evolution. We are fighting over the meaning of The Koran. Sherry had a copy of the book there and put it over her head, as a sign of respect in many cultures, "The Fig".

It's the United States and we have freedom of religion. <u>Meditate on Being</u>. Catch the vibe. That's your song BEING

They all bow down like Muslims. Jesus, <u>Isa</u>, peace be upon him. They bow down because what they just saw was sacred. Why is it sacred. I meditate. Frank taught the crowd to meditate, either eyes open or eyes shut. You get the image then you get the imagination. Not all people who have taken the name <u>Isa</u> are the Remedy. It's like latinos taking the name of Jesús for their young boy. It's common in Islam. We are so stupid in the west, last night someone in the army burned <u>The</u> <u>NobleKoran</u>, out of his head. It caused 4 week of riots in around Kabul.

He put on repeat the above 3 videos. Zen is the evolution. The videos are your <u>fetish</u>. <u>Being</u> is <u>Zen, which is Being</u>. <u>The videos are a type of Being</u>. Sherry was fairly dry. You reach the top of the Teton. You are dizzy. Mosque or Cathedral or middle Teton. That's the top. The entire crowd was dancing, dizzy, drunk on the movements of our Sherry. She was the incarnation of Shiva, a Hindu Zendess, dancing. We had images of all the great religions. In moments of Babylon.

There is a picture of a girl's toe. Does she want you to bow down to her. What is your religion, or not. The images you see today are a type of Being. <u>If you do not believe in Zen, then have a fetish of nature</u>. Just

have a heart and let the rest of us have our Zen. The crowd prayed like a bunch of Hindus and then Like a bunch of Hindus, in this dance of love, of Zen, of beyond Being, to the here and now.

I dreamed of a box full of shoes, said Sherry. I have a live foot. It's next to my toes. <u>It's my fetish</u>. Go home. Curl up on the sofa. Frank's home is Ithaca and he is not there yet. Tape an iphone of your meditation and E-mail us with the video. We will judge it and if it's good we'll turn it into our next DVD. It was a peak experience for the whole band. We all got off on the crowd's cry. Someone yelled our, I believe in Zen, or not. Sherry could feel cold. Like ice. At the mention of or not, it was part of some state's constitution, you have the right to religion, or not. Frank had been living the or not, for the past 10 years. He finally found Zen, the feeling of Zen.

-3-

It's the afternoon and we went to the soccer field. It's Sunday. This is the proof of Zen's existence through materialism. Run a correlation. That is connect one thing up in the ball game that we were going to play, with another. When you walk through the streets and the kids are yelling at you, you are either in a famous band like us or they hate you. If the dogs stop barking, who's to say it isn't connected to something a, connection of the crowd to all.

The same is true for Zen, and politics. If Frank is making love to Sherry and there is thunder, either it is a fantastic experience or Zeus is mad at you. Zen could be your Sherry. The President of the United States of America is not Zen. Frank does not even think so. But neither does the President of the US think he's Zen. Talking softly of Zen is a peak experience, might call it prayer, tuning in on to Zen, whatever that is. Half-blacks have equal protection.

But for now he has the power of the Presidency. And Frank respects that, for now. We are going to play a game of soccer not totally unlike the balloon game of yesterday. We are going to kick it. And someone will say something. It's a correlation. Of politics and economics of the now in the United States. Everyone carried the peak experience of the video and dancing to PE. Us playing ball, physical education.

The answer will be the correlation. If you get it right then the waters part and they let you score. That's the game. It's trash-talking, free speech soccer. Frank copied it. That is he defended NFL lineman trash-talking and turned it into a game. You can use your head, in that it's soccer. Someone on the sidelines had a cup of coffee. As they kicked around the ball, a Zen ballgame.

- - -

It's an uncanny game. In that nobody, that is me, knows what will come out. They could swear. Or give some directive to Congress. They stay clear of the United States Supreme Court. Nobody is that smart. It does not thunder much in LA so we leave Zen out of the picture, for the most part. The soccer field is a shrine and the shrine is like a slice of Pomegranate. That's the contract.

They have debated the existence of Zen through 500 years of modernism. And this game will not stop the debate. But it might stop Washington. We are video DVD-ing the game. To see who comes out with the best ideas. Frank thinks his ideas of contracts have the answer. It's beyond Con law, it's the contract between you and Zen, what do you have to take. Frank is like <u>Ahab</u> with Art. I contracts.

If the ideas are good, like before, they go in the band's "State Police" videos. We can edit the video later. And Frank is an Independent. But he is shifty. He writes for an audience that is half Republican. He has been changing on this. Especially state's rights and State Constitution in his defense of Capitalism. This is Republican, shouted out our Sherry, in the Rocky Mountains, or in the South, beyond Art. I contracts, of the US Constitution. In LA it's a Moderate Democrat.

We are on the soccer field. And the games are about to begin. One team is yellow and the other team is red. International political economics is fair game. Frank is the ref. He leans on a cane as is his custom. He knows all the ref signs. He holds up his index finger and tells the games to begin. The people on the sidelines come towards the game, that is going down. He has a megaphone.

Someone yells out physical education and the response is political economics. Frank yells out PE and throws up two arms at a square as if someone had scored. Frank has a unique sense of humor. But he is harmless. Since he's famous everyone loved him. It's gallows comedy, as they kick the ball around. Only a few know the real meaning of PE, but they play ball as if they did.

- - -

I grabbed Frank's cane and he fell. He is handicapped. We have not talked a great deal about his handicap. But it's there. He pulled himself up by the bootstraps and got up. Or got it up. This is the second period at Pomegranate University. I switched two chapters for two chapters on this 4 chapter journey past PE. Don't worry if you didn't get it, it's just a minor point, Zen. Frank folded his arms, thumbs up.

Frank had a megaphone. Where he could shout out the soccer penalties, that is as Frank wants to interpret. Frank mumbled that it's about how we go beyond PE? Nobody knew what PE was, he yelled play ball. And the two teams began to kick the ball. Frank had been transformed by the peak experience with our Sherry, who was sitting down on the sideline, wiggling her bare toes, *Nausea*.

Frank said, women are Zen. Because they have been put down. I and Sherry share the Church of Zen belief that mankind is Zen in waiting. I have not felt the ideology, but I can tell you she is female. They have a broken heart. Thus they would feel mercy. They are my judge. Somebody kicked the ball. This had made him say things he never would have said before. Things of Zen, as felt between his Sherry and him, from the last hour.

Frank said, we evolve. Imagine the evolution of creation, the Big Bang. A fish evolved out of the ocean and land animals were created. <u>Homo</u> <u>Erectus</u> was our common family, some 1 million years ago. A person kicked the ball. Nobody disagreed. Score. Don't worry if you didn't catch it, people don't in the Rocky Mountains and the South. They call them vulgar Republicans. It's class.

Frank took the ball and gave it to the other team. They threw it in. He said, PE is gone beyond because I want Being? And Paul wrote about like his wife's death. And he was PE? Did he go back to being modern? Am I modern because I want Being? The other team kicked the ball. And kicked the ball. It was a run. It was a score. Perhaps only 1 person got it but they were playing ball with our Frank. It's a contradiction.

- - -

Frank held up two arms at a square. Then he asked is China postmodern? Is Russia Postmodern? Isn't Chinese self-criticism good for the body? I have PE self-criticism? Isn't self-criticism good modernism? Somebody kicked the ball. What would I do to the Museum of Modern Art? Isn't postmodernism the mistake of hubris? Kick it. At this point nobody got what Frank was saying, he was passing his Phd orals. And it made sense to him, he looked at his Sherry, who blew him a kiss.

Frank said, PE was *Time And Narrative*. I want to go back to

modern Being. Paul even talked about death in the end. He wrote about the "Song of Songs". The lover as Zen was there. Sherry is my lover, still. It fits in with my Church of Zen. Prayer as sensual. I worship my lover. That's why she is my Zen. Score. We are Zens in embryo. Frank had no heart, he was throwing out everything.

Frank grabbed one arm's wrist with the other palm, and said "Holding". He then pointed up his index finger. He then said, I am Independent. They are the under 30 generation and the generation over 65. I claim the middle-class for the Democrats with the defense of Capitalism, with obligation of contract clause with Art. I Contracts of the US Constitution that "No state shall impair the obligation of contracts". Someone kicked the ball into the end zone. Is that a Moderate Democrat? What about the trillions National Note?

That's a Moderate Congress? Get out more.

Hansel said, I would have blocked that with *Ogden*. Frank said, holding up two tight fingers, State Constitutions in right to work

states with 42 USC 1983 don't hold, though I love Title 42. The Federal Constitution and the obligation of contracts is still the civil rights of contracts. Somebody scored. As if they were in 2087. Our Frank didn't know how advanced he was, it was amazing that the crowd could hear him. Liberal Independent.

Frank said, the problem with Title 42 is the vendetta. These statutes were enacted to Counter South. The history of the Jim Crow South, and the Rev. King, is that one fights an entire town of hate. True it's a counter to the police state of "State Police". But in the Rocky Mountains and the South the anger you get is hardly worth the no money for rights, like under *Davidson*. They kicked it. And you don't need the death threats for being a civil rights worker. Nobody kicked it. Like Section 1983, the tragic flaw of the Republicans heel, their denial, of civil rights. Frank made like a sign of playing with a bow and arrow, like Odysseus in Ithaca. Then he said, Section 1988 pays your lawyer bills. That's the remedy for "State Police". But the reality, is that nobody hears what you say. If it's law and order then let's have law and order for the people. You might just score. You could be in embryo. Then he picked up the ball and threw it to the yellow team. They put it in play. Kick. One person heard our Frank, who yelled out to our Sherry, patterns.

Patty said, China and Russia are postmodern. Frank is postmodern too. It is self-Critical of modernism. Paul, with his metaphors, was post- existentialist. That is post-Modern. If you see someone with the fire of evolution, iniate it with water. Like the revolutions in Egypt and Tunisia. In your mind, if you see someone drinking gas in order to spit fire on the belly, throw water on it. They started kicking the ball.

- - -

PE was back in trope. This time she kicked it hard. The water of evolution is like the politics of the world. And as the world goes so goes America, now. Kick. Somehow I feel like a new world is about to be born. I can't stop it, said Frank. I can just throw water on it. Democrat or Republican. Kick. Went the two sides. I got it, said Hansel this was America in 2050. The year China goes socialist.

Play ball, yelled Frank. And so they kicked the ball back and forth. Frank yelled like some general, different commands. And the band played ball. There were about 400 fans on the sidelines, watching us and watching our videos. Pablo said, Cruz. Hello Pablo? Get it? Kicking the old can around? Sometimes I wonder what he's doing here. <u>Black</u>. Pedro was on fire. He ran down the field faster than anyone there.

The yellow team blocked. Pedro was a red. The two sides yelled back to Frank. It was like communion of free speech. Sherry was on the yellow team. She sang back to Frank. The words of his songs. Forget about meaning, you caught me. In a big way, Russia and China especially are postmodern, because they gave up on their 20th century feudal revolutions. Frank just got his like Doctorate degree. It's class.

-4-

Frank called a time out. As he gave a lecture to the band and the fans. Picture the creation of the sun. Throw yourself into that creation and picture yourself there. At the time of The Big Bang. And meditate with your eyes open. That is what you are learning to do. To do it at home. Then you are a poetic scientist. Like with our videos. He explained that he understood Russia and China, but that was not his postmodernism.

Did you see a type of creation of the sun. I got to earth. Did you see the creation of you. Open your eyes. What do you see. Waves of light.

The fall of a leaf. You see the fall of a leaf is like the creation of the sun or the creation of you. The palms swayed in the Santa Ana wind. Which caught our Sherry's toes, and her now almost wet body. She was almost dry. Frank was not orthodox.

What's going to happen is that I want you to create images with your mind and create your imagination. They all looked at each other. Then I want you to create a this is for that with your images. The images follow from each other. Those images are your proof. And follow your heart. So that it's not broken. Just keep reading. It's materialism. See a symbol. Then look for a correlation. That's poetic proof. That Zen exists. We all have different views of Zen but you must find Zen so that you can make it home. That's philosophical thought. What can you do with that, give proof that Zen is real to your life. This is not any one church. Zen sees all people no matter what their proof. Look for a sign or an icon. Don't be a strict Dada, let the belief be, it was for our Frank. It's we who have lost Zen. Now empty your mind of the videos.

Close your eyes and look for an image. Even Zen on the Street. Butch Lautsky was in the crowd and he did not play ball. Close your eyes and I see a big building. It gives the learning of the academic modernism of college but it forgot about our videos. Don't worry, it's a proof of the existence of Zen. The passing peak experience, yes Frank and Sherry had finally found Zen, with help from the crowd, a party.

Materialism is like reading a book and at a key point thunder goes off, Zeus a rare sight in Los Angeles? It's at that time we want you to get inspired. Half way to seeing Zen. Frank had done this since he was 21. When <u>he followed William Blake. The marriage of opposites</u>. That had guided him ever since, like with his two albums. And the images in the videos. That's it, the enemy, who ever it is, is buried.

Reading, you run a this is to that with what you think. Tropes of Zen intentionally trying to reach you. Like President Obama getting tax credits to hire a vet. It takes both sides of politics, like what I try to do. Then you are awake. Like Zen telling you to get out of a Halloween party. And that you needed to be bipartisan. This was hard for many people in the crowd.

Pablo stood up and told people to go to whatever political party they were in. Some were in the Teabaggers, now. Most were Republicans. Frank was giving them, Captain oh, my Captain. The tea bag party was like Thoreau's tax protest. And the Freedom of contract. This is a major climax of the plot's theme. In wrestling it's a reversal, as it was in politics. Frank was like our President Washington, mixing church and state. Like The Teabaggers are in reality the Libertarian Party. Or, the Constitutional Party.

Frank said, I've already read Thoreau, but I can't understand his protest in light of the tax protest of the Tea Bag party. And their freedom of contract? <u>Butch Lautsky was part of that movement in that they wanted a revolution.</u> This was Thoreau's text on Civil Disobedience, something that Frank was against? Of this, it's like he had climbed The Grand Teton, and was helping up his Sherry. Nobody else could understand. It is commerce.

-5-

Democrats, as many as there were, had something of common cause with the US Constitution. Frank worked both sides of the political party. <u>He told the crowd about the obligation of contract clause and how it was a peace offering of like the Democrats to the Republicans, a tactic of Frank. Like tax credits for vets, by Obama. On the State of the Union address, on January 23, of</u> 2012. Go to the "Center".

Frank knew that he could not speak for the Democratic Party. But he figured the he was part of the people too and he could deduce and think. And he knew how controversial his belief was. And he made it more than a belief. The President put it in everyday language and it into practice. Don't worry, Frank is being bipartisan, he just doesn't have a heart. He is lecturing the Political Science department at Pomegranate. Fishing the cosmos. To get the Republicans to vote Democrat!

People mimed Frank and he knew that this was a good sign in that they were showing him that they would play ball. He threw both hands up at a square and yelled, score. They all followed. Frank was having a vision about the meaning of life. And the possible existence of Zen. He was a fish. But he saw the water, something people Aren't supposed to do.

-6-

Evolve, Frank said. He could see into the new year, with a little help from his friend. Political economics means <u>factories</u> and <u>export</u> and a resigning of NAFTA, where all our jobs went south. And Frank wanted to adapt to the good feeling about Zen he was getting. Something that the crowd could relate to, whatever their belief of Zen, he was choking on the smog, through the green party, like even talking to the Chinese. Like a Moderate Independent, with the National Note, Trillions.

What about *The Phenomenon Of Man*? The evolution of Zen Consciousness? Dada met the author when their family had gone to Europe, when he was very young. He was 50 years ahead of his time. In fact, 50 years from now. But it was as much a part of him as the use of the US CONSTITUTION. He was like a George Washington who mixed church and state, but it felt so good. For Catholics.

Natural metaphors lead to Zen's consciousness. And that would be his intention from here on in. Sacrifice, said Frank. The video playing all this time. <u>Self-consciousness and self-criticism</u>. Butch Lautsky got up and left. Social Darwinism is not good economics or part of Capitalism. GM needed a bailout. And it gave the government back in one and a half years. It was just a loan. Like a Moderate Independent.

Capitalism did not believe in survival of the fittest. Don't disagree. This is a big deal with Republican candidates of the Presidential election of 2012. And the not self-conscious of econ or self-Regulating nature of the economy, which caused the 2008 stock market crash, because of the relaxed regulations on banking. Frank is being Independent. But

it's a major point for the Economics department of the University of
Chicago.

-7-

Primate evolution was not a good metaphor for economics. We
hear a mime, said Frank. He had reached a heart of a baboon. But
this was Frank, always searching and always thinking. He said, some
regulations were void as they applied in particular cases, under the
Federal Constitution. Like Vincent.

Romney said capitalism was survival of the best, a bad metaphor to
mix with economics. And he was a Moderate Republican.

Local contracts, said Frank, are not void against the city, under Art.
I Contacts of the Federal Constitution. Frank said that he knew how
controversial this was for him to say. But that this was his defense for
capitalism. It went beyond his videos and crossed into his new work,
"State Police". He had an eye-opened market. People who heard him,
mainly graduate students, were getting the different sides of his open
heart. Democrats needed to go to the "Center".

Primate evolution had kicked the ball to contract people. And
there were plenty of real republicans in the crowd. But they did not
seem to believe the bit about how Capitalism was not a metaphor or
the metaphor of survival of the best. Frank thought that this was funny
in that he was like a life guard saving a life. But this was his major at
the University of California, anthropology, and he knew the President
needed a heart. Like a Moderate Democrat. Both were <u>black</u>.

<u>One in four homes in the US are worth less than what is owed</u>,
said Frank. For the co-op, group homes was the answer. House the
bankrupt in group homes. Put <u>factories</u>, as if running for President of
the United States, in another bankrupt home. Where will we all evolve
to. With the Federal contract clause, Democrats have something to say
to everyone, the under 30 like his band, the over 65 on social security,
and the middle-class Democrat running a business. Who would hear
him? Evolve our capitalism. Frank went on, like in Great Britain a
coalition of the left and the right. And stop all this bickering. Tax the
rich for revenue. Funny, it would be like the Tax Act of 1981. Nobody

laughed. I agreed. Frank went on, tax rights for hiring all people. He used the megaphone. Tax all corporate profits. It was like Great Britain. A new way to run the country. No taxes for manufacturing Corporations.

A Production Act, said Frank, like he explained to his Congress person, where The Fed gives 1% loans to people to go into <u>Production</u>. Correlated with tax breaks. Stop sending all these factories into India. Find something to produce here at home. This is like a 2012 Presidential platform. Pre-2016.

What is the meaning of life, said Frank. Care and concern and Being. Benefits are too low. Don't tax the poor. Raise revenue on the rich.

That's how we can lower the debt by Trillion. We needed the loans to save the banks, that was the problem in the Great Depression. It was a Cal Democrat who knew this. The students in France are wrong. The banks needed saving. Even President Bush knew this. Bipartisan? This anti-novel is full of presumption and propaganda. That is normal. Leo Tolstoy had a theory of art that he called – infection. The writing, here, is like a virus. The cure is the reader. Waking out of this illusion. Fiction.

- - -

Moody won't downgrade again our nation if we do the above. If we have a high national loss like Trillion, that's what gave our nation a downgrade. But we need Moderate Democrat Revenue to bring down the loss, that means a tax act with bite, like the above, and production going again, remembering the UAW. From the perspective of a Democrat Presidential candidate? Who would hear him? And not think it's a pain in the head? Like the President's cut of a half a Trillion dollars out of the Defense Budget, by his pulling US troops out of Iraq.

-8-

Being is being here and now. US thinkers ponder. You reach space, absent time. Absent Zen. Meditate on it, said Frank. Lover's can create a tropic experience? What do I get? Knowledge of the here and now. Time of PE is timeless. Politics of Great nations, like Germany, have their political parties work together, like Great Britain makes it work, like me, said Frank. Sherry united with Frank. Paul's *The Just*. Bipartisan, which was the University of Chicago putting down Harvard University.

- - -

A novel of Being, of PE, in its many meanings. Everybody loves Frank. <u>He wants to unite the opposites of America</u>. He is the prodigal son coming home. Wait till the sun comes out and follow it's rays, said Frank. It's a petition to the people. Something you can do in politics in America. This part of the novel is about something nobody talks about. Ideology and Zen at a University. This book is born out of weaving an illusion. The point is that, while there might be some good ideas, here. Is that we are to change it, the illusion in our lives. Awake now. And doubt ideology, hiding the fact that you are alive, in Being. That is the meaning of the title? Aristotle.

You need a coalition government. Something you can't do under Constitutional law. Today is Sunday. I'm turning this into a novel, said Frank. Nobody laughed. Religion is a sign is a symbol. The sign of Being is Zen and you get that sign through a metaphor, like our videos, said Frank. We say be bipartisan. Something the President wanted congress to do, he already cut a trillion more, to make sure that Standard and Poor's didn't downgrade the US again, the way they kept doing in Europe.

Follow the rays of the sun and you get an idea. I'll narrate the timeless. Mysticism is being. You know the passing of time when you narrate it, said Frank. That is my goal but now Enrico Pelican is <u>recording this time. Center in on a point, and see Being as a trope, swirl,</u> you have drunk gas to spit out fire. That's a metaphor. On why Pablo Picasso painted so good. They said that of him.

Now you can kick the blues. And a sign will guide you. Like a Sufi or an dream sign with Paul at Chicago. Close one eye slightly and you wish to see a Eliade sign. When Frank was in Chicago he took a class with Eliade. He waited for office hours. Frank was the only one there, and asked a stupid question about Myth and ritual. It was stupid because Eliade was a yoga. Awaking out of our myth in this book, Water in the belly, is the goal of its author. the fact that all novels are dead, or as PM once said, they are full of illusion. Correct PE is to Be alive and know it.

- - -

Eliade used religious images, like an icon, to give rise to imagination. He wrote on international images. Of all peoples of the world. Of the material of particular people. People all over the globe use different symbols but their signs lead them to a personal relationship to Being. He like Paul was timeless. Like half the world, before 2050.

Eliade was beyond Tunisia and Egypt what he wanted to know was what was like the "Song of songs" of the Sufis. This was beyond class and guilt. It was the History of Religions, Eliade's world known authority field. Frank was not like a Luther. He was like Eliade and Paul, putting into practice the customs of a particular people. Like a religious Moderate Democrat or a Moderate Republican. <u>Civil religion</u>.

Evolution, for Frank, was the seeing of a man drinking gas so he could spit fire on the trope. He didn't want to explain his metaphors, like Jesus in the New Testament. Some symbols can't be explained, especially when they deal with the relationship between man and Zen. <u>Frank's art was like a Suf i meditation</u>. Like the "fate" of Dead Zeus.

That's what meditation with one eye partly closed is like for Frank. He does not see Being. He gets like Paul's interpretation. It is as if his eyes are on fire. There is no harm, of course. It's just a metaphor. The fire is the fire in his eyes. The gas he drinks is the fire of Being. He's not drunk. He's sober, in his vision. It was evolution. Frank as at the Harvard of world religions. The water in the belly.

Feeling is what it is. Drinking fire is his bliss. Not real fire, the fire of seeing Being. He had gone beyond ideology. He had reached the point beyond pain with what he called the burning of the mind. It was his brain that was water, like the images of the imagination of Eliade.

Frank was sharing with the crowd the spitting out of fire. It was his ironic free speech that he shared in his songs. That sold so many millions. He was beyond Egypt with the fire of his words. That's like the metaphors of tropes that Paul was so fond of. Eliade could call it material, the unity of Zen and People, through what could be called the fire of language. The water in the belly, a Zen picture. No metaphor is a Ricoeur <u>Metaphor Vive</u>. It soon becomes dry and we sink back into the illusion of sleep, that is this novel, the goal being to inspire, innovate, collaborate and liberate.

Slightly closing his eye, ever slow slightly, he had become what he hated so many years ago, a public speaker. But he knew he had free speech, the power of language to express his bliss, fire. He was seeing in his mind's eye water. It was nature Materialism, because it came from his mind. And reached out to the crowd, with the metaphor of drinking gas to spit fire.

Natural metaphor, like Paul suggested, was what he was doing. No touching his face or any thing, this was like pure materialism of Eliade. Just sit there and breathe the fire coming out of Frank's mouth. The flames of his mouth, pushed him head over heels. You ask what does the gas represent. It means the free speech between him and Zen.

This is a natural metaphor for those that don't like the idea of flames

coming out of Frank's mouth. We don't intend you to take the literal meaning of Frank's words. It's his state of trope. Go read Eliade's many books. <u>The bliss is symbolic of his spitting out of fire</u>. If you take him literally, I suggest you read Paul Ricoeur's *The Rule of Metaphor*.

The title of this novel is a metaphor. One thing stands for that. Like Paul explained regarding "The Song of Songs". The signified is Zen. <u>Water in the Belly</u> is symbolic. It is tropic. The feeling in the body of a world yet to be born. <u>A woman's being is on fire</u>. This time the eyes are not flaming. We have a different figure of speech. It's more than mere being. It's the flame of Being of a woman in the process of birth. If you can liberate yourself from this text, and start reading with an "interpretation of Doubt" just for a moment, then you can read the Ricoeur thesis that "narratives", take the space after birth.

It's a metaphor like the burning bush. It's giving respect to half the human race. In the words of Paul Ricoeur it is a trope. I recommend his book. But to understand this novel's title one needs to read the collective works of not only Paul but Mr. Eliade. Water in the belly.

The Burning Bush of your belly is like the future being born, the children of next week. And that future is on fire with the hope of a small child taking milk from its mother, protected by a father like a parent of the Constitution guarding the children of its country. Fire in the belly, is a starving Zen child yelling for food.

The <u>Water in the Belly</u> is the children of the world holding out for its next meal, not sure of where it will stay the night, protected from reality by the Constitution and The governments of the earth, for sure a vision of the whole globe, not of our one small country. It's s metaphor for the future. Nations are starving.

A fire of Europe unsure where it will go but sure that it will survive the night. The belly of Ireland and Spain and Italy and Greece and Portugal that will give birth no matter who the doctor is or where be the hospital. This world trope cannot be stopped whatever the good intention of the United States of America. That's the water in the belly. Language is the problem. That's why this novel is a rite, a rite of consciousness. For some this means a cup of coffee to awake, sometimes we might wake up to existence. Or, at least see the means of production, of our own political economics, beyond our illusion of words.

This is international political economics, presented in a symbolic way, through what is called a trope, which is a symbol that has no literal reference in the real world outside. Like the future being a Moderate Democrat or Independent. The signs of the allegory-like symbols used to present the meaning of the metaphor. There, that was understandable. In a symbolic way. <u>Water In the Belly</u>. To keep away the feelings of hunger.

That night we thought of the Starving Africans as w e talked before going to bed and thinking how lucky we were.

Chapter 13

WEDDING CONTRACT

-1-

In the vision of the fire of the belly can give forth satire children. This is the case with "State Police". Then there was the shootings in Tucson. And the silence on the far right about the deer hunt 2nd Amendment from Teabaggers. Some people at least know how to mourn. No free speech protests. Just 6 dead; and 12 wounded, including the congress person. A lady. Who gave up her seat in Congress a year after the attempted assassination, she was an Arizona person of the people, Democrat. Of course, you did it that's how society went around and around, To make you feel guilty for a crime you did not commit, simply because you had a hunting riffle in the back of your closet. Guilt and Punishment. Though the US supreme court held it legal to own a gun.

<u>I am Frank</u>. <u>Enrico is no longer the narrator</u>. This is the return to the trip home. The last 4 chapters of Homer were his dream for Odysseus. That is me. I am a prodigal. I am trying to start over. But it is hard. I have already made my money in a trade of question. But I must move on to home. Some months have passed. And the thrill of ideology is gone, but I have a memory of the wet inate into the world of the "Song of Songs", where Zen started to be possible, in the spirit, that changed my life forever, a mind changing event, of the poetic. Something that I never felt again and which I don't know how many times in my life such an event will happen again?

The tragedy of the Saudis bombing Yemen, causing mass starvation, with their political assault on Shiia class, is linked what mass starvation in South Suddan to name but two, is some contrast.

- - -

Federal courts, not controversy, have for almost 200 years been lost in a material haze. National Constitutional obligation of contract clause is the one Federal choice to defend capitalism. It says no to the states, Also not controversy. I am America. And I need the contract clause to defend my music. I am still an Independent. Bipartisan.

I can see it, the Republicans are going to take over Washington. My one thing I will grab on to is the obligation of contract clause. The conservative US Supreme Court still wants the Constitution's original intention. That is my <u>one</u> home? And a return to the early Chief Justice Marshall court. I am going to propose to Sherry soon. That event months ago changed my life so much, I felt I should have a chapel wedding. I could be a bipartisan Independent. A moderate and not a hawk. Like Mr. Blair, of the UK, we need to find the "Center".

Vincent, my brother, is a Republican. He was in need of a way to validate the US Constitution. Against the city of Los Angeles. It could have been New York City. The issue was the same. The obligation of contract clauses of the New York and California Constitutions do not exist, in that they are not right to work states. I will give Sherry a ring. Which will mean so much to her. Girls are like that, like the majority of the people in the United States.

-2-

I can see President Obama start to reflect the attitude of a Republican. Like his use of tax credits. He wants to influence the Republican House. Where they have a bunch of jobs bills, that they can't get through the Senate. The 2010 Tea Bag party must not be a failure. They could hear my obligation of contract plea. The country is going to the right, but The President would save social security and stop a <u>class struggle</u> finished by the people of the United States. Congress controls it.

California state law enforcement officials legalized the legal, medical use of Mary Jane. Justified by some city and county law. Then the National FBI made a raid on the business, something that I had expected for 10 years, given Federal statutes. But that was the real Federalism, where National law rules over ironic, conservative States Rights but that was not the point. It's that the FBI made a legal business, as if it were a Mary Jane plantation. Federal law preempts state and local law. But they got charges like Vincent.

Some kind of Universal Health Insurance is a necessity for all of America, if not just like Medicare. President Obama had his health plan. It was just justified by a Higher Federal Court, in Washington DC. It will make it to the United States Supreme Court, where state's rights advocates oppose it as too costly. This is fire and birth. But whose birth is in question. This holding will start to cause a <u>class war</u>, in June of 2012. In 2017, it was no joy.

-3-

We have been at the co-op talking about politics. I am Frank. We are on our trip towards home. We have free speech to talk about both sides of politics. But I am a Moderate Independent. I could organize. The under 30 have the politics of "Busted"; and the over 65 have the album "White-Collar Crime". Go back and read the songs in light of the last chapter. The songs were political and were meant to stir the emotions. Like the suitors in <u>The Odyssey</u>.

<u>It's the over 65. They are the silent voters. They think that they are Republican. They are so wrong. The Republicans want to take away their Social Security and their medicare. The Democrats want to protect their retirement.</u> When will the over 65 wake up and see which party is on their side? Though the over 65 are too old to protest at a peaceful assembly? But we are talking about politics at the co-op.

Democrats want to protect the middle-class, that is my vision of politics. The Federal Constitution's obligation of contract clause. That is like coalition politics. It's like Moderate Republican or President Obama using tax credits. We will talk later about this clause. Everyone is a person. I am too. For peace and commerce. Obama got us out of

Iraq, finally. Thus saving a half Trillion dollars from the National Debt. By the time of the 2012 election there are going to be a lot of mad people. All over the US. We talked about this at our co-op. We had free speech on both sides. Sherry was a Republican. And liked us finally talking about her party. The Republicans. It was like all the free market and get government regulations off our backs. The AFL-CIO had one big target on its back. They were not the UAW. But 23 states are right to work states, which would make it easy to have Art. I Contracts, incorporated in the state constitution, which would mean there is no need for a Title 42 action. Those states are not union.

CEO's want to strip the unions of all their power. But not GM of the UAW. There is a way to unite business and labor. And not export labor to India. Hansel started to rap too. It was going to be an avalanche against labor. We needed a coalition between the everyday people who used contracts and statutes and the real people who worked and the people who managed. Just like the need in the nation. The unions are loosing power politically, around the United States, But not at GM. Or, Ford. It's City governments around the US, like San Jose, California, where they want to drop city worker pensions, down 65%.

Teabaggers scared me with their state's rights and libertarian national politics. They took Congress in 2010, at such a level that you would have to go back to 1947 to find such a takeover. They controlled the House. And stonewalled all of President Obama's jobs plans. The really rich pay 15% because of capital gains. We need that at 32%. And tax the rich who make over 1 million a year. Sure it would stifle investment, we should make a like Reagan tax act, keeping the estate tax. There, I'm bipartisan Independent.

It looked like the Egyptian Revolution. That was their metaphor, revolution, the people from Egypt and the Tea Bag party. It hit me in the heart, American politics being that bold. Though it worked, it makes my hands tremble, to hear our Hansel. Talk about The right Wing of the Republican party. Who hold the country hostage.

See a Republican President. Like fire in the belly. And if it's not that, it will be a Republican Senate. Better anything than a Republican Congress and now a Republican president. If I could only talk to the over 65 voters and tell them that it is against their interests to vote Republican, on Social Security and Medicare. This is so democrat I can hardly stand it. I can't stand the hypocrisy. It's all money for the Pentagon, and cut money to health care; and the EPA. and to the department of state, which should be helping with world treaties. They leave us homeless.

Republicans would love my idea of the Fed Constitution's obligation of contract clause, because it voids regulations. Just not Federal regulations. But it's my idea. Like State Constitutions and states rights. And I give it to the Democrats, in an attempt at coalition politics. The Democrats will have to give it up for commerce. Just in, the US Supreme Court heard the case of The President's Universal Health Care, which won. For now. And class revolt?

We are still in our co-op talking as we will be all day today. Sherry got animated when we talked about her Republicans. She liked the Bush of 2008. I reminded her of the mistakes into Iraq, which President Obama pulled us out of, and the torture of the CIA. I gave Sherry an engagement ring. She cried.

<u>That reminded me of the under 30 vote and our next album "State Police", which was taking a long time to get pressed. That under 30 group of voters were in essence democrats</u>. That was the way I wrote the coming album. But it was sarcastic so you could read it any way you wanted to. The youth needed help with their tuition loans and money to go to college, in California tuition spiking up 10% each year, because of the state's deficit of 3 billion dollars, a tragedy found around the United States. Who will pay for pensions? And paid Vouchers?

The CIA's torture was under the Republican President Bush. In Iraq and that small Territory of an American base, off a Cuba Bay. The Bush years were marked with mistaken action. Did we really want to go back to those Republican years in international Relations? One presidential candidate said bomb Iran's nuke plant. Is that what became of compassionate conservatives? <u>And another said take away the Federal subsidy of the Poor's food. What about starting a class war?</u> What about the poor and their safety net, as seen by Romney? Where are the jobs? How could he keep winning? Put his company into the tax code, like a blue print or how to start to fix up a business? What about treaties, everywhere? What could he have done for Vincent?

-4-

We are in the co-op. <u>People use signs all the day long</u>. A signal, the signified of which is culture, not the thing itself. There is an apple tree. I say, apple. The meaning, by modern linguists. We were talking of that is what is in your and my mind. Not a real apple. This doesn't always work. There could be a real apple tree. If somebody threw that apple at your chest, you would see how real that apple was. Pablo reminded me of this. It's like Zen. They say that the referent to a sign isn't Zen but culture, which would block my ideological experience. This issue I deal with, the birth of my materialism. My wife is my Zen. I am like a fish, in water, which is like Being, which is like Zen.

In 2008, Wall street was the sign that hit us. It was a Republican administration. The band was there. We were there. We got into the MBA school. We got loans to get in. We remember like it was yesterday. We could not get a job. We formed the band. You laugh. But I am a professional music writer. And we made millions. We would love them to tax the rich. But Congress signed a pledge not to raise any taxes. <u>The so-called trickle down economics, or Reagan, being behind the supply side econ, put down by the Chicago economist, Mr. Stigler, a Nobel prize winner.</u>

- - -

I think I am going blind. I think I see what's coming politically and I am powerless to stop it. I can't see into the future but I see a change is going to come. Thus, the title of this novel, <u>Water In The Belly</u>, there is future that is ready to be born, and it's at a world level, not just America, like the President of Italy quitting, hitting world stock markets. And The Republican economic plan—lower taxes, and the rich will want to invest—was Put down by the first President Bush, as <u>voodoo economics</u>. Back to symbols, how can we get to the reality behind the sign.

Like the apple. It's Not just a sign. Sherry comes up and sits besides me and strokes my shoulder. Evolution of ethics is Republican too, she said. Pluralism is Democrat. The voice behind the sign, is an echo from Western Civilization. I went on, I may not understand everything about all things but I know we need a Congress that is willing to be bipartisan, which the Tea Bag party faction of the Republicans, refuses to do.

Republicans have symbols too. Like the haunting of the Tea Bag party. Sherry reminds us. They were capitalists. Capitalism is my love too. I love Sherry. Why could not we have treaties, based on class like Islam or with China, or not the nation and the world be run the way Sherry and I get along. We love each other. I am a realist too. It's coalitions that are stopped, except in London. Where half of Parliament is like republican and half is like democrat.

Democrats back the votes, most of them. Republicans fly the flag. Sherry is a Republican. I love my wife. I know my politics are not with Vincent's Republican party, I only seem half-hearted. But my President brought the troops home from Iraq. And will bring 30,000 troops back from the Kabul area. I love the troops, but want them home from foreign wars.

I was once in Air Force ROTC. I played trumpet and took a class on military tactics. NATO backed the revolution in Libya. I like NATO nations. And do not meditate on a world police force by US troops or think they should go into Syria. There already is too much imperialism. I like the Constitution. And think that the Treaty clauses are the way to go. That's my tactics. My tactic is to get many treaties with our enemies. I kept on talking. Vets are our fans. That may sound funny to you.

But what I wrote backed law and order. I saw last night on TV where the remains of one head was put in a trash dump. That's what vets get when their remains come back from like Kabul. The President wanted tax credits to hire returned vets. Then he would get a job corps of Vets to police the US, if protesters got violent?

- - -

Republicans, who own their own homes because it was their investment in the future, are suffering. Especially in Las Vegas. It's not that good in California, here, and in places like Florida. They invested in their homes because they did not want to invest with brokerage firms, in like the stock market. They need a Democrat like Obama who hears. Meanwhile my wife sings in the shower.

<u>I went on, the stock market responds to like Europe, Greece and Italy. What about Spain and Portugal and Iceland and Ireland? And The Euro? That's what's in back of the brains dealing in the world stock markets? They had merchant banks years before US 1999 legislation that allowed banks to trade in stocks. We wanted to be like them. This throws the cause onto Europe, not on us, for the Wall street stock market crash?</u>

- - -

Vincent was at the co-op but all he could do was think about real estate. He was a Republican and my heart went out to him. It's chapters, before we tell his story. We talked about PMS and PS and the questioning of assumptions? All I did was question the presumptions and assumptions of old people who said that they were a Republican? This is funny because at the end of this novel I slowly become.

PMS was a way of life to me? As it was to my Sherry. But I was the one who studied political symbols. My songs were PMS? I wish I could explain all the things and thoughts, the contradictions, that were running through my head. But I knew that the band, who was listening, knew about what I was talking about and how it related to my Sherry. That means, again, postmodern symbols, like water in the belly. Like the revolution in Syria or the smelling the air where the Koran was burned in Kabul. Talk about some ticked off Arabs. It was a bad act, and should never have been alone.

PS is like the Chinese, with the best economy on planet earth. They had self-criticism. I understand their defense of their territory and their dislike of Tibet and Taiwan. They are internal affairs of a country and it is not our business to critique them. You don't question their assumptions. Post-structuralism, PS. Here the reader is like a spy doing espionage on these letters to decipher the meaning, stop reading for a second.

PM and an S is what we deal with. I told the band that I did waffle when it came to Zen. But that it was like that we were a whale in an ocean. That was a sea of signs. We don't notice the signs at all. The problem is that we did not know we were in the sea. Take PS? <u>When we started to Question the sea of signs it did not work, the way a whale does not question the ocean.</u> Most people don't understand PS, the concept of defamiliarization. Almost always, we never do it with Being.

Millions call that sea or ocean, Zen. I was trained to say, I do not call it nothing. That's me and I am weak. But I don't question Being, which is like a sea or an ocean. Still I question. I don't want to be a fool. I am an agnostic theist. To the ideology my faith waffles. I am confused. Now. But with my obligation of contract I sound like someone in politics. I am human. Then there was my wife as my Zen. Not popular with Republicans.

There was a long pause in the conversation while Sherry passed around some crackers. Pedro asked, what's reality? I felt he waffled too. Symbols?, Sherry said, the icon in a glass candle of the Mother of Jesus, ironic. I said, yes, it's like the water in the belly. A new world would be born as of 2012? That's the metaphor. It's a trope, a non-literal metaphor. I can't predict which side will win the election, but it will be a new world, for us. We had to be bipartisan. To get the vote.

Like, drinking gas to spit out fire on the belly blues. That's a metaphor. A trope, not a literal symbol. The gas is you. The fire is my mouth. The drinking is the reading. The spit out is free speech. The belly is what gives birth to a new world. It's the blues I think. It's a parody of a metaphor, then. Why didn't I use that as the title of this novel? It was, but it was too confusing, so I made it more simple.

<u>Water In The Belly</u>.

That's a trope, it's a type of metaphor. A type of symbol or sign. It's not reality. It is used to explain reality. Like in a poem. Or, a scientific theory. The theory is not the reality, like the Big Bang or Zen. Our ideology is a poem to explain evolution. The teacher gives us mellow words to keep us calm not like spitting out fire on the belly. Like they are doing in Syria, in spring of 2012. Because nobody understands it. But in reality the Big Bang is anything but calm. It's a trope, not a literal metaphor or poem. We measure its effects.

Sometimes I doubt my tropes. I doubt my metaphors. That's like a whale doubting that it is in the ocean. It's tropics. Sounds like Vincent. He can't believe he ate the whole thing, the entire Republican line, not a good thing for a fish, eating on a line, who knows who on the shore, who knows where the trope of Vincent's will go, or who knows where it will lead. Not good for the fish. It's like, Whales swimming in the ocean talking to each other. We are like that whale. Alienated.

It's a troooooooooooooooooooooooooooooooooooooooooope. Not a literal symbol. That is *The Structure of Scientific Revolutions*. 500 years ago someone said that the universe did not revolve around the earth. It doesn't. The <u>entire</u> Greek world was wrong? And did the guy who said offend the reality of the tropes? He laid it out, the Greek world was a trope. It was a non-literal metaphor. The trope. Like Zeus.

Hansel said, I still don't get PMS and PS? I told him to think of them as symbols. Non-literal metaphors. I told him he had PMS and that if he asked me again I'd give him my PS. Pedro told him not to worry in that they were like the trope <u>Water In The Belly</u>, which Hansel didn't get either. <u>Nobody got what a trope is</u>. The meaning is that sometime in the future, a new world will be born for us. Out of the bankruptcy of civilization's cultural critique. If some ball player pleads- free agency.

- - -

I said, Hansel one day you will find the method to go home, for me my iphone is my trope water in the belly. He understood that. A trope is a non-literal metaphor, which says this thing is like another thing. It's what good poetry is based on. Like a good scientific theory, no the theory is not the BIG BANG itself. The theory is not the data, which can be read differently with a big leap in a paradigm, or a scientific poem. Math is our model. It is not the thing itself.

I studied, up to my Phd orals, science and symbols. At the University of Chicago, where they first split the atom. Thus proving that there was atomic energy. And where in 2007 they found Neutrinos, particles that went faster than the speed of light, thus proving, at the Fermilab, that Einstein was wrong. Where, in economics, they got nobel prizes, in the last quarter century.

Who could doubt that?

The Structure of Scientific Revolutions, the author of which taught at Chicago, anticipated this falsification of Einstein. Like sign theory is made poetic by tropes. A non-literal metaphor, a trope says what you know about the world is wrong and I am going to give you a sign, like a whale in the ocean, which will blow your mind. That's Wire In The Belly, like the use of the word trope. Like the below.

Drinking gas to spit out fire, was a metaphor told to Picasso, as to why he painted so good. My mother once told me, Picasso is not on trial, its our reaction to that Symbol. She means trope, but my dear mother did not go to Chicago. Now my Mummy is Chicago, I adopt each department that gets Nobel prizes, So I can better understand my school. Like <u>Culture in Practice.</u>

-5-

<u>Denotation is from signs and we deduce meanings. Poetry, like water in the belly, tells us to think. Symbols are food for thought. One teacher I had in Los Angeles said we all are the whales in a sea of signs.</u> The sea was not Zen, he said. What a thing to say. Something I used to say to my Sherry. When I was an <u>atheist</u>, now Sherry wears my ring. Am I like <u>The Stranger</u>?

- - -

Something is ready to give birth that the seas can't hold. It's the water in the belly. The whales give birth and a new generation is born that the ocean protects. That's poetry just as the ocean is Zen and we are the Whales. Of course we don't know the outcome of the election and I don't want to hurt you with my party, but a change is coming.

This is hard to read, like deciphering a trope of this sentence. Slouching towards Jerusalem, what is it that will be born?

Let academics call the ocean ideology, I say let them pick apart my trope. It was not literal. They missed their soul, a metaphor for them. It's a trope. Like the water in the Belly. Then there was the oceanic feeling of the mother giving birth to a new nation. Let's just not forget how tied to the past we are. The trope of a type being the Whole, that is a trope, poetic, a type of Jesus is like the whole of Jesus. Take care, its poetry. Being is Zen.

What are signs, said Hansel, pointing. They are like street signs that say, Los Angeles 33 miles. The point is to follow the sign not to grab onto the street sign for security. There is a profound lesson there, that should not be lost. We follow signs. I put my hand on the wrist of my other arm. I think and type in metaphor and these signs are types of different things, I haven't worked out me ideology yet. The Church of Pride, the belief in humans as God, tragic.

When the signs are not clear, don't reject the sign. Whales are funny that way, they like the sign of the ocean as their Zen, even though they have never thought of it. In the NFL certain signs are clear. They are signs. Rules. Penalties. They don't mean them poetic. There are those who would penalize my religion. I plead the 1st Amendment, to free speech and a <u>redress of grievances</u>. I have a right to the evolution of my ideology, even if it's different than you. My wife as Zen.

I think in metaphor. For example, Neutrino only went very recently a fraction of a second faster than the speed of light. I say Einstein's theory of the speed of light was basic, universal to the speed of light. I say Einstein's theory is still in force. That doesn't put down Chicago, but I wonder how Einstein might feel? That's like a paradigm change, a counter example than the theory of general relativity. My politics are my character, not a political platform for President. My character is complex, either bipartisan moderate Democrat or moderate independent. But it's Bipartisan character. I like the blues.

All day long signs are coming out of our mouth. Pedro rubbed his eyes with his fists. The conversation must have made him tired. Signs out of your mouth, like the Church of Zen, a boat I am almost in. And what do the words refer to, said Pablo. We don't really know what they mean but by convention we get the general idea. I am engaged to Sherry and that will be my new world, the water in the belly.

It's like a symbol coming out of my mouth or pen. I got that I was their teacher. Both on symbolism and science. There are green go signs. We do what the sign says. What to the tar and Vincent's case? We are not Einstein, I said. Signs are a mode of communication. I was once told by a friend, symbolic, on a red light you stop and on a green light you go because no good driver would ever run a red light. He wasn't talking about cars. <u>The conversation was in tropes</u>. Which nobody got like the not literal title of this novel. Slouching towards Bethlehem, what sort of Being will be born?

"State Police" was our album in the works. We deal with yellow lights, tropes. We all are like whales swimming in a sea of cultural signs, the album will deal with Amerika, but except for the remedy it was basic universal, unknown to many protesters around the world. That's why I was sarcastic. In a police state, a red stop sign means stop. To that extent we all live in a police state. Like the tragic hero of <u>The Odyssey</u>. I am a life guard, as Enrico Pelican knows. My intention is to save lives, as many as I can. The signs of a whale are all around. We are so familiar we don't even notice them. And we swim in an ocean of signs. During a riot, the sign is a red stop sign, no matter what you think your defense is. I went on talking. The talk being a stream of signs we don't even bother to think about. In Water in the Belly, what will be born is my Character, out of the tragedy.

When the CD "Busted" hit, it was like everyone was busted, I said, that was my intent to act like the police. Everyone swims in an ocean of signs. You don't want to be caught in like the Arab spring, in Egypt and Tunisia. The life guard can't save a body that is caught up in 50 feet waves. That's how big the Arab Spring was in the history of the world, a string of revolutions, not since Europe 1848.

- - -

Some signs are like sharks. Nobody should be swimming in those waters. Better go back to the whales in the ocean, unknowing that the sea is their Zen. For us it is Being. The whale swims in the sea and that ocean is part of her Being. Of course, this is just a metaphor. One thing is like another thing. It's good fish food. A symbol is this thing standing for that thing. The thing of water stands for the thing of Zen. VVVV   VVVVVVVVVVVVVVVVVVVVVVVVVVVVVVVVVVVV VVVVVVVVVVVVVVVVVVVVVVVVVVVVVVVVVVVVVV VVVVVVVVVVVVVVVVVVVVVVVVVVVVVVVVVVVVVV VVVVVVVVVVVVVVVVVVVVVVVVVVVVVVVVVVVVVV VVVVVVVVVVVVVVVVVVVVVVVVVVVVVVVVVVVVVV VVVVVVVVVVVVVVVVVVVVVVVVVVVVVVVVVVVVVV VVVVVVVVVVVVVVVVVVVVVVVVVVVVVVVVVVVVVV VVVVVVVVVVVVVVVVVVVVVVVVVVVVVVVVVVVVVV VVVVVVVVVVVVVVVVVVVVVVVVVVVVVVVVVVVVVV VVVVVVVVVVVVVVVVVVVV fish food. Those in California and Chicago are whales too. They are some of the biggest whales in the sea. Better throw them some big fish food for they are hungry. So I have myself and my non-literal metaphor or symbol, drinking gas so I can spit fire on a belly. It's not the trope that's on trial, it is the person reading the symbol that is on trial, like the judge of a Picasso painting. Drinking gas is like reading Wire in the Belly, spiting fire is the readers interpretation, ready to be born.

<u>Tropes are what we call it, I said to the co-op. And the real reference is lost to the Poetic image that feeds our imagination. Don't have it yet</u>, don't worry, think of it as a complex metaphor, this thing stand for that thing. But the water in the belly is like an ocean where whales feed. These are multiple symbols explaining the title of this novel. Like spiting out water in the belly to put out fire, for example. I need some water.

We don't see everything in a poetic image. We don't recognize all signs everywhere but we can read the street sign that is green and says go. Just figure that you are on a freeway. Read the signs. If it says Disneyland in 50 miles. Don't grab onto the sign for security. Follow where the sign leads. That's the key, don't grab onto the trope that says water in the belly, follow where it's leading, the future of the birth of a new world. The intention of the sign, is the rebirth of the prodigal son, a material thing. Like a wedding contract.

Whales are my favorite metaphor. I grab onto that sign. And turn it into a trope of Zen. These are not mixed metaphors. They are multiple metaphors, I said. That's what they are there for. After all you have a whale swimming around in your brain. Let it do the driving. And don't be that self-critical. Like a whale, we swim in an ocean of signs, we just don't recognize it. The referent of the whale is us as Zen, in a sea of signs, Zen too. The Church of Zen.

The co-op was tired of symbols, this for that. And Sherry was a good drink. She passed around sherry for all. We all had a glass of wine. It was sweet. It took away the tropes of the whales. Not all signs make us feel good, I said, knowing that the wine would mask my non-philosophical intention. She showed off her ring. Like *The Iron Heel.*

-6-

Take the Tarot. It's material to me, said Patty. I held Sherry's hand. Some say that there is an intention behind that, like Zen, said Pablo. I don't believe it, sometimes it's by accident. Yes but it's symbolism. It is a whole new world for most people. It's not Zen, it's by mistake, I said. Put the tarot on the internet at Google.Com. We met the next day to talk at the co-op.

13 is death. 6 is the lovers of The Tarot. 11 is trial. 15 is the Devil. 18 is the moon. 19 is the sun. 9 is the hermit. Is that my intention?

No it's just by accident, I said in my writings and I said, in my novel and my songs. Still, those are signs, said Pablo, putting his palm over the backside of his other hand. Yes, I said, making a peace sign over one eye. These are like NFL signs, get a ref book and see their meanings, or on Google. Where else would you get its meaning?

Whales have a special language, like mimes, said Pablo. He had grasped what I was trying to say with symbols. I said, I like mimes.

Vincent was the only one not to have wine. He bought the bit about the whales but not the bit about the mimes, which he hated. It's a controversy, these non-verbal signs, but they are like NFL penalties, and you give them when someone playing makes a gross mistake, in parody. The mimes drove Vincent mad. He wasn't educated like me in symbols, this for that. Signs are language, I added. They are a natural part of life. I enjoy talking about symbolism, I got a masters degree on them from what must be the best school in the world in symbols, this for that. I wanted to educate. But when I explained my passion in symbolic terms, like wiping the gas off the belly, only few could follow. Signs, I made the peace sign, something the band could relate to.

Symbolism, this thing for that thing, I said. It's just that sometimes we get whatever feedback, where there are no mimes. I had some more tea. Justin, a few weeks back, had been busted or he was put in the hospital a real dirty trick, like a real political prisoner for his LGBTQ signs, behavior. They put him in a hospital. Based on 60 year old theory. That said to be Alice was to be mad. We got a writ and sprung him. He was angry.

You were framed, I said to him. He couldn't look me in the eyes, his thing. It was Alice theory, he said. Don't talk about it, I was a political prisoner. You were, I said. You should talk with Vincent, he won't bite you. They got both of you on your odd behavior. That was the cops giving a penalty to a class of a person. A status crime, it just started to rain, and made us depressed. LGBTQ marriage was to come.

You are a hero to the people, said Pedro. They tested his signs and symptoms. They got his confessions. Just like "State Police". When is that coming out? Not for a while. Things around the world are still in a state of flux. In the last draft of the last song I wrote I said that the protesters would end up in a jail ward. That's civil death. Like the law calling you out, and you having a type of record. KaFkaesque.

The signs that they gave him made no sense. Vincent too. They wanted their symptoms? The symptoms of owning property? The signs of lost dreams? I heard them. The sign of staring into someone's eyes? Both on trumped up charges. The symptoms did not refer to anything. Sometimes signs do not refer. They made both of them mad, which they took as a bad sign. Sometimes a cigar is just a cigar.

You see through somebody's reality. And it makes you mad. Don't doubt it, some people are crazy, like Chuck Noon, who the band sprung. The sea of signs for the police were symptoms of bad behavior, all they are really interested in. The police deserve honor, for what they have to see and to judge every night. Or in Chuck's case. Noon Chuck was wrong, he was not set up like Justin. Resist authoritarian ideas?

Football ref signs, like mimes, are for everybody to see. Mimes use them to call people out. Football ref signs, I said, bringing both arms to the square. The police were watching and they scored. There is no Title 42 claim for these brave victims? They might as well have been homeless, brought in on a general sweep of the streets. There is no right to be homeless And sleeping on the street is not peaceful assembly. We married.

One singer, in one of her earlier CD's at the end, introduced her audience to Christianity and Revolution and their entanglement. It was quite the wedding gift, we were shocked. It was like Christian Nautsky. Or what comes after, with so-called late capitalism. Like a serious Republican Revolution.

We went to bed, not thinking that a January 6, 2021 could ever happen.

Chapter 14

PREGNANT SAILING

-1-

Signs can be a work of art, I said putting my palm over the back of my other hand. Yes, I said, when I was in Seoul, with more taxis than New York city, they had art all around the city. Some of it was postmodern.I know it when I see it. It had modern art mixed with the Gothic with classical Roman. So we have various types of postmodernism. The above is in visual art. In politics, it's Russia and China. And in this novel, it is parody of Homer. HEre, this is The Odyssey Sailing.

We went down to the San Pedro Harbor and got on a friend's boat. We talked with each other as we prepared the boat and thought of the trope of Zen and started to sail it. Someone said we were like swine.

I taught English in Korea. By your students you will be taught. My students taught me about how the people of the South really feel about the North. They said that half their extended family was in the North.

What they said was the opposite of the official American line about the war with the North. This is so controversial I can't even mention what they said, without there being like charges in the air. The bipartisan nature of my character is in the process of being born.

I said, Rome is like a postmodern city. They have modern buildings next to 1500 year old ones which are next to old Roman ruins. It's the eternal city. And that's just the ideological type. The Reformation art is priceless. We don't have anything in America that can touch it. It makes

American art and cities look like kitsch, plastic. In the 1960's the movie *The Graduate* popularized the term plastic as something Kitsch.

Hansel said, why did they revolt in Egypt? That's a good question. They did it with middleclass computers and software. The government shut down the internet, to stop the revolt. The poor can't get on Facebook and Twitter. I thought that revolutions started with the poor. That's why you need to go back 150 years to find anything like the Libya revolution and the Arab Spring, the mass revolts across the Arab world. We were like strangers, on the DL.

Then there was British imperialism and colonialism in the mid 1800's. In Egypt and India. Now there is a poor place for you. Better hide America's brand now in the mid-east, so we can sell more albums. There is the American middle-class. Only 1% are vets. But the US worships its vets. Still, the President of the United States pulled us out of Iraq, a controversial war. <u>The</u> <u>Odyssey</u> cites <u>The</u> <u>Iliad</u>.

I said, we're rock and roll not the US brain police. At least when you talk of Zen you have an audience. 80% of America goes to church. I have my daily doubts. It's my struggle. I was trained a scientist. Proof for everything. A whale metaphor is not proof of Zen's existence. Still, Being and the "Song of Songs" gave me hope, like I have never had before. It was my one moment in time that gave me a taste of Zen, intoxicated. Both of Homer's classics, are tragedies. We all are like strangers here on earth. We all have out tragedy. Critical theory can help us with out illusions. <u>The</u> <u>Iliad</u> gets repeated signatures.

Given the Arab spring, you might have thought that the Tunisia and Egypt revolutions were a CIA plot. But the Democrats don't work that way. <u>That would be the Achilles' heel of America</u>. Like the Shah in Persia. Then there was the revolt by the students in Iran, in 2009. That wasn't a US plot either. The head of Syria killed 7,000 people under the assumption that the revolt was a foreign plot, at First.

Sherry said, we're artists and we must ask these questions. That's why people buy our records. We give them the truth. That's the key. If we lied people would loose faith in "The Cherry". If we lied we would have lost cherry. Yes purged from the minds of the world. So I continue to explore the tropes of politics and all the world to get new material for new songs. World Zen to redeem the prodigal son, Odysseus.

Tunisia was like a police state, the "State Police". The world will see in our new album the truth about revolt. And outside America and proof, there is no remedy. Just buy our album and see what symbols do to explain bombs. Curl up and listen to our songs. I am a <u>primitive</u>son, I said. I understand world culture. And it's not pretty. It's funny in a <u>black</u> comedy way that across the world the above album is the norm. Like Syria. The US is factually like Russia when it comes to protesters. We get the collective guilt of the world. And we should not be guilty, for not doing anything in some countries. They bought our albums in Libya. We were a hit. US and NATO. The meaning of life, I said, is to go to the ocean of signs and pick up a sign or two that you can politic with. Hold on. Doubt just now and then. Sherry held on to Zen and a wedding ring. Odysseus is homeless.

President Obama got us out of Iraq, I said. And 30,000 troops will come out of Kabul by next year. We are 22nd in the world in education. You can see it in the faces of people on PBS nightly news. We follow the war and the Euro. And ya'll are the victim.

My father was very young and the man was very kind. It was a controversy. Some people did not like the fact that the author was an anthropologist. And believed in evolution. Others didn't like the fact that people would merge with Nothing? But in the end he got the okay from the Pope at the time. It was almost a new religion? Thus, the controversy? I was ready for it?

We made it past that ship. We sailed out into the ocean. We had a 33 foot boat that was called a, yawl. It had a big mast at the front with a little sail attached and a smaller mast at the rear. The mast is the up-right piece of wood that holds the sail. We spent a good 3 hours in the ocean. We got there early in the morning. We meditated on the big ships in the harbor, and on the clouds in the sky, and wondered about Zen and we still related things to "Song of songs". How does your life relate to Zen?

And now to Zen Consciousness? How would you say that in tropes? We talked as we sailed the boat out of San Pedro Harbor.

The wind, now, came off the bow, the front of the boat. We tacked into the wind. I pulled the tiller to the right. The end of it hit my rib. I looked at the wind and thought of Being, and thought how I was like that anthropologist, priest. We evolve into Being.

I looked at the clouds. And ran a connection between what I was thinking and the clouds. It was the mystery of Being. And the evolution to the "Song of Songs". I kissed my Sherry and doubted the existence of Zen. It was the scientist in me. But I never told my wife. I was Being and I was Zen. I doubted my own metaphor. What's proof. That's legal proof, I believe in Zen beyond a reasonable doubt. In a court of law, I would be not guilty, of believing in Zen.

- - -

It was not a pathology to doubt your own metaphor. It was science. The Church of Zen said that you could have the Zen of your choice. I chose "The Song of Songs". It's ideological <u>agnosticism</u>. Like they said of the above anthropologist Catholic Priest. I was not guilty beyond a reasonable doubt. We later would convert to the Church of Pride. Which turned into spitting fire on the belly. They were similar, an <u>agnosticism</u>. I just called it Zen, and everyone was happy.

All this went through my mind, as I stared at the Being of the clouds. I am not Catholic, I believe in the "The Song of Songs". It's mysticism and a correlation of metaphor, this thing for that between one thing and another, like a symbol, this for that. If this confuses you you can join the club, the scientist who uses metaphors. And the proof of guilt, which I now did not have, beyond a reasonable doubt. You academics will note the room for doubt. Zen is not with me every moment, all the time.

So not thinking about Zen is doubt. If you have any doubt, go talk to a good defense attorney. It was Dreyfus, at Cal, who kept me with being in the world. Despite the contradictions and unity of the two. With Ricoeur.

- - -

I said to Sherry, Zen is like a court of law. It all revolves around proof. Sure my correlations tell me that there is Being. But I am weak. What are the right ethics. Paul takes us back to the Greeks. After Homer. Ethics, says Paul Ricoeur, leads to a good feeling and is different than German <u>SiNN</u>. We always had ethics while we were together.

I told her, that's the "Song of Songs" evolution. That was the Zen I chose to worship along with Being, not one being, but the whole of the Universe. That was my Being, that The Church of Zen said I could worship, and we are protected by the First Amendment. Pregnant, Sherry threw-up over the side of the boat. I ducked.

I told Sherry, Paul said that Kant's morals was different than Greek ethics. And I chose ethics. And the evolution to "The Song of Songs".

That is my Being's Zen. The Zen of Nature's Zen. And why we don't recognize we are in Being, in the first place.

Time structures the day and night, and the tides, so intentional. It is the Sun and the Moon. That's what I guide my boat on. The sun gives me the relativity of Time. It will be a full moon tonight. That is the sun's sight. The tides of the Moon guide me. This is the scientist in me. Like the Fermilab's Neutrino. Faster than light, Ricoeur.

The time of the sun tells me where to put my boat. I know that I am playing with Being. That's my narrative. An evolved post-existentialism. With Being. And Paul Ricoeur's "Song of Songs". I am a mime of Being. And I got it, he just called it here now. I don't doubt the first time I felt Zen on the green, when Sherry danced like a Hindu. It's the feeling. I was like Odysseus sailing with my crew.

I looked at the sail and the wind died out again. I could no longer deduce Being from the coldness of the wind. I meditate on the weather and how that hits my heart. Now, that's how I guide my boat. From my heart. I am not like a weatherman. I note the weather, that each day is evolving and universal. But it is the feeling, you get, of Zen.

My Material is like that. I mention morals of Kant and I come up with the ethics of a candidate running for President? I am a Democrat? Let me just say that. Sherry and me, we were two consenting adults. That's ethics, as I read the Greeks. I felt guilty because of our Common law wedding. So that is the reason we got a Zen wedding.

Calypso is our record company. And it was either Calypso or Circe that took over our Odysseus. The way that my record company dumped a bunch of money on me. I am that Odysseus. Just looking to go home in peace. The lotus-eaters are worse. They totally make you forget about home. I am at a home, and sailing.

I am an agnostic and I don't like people asking me if I am Buddhist. I forgive and that is enough of a Buddhist for me. Being is meditated in time. I guess that makes me like a little Jefferson. Not fragmented or afraid of the end. I feel my heart. And the end times are Being. Like me becoming a father and taking responsibility.

- - -

I would like to think of me, as someone on first base. On the team on the Giants' first base. I then go from first base to home and put out a man coming from third base. While saving a batboy near home. It's impossible. Paul's PE? I needed all the Zen I could get to redeem me.

PE is escaping heart meditation. It's mime meditation. I saw the sail go limp. The wind had stopped. I wondered how Sherry was. I was seeing the CCC? I took inspiration from the sail. Being isn't the wind. It's an effect that moves a part of Being. Like I was moving my Sherry. She was pregnant so we were careful.

-2-

Nausea is one of the best books ever written. It was written by Sartre, Paul's fellow from France. And yet they are as different as night and day. Paul shares Sartre's love of philosophy. I don't know if they ever met or if they were together at the University of Paris. Sartre was like Ricoeur's father, that was like the relationship between.

It ended with a <u>black</u> woman singing. He was an underground fighter and feelings of America were on his mind. What's the culture of Sartre's book? It was pro-America, and that is enough for me. He meditated on the mime tree. From nothing, he reasoned Being. The <u>black</u> woman singing. You could say that it was a classic book. I read it. It would be in the top novels of all time. Sartre and Paul liked praxis.

What caused the two people to separate. Paul was also into Philosophy. Sartre was given the Nobel prize for literature. He turned it down. Culture is the author. Just stick to the book. That is Chicago's CCC. The environment wrote it. Like this novel. It's 10 years of America. The wind came off the bow, and we leaned over the sea.

It was a journal that went from day to day, Sartre. I have to admit that I would not march with the "Occupy Wall street". Too much anarchy, on the side. But Sartre marched in protests in Paris. Paul was too humble a man to take sides politically. Literally, he was too occupied in meditation. That's what I remember about Ricoeur. A humble, honest person. Postmodern philosophy, putting down Heidegger.

This so-called radical, Sartre, wrote *Being and Nothingness*, saying that what the people of the world needed was freedom, he got from US. The wind is picking up. But my heart is in one piece. It's Sartre. A man who I read word for word. The wind came up again and we leaned out over the boat's side. Like the "Nothingness" of Zen tragedy.

The CCC was Germany in occupied France. And both Sartre and Paul were vets. That's Chicago Cultural Critique. It's not what people want. They want to critique the writer. Sartre produced works of art. The issue wasn't him. It was the culture that was in the work. I thought about this as we leaned out over the boat. As the wind hit our faces. It's what is Frank Holmes' culture and his family. Zen is "Nothingness".

I told all of this to Sherry. She is wise beyond her years. She understood me. This was my PE peak experience. Meaning isn't ideology. It's like the German's <u>care and concern</u>. Something that Paul ate half of. He was held a prisoner by Germany. Heidegger, author of *Being and Time*, was German, which Ricoeur spoke.

The wind caught the Being of the sail. And I pulled on the rope that was connected to the boom. That's sailing. It was some wind. Like catching a wave in surfing. The wind was coming from the stern, the back. I saw the sail and thought of Being. Like Homer.

Aristotle, key in CCC, talked of tragedy. *Being and Time* started out with a question of why was their Being at all? The issue for CCC was not that the author was a German prior to W W II. It was what was the picture he painted in the book. I can't emphasize this enough, it's not what Heidegger did during World War II. Here, novels are different. It's what is my culture, in this novel. Not what is the novelist's culture and family life. It's the culture between Sherry and Frank. Not the novelist and, for example, his wife. Being is "Nothing" to me now.

Tragedy, in CCC, was the sin of pride. And the American's. And of those who read his book and did not ask why Being was? Put in Chinese terms, why did the reader fail to have self-criticism. The wind shifted to the right side of the boat. And the boom shifted right with it then I pulled on the rope that was tied on the boom and sail.

The meaning of Being was visible to me in the sail, in that I saw the care and concern for the whole world. In CCC terms, it's me Frank seeing the meaning of Heidegger's world of the book, not about the German People. Just like you don't blame the German People, generally, for starting the World War II. Give us back our unity.

I pulled on the boom. Some have called as a peak experience, Heidegger's Question in the book that why is there Being at all? People spend all their lives ignoring, totally, this question. It was the meaning of Existentialism. It said how could you be authentic? It was facing your own Death. Like Odysseus, with the Trojans.

PE said that such an ism was wrong, because it centered in on death. Paul's *Time and Narrative* said that death worship is wrong. And for 150 years that's what existentialism worshiped. Paul started an entire new school. I called Paul's work PE. That is Ricoeur was too humble to name what he had discovered. I knew it right away, as putting down Heidegger and Sartre. Ricoeur's PM.

Nausea did the same thing. It was called modern. Paul, by way of contrast, was postmodern. By definition. He got a modernism and put it down. I saw Paul in the Chicago church praying. He was too humble a man to call his work a new 'ism'. But it was. Postmodernism, like the Chinese by Deng Xiao Ping, went beyond mere materialism, but married Post-capitalism, PC. Paul was post-existentialist and postmodern. That's two types of postmodern, Paul and the Chinese.

Russian's too did their own version. Capitalism was modern. Like Adam Smith. They went beyond belief. They, too, became postmodern. So the idea that PM is new, is silly. It's almost half of the human race. And they are our friends. When the wind came off the side, I let loose the rope of the boom, and faced the new waves like PM. Like Homer. Live, I said to Sherry, as I reached out like Pride on the cross.

Republicans are revolutionaries with the Teabaggers. Then they became the rich class against the Federal government. The wind shifted back to the stern. The Tea Bag party is still modern. They hate Russia and China. They don't know that the Tea Bag party started the Arab Spring? And was in reality too M. Just a little different. That's a living contradiction.

It's not bad to be modern. It's just that being against the Federal government, May make them a hero in their eyes, but it doesn't make you a post-Modernist. There is too much in foreign relations that you have to go against. Not all Republican candidates are modern. But I am a Democrat. Almost. I am like Romney, I have shifted positions enough to make one question what party I am in? I am like a Moderate Materialist, because of the national Note. It's just I know what people will say and I cover my tail. It's my character's redemption. Ideology of the Church of Zen, not Republican. That is my character? Bipartisan Pride. Don't question my Materialism, feel grateful I have found at last. I looked up at the sail. And it caught the wind. And I thought I was Being. The response of the wind was Being. Being was not Zen, to our Paul. I added that later. I just was buying Paul's brand of Material. Is Being Zen. It's like my crutch. I am handicapped. Most people missed this about me, and I don't say it much. I am crippled. Like an <u>Ahab</u>.

Cosmic theater, here, doesn't reject all Victorians. Some of my best friends that are Republican like Art. I Sec. 10 of the United States National Constitution. We will deal with the contract clause in other areas of this novel. <u>This narrative is about my character, the key to this novel, how I changed from an ethical agnostic to an ethical Buddhist, it doesn't all happen until the last chapter in this novel</u>. That's what keeps you reading, will he end up now, as my brand of Zen?

<u>Have we cold feet about the cosmos</u>. The wind came off the bow, a good tack. Begging at the gates of Eden. I still have on my Greek, and I don't mean modern, mask on. I know how you feel but it is a whole new WORLD. Sherry was just a little bit pregnant. Our Ship was like Odysseus Sailing.

-3-

The wind shifted to the stern. It's going to be a little bumpy ride. I moved the TILLER. <u>Just like James Joyce. Tiller to trouble. Feel the wind. Let it help you catch a thought. Meditate on that thought. Relate it to your Being. This is Zen sailing. I am pregnant with Zen sailing</u>. That's a trope, you should know me by now. I have gone through so much I am like writing this to my kids? 11% of America is atheist? Hence, if I am a good American, I must believe in some type of Church. It's like I can lean over the boat, and if I look down, I might think that the earth is not round? The dead Zeus, gave you your "fate".

I meditated on the sisterhood of the wind. What do you do when the wind comes not from the bow, but from the stern? You give the rope some slack. You have reference problems. How do you think Paul felt. That's how low Odysseus got.

They are only social signs. Just remember Being, the thing behind the wind. You see it in your sails. In that, you can get traces of Being. Paul hated Being. He formed *Time and Narrative* as a treasure against Being.

- - -

"Traces" of Zen can be caught by reading almost anything by Paul Ricoeur. He was a historian. Who remembered his own Zen, not Being. He had PMS. *The Rule of Metaphor* was like an analysis of the tropes of Jesus. He put living metaphor, from the French, with his work on stories. You don't grasp Being directly.

We kept sailing and Being involved with the most dense ideas of our marriage. CCC of Paul dealt with Aristotle of the ancient Greeks. Not to mention tropes, non-literal symbols. Which was meant to apply to the spirit of the P.M.? The way Jesus' parables seemed a riddle to his enemies. Like water in the belly. You got tropes.

Paul, of the new testament, did not always speak in parables, like Jesus. Do you remember, Paul listing qualities to have and he said the greatest was charity, or love. The Romans crucified Paul upside- down, for going against the government. Thus, people speak with not literal tropes. This was a step beyond just symbol or metaphor. That's why the Christian right doesn't trust the Government. Beings threat.

CCC can be used to see that Paul? He had rank and Roman <u>class</u>. He spoke where Jesus knew what the Romans would do to Jesus. CCC saw a mistake in Paul. He had a thorn in his flesh. Our tragedy if we don't get our act together somewhere in this novel. Don't worry, we did. About a half year ago we got married. For the South.

Common law marriage, in California, is not what it's made out to be. When we did gigs in other states our marriage was not recognized. It made us feel constantly charged. It did not matter that we were in love. The road to Zen is paved with good intentions. That's why we got married. That's part of the theme here, redemption of the prodigal. Like Zeus and the Greeks.

CCC, in our jungle, meant money, looked down on by Paul the Apostle. Quick, look at the sail and traces of Being. I mime Being. Is that proof of Zen? Center in on Paul of the University of Chicago. The most humble of men, but he took on the issues of <u>existence</u> and ethics. He took my case. I, still, don't know Being.

Aristotle, who deciphered Homer, came down on the side of ethics. That would bring you happiness. Not the Romans. Aristophanes, the Comic Greek writer of *The Frogs*, made fun of his society, much the same I made fun of the world, in my songs. Fun of tragedy.

The wind shifted. I hit the tiller. And I moved toward the boom. It's the wind. Look at the sail. Look at the sail. We are not looking for Zen. Like Paul. We want to expand your mind. We want to take charge. CCC would now view my novel as a tragic comedy, because of our stance on Zen. We are rock and roll stars, not a philosopher like Paul. The wellness is that they do give Constitutional Full Faith and Credit to our California marriage. We couldn't stand the doubt, so we got married. For the rest of the world.

We don't want to talk to the author of Being. We want the signature of the wind. That is Being enough. We want to go beyond the sail and see the clouds. Then we sail. The sailing is getting better. With Constitutional law. And wondering why we exist at all.

Watch the boom. It's shifting even as we speak. Good look at the sun and its shadow. The shadow moves. That's time. Paul's Zen. PMS is Paul. His friends liked PS. Use it to interpret time. Of Paul. The ethics of love. I am like talking of 175 years ago.

PS says it's the metaphor of the thing you should see, like the fire in the belly, the fire of being born, of recognizing that I am an Odysseus. You don't see Zen, don't worry, you will, it's life ready to be born. A burning in the Bosom. That's Zen. <u>Homo</u> <u>Dei</u>.

PMS is the author, in this CCC. Why won't they let the prodigal go home? Like Odysseus. The hero of our story *The Odyssey*. It's a classic story, Brian. From *The Life of Brian*. It's like the Greek of Aristophanes.

- - -

The Who's *Tommy*. Someone's Being you don't want to be.

We are the characters in a play by Zen. Comedy ends in marriage. Just not our California marriage. Marriage is a fundamental right.

And they wouldn't give us Full Faith and Credit. A fundamental right means you get equal protection. Were they wrong? Yes. Were we wrong? Yes. Those are the contradictions of reality. Like 2015 for LGBT. The cool breeze came off the bow. When you are too close to creation you are too close to Zen. And it doesn't let you see it, all you see when you are home, is the stopping of the barking dogs, next door. That's what I am. A trope. I see Zen in people. And in the correlations of being. That's just my character. That's all the Zen I get to see. <u>Homo Dei</u>. Have mercy on my tragedy.

-4-

I reached back, thinking of Sherry, and placed my hand on the stern. With the other hand I put my hand on the tiller. What was it, tiller to trouble. And we were in need of some Zen. The wind was at our back. But more. The boom was in the water. Homer.

TILER TO TROUBLE.

We did. We put tiller to trouble. And that was the remedy. Thank Zen. The mystic's *ayat* is seen in this CCC? Paul's signs tell the reader where to go. The metaphor is Zen's way of talking to me and also like a trope sign, here. The wind tells us where to go. It is Being in back of the wind that tells the prodigal which way to turn. We long ago got the wind to our back and got married. *The Noble Koran.*

Cultural relativity tells us the way. No way are we going to let the Arab spring occur on US soil. Republicans have their own heartbreak. Like Tunisia and Egypt tell the United States of America that their revolution is in the wrong jurisdiction. Muslims are good and bad. We do not give our spy signs to pan-Arabia. Now.

The tiller went to the bottom of the boom. And the boat shifted around. *The Koran* can be a guide to treaties. It's author, Mohammad, peace be upon him, would in no way endorse pan-Arab revolution. That is where we draw the line. Libya was a war not evolution. Like America, I was slowly getting redemption. Like from a Muslim *ayat*, or Islamic rule or law or trope sign. How controversial. That's me as a prodigal.

Their book tells us of their <u>behavior</u>. And evolution of Egypt in no way should be universalized. Even now as we speak, there are countries that reject the notion of revolt. These are Arab countries. The Saudis are reluctant to adopt even modest reforms of like Tunisia.

This was tragedy. All in the name of the people. Jurisdictions like Tunisia can not even plead necessity, to the Saudis. CCC sees tragedy almost across the board? If we were in a mystice challenge, pan-Arabia would need doctors not justification of arrests, tragic.

Do CCC on Snow's <u>Chrysalis</u>. It was about a good CIA agent who taught at the very same UCLA. He was liberal in 2003. But in the wake of September 11, 2001 he found the need to become conservative and quick. PMS was the title of the book and narrative. It was "Sympathy for the Devil"

And with that I saw the light. I needed to become more <u>Democrat</u>, for no other reason than I did not want to be misread. I decided then and there to become a Democrat, if the water in the belly was right I needed to go through my own prodigal rebirth. And the next several chapters deal with the ritual process of that rebirth, to becoming a Democrat. It's really funny, now, I am not like Mitt Romney at all. And what I needed was Buddhism? Not Politics, like Mitt. What I need is liberalism. And for the rest of this novel I confuse Politics with Religion, in order to cure the prodigal. It was, in part, like 2017.

I decided that Art. I Contracts of the United States Constitution was too important to my family and myself to leave it in the hands of the Republican Party. For some this is just cosmetic. But for us it was real. As if we were in Russia.

And with that I turned tail and ran as fast as the wind would take me, back to the San Pedro harbor. I thought about that Catholic, anthropologist Priest and I could identify, now and forever, with his idea that we all are on an evolution to be like Proud. I think that was the Church of Pride.

- - -

I wasn't sure what the Church of Pride believed, but it was a tragedy.

<u>Homo</u> <u>Dei</u> For me. I had projected my wolf nature onto the cosmos. And boy, was I ever wrong. As for PE, I would play ball with Paul Ricoeur. That meant Time. So you are watching my evolution and contradictions. I will never be an orthodox Church of Pride. I was saved, out of my doubtful <u>atheism</u>, by the Church of Zen.

We made it back to the *Queen Mary*. And we had the wind to our back. These were a lot of changes. But Sherry would have a fellow politician to share her bed. Old ways are slow to change. But this was the right start. So the wind changed. And with that I took her to her dock. The one that didn't touch Medicaid.

I told Sherry all of the above. And you could have hit her down with a feather. She agreed with me for all of the right reasons. I will live up to my promise. And I wouldn't let America go down the road of the countries of the Euro, so deep in national eros that their country, like Greece, would go under. The opposite politics of Hungary but the same result. Balancing the eros on the backs of the poor.

Pregnant, Sherry leaned on my shoulder. We got to the car and Sherry threw-up again on the ground next to the car. Rational contracts told me that we did in deed made our chapel law marriage church-legal. After we got married, many months passed. I was to find out we were expecting a baby girl, some months into our marriage. This was a shock to my system as was the change in politics.

The pregnancy helped to make me a Democrat. The Presidential fight was way over 8 months from now. I was being born a Democrat, again. I was old enough. We just talked about life and everything after our church wedding. Mitt was the Republican, a man, candidate for President of the United States, in 2012. On brief, we need an election that would bring in red and blue states. U.C. Berkeley profs and "The Chicago School" of economics together. That is to say that what I'm giving the reader is ideological rhetoric. I'm a half African American, tan in color, letting 2017 take me away. At the time of 2012, with a tail. <u>The Odyssey</u> goes on. Odysseus doesn't need to sail anymore. I was the stranger. But not in my own bed. The suitors wanted, but could not have, my wife Sherry. This was Oddyseus.

-5-

I am positive about the so-far tenure of chairperson yellen of the US private Federal Reserve. She was in the elite club of Mr. Bernanke, in the housing collapse of 2007, Mr Greenspan who was blamed for the Mortgage crisis, and Mr. Volcker who allegedly was one of most hated men in America for his role in 20% inflation rate during the early Reagan years.

For close to over 4 years, Yellen kept the interest rate at about 1%. Then after the Obama years after the election of the new president, she chose no tot "stand her ground" and fight the Trump administration. She raised the rate 0.25% four times during the next year about. I'm not sure what the change would do to the highest stock market value, in the history of the fed? I know it would benefit wall street investment banking firms. But it would hurt the middle-class people wanting to get a mortgage and home in the future. I know that increases in the Central banks interest rate helped to put coal on the fire of inflation. I'm not so sure what this would do to short-term and long-term international trade? Or, how this would help the devaluation of the dollar, like the way that the Chinese did to their money to help exports? If they do that, I don't know. Inflation was at 2% a year.

The Credible chairperson yellen was a professor of Economics. And was probably trying to teach a lesson, <u>inter alia</u>, to the world. She said, she did it because the economy was good with low unemployment. Samuelson's <u>The Great Inflation and it's Aftermath,</u> stated that high inflation was justified by Keynesian economics. Rising inflation stimulates a rising economics. Business "cycles" are not self-regulating, as the Republican's believe. Keynes and Galbraith, also from Cal, said that technocrats could control the economy for the better good. And that's what was in the back of Chairperson Yellen's mind.

In 2022, inflation is at its worst in 40 years, compare with Fishback, Rose and Snowden's well worth saving: How the New Deal Safeguarded Home Ownership. The government holds the key to stop 2007 housing failures in light of Keynes "investment".

Chapter 15

TIME DREAM

-1-

Dreaming, I saw a Materialist, who mirrored my every move, like my Dada, who needed a prostrate operation, sure he can have that operation, but a good doctor will leave him, like with a 10 year sentence, to get his business done, and a bad doctor will leave him, blue all over the place. Dada never got over this recognition of prostate cancer.

- - -

Like my grandfather, I was my father in various stages, of the joker of Dada, a wolf like one of my songs, which I revolted against, in my way home, suddenly there was a pyramid of Time, on my belly, and like Dada I told myself to sit down, this wasn't a logical contract, it was a freaking dream. Time is altered.

I saw a foggy Chevron station, and I went in, because I went to the University of Chicago, they called it pig and I caught someone throwing an egg, at it, and the egg hit me, when Time is short, there are few friends, as Chevron was a friend, it went all foggy. You should have got me by now, I am telling you my dream.

Then, I dreamed of Sphinx and a Materialist, and they asked me the meaning of life, I told them that I was supposed to ask them that, and the Sphinx which was in Egypt, of the Arab spring, said law and order, I just laughed at the contradiction, and they both said that the meaning of life was revolution. I easily did not buy, my "song" didn't like the term revolution, they went for the term progression.

Isa, of Egypt, kept talking to a crowd, I had my legs wrapped around a pyramid, and I turned into a tank, in Syria, which had its own territory, but which was the target of all the collective Arabs, and the king of Jordan told the President of Syria, to step down, what was I doing in my tank. This was the last hold out of the so-called Arab spring, and very bloody. And the crowd of suitors.

Then the scene changed, and I faced the Dada of Time, Mr. Mann, author, of "Snow" of *Homo Dei*, and I saw swirls and storms, which hid the Chevron station, I thinking I could never touch a Mann, who was my master, and I worshiped at his side. Then I realized that such was the sin of pride. I had seen Mann. I got there by briefly reading Homer's other classic *The Iliad*. Stay there stranger.

Colors came to my head, and I could not get them out, I thought that the eight hours of sleep should do my head, in my Odyssey, through Paul's Time, which came in my brain, like the 20th century, still alive in me, but going fast with Paul, with his PE. The modernist Mann was guilty of having an Achilles' heel. This was a major discovery, especially since Mann got the Nobel prize. Rocky.

I knew that like Mann's Hans Castorp, I was in, for the long haul, like a modern <u>Odyssey</u>, I wanted so much to be like PE, but I knew that it was my sin of pride, like in the other Homer, I wanted so much to play ball with the 21st century, and I felt, in my heart, that heartbreak? Time. Which was Paul's history, which is what this novel is all about, and academic like Mann's *Magic Mountain*. Not a swineherd.

The symbols of my dream, would tell me where to go, like the signs of society tell me when my heart is going to break, I saw more symbols, and metaphors, like this for that, like the water in the belly, the being alive to be ready, to give birth to a new world. My new world was giving with Mann, and his *Homo Dei*, so close to the Church of Zen with the "Song of Songs". The past and the future of my dreams are the ideological propaganda, from a non-intentional mind, my subconscious. Odysseus and I were tragic.

This is me changing. And I am serious, this is not parody. For as long as I can stand it. I hate judging my character against some ideology. It's always been that way. I want to hold on to Obama and to the Church of Zen.

I am Frank, I am not a Mitt and this is my Odyssey, through 10 years of the United States of America, at the dawn of a new century, playing ball with Paul, and his PE, as I call it, and with his living metaphors, like a waking dream, full of symbols, this for that, Arab for Teabagger. Time. To have their revolution of the Tea Bag Party? This was history, though it was mostly. To Obama's plans. *Ayat* means signs. <u>I saw signs of yellow and red, symbols in a dream, like PE art sometimes the signs do not mean anything, PE drawing on modern art, pluralism, gothic and modern and classical Greek, like all together in a dream, in one ball, this was Paul's PE dream for me. This was artistic postmodernism.</u> So different than simple modernism. It accepted the different periods of art, not reject them. I accepted the different periods of art, not reject them. I was <u>The Stranger.</u>

Signs point the way, in society, sometimes they are absurd, in a dream, symbols of a dream, are this for that, Paul's living metaphor, my Egypt for Tea Bag party, water in the belly, but not pure libertarian, hate of all government, but metaphors, for Paul's just, contract rights, from Europe. Time. The birth of history was seeing the stupidity of Republican Candidates for President.

Symbol or sign, in my dream, like Paul's Freud, sometimes for you, sometimes for me, sometimes personal and at other times public, history talking to us, in our *Ayat*, this for that, living symbol, this for that, Tunisia for Teabaggers, history, not me, talking. I just add the living French metaphor. A living metaphor is like drinking water to put out fire in the belly. My images, like my economic politics, come from the bottom up, not from the top down, as if to dominate.

- - -

Put water on the sparks.

I still liked my tropes. It's just the Republicans who make me uneasy.

Ripple on the water, a sign, like a Muslim sign, this means for that heartbreak, or ripple on the ocean, we are a whale, and it's an ocean of time, of history, Paul's time is a symbol of historical change, water in the belly, the drop of the heart and the loss of knowing what history will bring, I don't know, I just dream. We don't know what history will bring, so like Romney I change my positions, relative to time. I call that vision. In that we are united. But I feel more Being, than Church of Pride. At least I'm modern.

The dream changes from the ocean of Being, to the sea of Time, I note the change of narrative, in my dream, the narrators change and the metaphor changes, as the politics change, I had now a new friend, asleep now, in need of help, I can help, just hold on for the ride. This is so new I don't know how to play the game of politics, I put down my party.

I dreamed a new dream, waking, at the right time, the police cleared away, occupy Oakland, now is not the time for camping out, so I get new metaphors, but water in the belly is constant, it means change, birth of a new world, I told you about living in the US of A, and you know I am a writer of tropes. Drinking gas to spit out fire on the belly, a living parable, like those of Zen. Get me my Mitt.

We haven't come out with our third album, but it fits, time for change, kids, that's what plot does, and now I still follow our President disarm Iraq, we need a bipartisan collective dream, to keep us from becoming Greece, not Homer's but one on the brink, with its National Note. How close are we to Greece, here and there, anarchy against local businesses, rocks against the business front.

- - -

Work on our National Being, is stalled in Washington, people there don't see how our bipartisan response, ripples into Wall street, and no Bang, it's not new years, I just changed my waking dream, stay tuned, it's bound to be a bumpy birth, time, I am so bipartisan, where are the rest of the republicans? Not Bipartisan. It's the only way to get rid of the Congressional deadlock, whose popularity rating is at 13%, the lowest in 50 years. It's still the Republicans.

Dreaming, I saw myself turn from a wolf at the door, to a life guard, helping the world give birth to a new world, the sign is a bipartisan Speaker of the House, he must change, I see in my dream, or we can't stand the heartbreak, it's not either or, it's both and, just follow, downstream is our nation, our world. And upstream we are polluting the river, with our waste, against the people of the US, quick I saw a republican from the house, in my dream. And am I ever not him. I can take Mitt, but I jump back, not knowing if Romneycare would work for the country.

I dreamed on, and there was like a brown wall over my head, there is a Mummy and it's King Tut, hear the king speak, he's got free speech, it's at the University of Chicago, seeing the passing of Time, history, of the Chicago Commodities' exchange, of Wall street, what will we tell our kids, of our dream. My political dream is like Obama, first left, we change because of the rocks in the water. then right, we change because of the rocks in the river.

Keep cool, and King Tut will whisper to you, is the Senate stonewalling the Jobs bill of the House, it's all who will win the elections, can't give in, the other side may win the election, as Wall street waits, I floated down a river, that passed a magic mountain, which turned into King Tuts' pyramid, is it the Nile, I paddled on, in my dream one thing is turning into another thing, so difficult to follow, like my politics.

I saw my Mummy naked, I rushed to cover her up, then a red fox ran into Sherry's Belly, what would it give birth to, I turned into a howling dog, I didn't worry about mixed symbols, that's the nature of a dream, this for that, and this turning into that, it was red fox, so pretty, the fox was a girl. This, the girl, was turning into that, the fox, as living and moving metaphor that was my dream. Like Lacan, PM.

The fox ran into a pyramid at the side of the Nile, which turned into the Chicago River, I watched the passing parade, going down the river, but what about my red fox Mummy, was she safe, of course, if we could keep it in Greece, and keep them with The Euro. Keep it in Greece because Homer was the Greeks, and the Greeks were the Achilles' heel, sin of pride. *Homo Dei*

The problem with the Church of Zen.

Then I turned into a coal miner, but it was strange, I was still on the river, then I turned into a miner of gold, Mummy loved me, she said, just keep it in Greece, and worry about the gold of The Euro, these were dream symbols, this for that, and dream signs, that, the miner or the mummy which was I, I was what I saw, twisting and turning, the images turned into each other. I'm still the stranger.

Dreaming, I was howling in the mine, I had free speech, we were a mile down, what was the meaning of that, not The Euro, I had turned back into <u>red fox</u>, as Freud once said, sometimes a cigar is just a cigar, and a fox has got no place where it can lay its head. How could I howl, I must have been in pain, then the fox, turning and twisting the symbols and tropes changed, not literal signs. It was my Zen suffering.

The red fox hit a piece if metal, and started to bleed, I thought of my Mummy, then red fox started to get on top of me, but I was prepared, I had seen the fox before, then I got down on the fox, a fox is quick, quick as a black cow, I kept dreaming, I was in a coal cave, not lie Freud, the fox didn't mean anything, it had no meaning it was structure of a symbol, like math symbols.

Sherry stopped the purple bleeding, then the scene turned into a part modern painting, a Kandinsky, lines and pyramids, colors everywhere, I looked at the art and it was weird, were there little figures of realism, caught between the lines, or was it just my dream. Like a modern painting, the signs had no meaning, a cigar was just a cigar, and a line was just a line. The hawk and the dove.

The Kandinksy went into a Republican cave, the storehouse of art, modernism accepted by PE and PM, that pluralism that accepts all forms of art, even my primitive attempt, that's the PM of a Seoul relief, seen catching a taxi, driving Into Insadong, the artist area of Seoul, where they had Postmodern art in the street, so much more advanced than us.

In the center of the cave, had abstract art, the haven from reference, the cave being our home, our co-op, from where I am dreaming, I could smell an odor, it was the smell of dinner, my Sherry turning into a cop, seeing my attempt to pay the property taxes, due on our co-op. In the cave I craved modernism, for its lack of reference, so my ideology turned into a drag, in the cave, which was just a simple cave. You will get used to Mitt? PS.

We were in a group home, a Time co-op, our fire cave, there was more of that <u>black</u> cow, that we all ate, in that we were hungry, there was the smell of coal dust, covering up the odor of the <u>black</u> cow, it was a little chilly, it being odd for Los Angeles, my home for so long, LA becoming a Mecca for modern art, something I loved, because I could see, its reference to nothing. The "nothingness" of Zen.

-2-

I turned into a cop, the next night, in my dream, it is typical of my *Ayat*, of late, what do other soccer clubs do, it is my obsession with reference and the signified, Zen, of late, I did not know, crossing my arms, as I lay in bed, still dreaming, playing kept my heart still ticking, because the Occupy Movement Had turned into anarchy, in the eyes of the Isa. The "Nothingness" conscious was the goal of zen meditation.

- - -

What am I to make of the revolution of the Teabaggers? Was it really a revolt? Was it really water in the belly? It wasn't Egypt? Isn't it a play on words? I am not a libertarian, against certain forms of government. I remember who I am. I am a bipartisan Democrat. I stopped my dreaming, in 2010 they took the House, I could read the writing on the wall, the people had elected a Libertarian congress. They would buy my Art. I Contracts argument, straight off. I just don't know about Federal Courts. How can we get back Republican voters.

It was by vote, not by revolt. Anarchy is what took over the "Occupy Wall street" movement, in certain cities. My songs were never for anarchy. Nor were they for international police power, "State Police" was sarcastic. I saw the need for a strong national force, time, what about the Presidential vote for next year? Who would I vote for, me and my bipartisan party? Vote for PS.

Dreaming took me over, to the young initiate, I say keep digging, and above all, keep dreaming, for when you have lost your dreams, you have lost your soul and your heart, it doesn't matter if it's a gold mine or a coal mine, its <u>industry</u>, there is always a job for a good cop, keep looking for the next bit of evidence, if you have problems of proof. There are good problems of proof of modernist reference, symbols meaning nothing, so good for a defense attorney.

In my dream, there was a Greek miners strike, a threat to world stock markets, it was down low, where music of the red and the black filled the mine, owned by a world corporation, in fear that the strike would spread, to its other mines, where workers were peaceful. This was a dream of realism, not modernism, who do I side with, solidarity or the world stock markets?

Greek management, aware of the economics of the workers, were still in fear, if they could not control labor, which supported the Greek government, which felt it could fire workers of other areas of the system, this all being connected management and labor and government, deep in eros, causing harm to The Euro? This was the realism of my dream no more non-reference of modern art.

Republicans, at an international level, all were in fear, of Greek cure, which Was a threat to all Europe, which had the stability of Europe, to consider, Where in Spain and France, workers were in sympathy, which went back a century or two. Time. This was realism, no twisting and turning images, just reference to Europe of the here and now. Voting. The Euro, in my dream, waffled as to if they would let the strike continue, and the governments of France and Germany, were dead set to see all of Europe continue, bigger than one small strike, which nearly brought down, Europe. This was modern politics, ironic as it was. Like the Greeks, solidarity of one union siding with other unions, Like in Oakland, a strike to shut down the Port of Oakland. They were so radical they burned the American flag for the cameras. It was legal. <u>Back and forth, I and my wife were like management and workers</u>, the red filling my ear, and hungry mouths to feed, which in my dream screamed out for mercy, the Greek National Cure, however, did not hear The claim of Howl. Time, in Greece, all unions, government and private, Went on strike threatening the socialist government and their cure.

Defense of Europe was greater than the howl, of hungry labor, Greece being the test case, of government and labor, the national Note notwithstanding, people need to eat, and the taxation of real property, long a resting place for the rich, was now that of labor. The middle classes owned their own home, so increasing property taxes, was a direct threat against the people, who were striking.

Everyone, in my dream which changed to the US, was using NFL penalties, exchange one for another, and the adults seemed to know the sports signs, but there was one group, that did not believe what was being said, they would not play ball. This was art too, realism reference, what the modernists were rebelling against? Like Proust.

NFL language, penalty for mistake, was not enough to solve the deadlock, in congress, which had its own international cure, one side calling out, the attempt at bipartisan politics, not the usual in America and California, where it was one side against another? This was especially true for 2011, where people were anti-bipartisan because they didn't want the other side to look good, a stupid reason.

Holding sign and touchdown sign were not given in California, a mirror of National politics, where both sides of politics only cared about their next election, in my dream, which was strangely like reality, of a reality TV Program. What was needed was one party calling for bipartisan cooperation they would look good in the eyes of the people. I kept on dreaming, the brain police knew of the downgrading of our country, because of the necessity of US cure. But the time had come, in my dream to put up or shut up, it not yet being as bad as Greece, who were on their own Homer's <u>Odyssey</u>, for home. I fluctuate in my politics like Romney. He is bipartisan. It's stupid to have Newt say they need a real conservative, to beat Obama. A Bipartisan candidate would have the best chance. The sign of the dove.

The red cave, in my dream, was where the fox and the raven could work Together, where Sherry and I shared a drink, which seemed to calm our hearts, which needed a stability, to what we helped, to create, paying in cash, for things that went on the national cure, index of bankruptcy, at the national level, Obama wanting to cure defense.

National bankruptcy signs were not just for US and the Greek. In my dream, I saw the student protests turn ugly, and Democrat law and order was the heart of the day, nobody but nobody wanting to side with the street people, who were for anarchy. Time. Romney was for taking back the half trillion in defense cuts, by Obama. I did not want that Mitt. I am a hobo at home.

My dreams, right out of the nightly news, became a world nightmare, students, workers, everyone on one side and the President of Syria on the other, oddly I could see his plight, sans the killings, I had become a Democrat, at a world level, more siding with the students, who we didn't helped to incite. That was the major reason for me changing parties, to redeem my character, there. Is it because I'm black.

World Republican dreams were damaged beyond belief, with the US President pulling troops out of Iraq, and 30,000 more out of the lager Kabul area, where we had gone in 10 years prior, by a Republican President. I was like a Thoreau, no foreign wars, and I wasn't for a Third party. Like the Republicans after the last civil war. We imported opium into the homes in Ohio.

- - -

Republican candidates for President, looking like suitors, in light of the President of the United States of America, could only utter a patriot slogan or two, or why it was okay to torture, against the eighth Amendment, President Obama being a Constitutional professional. I pick and choose my platform I am me, not a party, I just don't want to incite a riot, pleading Occupy Wall street.

NFL refs should blow the whistle on such suitor foolishness, coming out of the World Republican vision, damaged by wars and pity of wars, fought as if it were the patriotic thing to do, international Republican, sans Bipartisan vision, was childish, I was ashamed at my brother's party. And that was an understatement, with Romney for taking back Obama's cuts to the Defense Department.

- - -

All Republican DC, added 10% in 2017. Banana republics could do better, I stop myself, international relations being my profession, before I made my millions in the record business, "State Police", not out yet, was a parody. I can see the signs, Obama would destroy the world Republican non-economic vision?

Transnational Republican cure would come out of the flesh and blood, of the middle-class, and the poor and the old, who like a child vote Republican, cutting out their own social security, I have not yet seen a good bipartisan vision, so badly needed, with a heart.

Bosses, an MBA taint, are Republican territory, unfortunately we have our own Euro question, I am not running for anything, I write parody, but cutting Social Security is not my idea of the American dream. In question like little Italy, I am more a Democrat bipartisan, though with Thoreau on foreign wars and the green party. I am for the rational police Greece and Italy sided with bosses on national cure, the issue not yet redeemed or dealt with by bipartisan Washington politics, an international issue, which we can't forget, but which we wait on eros nightly news, for an answer, a response that has not come. It's congress that is at its lowest point at 13%, and Obama at 47%, enough to get reelected.

It's Congress.

I have no party that represents my opinions. It's all compromise. Sherry, a sheet over her, was naked to the core, she being a Republican First, but she singing the words, to my parody. It is as if "State Police" would be taken as literal, international states and people doing battle at the extremes. Time, so why am I a bipartisan Democrat? It's the National Cure. I don't want them to down-grade our country again, like they did to Spain. Wake up, Washington Irvine.

Foxes have holes, but the son of man has no place to rest his head, it's as if we are on a fox hunt, in the red cave, it's as if they are coming after me now, the issue is what to do about the Persian Gulf? I saw a mountain next to a Pyramid, in 2009 the students of Iran revolted, now its economics, the Iranian Youth started the Tea Bag party calling for a revolution? Time changes, it's the same dirty issues.

- - -

Tea bag protestors have no international theory. In my dream, the Teabaggers kept saying no to everything, when in reality they are trying to ram through The Democrat Senate job bill after job bill, I cover Sherry with the sheet, she trying to go to sleep. So with that Why am I a Democrat, again? It's the National Cure. Where's their Bipartisan politics? Where do I vote?

-3-

I vowed never to drink again. The wind had gone to my brain. I am in a pond and dreaming again the next night. I dream of a red Adam Smith, in a pin factory, the hands of Zen don't run his economy, and all we do is import from Kabul. Just pull all of the troops out of Kabul and we beat back <u>Al Qaeda</u>, we killed Osama Bin Laden. And the <u>Talibani</u>s on the run. We have 100,000 troops there. Obama would bring them home just like Thoreau. And have the local Muslims fight.

That's Material laissez-faire economics, the pin factory is in Kabul, where I dreamed more of export, where they dump Time on the streets of New York City, where they dump time on western civilization, from Kabul, imported into the US. Time. Have the vets go door to door selling something. Like suitors.

Dreaming, I saw the Christians, looking at the ceiling, where I saw a number of faces, then I looked at the images behind my eyelids, I had gone to sleep, dreaming of a red cave, next to the tomb of Zen, Mary crying, and I giving her comfort, someone was mining.

I thought of "The Cherry" and thought that such was a good name, we being like children, a cherry, in our songs, but it was all we had, we couldn't get employed, and there is the "State Police" parody album, not as childish, more realistic, of what the people in Greece face. They were a socialist government.

Dreaming, I got a Material Sec of State and used my anthropology to form treaties, with all the warring Indian tribes, like the US in the 1880's, All the Pashtuns, the Hamas, Pakistan, Iran, Syria, Israel, Kabul. The International Material Treaties got us. Elected.

In my dream, Kabul turned into revolting Cairo, without any US targets, Soldiers, to Kill or bomb, I making sure we had a Transnational bipartisan, Democrat tactic, in continuing to withdraw troops out of the country of Kabul, like President Obama did in Iraq. We are no longer fighting the cold war, like Romney seems to think. He thinks talk softly and carry a big stick. What abou thte Congo.

-4-

<u>I dream of the people, no more civil war, no more bombing</u> mosques, we were no longer the target, and the people slowly followed *The Koran* with legal trade, something that their book dealt with and not the illegal, suicide or killing, the waters parted, we had done the impossible, we interpreted *the Nobel Koran* it was to be done, we had done the real Thoreau thing and got out of foreign wars.

It's what will the sec of state do for Russian OiL. As the budget is cut, to stop peace negotiations.

Throreau civil disobedience, I left for my Republican brother, Vincent, with his rental apartments, all of my dream was starting to make sense, Thoreau was US Historical key, to International Peace. Obligations of contracts are like treaties. And low National. It's trillions in tax revenue.

Thoreau used his civil disobedience to protest a tax that supported a war with Mexico, this is the real history of the Tea Bag party, friends with Democrat, and linked with My Transnational Democrat vision, of peace, it all hinged around Thoreau. Time is Paul Ricoeur. It's all the Other.

The green party hinged on Thoreau at Walden Pond, and Immigration hinged on no war with Mexico, this was a unique dream of Democrats, but something, with bringing down National Cancer, was a dream of Time, a Time dream, something I evolved out of my anthropology, MBA background and rock and roll, my heart. Even if it doesn't look straight Democrat, I pick and choose my issues. I am not running for national office. I am an old stranger.

I dreamed on of Democrat Time, I wondered what they would do to tax Tea Bags, and how bogus was Adam Smith's invisible hand, where there are really markets that are irrational, a point most Republicans will not admit, because they want to do away with all regulations, like 1999? Time. I am a compassionate Democrat, with low national Cure. Neo-Keynesian trade cycles exist, like 1928 and 2008, unlike some economists, who need to contemplate Time, cycles exist on the stock market and on the real estate market, <u>they can keep dreaming, but it will not stop the existence of the trade cycles</u>, I actually read Keynes famous book, and I distinguished it.

The more that things change, the more they stay the same. It's the Time of the History of world tropes. World and US legal precedent. It's Time like that, which rules the conflicts. Like 2012, 2020 and beyond.

Voodoo but a red contradiction.

-5-

I <u>dreamed</u> of the Republican Tax Act of 1981, Keynesian in the inducement to invest, and I thought how that would be a good bipartisan return, its high tax brackets and its estate tax and the inducement to buy rental property, I saw all this from my Mars Space Station, all red. It had an estate tax.

I dropped down on the planet mars and thought how Congress, in trying to cut dollars off the national eros, were like Martians, unable to get the job done, how I just threw in the towel and The Republican tax of 1981 could help, we talked in this space station in Russian and in plain English. It could be a bipartisan compromise to choose such a plan, part Reagan. Returns like Odysseus.

On Mars, there were rows of streets the houses of which were celebrating Holidays, there were lights of every shape and color, some houses were drenched in lights. There were no regulations of lights, and I thought of Vincent, business is like lights, harm, as an Egyptian revolt, like water in the belly on Mars. In Time.

Teabaggers were on the Mars Space Station, trying to think of more than taxes, I made friends with my Democrat brothers, but they did not seem to believe the Russian that was breaking their heart, I told them of Vincent and Art. I Contracts, which they liked I told them, not dreaming, that such contracts were not Russian.

Mars was a foreign place, the Holiday lights, though, were like unregulated contracts, something that made the Russians almost famous, they had their vodka and the attempt to regulate, but not on Mars, in my dream, to me I was the Christmas lights like a cease fire that happened in World War I.

Martian freedom of contract, of unregulated Christmas lights, were so fantastic that I could hardly stand it, this was no fantasy, it was a real Christmas, with no talk of Santa, it was realism, and the Russians had their own Christmas.

The next night came and went and it wasn't for two days that I was dreaming again, I dreamed of an oil rig next to a pyramid, in Egypt, it was BP not Chevron, my schools token, they thought that they had freedom of contract, international regulation did not crow their mind? Regs are a necessity. In Time. And money.

The pyramid scene was a hip view of liberty of heart, it was a depressed economy, in Egypt, after the revolution of heart, so the government let them continue with their research, and <u>oil ownership of the mode of production</u>, it was California and Chicago in Egypt.

Then I saw a painting next to the scene, it was Vincent's rooms, the ones so simple, then I saw a field of wheat, and a bunch of crows, but Vincent could not find his heart, there was Vincent's apartments, outside of a café, all these broke Vincent's heart. The same as Time. The pictures of the humble potato eaters, came into my dream.

It was BP's oil spill, but that was not Vincent, they are one picture, but two different visions, Vincent spilled no oil, and the two scenes are distinguishable, and the Russians could see that, the scene changed, to pyramids after Pyramids, and boom they regulated BP. In my Time dream. But 2 years after the oil spill and they were advertising for tourists, it was so clean. The above, the Mahattan Project.

I dreamed of the necessity of national and transnational regulation, and a situation of no conflict with those and states' rights and local zoning regulations that Vincent faced, and how it broke his heart, politics of Thoreau and civil disobedience and Constitutional law enforcement? I can't speak for anyone other than my brother, but for him it was civil obedience. This was ironic even the 5th Amendment.

I kept dreaming, thinking Thoreau would want regulations of the heart on his Walden pond, these are not contradictions, they are two different scenes, "Civil Disobedience" went on, I read, agreeing with President Obama's withdrawing of troops out of a blindness Iraq. In Time. The human marketplace.

<u>The Mexican war, I went on, was an example of a government cabal.</u> He then goes on to the Revolution of 1775. He had a call to revolt. The Teabaggers go back to the Boston Tea Party, but they stop short in their reading of Thoreau. He did Time.

People should cease to hold slaves, he said, but what of the banter that Capitalism is slavery. Sure a capitalist can be a slave to his business, but this is using one word in two opposing ways, thus the blunder. Capitalism is a civil right. It's in the original intent of the US Constitution. That is the other reason that I am a "Song", defending capitalism. Let the Russians laugh. With their oil, a stranger.

The last Kandinsky just painted was done under the protection of the United States of America, lines and pyramids, colors of blue and purple, modern yes but it is timeless, with a heart we can get beyond a symbol, which takes us into the modern of our own lives, forms like the myth of the modern return. It's timeless.

Yellow dog contracts and oil spills are heartless, unlike the above Vincent, my brother who we will talk about in the next chapter, but like Van Gogh, suffered for his capitalism, yes he was a business man, and yet he sold but one painting. He was ahead of his time with his art, like a meditation on nature, That's Van Gogh.

Like Van Gogh, I bought what my brother was selling, it was a vision, of free capitalism, I put that together with the heartbreak that is now called Con law, by law students, a vision of how much power they feel that they have with the US Constitution. It's the free market, that's why I changed to "Song of Songs".

Vincent sold me his painting, yes it was capitalism, but it was more it said let go of my property, he was middle-class, he had more the merry of Holidays, but for him it was regulated, they said you can't put your Christmas lights here, they lost the heart of materialism. And the heart of Christianity. They were talking in Russian.

It nearly gave him a heart attack, he had health problems ever since caused by people who lost their heart long ago, the sphinx is still there and I am still dreaming, something that Vincent can't do for you see he lost his dreams, when he lost his heart.

In the background, were rows of palm trees, in the sand, it was, the Sphinx talking English, still Egypt in my dream, having just gotten a little Twitter from my brothers heart, there is a rainbow, over Vincent's duplex, opal the color of Vincent's contracts. Got Time, The regulation of the city with a compassionate conservatism?

- - -

The sphinx wants to take charge, what is the riddle of man, I have a new twist, <u>it is survival to get customers, to fight the government</u>, who don't understand, I had my state obligation of contracts, and I made it big, now I take Vincent's cause, which will take congress? Which said the government is capitalist

But I am not a stooge of them, what I give them is my vision of Transnational Democrats, I can take my brothers cause, and they will hear me, with my Thoreau and US Constitution, they are not jaded and call it con law. Frankfurt stock markets, are seen by the Frankfurt school, with it's Critical Theory, as fascist pop culture, plastic ads on the TV. Illusions of consumer fascist demand. I want it, I want it. You can't have it.

I am dreaming again, I take lost causes, I'll take your cause if jobs are important to you, I'll plea for the obligation of contract, if you are labor or management or run your own business, which is best, I have the door to open the heart of the government, the sphinx, I talk back. Or, are we blind. It raises revenue, from voters.

Pyramids turn yellow and the sand turns blue, California's colors, basic universal now, we will rebuild the economy of Tunisia and Egypt, the Dean is a Democrat and I have free speech, and it ballooned into the Constitution. Free speech to talk of a fair market. And the Dean is good, yes he can paint too.

They are the colors of the UCLA. Where I went to pre-school. We danced and made bread and learned about <u>Africa</u> where we played in an old Palm Hut and played in an old California house and made balloons that we floated over the UCLA campus. I loved school ever since, it was like the new home schooling, learning by playing at what you do. It was like Vincent with a tin cup, begging for money. Saul Bellow.

Materialist, I told myself, must be the water in the belly, giving birth to a new world. If I am wrong, I will stand shoulder to shoulder with them with the lights we share. To me, they are Thoreau, no matter what they say about my Transnational Democrats. And that's Time. The Tea Bag party had no real foreign relations, just The American flag. With Mitt, Who will play ball with him? Social Security?

And I want you to get the water in the belly, no matter which side wins, I want a government enforcement of capitalism, the way my brother Vincent never saw, my bipartisan vision cut across party lines, and you are not the opponent, I want a win-win vision of the earth. Therefore Thoreau on foreign relations, the government in foreign affairs is best that does the least. Just give social birth.

I saw the sphinx, in my dream, and he said, welcome to reality, we hear the poor, <u>The Habitat for Humanity</u>, where millions of the poor can be housed, my heart is in my throat, and it's a conservative US Supreme Court, who I can't say how they will accept my President's Health Plan? In June of 2012? This one is the monster, whoever wins will probably take the election. And make the other side like the underground. It's as big as *Roe v Wade*. Who will house the retired?

Egypt is on a pilgrimage of white, I was asleep, but I saw someone running of the Democrat ticket, and it was me, I have gone through so many changes in the last 3 years, my head is swimming, and so is yours, the President is not the barking dog, prodigal son, it is me, and I can't put out the water in my belly. What of Mitt's Health care? If The President's Health care doesn't win? What of 2017 and beyond.

Dreaming of Egypt, I slept on, I heard my song of "Third World Revolution" it was not written by a radical, I said if you want a revolution count me out, we were an Underground rock and roll band and now I've turned Democrat, how's that for a plot? And a character transformation?

-6-

<u>I went to sleep, and I was in a Van Gogh painting, a green bedroom,</u> who knows what affairs were there, I fell asleep, my entire vision turned to a large palm tree outside, there was a native climbing the tree, how could this be, it was in France, dreams for you, symbols, this for eros, where did they come from? I was Vincent selling his Van Gogh, it was free market capitalism.

The sphinx appeared, suddenly we were in Egypt, it said go through the Congo line, like this book's 3 parts, and it meant it, I was in a ritual, and I was to become Osiris, and Sherry was to become Isis I knew this from *The Egyptian Book of The Dead,* it was sacred in ancient Egypt, we were initiates, to become Gods. Rituals of transformation, like this book! This was way before the Muslims belief in rituals of just one God. ISIS!

In Time, in Egypt, I saw Isis say, why is this meaning of life? We started to talk and she said, get beyond the red ideology of time, and I told her that I did, and she said good, now you are Zen, let it go to your head, and Osiris agreed. That's the meaning of the rite. It was an ancient Egyptian Ritual to become Zen. Home Dei 5000 B.C.V Tragic.

In my dream of time, I was amazed at how fast the moon went around the globe, and the Sphinx said that it wanted to make one thing perfectly clear, this was not Islam as seen in The *Koran* where Allah, the compassionate and the merciful, was their one true Zen. After More months passed, Sherry was rather more pregnant.

On the contrary, Justin, a gay, looked around at everybody with one eye wide open, and the other slightly closed, he saw everyone, like a black.

What's the meaning of my dream? It's absurd. Ricoeur in his study on Freud wrote on the "interpretation of doubt". That is, question every text. A dream can be slow PE. We have such narratives, I said, to take the pace every night for the time between going to bed and waking up.

That's part of his PM of doubt and his PE of stories. That's Paul's theory that, awake, we don't think about death, we just have mythological and real and fictional narratives that take up the Zen. Like Homer's The Odyssey. In Ricoeur's Freud and Philosophy, he deals with the problem of the interpretation of meaning, calling it the "hermeneutics of suspicion". Herbert Dreyfus, in his Being-in-the-world, written after Paul on Time and Narrative, regards "Being" as still needful, after Ricoeur. I sat in Dreyfus class, at Cal.

Sanity is a "behavioral health" that seeks justice, affordable housing, and food and meaningful employment or time. The search for justice is the universal meaning of life. As Aristotle said that is happiness. See his Ethics.

Tragedy is the loss of happiness; as the sign says: There is not parody of one American dream, but 330 million people who achieve their own happiness.

Chapter 16

AMERIKAN TRAGEDY

-1-

VVV The American dream is a tragedy. Federal or state, governments generally want law and order. They take it as an attack on their manhood when they are challenged. And they want to go duck hunting after you. Charges, by police power, have the effect on one as if Nausea was the rule of law, which is how it made me feel, which it is not. Where is there justice? How can you go enforce it? I felt like Vincent's Dada, in this <u>Odyssey</u>.

Why put up with this? To paraphrase a good Woody Allen joke, I have an Uncle and he thinks he's a turtle. The response is why doesn't someone tell him of the delusion. The response was basically we need the eggs. This looses the original humor, when one realizes that turtles are a protected species. One doesn't want to eat its small eggs. Why do I like Art. I Contracts? I need the eggs. I wonder who can relate?

I told Vincent that his constitutional rights were like <u>Habitat for Humanity</u>.

- - -

Basically, not withstanding the original intent of both Federal and some state Constitutions, <u>it's a Mexican standoff</u>. But for purposes of this discussion, the police have the guns. How did we get to this situation, which created Vincent. And the intent is to crucify if they catch you hiding. Faking like, The other.

Capitalists are the Indians. And the government can do what it can get away with. The government is not a Custer. Felt the charges, Vincent did. And he was a small egg farmer. Basically, I left. I can't stand the heat. It drove Vincent mad. That is he got mad. I became Sympathetic because of my brother and his case. I had compassionate materialism. His case tugged at my heart strings.

Enter economists and the University of Chicago Law School. Chicago is a unique animal. In so many years, the Chicago Economics department has won 11 count them Nobel Prizes. Chicago school, as it is sometimes called, directs the economics faculty to give its ideas to the business school and to the law school. Thus the econ Department is a big think tank. It was my own idea that, by definition, Article I Contracts should be controlled by Congress. And Prof.

Sahlins This is a factory. They have a law journal encoding all of this. They are also big into Constitutional law. How do I fit into all of this. My main professor was the best Anthropologist in the world. He wrote a book *Culture in Practice*, where he pointed to the economics department and said, get them. That's how I learned about the biggest conservative, economic think tank in the world, especially since the business school and law school give them feedback. Let <u>them</u> solve this.

Capitalism and Freedom, by Milton Friedman, enters here. Almost by himself, he solved the inflation of the President Carter years? For a Republican President. Uncle Milton, as his friends like to call him, had the theory in the above book, that if you could get capitalism then not only would you get economic freedom but political freedom as well.

Vincent tried it and it didn't work. He got bombed. He and his egg farm.

Milton got a Nobel prize almost just for this work. Being a scientist, he tried it in Chile. It didn't work. Friedman is the idea man behind the Republican party. And others as well. Libertarians love him. He did not know it but he was for the civil rights of contracts. And against economic Jim Crow laws. See Reich's <u>Supercapitalism</u>.

I tried Uncle Milton's ideas and with our recording contracts we made a bundle. There is the Constitutional Party. Not as well known. I chose to draw. From an Anthropological realist to a materialist. I adopt their candidates, I learned to defend. Like Paul Ricoeur on contracts, *The Just*, the way to turn around this story. Paul's one book was a put down of a major writer on contracts, at Harvard law school. Human Capital is useful. In times of Contracting you want to be very critical, so as to not sign you're your rights.

- - -

That's the Chicago School. With several Nobel prize winners. I started reading old law journals from about 1986. The key ones were Chicago, Yale and Harvard. All on the Federal Constitution's Art. I Contracts, that states that <u>states can't impair the obligation of contracts</u>. The picture that they painted was grim. They reviewed several cases, and I can tell you that I didn't look good for Vincent's eggs. Stay where you are, stranger.

What does that mean? That's the Billion dollar revenue. I don't recall all of the arguments. But Exxon, a spin-off of Chicago's Standard Oil, if I recall and my memory is poor, tried to claim a tax was an impairment. It lost. But the idea stuck with me. Taxes are powers not impairment. Chevron was a spin-off too, along with Mobil.

Capitalists, like a bunch of rebel Indians, exchange things. Capitalism uses contracts. Enter not the competition, but the government. Since *Ogden*, the Government has taken away what some have called the freedom of contracts. Federal government, which I like, does it often.

States have con law contract clauses. That's like Mike the nuclear bomb test. It's overkill. You've never seen such hate as is associated with civil rights law Violations. That's the alternative to Art. I Contracts and *Ogden*. I got the idea from several Reviews, The state constitution's contract clause is baby. As is the fact that it's material states' rights. State courts will follow <u>Ogden</u>.

See Don Quixote.

You want to end up like Mike, try 42 USC 1983. I tell you are Vincent. So why do I give you such ideas? I got hired by a University. That keeps states from acting like the South. They killed civil rights workers in the South, in the 1960's. It's like my own self- portrait, in the way of a journal.

National laws keep states from acting like the South. They will turn you into Vincent without remorse. I had a friend named Andy. He said make Capitalism a civil right. It is. A rational contract. Under Art. I 1820's Conracts of the United States Constitution. And your chances are 1 in 100 of prevailing. Especially if your name is Exxon. How do you win? Get the 1828 *Ogden* case.

- - -

The Constitution's contract clause shows the Founding Father's intent to support of Citizen labor. The civil war stopped Slave Contracts.

Custom is the rule of law even in the old south, of zoning regulations.

I would attempt to protect small business, like Vincent's rental business, from the city and the zoning department. They do that with police powers. <u>That means they charge you like a criminal</u>. Then you are looking at "Busted", said Shaw, making a joke of 1 of my CD's.

That's the good news. The bad news is that you will end up like Joe Paterno, the best coach in NCA A history. Why go on? Because there is that 1 chance in 10 that you might win. And heck, it's a defense of capitalism. Mr. Paterno died last week. Vincent is the other.

Jim Crow laws excluded you if you are <u>black</u>. The idea is that being a capitalist is like being <u>black</u>. Just ask Vincent. In law its on all 4's, as they say. Capitalism is to be black. National laws protect you, by the National Constitution. Give 'em Hell Harry. Like the Irish.

This would not exclude all state regulations, but it should have mercy on that one man who is unjustly accused of a crime. On one man who has private obligations that are impaired, said Andy. Amos and Andy always my father's favorite sit-com as a child, It's like going up The Grand Teton. Or stock Exxon in a corporation, where now you have to stop all those state oil well regulations, that take away 12 % of your income, when you only took home 13%, that's a slim margin. Something like Mitt. Shaw's nickname was Amos.

The National Constitution if it can't do that it doesn't exist. Capitalism is a crime. And if you buy that let's kick out all the vets, who gave their limbs for the Republic. National laws are useless. We might have lost World War I. Enforcement of Constitutional law is what we fought the Japanese for. Vincent also a mulatto.

National laws do protect us. The same is not true for city zoning departments who would separate the capitalist from his profits, said Shaw. What a comedy of errors, if it weren't so tragic. That's why we have National Laws to protect us from such errors. Its <u>black</u> comedy.

The "Occupy Wall street" protests got their way. But Federal Judges won't let you win on this one? Why? They are not Communist? What are they afraid of? The people? The people got to Occupy! Why won't they give a capitalist his protest? The point for Democrats, is that now, in 2017, the Republicans have taken all 3 branches of government; if Democrats can get to the "center", they can win back the middle-classes that voted Republican in 2017.last year. And you're your enemy.

This is like a detective Novel in many ways, with its <u>clues</u>. That's why the reader is like a Sherlock Holmes. What is Capitalist? What is not? Why? What of Nautsky? Lautsky? How does Holmes <u>Not</u> look like them? It's hard.

From the John Birch society.

National laws do not protect against Federal legislation. Zoning laws operated against our Vincent, the moment they got their way. They got notice of his capitalist criminal zoning breach. I will continue. Because I believe in and defend the Federal Constitution.

State constitutions are crippled by the heavy Ogden case, and I'll go out on a limb, misprision statutes did not apply to our Joe Paterno. He was the best college coach of all time. I'll say it, I am not Joe. Zoning laws irrationally enforce itself against family business, like Vincent. Here it comes, starry night. Vincent's eggs.

War rules. <u>Local law is international law</u>. Power of the law can cripple a family business, even when it has obligations to enforce itself. And that would exempt the family business from the law. National law begs to be enforced. As do local police powers. Was it <u>racial</u>?

Vincent was told to pay $50,000 to get paved parking spaces, it was tarred, even when he had obligations to a group of Chinese students, who used bicycles, thus negating the need of city regulations. Republicans can relate to this. Excess regulations on the fair market, like Candidate Romney is on record saying. That was in LA on property where all they needed to do was tear up the back lawn. The same in New York, would have cost you $150,000. That assumes there is enough turf for 18 parking spaces. If not perhaps just sell.

But my own hands do tremble, when I attempt to justify my Brother Vincent. So in the interests of my own health, I offer from here on in the case for regulations and police power, the state of California. That way, the Federal Court will hear you.

While Vincent was on the bus line, and he contracted with people that are poor, and did not own a car, poverty is not a defense of equal protection. Enforcement of regulations, is a necessity even if it seemed not to apply to my brother, in the name of law and order. Tell that to Occupy Wall Street. How many of them were <u>black</u>?

Custom is the rule of law even in the old south, of zoning regulations. Enforcement is not blind, the city seeing in the other owner's gross violations of the zoning code, like cars parked on the lawn, leading the city to one conclusion? You don't have enough parking spaces, which must Be tarred, paved. Republicans say that by 2027, one quarter of Social Security will be cut, from the budget. We're dying out here. If you're over 55 by 2017, you should vote Democrat, in the next few elections and beyond. The same for the rest.

It is not National law but Federal law that applies in this case. National Laws do not exist, they are a fiction, like this novel. Vincent had the land this is true, but he had notice of charges on Management of rental land, where zoning laws as to parking are violated. They sent Vincent a letter telling him of the 2 criminal charges on his person.

Again, being on the bus line and students walking to University, are not defenses as poverty is not a fundamental right in 14th Amendment cases, a plea that Vincent considered. And being in exchange for not having a car is a poverty equal protection claim. Property is not a case For equal protection. Never because of his <u>race</u>?

Tar of parking spaces, allows for subsequent owners, who made no poverty claim, to be in substantial compliance with city regulations. His so-called exchange was Time, unlike the city claims for full compliance. But the charges were on my brother, which drove him mad. And other. The city sees as basic, mandatory its zoning laws. If exceptions were allowed it would have a log rolling effect on city enforcement of dirt parking spaces, which were a health problem, in the city of Los Angeles? That's what the city and the DA have to say? Can you Overcome the presumption? They ran it like Jamaica roots?

-2-

Yellow dog contract and *Lochner* are examples of so-called freedom of contracts that were popular over 100 years ago, contract so-called liberty permitted the worker to exchange a right to a job, in exchange for working a 16 hour day. That was the obligation of contract. Can you overcome the presumption? You can't see a thing? That's bad law. So-called National law would see a State Constitution's contract clause linked with a Title 42 claim, in defense of capitalism? This states' rights approach, in a right to work state, however, is like sticking ones face in a bee hive to get some honey? You will be stung? Can you overcome the presumption? Have you seen the eggs? We're wounded.

To say that the city made Vincent's contracts not rational, is like saying airplane security at the start of this century is not rational. There is a <u>rational basis</u> for basic uniformity in the two situations. He had the 1st Amendment right to redress his complaints when he first received the charges from Los Angeles City? Why did he get mad?

Law is not expected to have a heart, and it is basically mandatory to all people in city. And separate but equal, of Jim Crow, is totally different from capitalism? The poverty argument of the 14th Amendment does not trigger equal protection, under *Yick Wo*. Like with Justin? It's a fallacy of argument by metaphor? Can you overcome that Presumption? State and Federal Constitutional law of the obligation of contracts, is like warmed over freedom of contract and liberty of contract <u>substantive due process</u> claims of a 110 years ago, where coal miners exchanged the right to work for unsafe conditions in the mine. It's the tragedy of the US Supreme Court? Can you overcome that argument? It's apples and oranges. Why are Capitalist landlords like <u>Blacks</u>?

States' rights and state statutes are there to protect capitalists from depression and there is no need to bring out Draco and Title 42 to remedy the situation? Metaphor does not connect civil rights laws and capitalism? Capitalists don't own slaves? The symbols are all wrong? Or, are they?

It's true there is an Art. I Contracts Constitutional right to keep the <u>state from impairing the obligation of contracts</u>. This is a civil right to capitalism. But it's against States' Rights. And it's a power play between state and city police power and the all more Important Federal law, crippled by *Ogden?* It is not a slave contract.

Ogden can be questioned in the case that argued for obligation of contract. The reader is encouraged to go to a local law school, look up the case on the computer and then go to the US Supreme Court case. It's only a many billion dollar question, like if *Exxon* would have prevailed. Vincent's case feed all those chicks. This is a cultural as well as a suspicion critique. A detective looking for clues. Culture, CCC or Critical Theory, of the Frankfurt School lives at the heart of the crimes committed by Vincent Holmes.

- - -

A <u>black</u> Vincent, in the South in the 1960's, would have been crucified for starting up a family business, and would have been the mark to the city zoning department. To be a mark, is slang that he would be the victim. At custom, he had no redress. The custom of the Jim Crow laws. Citizens are invited to so think outside the regular framework. Why not? But don't create Mike.

Under color of law, Vincent had his obligations of private contract. No it's not hopeless. It's just that there is so much money involved <u>Exxon</u> is just one of many clients who can employ the constitutional contract clause, with customers. Under color of custom, zoning charges were enforced without regard to national law.

Bus line obligations trump, in New York City, the need of $150,000 worth of tarred parking spaces. The city, however, is more hard to prevail against than laid back Los Angeles. States' rights in either place don't prevail as they would on a Bull farm, in Texas.

Metaphor makes you think. I think it's a Bull ranch in Texas. Whatever, the point is that symbols are food for thought. If I could have made you think with the above, I am not a failure. The defenses of the city are real. Vincent, wrongly, wanted <u>equal protection from all the people around him in the same business</u>. Who could have informed on the place, out of jealousy? Why wasn't he mad prior to the charges? Why would no attorney take his case? Why didn't he redress his grievances? What made him mad? Did he become a mark?

Redress of complaints against the government, as in the 1st Amendment, is real and the lack of which made Vincent mad, but not in the same way as a rich Republican? Vincent was poor. Like a child, he felt his redress was free speech, in a unique way. The US Supreme Court will hold against you. Mr. Tribe, of Harvard, tried to argue the case and he could not make a case for the under- dog. Of course these are contradictions. This is the 21st century. HOWL. That's right, instead of having a lawyer, he went out in the street and started to—<u>Howl</u>.

Law and order had to prevail. The police power busted him again. There is no way that free speech can do away with other laws, notwithstanding that the bill of rights and treaties are the supreme law of the land? Anarchy would do away with all zoning laws? This is just a plea for the enforcement of the Federal Constitution, in my brother's case. <u>A case in need of a good detective.</u>

<u>Walking to school, instead of having a car is a fair exchange</u>. The issue was the Federal obligation of contract clause not the 14th Amendment, Where poverty can't be plead. But poverty as a contract clause exchange is a legit obligation the Federal Constitution protects from impairment? Can you see this? What if you were a juror? This is a test? Was it like a civil rights abuse?

Here, the Federal Constitution protects the poor? And such was the obligation for not having a car, which trumps States' Rights and City police power, by the zoning code? National law, or whatever, prevails for the Chinese students with bicycles, and not a car? Can you see the issue and the connection of the China students and therefore not Needing parking spaces? Why not? What I have done was to <u>defamiliarize</u> this story in order to use Ricoeurs "hermeneutics of suspicion" used in theology with the Critical Theory used by the Frankfurt School. This is to shock the reader as to the outrageous things in this case.

- - -

National Constitution law sounds like a redneck, <u>black</u> man pleading trying to void Federal law and secure States' Rights? But I like it because it shows the futility of the claim of Art. I Contracts of the Federal Constitution that states "No state shall impair the obligation of contracts", since *Ogden*? I can't say it enough. Can you give him the respect? That's the economics clause.

Injunctive relief of a section 1983 claim can be made to the City, which uses state police powers, and their impairment by 2 criminal zoning charges? But as in *Exxon*, taxation is not an impairment. So here charges, arguably, are not an impairment they are a power, like taxes in *Exxon*.

If you see the multi-million dollar above argument, the entire Vincent case is won? That's scientific talk for, Vincent does have a case. But injunctions are before the fact to the charges? And arguably no amount of due process is correct against zoning criminal charges, that is they are arresting you. Can you empathize with Vincent? Though you are not like him? What if it were you? With different facts? An other? To me, it is a question for the US Supreme Court as to if Art. I Sec. 10

sees police charges as an impairment? Tax power is not an impairment? It's another issue for The Chinese with their bicycle obligation and the court as to if the threat of charges by the city is an impairment? Go reargue the early Chief Justice John Marshall holdings that do find impairment in the state. It wasn't always this way. What happened in history that caused the *Ogden* case? When can the city allow an exemption? It's a political issue under color of custom. That's why I say let Congress rule under this Article I case, which means by definition it should be controlled and taxed by US Congress. Billions would go to city, State and Congress. ? Now you are in little Italy, in New York.

-3-

Section 1983 is used with State Constitutional impairment of obligation of contract clauses, like in right to work states, like on the farm. Also applicable, are the Thousands of state statutes, with Title 42, like peaceful assembly, so easily set up by people into anarchy? It's all like the Nuclear bomb test—Mike. Like Standard Oil?

People like Vincent, are at the mercy of state police power. Contract is private, not public. It's wrong to say the city acts like the South. They use police power. The former supported slavery, while the latter keeps capitalism? Could you be a slave to the zoning department? Slavery?

Federal, not national, laws prohibit the above. Civil rights of capitalism, is no joke? Though some people will laugh. But at this point of The Republic, we need all the jokes we can get to keep us out of a depression. Economics is the prime mover of all other Rights, that's Milton's vision. He's King Tut. Or, the Easter basket.

This is a novel, not a legal brief. But brief it is, when seen in light of the world economy, and the fate of Europe? Vincent is just one person, where I find common cause and common heartbreak. Police abuse people every day, so why can't state police powers of the zoning department of Los Angeles? Foucauldian Criticism, cultural and literary, of power and its misuse can be seen in the Hermeneutic analysis of the <u>context</u> of our one character, Vincent.

The Latino Mayor was chosen because of his power of seeing racial abuse. The Metaphor, <u>Water In The Belly</u>, tells me capitalism is like race, a symbol, this for that. The President of the United States tells me with his teaching at Chicago, he sees that symbol. People are abused by police power every day, like last night at Cal? Federal power can't protect, if anarchy disrupts peaceful assembly, granted by the 1st Amendment, like the redress of complaints, also in the 1st ? It's a redress against the Government? Just like our Vincent, A Starry, Starry Night, do you know how much that Work of art is worth ?

States' Rights can abuse capitalism. But our Vincent is a different animal. He had no Republican Lawyer. So he thought he'd use his version of the 1st. It was his form of free speech. He went out and started to howl. To the people around it must have looked like anarchy. He hit the streets and started to yell about abuse at City Hall, in LA. We all pity someone like that. By <u>The Stranger</u>.

Section 1983 would protect the students, on strike, to reconstiture their classes, the way that I did, at Berkeley? But who is to say what's peaceful assembly? Berkeley taught me the mean power of a mob. I protested in the classroom, where friendly students heard me and my teachers didn't try to stop me for my free speech, that is my Professors protected me. I cry when I think of my Cal. And how the Peaceful assembly in Oakland was subverted by anarchy. There were raids. There is a where and a when To redress one's grievances.

-4-

All zoning regulations are not abused? By a Title 42 claim? Sole obligation of contracts of one sole individual are just enjoined from wrongful enforcement, like Vincent, like the students at Cal, painting their own picture, of the streets of power, the power of New York, the ways of money, a mirror of the Greeks? When was Vincent abused? By a law? <u>Was it a hate crime? Was it malicious? Against Capitalism?</u>

- - -

Federal Constitution protects both the ways of money and the students? Vincent gave up his power when he turned to the wrong side of the force. Students and Capitalists try not to walk on the wrong side?

The National Constitution protects them both, it's funny and ironic? You just have to step back and see. Vincent's the other.

I see them both and I remember like a fox. Wall street is like a lot of small business people. Where is their peaceful assembly? To protest graffiti? To protest Italy and Greece? To protest the near downfall of The Euro? To protest the threat to Europe? The inaction of Congress on lowering the National Cancer? Tragic?

The students want post-capitalism PC. Like in Asia. They want National and State and Local regulation. They want to sell their beads, by freedom of contract? What's SOLDARITY.

Federal Constitution is the answer to both wall street and the students. Congress and State legislation and local laws are what they want. Trumped by the Federal Constitution. That's the way it works. The 1st Amendment is the highest law of the land. Though not the highest, the Federal obligation of contracts protects our Capitalism? Can you see these things? Then you see the importance of Vincent as a token capitalist? Where is Romney's Bain capital? Due process?

I am a capitalist. And a new Democrat. And believe in most regulations. I also believe in the Federal Constitution. We all would be like Vincent without it. We can't know about all Federal laws and I can't do much about National Statutes. But state and local regulations, however they are enforced, are subject to the original intent of Art. I Sec. 10 of the Federal Constitution. Controlled by Congress.

It is the small business of a Vincent, like the street artists in Cal on Telegraph Ave., that is attempted to be protected. The Federal Constitution does that, not undermines it? The clause that states "no state shall impair the obligation of contracts", protects those street artists, like Vincent. Habitat for Humanity.

Jim crow laws that are like the ones that went after our Vincent, and people like him, should be kept in check by state statutes and Federal law and Fed Constitutional law? Vincent was mad and the business students are mad? Because of abusive practices? By the government? In another context they call them Republicans? Or, Section 1983 needs abuse of state law. So it can't be used by the Fed Constitution's

Contract clause. The Fed Constitution is the fastest way to find Fed law. My heart is Breaking for Vincent and the students and Wall Street merchants. They all are abused everyday by violations of their Federal Constitutional rights? What about Democrats? Rasta? Customs of police powers, we are not talking about the National FBI who are controlled by the Bill of Rights, need to be regulated, like old Jim Crow laws? The civil rights of contracts is no joke. But they should buy our "State Police" album when it comes out. And I wasn't "Busted"? A candidate for President?

Criminal zoning laws regulate the Berkeley street artists. There is common cause between the right and the left. That's why I am a Bipartisan Democrat. I gave up conservatism for Ash Wednesday. Right now I am worried about Congress. Their inability to solve the Cancer of the Nation, means we are heading towards Greece? I side with the US Supreme Court, mostly.

Berkeley street artists, and I was a street artist in San Francisco where I sold the play *Reality*, have a good sense of comedy, they are not into anarchy, as with some protesters in Oakland, so absent the custom of color of the County or city police, there shouldn't be any problems, absent a violent mob, mad for different reasons. No problem.

Vincent is my point. Both his rental business and the mob, both mad, faced criminal charges by the police. It's a shock. Like a Wall Street Ponzi scheme. Like wall street churning brokers. What if a Democrat stepped over that line? Can't you see we are all in this together? Why can't we be Bipartisan? In solidarity with the police?

Like our tunes "Busted". The national eros is broke? Italy and Greece could be joined by Spain? And then what? Portugal and Ireland and Iceland? With France and Germany as the last wall of protection, how will they collect revenue? To pay their National Rosa? Where does The Euro go? And with that Europe? That's where Wall Street is. There are so many multinational corporations, Wall Street is everywhere. And they want to charge you for a matter for Art Contracts is everywhere in the state? And their protesting Wall Street? Which rises and falls with now The Euro? Will the dollor follow? Tax the clause.

Bipartisan anybody. Surely you see the connections between an angry mob in Greece and police force in Berkeley and the criminal zoning police power coming after Vincent? There goes Vincent and there goes the Euro? What goes next if in the next two weeks Bipartisan Congress can't lower the ethic by 1/2 Trillion? Where's the light?

It's because of the cure that Standard and Poor's downgraded our National worth. The same is true of Italy and Greece. Then Spain. That makes borrowing money cost more. Berkeley is like Greece. Ask Milton. He dealt with inflation. Where's our Vincent now that we need him. And he used to play trumpet in the UCLA band.

It's bias. The whites hate the blacks and the poor hate the rich and the Germans hate the Muslims and the students hate wall street and the cops hate the criminals? What if running a business was something you get busted for? As if it is in most states of the Union where state agencies control all sorts of businesses with state police power? Was it a crime to run a business? What if they won't stop in Greece? What if Oakland Happens to Berkeley? Would we all turn out like my brother? Bias is the problem with a type of Jim Crow customs of color with criminal zoning police power. What are the laws like in the above countries? Who is subject to bias? City Hall putting a $5 tax on glass, Catholic candle icons? The rich? The poor? The last two are the guild of the rental business. <u>If police abuse students, then couldn't it have been a mistake to throw two criminal charges at my brother</u>? How can you take the position of the zoning department? When you see the word Republican or Capitalist you can use the word material? Some of those things can hurt. Like socialist Greece.

Jim Crow was backed by the police for over a half century without anyone doing anything about it? What if the laws made for the landlord turned out to be anti-Rich Jim Crow laws? What color of custom have we found as it relates to the rich? Criminal? Like those poor students at Cal? Or Greece? Or this place?

My Sherry is America. I am America. I am prodigal but I am heading for home. The reason that the like Jim Crow laws are so <u>abusive</u> is because they were backed under color of custom by the police powers of the state and city. We saw it all in "Busted". I do want the legalization of drugs, I want business legalized. Voting in 2016.

<u>Notice</u> of Vincent's business violations, was backed by heartless abusive police powers, for a mistake like smoking in his home? That's a type of abusive police power, kept going by color of custom? Capitalism is like being a black man, and abusive power needs an injunction?

And since its criminal charges would it not be more correct to say that the zoning department had undue prosecution? What I'm doing is like talking like a linebacker coach to a state-run University like Cal. If you can understand, you're like an NFL-bound down lineman. In looking for a safety, that's you. Well illustrate this, later.

Capitalism. Like Minneapolis zoning, multi-family. Anti- Trump

Zoning departments are like the police stopping someone for speeding, when the ticket was wrong? <u>It's abuse of process</u>, for our sweet Vincent? The Cal or Greece students and workers face similar abuse? Why would all these people have so much in common? A Candidate for President said this next election as like 1860, trying to stop a civil war. Just like the 1969 underground movie "Alice's Restaurant". Farm workers live through Economics.

They are not all crazy. They, of course, are all different. They all faced the "Busted". For a redress against the abusive government? In the US protected free speech, so much so that it's the highest law in the land of the United States of America. What of London's riots and firebombing? Are they going to treat Vincent like those criminals?

Like Oakland once the people of anarchy arrived? Peaceful assembly, one of our Bill Of Rights, was as they say set-up? It turned into a mob and the peaceful street people, protesting, were rounded up, just like Vincent? And they were mad? In the tank, they found common cause?

Capitalism is slavery, that's a good one, to break your heart. But a slave to whom? To regulations? Yes, all good Republicans can agree with that. But where is their action? Would they find common cause with our Vincent? Even with his mistake? <u>Abusive state powers</u> will eventually get self-employed Democrats. The US Supreme Court frowns on <u>Lochner</u> – like Contracts.

What I am saying is yes there is common cause and the remedy is Art. I Contracts of United States Constitution which says "No state shall impair the obligation of contracts". Materialist be the judge. Is a criminal charge from the state and city an impairment? If so, then it's unconstitutional. What's so confusing is that landlords are pitted against renters. And renters get charged? Here history is turned on its head. So we are blind to it? Can't you defend your landlord? Even he has a defense? With my Congressional Control of Art I Contracts?

That's the issue. In back of this entire chapter of this novel is that one question. The rest is for the local and state and federal and congressional and world jury. I say that the plumber on the left and the street salesman on the far right above have common cause, be they Republican or Democrat. I am a Democrat so I know how they think. When could a Republican be like Vincent, without his yelling? That's the issue before the court today, as the sun is shining down. The following is a case we had in moot court in the law school at Pomegranate University. I argued the case of Vincent. This is a civil case, not criminal. We had a video tape, the entire case. It was moot. Since Vincent already lost his business. Because of the zoning department's charges. He was arrested.

-5-

City defense is that it is immune from a section 1983 claim, by *Rhodes*. This is a far reaching defense. The issue for the court, there, was given the Kent State killings, in one of the outrageous cases of the 1960's, does the head of the state have immunity? The answer was yes. It is still good law, and I think they are in a Federal court, in this moot jurisdiction. Under Title 42 of the United States Code, Mike.

The City says that money is scarce, and they plead *Davidson*. This is a good case for the city or state in that the US Supreme Court held that there are no money damages, for violations of Constitutional rights.

The state says it will not hear argument by metaphor. This means the Jim Crow Historical issue, can't be united as being like capitalism. Nor is a capitalist a slave. This is different from the metaphor, fire in the belly, which deals with the <u>Water In The Belly</u> that gives birth to a new world, for me reformed Democrats.

States' Right claim is made to the State Constitution, of Selma the tie to this venue. It states in essence "no Obligation of contract shall be impaired". Section 1983 requires a breach of a specific state law?

The State Constitution is the highest law of the state, its obligation of contract impairment clause Is in the state's Constitution?

I am pro se. I represent my client, Vincent Holmes. We are not letting bias come into The Federal Court, by letting evidence be allowed as to how he acted <u>after</u> the city brought 2 criminal charges against him and his rental business. It was a breach of the peace. After he was given the information he was told by every lawyer in the City, that he had no case. It was after that that my brother went into the streets and started to howl. It was on that, that he got arrested. The arrest we do not dispute. It's Article IV of Con Law.

The state starts out. They are the defendant. The jury was chosen. The state claims that it is not guilty. And the reason, it claims, is that criminal charges are not an impairment. It cites *Exxon*, which was a Federal obligation of contract case. It says that like Exxon, but not identical with it, criminal information is an impairment? And like them, taxation is a power and not an impairment.

It added it was immune from suit. It was my turn. For the jury, I explained that Vincent, a name which he hated, had a business, two houses, one and a duplex. One day, and this was a day he would remember for the rest of his life, Vincent was working around his landlord business. Then to his surprise, he got a letter in the mail, from the City telling him he was charged with two crimes. Socialism?

It was from the zoning department charging him with not having enough parking and The parking that he had was not tarred. He could not believe it. He had gone to be a Landlord for some status and here he was being treated like a common criminal, like a Wall street broker who was guilty of churning. Universal jurisdiction.

In the duplex, he had 3 Chinese, 1 Indian and 2 Latinos. That was in the basement. In the top were 3 white people, who were students too. It was next to UCLA. It was the year that UCLA took the NCAA

National Championship. In football. How we got in a Selma county court, first, is a surprise to me, but how we got in a Texas federal court is a fine point of the law of jurisdiction, he had moved there for a time. I claimed that <u>charges were an impairment</u>, and I gave several cases in a motion to the nice judge, he was kind to me. The state came up from Los Angeles, California. The state claimed that the counts were wrong, in that it should be from the Federal Constitution. VVVVVVVVVVVVVVVVVVVVVVVVVVVVVVV

In a motion, the state of California also said that the jurisdiction was all wrong. Also that 42 USC 1983 was a civil rights suit and that my claim that there was a civil right of contract was bogus. I won on both counts. Though the judge said it should be a federal constitution contract clause claim. He didn't like state constitutions. Contracts are property, the judge said. <u>Intention</u> is needed under law.

It got so bad, they nearly threw me out of court. But the nice judge said that I could have a hearing. Despite the mistakes. I played to the jury. I looked them right in the eye and talked to them directly. After California's motions the judge scratched his head. I could tell that he liked me. It was Universal jurisdiction.

I went on. I claimed that not only were the zoning charges an impairment but also that it was an <u>abuse of police power</u>, which drew a strong objection from California. I am quick. I stuck to the main argument that it was an impairment of Vincent's obligation of contract. Thus voiding the criminal charges. America is Prometheus.

I continued. Land in Los Angeles was expensive. Fortunately, Vincent was not charged for that. He forked out $50,000 to tar the parking spaces which came out of the lawn. There was no objection. Then I said that I knew that had I known of his mistakes of parking, I would have gotten an injunction against the city of Los Angeles, or the county or the zoning department, all claiming state power.

I talked to the jury explaining others who were landlords would not be as lucky as Vincent, regarding coming up with the land for the parking spaces. There was no objection. I mentioned that the charges were unfair to a <u>class</u>. There California objected. I filed a motion with the judge. On the class of the rich, a <u>status crime</u>.

I mentioned about the National Constitution's contract clause and said that I liked the State Constitution because I could get a Title 42 claim and I mentioned my theory about the <u>civil</u> <u>rights</u> <u>of</u> <u>property</u>.

California lawyers were asleep at the wheel, at this point. Or so I thought. I was for the under-dog. This is Iowa.

They filed a motion, that I had not shown an <u>intent</u>. That is a motive on the part of the city of Los Angeles. They were sharp lawyers. I made a few mistakes. The motions were in case California did appeal. Assuming that I win. I mentioned about the impairment was under color of state law and custom. It's a waste of time.

That was key to my case that there was a civil right to property. No objections now. Walking to school, UCLA, was key too as was the Chinese bicycles. I said that they exchanged for lower rent in stead of having a car. Also, the houses were on a bus line. I told the jury that this was Vincent's obligation of contract. A <u>rational</u> <u>contract</u>.

I mentioned that these obligations were impaired by the city and their charges. I got no objection and I thought I won. Police power rested with the state. I didn't have to overrule *Ogden*. That was the reason for the appeal to State Constitutional law? Like a good Republican Vincent paid the $50,000. The City filed a motion that I did not prove damages due from the state. *Davidson* on appeal undid me for damages.

I explained to the jury that I had a civil right to property. They held 12 to 0 that I won. I had defended Vincent. And that was enough. I cited the most recent case *Rhodes. So I showed that the state had immunity. After 3 months I lost on appeal. I did not show intent, Fortunately, I didn't*

plea for damages, and I was in the wrong jurisdiction. I needed a civil injunction. <u>This was a stragedy</u>.

Sherry was slightly more pregnant.

After this moot court, Vincent was never the same. He started to sleep with a gun under his bed, he was that criminally ticked off at the justice system. He got it wrong. The Contract Clause is dead.

Vincent and Dada are still <u>The</u> <u>Stranger</u>. One of the reasons that, in parody of <u>The Odyssey</u>, we have so many questions marks is that the story of Odysseus is marked with them like the introductory quote at the beginning of this anti-novel, with the quote from chapter or book

VIII. Paul Ricoeur's "Hermeneutics of Suspicion", as a theme in Felskis <u>The Limits of Critique</u>, should help the Justice Holmes, in the reader, to at least "hear" the advantages of capitalism. What does that say about the culture of Amerika. It says America is Prometheus.

Los Angeles had strict zoning laws unlike Houston, Texas. Still in both cities there is a "civil right" of property, contrary to popular thinking. Like now we have Minneapolis – type zoning law that would let a property owner take in tenants to solve the housing shortage world-wide.

In the classic Man's search for Meaning we see that social justice is a goal like Aristotle's Ethics where the good is the search for Happiness, justice and Pleasure.

Chapter 17

FOREIGN AFFAIRS

-1-

Pablo got a fan letter from his wife from Chile. She was a fan of the "White Collar Crime" album. Pablo wrote her about the upcoming "State Police" album and the very colorful, sarcastic Constitutional tunes, more songs I had written. She wrote him that she had a small boy. They had been separated for 11 months. The band was going to Europe for Thanksgiving. We got all packed and went in cars to the LA airport. It is, here that it gets funny. I do approve of what happened. I wondered whether or not to include it in this novel. But Pablo was in the band and in our co-op and like most members belonged to the Church of Zen, a liberal sect that believed in the "Song of Songs" as a manifesto. Critiqued by the Philosopher Paul Ricoeur. He didn't start his own dogma but it was in one of his works and it caught my eye. Felski says in her chapter "Context Stinks" that we should have a sense of play and seductions of art. To do this we inspire, and liberate with artefacts of the New Historicist and postcolonial cultural critique.

I am a member of the Church of Zen, so I knew that they at least believed in Zen. And were forgiving to a fault. I knew that they treated each other as if they were Zen, which means they respected each other as if the other person was basically to be treated like Zen. They did not do drugs. For that I am grateful. They, however, believe in the police powers of the state and nations. Pablo was Marta's husband. We arrived in Span, in Europe.

Pablo had been married for some time and was looking for new spice. The kind that gives me joy. He was a typical wolf and wanted one true female relationship. He never thought for a moment that what he was doing was wrong. In fact, he got heart pangs of joy that came over him, like the sea over a whale. Pablo wanted to be reunited With his old wife.

He had found Zen and now it was to reunite with his wife. It hurt him in his heart. And lungs in that the relations started him up again smoking *Salem*. They went to the top of the mark, that is to a bar at the top of the hotel biggest Hotel in Madrid, The Prado. It was in the artist section of the city and next to The Prado Museum. Where they would play Priest and Penitent. Pablo has a sense of play and I am recording their relationship, now a lot about the band.

The wife's name was, Marta. They went in their room. He had a smoke and she cradled her small son. Again, they fell in love. She could understand why he was so shy and he felt he was her son that she loved so much. He forgave her of everything, the band was in Europe this Thanksgiving vacation. We all were like Pilgrim's Progress. In the Church of Zen anything goes. It was his child, but he hadn't seen his Alma before, Marta had left for Chile while she was pregnant.

Marta ordered some wine. By the time it had arrived, he had already taken off his UCLA hat. He was a mirror to her life. What he did imitated what he thought she would do. And then there was the small child. They had ordered two beds. One for them and one for the child. They put him to sleep. 4 hours passed, as he cried at her feet. In this comedy. The band had their own rooms. Actually, Marta was Catholic and Pablo was Church of Zen, they thought everyone now was Zen. And they acted like Zen. Everyone converted some 6 months ago.

Then they went to the Prado Museum. It was right across the way. They went in with the small son ever so quiet. They were in a <u>trance</u>. At first they saw EL GRECO. This totally blew Marta's mind, she being a good Chilean, with good Chilean guilt. The colors and the suffering of Jesus. Who was crucified for less. She did not use Birth control. So they had to be careful. She was a UCLA grad.

Pablo was wearing his UCLA shirt. Where she had gone to school. He was saying, don't you see I am you. She got this. She was an economics major. She loved Milton. They walked past the massive PICASSO of the Spanish Civil War. It was in black and white. She stared at it for a half hour. Then she said, you are my Pablo. This was what Pablo wanted to hear, that his ego needed boosting, being like Picasso.

They spent the next 4 hours in the museum. With the small boy sleeping. As he could. They went by rows and rows of Catholic art, where Marta could see the blood dripping from the side of Jesus. She would be forgiven by her priest, in LA. Their flights arrived early that morning. Where the sun rises. They loved the Prado museum, and made each moment like it were communion.

Pablo had a vision. The truth was manifest of the truth of the Catholic Church. If Marta was Catholic, then it must be true and the Pope. They went through the Museum again and it was as if it was for the very first time, she showing the bleeding Palms of Jesus. She said that she needed to confess that she loved the Pope. This *meant* he too did not believe in birth control. And their temporary divorce had been a sin. An attempted annulment.

They left. And went to an outdoors café. Where she had wine and he had coffee and smoked in peace his *Salems,* They had a big salad with Italian dressing and baked French bread. The child had milk. They sat and watched the people for it must have been 2 hours. It was getting dusk. The band went their own way. Would they get back together again? Would he accept his child?

They made it back to The Prado Hotel. They got the key, she having a wedding ring and Pablo having one too. People pay attention to the smallest things, like the loving care of a mother of her sleeping child. They walked upstairs to the second floor, where their room was.

They put in the key and walked in. Their heads were in the cosmos, all spinning and swirling. Soul Bellow wrote a play about "birth."

He said that he wanted her to give birth to him which she did having learned how to play at UCLA. Then he said he wanted communion and she reached over to her sleeping small son and put the child in his arms to rock to sleep. Then he wanted baptism. She put some water in a glass and dipped her finger in it and made the sign of the cross over him. A sign. That he had convered to The Catholic church, it was a feeling he got, like a vision, from his old church.

They cried at each other's feet. Then they talked. Of "The Cherry" and how she had seen the band when they were in Chile. He had forgotten so much, now that the band was not on tour. She said that she loved him. And had loved his keyboard. She was a devoted fan and loved him as much as her son, Alma. Who was quiet all the time and rest on his mother's breast.

They lay awake. She wanted to know everything. And he told her about "The Song of Songs". It was about a lover and her love for her lover, Zen. It was a tune of a prophet to his lover, You want a prophet go to Mohammad, peace be unto him. But Pablo clung onto his old church, The Church of Zen, he was all over the place, <u>primitive</u>, he was the prophet, he mixed a little of his church with hers, spiritual things getting mixed, in eros.

She wanted to convert. And he said, no. Breaking her heart. He said that it was much too pagan for a Catholic, and he said, As your priest, I forgive you. And she said what is there to forgive. He was wearing his UCLA shirt and knew how the Californian government thought. They too recognized the Church of Zen, with their visions and signs.

They talked about Catholic, old California. And the Latino Mayor of Los Angeles. He had brought a demo of their not yet released "State Police" album and he played it for her. She laughed and laughed. She understanding the sarcasm. And international and Chilean Military. She loved it, it made her feel like home, back in South America.

He said, there are two levels. On the one hand its reality. On the other it's sarcastic. They have been waiting to release it till the people of the world see the need for police powers, given the state of the world economy. It's not all world riots. They were waiting for a 1984 but it never came. They were both guilty for separating as if it were a divorce, against the Catholic belief in heaven. That was his eros.

He said, it's like "The Police", in 1984. Pablo did not tell her much of his religion, at this time, in that it was a pain in his heart to think about LA. They talked on into the night as she was his most devoted fan. And wanted to know about the band, again, from their first album "Busted". The band had a party that night. We went out to eat and then to a movie, it was in Spanish, with English subtitles.

He explained their concept albums. They were from the point of view of the FBI. They were the police. He gave as an example "White-Collar Crime", it was a bust. He said that they were the government. They were the CIA. They weren't trying to incite riots. Like the Arab spring. They busted them. What if the Chilean Government got hold of "State Police" and understood the sarcasm? She had a small boy, Sherry was pregnant with a girl. They both just wanting just one.

-2-

"State Police" played endlessly. She finally got it. He said, we are the Saudis. We want law and order. It's transnational economics. The people who riot don't get it. Pablo talked about the Greeks and Berkeley? And said the two were one. And what riots needed was the state police? He was that much for law and order?

Pablo said, make love not war. He said that their band was like the Attorney General. Of California and the United States and all World governments. You just don't have to be mad. That's not love. He had been holding the small child all this time. And gave him back to his mother. His wife. Why so much guilt? It wasn't a divorce! They renewed their vows.

They were glad that they were in Madrid. But the country was going through eros problems. They had seen some protesters outside the Prado Museum, Italy fell. Europeans asked, is Spain next? And its real estate was like California. Pablo asked, were we crawling towards Los Vegas? Would something fantastic Be born?

They talked some more about the songs that were new for "State Police". And how they were all world order. Pablo laughed, I am even a moderat republican. He just thinks most Republicans are mad, because they are not Bipartisan. Pablo had on his DVD player Eric Clapton's greatest hits. Next to "The Cherry", Clapton was his favorite artist, when he heard him in heaven. It was perfect.

They talked some more about me. And how I was the leader of the band and how I had gone through so many changes and how I am the only one who writes the songs and how I was writing a novel. And with that Marta and Pablo went to sleep, she sleeping with her baby. The band went to sleep at 2 AM. It was a good meditation.

They woke up at sunrise and still excited about the time. This was the start of the second day. Paid for by Pablo. He was worth millions, too. He played electric organ. Marta's baby was right there in her arms. They went down to the El Greco café, attached to the Prado Hotel. They got only a few hours sleep.

As they had a meal, she talked about her mother. Pablo said, I love her now. Then she talked about the child and wondered if it was a pain in the head witness. Pablo laughed as he liked to do. He said, it really got warm last night. She laughed. She liked to play games. In this comic tale. Why did they separate? Why did she go back to Chile? Was it her secret SiNN?

Pablo, really, did feel guilt over the reunion, though he knew he should and he felt his heart drop. She was thanked for the baptism. And she told him not to talk, because Spain is a strong religious nation, and that she taking the role of the priest for sure would not be understood, it was her play. It, together, was their own religion, they would fight the collective guilt, so popular in Chile. That was his Zen.

He whispered in her ear, thanks for giving me birth. She answered, *De Nada*. Pablo's second language was Spanish. She joked. And then said, but why did you spank me. He thought and said, I thought I was spanking the child. Now I'm a pain in the head witness. Pablo just laughed. A type. Pity them, they were of no religion, where they made up the rules as they went along. This was the reality.

They finished breakfast then went back to the second floor and their room, which they opened up. They put the child on the bed. Now we can talk, there were too many people there that understood plain English. He had changed the boy before. Marta said, you are my baby I hold you like there is next week. They were intimate, he was her and she was the baby, it was everything.

Pablo confessed. He said that he had betrayed the Chilean Church. And that the Baptism wasn't right and that she standing on the bed with him crying at her feet may have been a symbol of giving birth but it was not being a good Chilean. She said, Zen then spank me. She was the joker. But he could tell better jokes. Bellow showed "social birth."

The child was 6 months old and went to her mother's breast. There, that's good Chilean. He was not laughing. And don't ask me about the father, you are his father, she said. He said, Our Nada who are in Nada, Nada be your name, Your Nada come, your Nada be done on Earth as it is in Nada. It was a parody of Jesus. Like some existentialist doing mass. That's like the Church of Zen.

<u>De Nada</u>, she said, as she held her baby. That's our Prado act. It's our joy, she said, holding her baby close. She said, so was last night, but it's not the last supper. That comes in one night, Marta said, nervous.

Pablo said, do you want to go to Paris? He started thinking of Homer's other book that's why it's heavy. Of the Spanish Civil War and one's Achilles' heel.

Only with my baby, she smarted off. She put her baby down on his bed. And they lay back on their own bed. 3 hours passed. Mom, Pablo said. Yes, I am your mom. I am the universal mom, she snapped. He loved it. I am Martha and you are Jesus, is that sweet enough for them, she said plainly. He always thought of the organ.

That's my Prado act, I just gave you an EL GRECO, she said, nervous, and I need protection. How about the Italian mafia?, he said, shy. No, we are in Spain, at the Prado Hotel, she said, heart breaking.

In the Church of Zen, we have no guilt. I am Zen. His church had the classic Achilles' heel of Homer's *The Iliad*. Still it's comic. We had planned to go to Paris all the time.

-3-

The band then flew with Pablo and Marta, in their reunion after months of separation, to <u>Paris</u> where they went to the Da Vinci Hotel, near the famous Paris Museum with the glass pyramid in front of it. The band had one big room. Where we planned on having thanksgiving dinner as if it were The Last Supper. This was so fantastic I can hardly stand it. We had the meal brought up to our hotel room. It was my idea.

- - -

Basic, it was a meal with NFL signs. They brought up the turkey, and put it on a long table, where the band sat around and talked, animated with nonverbal NFL penalties when someone would make a mistake. We ate the meal over a 5 hour period. Hansel pointed to me, who pointed to Sherry, who pointed to Patty who acted guilty already because of her bust so long ago, which made the band millionaires, Patty then pointed towards Pablo. And Patty nodded her head, no. We had Italian wine. We were Buddhist. Anything to be free and get rid of the guilt. That's the Church of Zen.

We toasted each other. Pedro leaned towards me and said, Is it I? I told him, no. We had some more wine and broke the French bread. The band and Pablo and Marta got along fine, it was such a long time that they had been with each other. Pablo put his hand on Marta's shoulder. Pablo's head swimming like a cosmos, as was typical for him, when he did something sensual. Eros like in <u>The Odyssey</u>.

These were the signs of The Last Supper, in part explained at the near end of this novel. Sherry whistled the French National Anthem. In my broken French I sang from the start of the national song *Allons Enfants de La Patria*, which is roughly translated to mean, Come Children of The Country.

Pablo clapped as he had his earphones on listening to Eric Clapton's Greatest Hits. He asked for more so I gave in my broken French *Contra Nous De La Tyrania* which roughly meant, We Are Against Oppression. The band clapped and talked to the person next to them. With everybody's heart breaking. It was like *Il Postino?* Chilean lover of a Chilean. They were international, so fantastic I can hardly stand it. Marta said, if that's the Church of Zen then I want to be a member. Patty pointed to Hansel, who leaned back, as Alice pointed towards Pedro, who shook his head in disbelief. Marta was gently feeding her child milk. The child, Alma meant soul in Spanish. A soul. The son never cried. Marta had long, dark hair and had olive-like skin, like a movie star. She was beautiful, catching the signs of The Last Supper, by Da Vinci. As is the custom of the Church of Zen. They were NFL signs.

Pablo meditated on the band as if it were a painting or art work, which it was. We were DVD recording the event for our song "Confessions", on our 3rd album. We were dressed in hats of NCA A University schools. Across the nation. We listened as Marta said, Is it I Lord? Marta looked like Penelope Cruz. With a child on her breast all the time. Penelope was the wife in Homer's Odysseus.

- - -

It was as if we all would betray each other. It was high art all to the American Holiday of Thanksgiving. We got pictures of Marta's Alma feeding. It was tender. It was sweet. The Church of Zen let people have the Zen of their choice. Pablo choose Marta, with her Catholic belief. Though he was the Church of Zen. What is to happen to South Europe? Like Homer's Odysseus, as an <u>Other</u>?

-4-

"The Cherry" then all went to the main Paris Museum, with the glass pyramid in front. We continued our act of the Last Supper, with our NFL signs. First we went to the Mona Lisa by Da Vinci. We talked as if it were the Last Supper and we pointed to her hands. It was the Da Vinci signs.

We did a DVD recording of the inside of the Paris Museum. For other tracks off the "State Police" album. We got the band looking at an El Greco, with its cool colors. Marta meditated on the painting. She saw the ribs of Jesus bleed, as if in a vision of the Virgin of Guadalupe. It was a religious experience. So fantastic I can hardly stand it. My heart is breaking.

After a half an hour of meditation, we went to a Turner, with its snowy storm, half Modern. We walked on to see a Monet, with its colors of red and green. The painting was full modern. Then we went by a Kandinsky, with its lines and pyramids. I wanted to read into the painting realistic little pictures, but they were not there. Only 1 critic saw the little Jewish life in the abstract painting, and was he ever criticized.

We saw a David, with its arms stretched, in front of men with rifles. The picture was protecting a small child. We went by some Picassos with right and left angles and a woman crying. Then a Picasso of a woman in front of a mirror. Was this the picture on front of Prof Milton Singer's Book? It was drinking gas to spit fire, that's why, it was said, that Picasso painted so well.

They had works of the Revolution of France. It was great history. Then we went by Catholic art. Marta stopped there and meditated on the mother of Jesus, she understood that she was that mother. Then there was a picture of a monk and a skull. We saw the "Yellow Christ", such a favorite of our Paul. It was all slightly altered. According to the Church of Zen. others meditating on the art. I stopped. People from Germany next to us gave us the Last Supper NFL signs. How universal was Leonardo. 500 year old realism. Marta's child was quiet, a type. Marta's head spinning in a universe. She having a religious experience.

We saw a picture of a large <u>black</u> child from Africa crying out. And then pictures of colonial France in north Africa. And Tunisia. I being a Vet, I could relate to the struggle for freedom and liberty. There were Oriental Scenes in one painting. So fantastic I could hardly stand it. It was all so modern, Pablo back with his Marta. It was the dark arts.

We saw the Big Bang creation of the Universe, in the next painting and then the evolution of <u>Homo Erectus</u> that scene, we having a copy of them in Pomegranate University. We continued to give signs of the Last Supper, of Da Vinci. I started to cry. We left the museum and went to a café where we sat outside and enjoyed the setting sun, its light just missing us. We were on the sidewalk and had a large salad and French bread. I had water. The baby had dinner with Marta. The French made customary signs.

We took 3 hours to eat and watch the people walk by. I was sober. The Child, a type of Pride, according to my religion, was quiet the entire evening. The Italian President quit while we were in Paris. It was over the National Note. It made the stock markets around the world fall. France was downgraded in its national worth, because of its National Note, to a level of the USA.

While we were in Spain, they had elections going from liberal to conservative, because of the National Note problems. You could hear the French and Spanish talk about the problems of The Euro. They were afraid of the return of a Franco type. Like Hungary, right wing.

We cried, wiping our eyes. Alma was Pablo's son. He kissed him gently. He loved them both so much that Pablo decided to bring her back to the States. There was room in the co-op. She would share in the coming out of the new album "State Police". Perfect for Chile?

I felt that Alma was my son, prodigal as I am like the economy of the US, The stock market going up from 6,500 to 12,800 during the time of the next election. But the housing went down 33% in the last 4 years, to unknown causes. What was it like in South America? Hadn't Argentina or was it Brazil gone bankrupt? Brazil's stock market is, now, one of the best in the world? "The Cherry"-played a lot of Notes.

We talked. Where would next years elections go? Where would people get a job? Could the President's party save our pensions, social security? Would we go on mass strike like in England? We talked on about bipartisan politics. My favorite subject. I love to say it, I am a bipartisan Democrat, a social materialist. I confuse this with my materialism.

We talked of the child and what the next year bring to the water in the belly? What would be the birth of a new dawn? Would Marta and Pablo stay together? I broke bread. And had a drink of water, toasting them. We clasped arms, in a sign of unity. We toasted the people walking by, many of whom recognized us from the funny pictures on our album covers. <u>Black jaw.</u>

We talked how we were populist. What did that mean to our business? What did that mean to international sales? We had learned enough? Would the world of youth get our sarcasm? Or would they think we were just like The Police, of 1984? Could we read the minds of the people of the world, Christian or not, world's peoples hearts? Were we preaching to the choir? What would the son Alma do? We remembered The Last Supper.

Marta covered up his head, in that it was getting cold. Could we save the Church of Pride with the first amendment and the National obligation of contract clause? Could we interpret the classics of the earth's civilizations painting, could I make the distinction between the Church of Zen and the Church of Pride, they being different? Would we rightly read world political elections? Da Vinci was right we all talk around the dinner table, is it I? Is that another Da Vinci code, of The Last Supper? Nato defences should have Russia.

Sherry did not go to Europe. When Pablo arrived, Sherry was there to meet him at our house. I felt like Alma all grown up. This prodigal was slowly getting material and the American dream. It's just that you try to get a church wedding first, then have your wife get pregnant. As Sherry and I and Pablo and Marta, so fantastic I can hardly stand it. And at that we cried. We know about the morals of many of our fans, who were not of the Church of Zen.Let alone my religion, the Church of Pride. Sherry was a month before the date she was to give birth. Many <u>black</u> feet, in the Holmes.

Jim Holmes, no relation, shot up a Colorado movie theater last night. He flunked out of graduate school. The biggest mass shooting in the US. Funny how reality sometimes imitates art, no intent US. Russia and China conflicts should be solved by Treaty clauses in con law.

Chapter 18

VINCENT'S BLUES

-1-

We are in the co-op, like they have near Stanford, and it's Saturday. The <u>band wanted my espionage again of CCC and PE and PMS and PM</u>. I told them that I, PC, which was okay, meant Post-Capitalism, like they have in China #1 in world, believing in the contradictions between Capitalism and State regulations. I told them I will but that I wanted to tell them the story, the real story, behind my brother Vincent. They said, okay if we must. I said, good. It's the Saturday after Thanksgiving. We flew back late Friday night. The codes are in parody. The Teabaggers were red-neck, brown-Nose, Joe 6-pack, football playing fans. This is the story of Lorenzo Shaw and Vincent. Both were <u>The Stranger</u>.

REFRENCE, I said, telling them of the so-called problems of reference That my brother had. He went absolutely mad, I said. They took his property. That is they, under penalty of law, gave him an order as to his property, that would cost him $150,000 in New York but in Los Angeles, $50,000 to be in compliance. It was that the city treated his capitalism as criminal, that made him mad.

To refer, I explained, is to point. A reference is a signified. A thing is pointed to. I said, Vincent became an object of reference. And this made him mad. First the city of Los Angeles pointed out that he was not with the program. Then his neighbors picked up the ball and started to point to him, the way they do in France, 1889. It is the pointing out of your faults, for no reason at all, that can drive you bonkers, especially when a lot in your family are doing it or if people are doing it, like your competitors, next to your business. Like a French Van Gogh.

But let me start at the beginning. When Vincent was a little boy, people would not play with him and then he would stomp his foot and yell for his Mummy. Or Dada. And then he would say "Gaga". He was such a mean little boy. He would yell and yell and yell, but Mummy never Came. Like in the CCC. Like his talking to his lawyer and the person stared at Vincent without a <u>clue</u>. And Vincent did not want to be punished. Being a good Republican. What if he was a Democrat?

Then he grew up. But he still had the nasty habit of yelling. When he did not get his way. Then I would come up and explain things to him. He got used to me telling him how things worked around here. After school he could not get a job. That's when it became a nightmare. Nobody would play ball with him, a type of PE. And his form of that, was to howl. There was an underground book named *Howl*. Vincent had read it and it was his favorite book.

He went from place to place all on Dada's money. He wanted to be a famous painter just like Vincent the famous painter in France. He studied book upon book of the famous painter. And copied his life. Dada was a shrink. And saw Vincent's reading habits and told him that he had something called problems of reference. PS. It was Dada who had the problem for naming my brother Vincent.

Dada had a business called Recovery, Inc. He assumed that all people were crazy and that they needed to do business with him, until they got well. I don't think that you will like the end of this story. For Vincent really was mad and the problem of not having a job nearly drove him to the breaking point. And he would yell and yell because he thought that his Dada was unfair. I am repeating, again, information, changing a bit, like Homer does in <u>The</u> <u>Odyssey</u>. That's one reason it takes him so long to get through the stranger period.

Then he would go out into the streets and scream and scream, but Mummy didn't come. The moral to this story is if you think you have free speech don't scream. Or Dada might get you. Of course you identify with the story, because you want to know what screaming has to do with contracts and how to get out of a contract. You just can't identify with a howl. Dada would say to Vincent, "Are you well yet?" Like I told you, this is <u>black</u> comedy, gallows humor.

Soon Dada got upset, or was it our Mummy, I don't know which. Anyway in a last chance bet, Dada bought Vincent rental units. And he learned how to earn money the hard way. 500 dollars at a time. Things went fine, for the first month. The money came in and he was happy. It was the good times of CCC. You could say that Vincent was spoiled rotten. And that would be true. Dada paid for my education at California and Chicago. CCC. Culture or DNA was cause.

Thenhestartedtoscreamagain. Therentersallheardhim. Itwasallinbad taste. MMMMMMMMMAAAAAAAAAAAAAAAAADDDDDDDDD, said Lorenzo. To our Vincent. Lorenzo was the first to talk with Vincent in I don't know how long. Lorenzo was our hero. He was a renter and on the college Football team. He knew all about running. At UCLA.

Vincent was a landlord. He was by one house one day when a tenant started playing with him. He said to Vincent, hey you. And pointed to his nose. The problem was that he had a bad case of acne. And he took it personally. Then he saw his nose in a tenant's car, outside mirror. Aristotle's <u>imitation</u>. That is to say Vincent started to imitate the persons behavior and point back, out of self-defense. Like Lacan.

The tenant was right and Vincent had what Dada called problems of reference. Or was it the tenant I don't remember which. He came home and I was there. Tenant had the reference problems, I said. And told him that the problem was not his. Like most of you. You feel guilty at first and then point back. It's a no-brainer. Vincent looked just like Einstein, but it was there that the resemblance ended. For he was no Einstein. Vincent was bipolar. He wanted to be an Einstein. The Einstein of property. As an aside, Sherry came up to me when I was explaining this to the band. Sherry was very pregnant. Vincent was <u>black</u>.

I explained to Vincent that it was a problem of <u>signs</u>. He asked what a sign was. I told him it was like his index finger. He could point too.

I told him that all his life he had problems of reference because he was the oldest son and that people wanted to be like him so they pointed at him. Like PS?

That's our first lesson on <u>semiotics</u>, the study of signs, which I learned from a number of people at the University of Chicago. I told Vincent. He told me that as a landlord he was able to paint some great pictures. I told him that he should concentrate on signs and see what the object was.

-2-

The University of Chicago was perhaps the best school in the world on symbols. Also in so many years, they got 11 Nobel Prizes in the economics department alone. I studied with among others Paul Ricoeur and Mircea Eliade, two world wide Authorities on philosophy and the History of Religions. That deals with symbols.

Eliade had a theory of the myth of the eternal return. I don't know what that is exactly, but it had to do with religion. If you're religious don't worry a myth is like what we would call a story of religion. He believed in the existence of Yoga and that it, or whatever you want to call Zen, could give you a sign. This was not problems of reference it was materialism and Freedom of Religion. Still, most people at Chicago would not tell you this. Or, Berkeley. They are both good.

Perhaps all his life Zen was trying to get in touch with my brother. In the remote chance that he would be like Zeus. He never had any problems with the police. Yet. But I am getting ahead of my self. We were back at Vincent's apartments. They were playing with him again. And I was not there to defend him. The people were giving like NFL signs to Vincent, penalties marking him out.

For those of you who read, actually, the last chapter on Da Vinci's Last Supper you should note that at the Last Supper the Apostles were giving signs to each other. That's what they were, so if you are lost go back to the last chapter, there you also find a material <u>code</u>. Decipher it. With the CCC and PMS. These <u>signs</u> were like NFL ref penalties.

Is it I, Lord?, said one Apostle. There is one problem. What happens to our Vincent is that he gets Crucified. That was the last time Jesus met with his apostles. That's why they call it the Last Supper. Roman guards took him away. And that's the moral of our little story. Don't.

In my church we remember the events in the life of Pride. Catholics, a good church, remember the sign of the cross. You should talk to a Catholic and ask him or her what the meaning of that sign is. Or, the stations of the cross that is what Vincent knew? Not the real PE? A sign you should be used to by now.

PE is a sign we have already discussed. CCC, Chicago Cultural Critique, is like you use the culture in a book, this book, the last 3 years of living so far in The United States of America, to see the text, not the culture of the author. I am Frank, the US has made me. That's the CCC. You don't need to be a master and memorize all the NFL penalties. Life's confusing enough as it is.

PM we have discussed? You play ball with PE and in the PM you go to sleep? That's my little joke. PMS is what I am doing now, I am a type? A hero. The title is water in the belly, that's PMS. Now you have my PMS? It's not a profile, its symbolism of a postmodern novel. It's my own personal meditation on the political economics for near 3 years, now.

You have already read that. To make it interesting I use funny little symbols or signs. The motive is to educate and sell my book. Vincent really was like crucified and he's my brother not me. Don't connect the dots, use the CCC, that's cultural America? It was first, the NFL signs, second, it was the zoning department's charges, third, it was the neighbors pointing to him once the hearsay got out that the city had a lien on his rental property? Was it that he was <u>black</u>.

Having gone to Cal and Chicago makes me a hero. They are very difficult schools to get a degree from. I say, <u>espionage signs</u>, because I want you to keep reading and use the above signs of a University, to tell me about what you see and read. It's my sense of humor. Like you could E-mail me your impressions? A clue?

Postmodernism is what I have just given you. In the PM it is right to kick back and relax and go to sleep when the time is right? You'll get used to it but you'll have to pay attention and use the above <u>symbols</u> to get the next chapter. PMS and CCC and PM of PS? They are easy to understand, in that they are common cultural signs that should explain themselves. Your environment or culture makes you.

-3-

Vincent was at the apartments one day, when a letter came from the zoning department. It was nasty. To make a long story short, he had to comply with the code. He had to make 18 paved parking spaces. He did and went broke. Then he went nuts. He screamed. But not before complying with the charges. He had to tear up a lawn and garden and fence in back of one of his houses. People are crucified for less. Felski's <u>The</u> <u>Limits</u> <u>of</u> <u>Critique</u> was based on the works of Paul Ricoeur. And his "hermeneutics of suspusicion". Vincent Holmes. He was living in danger, like Odysseus.

He thought he had a Constitutional right to defend capitalism. He did but nobody heard him. He got even more mad. Why couldn't he defend Capitalism? Because they broke the Constitution over his head. At least he went down defending Capitalism. Absent his emotions, he was the poster Child or Republican mark who said, no more regulations. That's what Republicans say.

Enter me. Who am I a law and order guy who wrote two killer albums.<u> Now I am writing a story about my times</u>. I have become a Moderate Democrat. I think I can sell my book, watch me. As for Vincent, my father, the doctor, committed him. Which broke his heart. It was baseball signs that they use in the streets that drove him nuts. And NFL signs. For he had problems of reference and did not like authority, any authority, he was not a Tea Bag party person. He, now, was a Republican. Who will be President in 2012?

It was the best thing for Vincent. Absent the Federal Judges overruling in part *Ogden*? If he had a defense, he would not have really stayed in a one room apartment. He finally found peace. He had learned that screaming will get you nowhere.

Visions are what Vincent lived for and the US Supreme Court agrees. You can <u>believe</u> what you want but you can't <u>do</u> what you want. His yelling through the streets of Los Angeles was his doing what he wanted. Visions were his belief. That's basic freedom of religion law.

I don't get too many visions, not unlike Marta seeing the bleeding palms Of Jesus. Vincent centered in on the pictures of Vincent Van Gogh. The crows and the bedroom. Those were his visions. He would see the night sky, and I kid you not, he saw Starry, Starry Night. Like CCC? M is Modern, like PM.

Say he needed glasses. But at least he did not Howl. A wolf would do that, not a human being. He got manic. That was the proximate cause. They gave him a bunch of pills and that seemed to control his <u>behavior</u>. He quit yelling. But capitalism should be on guard. Like PC. I plead the Constitution, not Vincent. His visions are his religion.

And no amount of talk can change his belief. Protected belief. As long as the Federal Judges relent, to use Vincent's term. Vincent liked the peace and quiet of *Walden*. That is what he wanted. And to get out of Los Angeles. After PC/M China, whatever? Modern stranger.

He became fixated on Death. And the court case that I argued for him. I didn't do a good job of it for I plead States' Rights in a Federal Jurisdiction. And the Title 42 was beyond belief. It hurt his case rather than help him. I should have just distinguished *Ogden*?

- - -

I think he just wanted to kill himself. The problem was that he failed in the one thing he did well at. Well, almost. He had a fantasy that he would get a gun, point it at his head and blow out his brains.

Few people could relate to this. Which left him alone and quiet. He didn't know he had free speech.

Being manic did not make him deadly. It told people around the problem with him was <u>behavior</u>. And there is nothing a shrink likes to do more than control behavior, first comes the diagnosis then the recital of evidence. That is not fantastic. The more manic he got, the more people left him. He became isolated. Without friends and uncool. CCC? Like Jim Holmes? They were bad.

He started to smoke *Kools* which someone was smoking when he was first admitted. He did not drink in that the booze gave him a negative reaction with his pills, which he needed to make him look sane. But friends left. One thing he never did again was howling through the city of Los Angeles.

Only once did he see someone put in a straightjacket. And there was the threat of an operation on his brain. They wanted to make him sterile. And he waited, religiously, this Vincent Holmes.

For the smoke breaks they gave. Cigarettes calmed him down. It was he was not manic. If he isn't manic and he's working then that was his wayout. Of the CCC? Culture or DNA?

Vincent eventually got out. But he had gotten in the habit. Of smoking. To stress him down. He went back to his one room apartment. Where he washed dishes at a local café. But he always thought about death. Still, the Hospital did him with a half a year of good meals. Some good in that he didn't own a gun, restrictions on his getting the gun enforced. How did not Vincent Holmes get guns?

-4-

Sign language of football refs, for the uninitiated, like baseball clubs and sign language for the deaf can drive you nuts, said the jock at the apartments. Vincent, agreeing with the football player, flipped the football player the peace sign. The football player flipped it back near his eye. An example of what people give you when you make a PMS mistake? Rita Felski, in her limits of Critique, mentioned in this recent book, that she believed suspicion was, basically semiotic, the study signs. This is just like a doctor's work with. "Symptom" and a detective's work with "clues". As with literary and culture criticism, as seen in this anti- novel.

It was November 25, 2011 when the group of us at the co-op got together with Vincent as he told his tale. He said, I am still cool, I am still a Republican. A couple of guys in the band laughed. He said, I believe in the National Constitution's contract clause. That was so long ago I can hardly remember it. So we are not back in 2004, or at the Michigan v. UCLA game. We are just talking about it, at the co-op 7 years later. The big game. Like a scientist, explore your mind.

Obligations of contracts are scary. Mad, said Lorenzo. A renter at the housing complex. He was a freshman on the football team, # 33. Vincent talked to us about the howling. It was bedlam. Stay tuned for he was crucified. Vincent explained about how he had a humble landlord business. With money coming in from our Dada. He felt he had CCC free speech and property? The right to due process.

He was 39 and slow for his age. I had heard the story before. The business had a duplex and a small house. He was a Republican for as long as I can remember. There was a football player, Lorenzo, in the small house. Next to UCLA. That's Lorenzo. <u>Hobby Lobby.</u>

He was very ideological but he liked to drink his wine, he was 17. That's 2004. That was the year after we wrongly went into Iraq. Not popular at UCLA, there. The year that UCLA won the NCA A National Championship.

We were talking the blues, at the band's co-op, to an electric manic Vincent. The Democrats in the band were trash talking about regulations. Something our Vincent, like all good Republicans, hated. He countered with Art. I Contracts 10 of the United States of American Federal Constitution.

As he talked on, manic, he got more and more electric, that's like he was highly charged. If you are a Democrat I am your Dr. Frank. I don't want this to cause you any anxiety, but this hurts. This is reality. And I ain't going to loose this time. We were just talking back and forth. 2 weeks into the term, Lorenzo damaged the one toilet. Vincent fixed it at no cost. Who is to say it was him. But the loss of money, about $ 300, was very frustrating. Vincent got heated. Then came the use of wine by a minor charge from the neighbors, also in the rental business. And Vincent covered it up and was charged by his neighbors.

Because to him the customer is always right. But he was wrong. It's rough running a business, said Vincent, electric and throwing off charges in every direction. Vincent's PMS?

You can see why nobody wanted to be around him and he was being rude to everyone in the co-op. He was a threat to all of us, playing the cop to a band who invented the term. He ran his business without any professional training. In the PS? Post-structuralism.

This is the completed story of a crucified Jesus, for those who are not deaf of otherwise impaired. Impairment of contracts, by the State or City, is protected by the original intent of the US Constitution, or otherwise. Vincent had a defense. But no due process.

Vincent told Lorenzo that in his upcoming game with Michigan, the opponents helmets were designed to intentionally distract the opposing player's vision. UCLA won the game. Thanks to Vincent. I had taught Vincent, about icons. Of the PMS?

I'll get to the big game later. It was only ¾ of the way through the season. But Michigan was # 1 and UCLA was #3. I'll tell you now it was won by trash talking. Which was protected by free speech. UCLA went on to win the Rosa Bowl the way that Stanford had done in 2001. But Michigan was the real test.

Back to Vincent. He kept looking for a sign from Zen and he was lucky he wasn't Struck dumb. He didn't want a sign from his fellow human beings. As they say, When you are in the service of humanity you are in the service of your Zen. They beat Michigan and that was enough, for Lorenzo had taken his case.

Lorenzo could read the signs of the big game. Lorenzo had the football team over to his house the next night to celebrate the big game victory. It lasted till 3 AM. They all had beer. But not Lorenzo for he had learned his lessons well. Still, there were complaints from the neighbors. He didn't know the PE?

It was near Thanksgiving and Lorenzo covered up well. But not his neighbors. They crucified Lorenzo as a type of Vincent the landlord, by the competition. Vincent the landlord was a National obligation of contract Republican. The tragedy is being told. didn't go the neighborhood. Vincent knew some law that governed who could now stay at his houses. He, like Lorenzo, showed no bias. Vincent put up a sign—For Rent. This meant for any male.

Some Chinese came. He rented to them. And no, this is not a Cheech and Chong joke. These were just the people who came in. The students just played and laughed. Vincent signed the contract that the Chinese would use bicycles and not cars. Of course, the Latinos had cars. They were customized and were so cool I could hardly stand It. This is world criticism. Like the French men, Mr. Derrida, who Ricoeur disagreed with and Mr. Foucault, all of whom had a base in Heidegger's <u>Being</u>. They all had a cultural critique with the CCC, Civilization Cultural Criticism.

That was the Federal obligation of contract, and Alice was 11 at the time and he stayed with us. These were their crosses to carry. The Chinese moved in, strangers to the United States and UCLA who loved them. But not Lorenzo for some reason. I guess it was the drinking of wine, being under age.

Strangers at the gates of Eden. Heaven's gate. That's when Vincent learned of the Chinese—"Two Whatever Philosophy". It was from Deng Xiao Ping and said that they didn't need to follow the philosophy of certain Marx and Lenin. That freed them to go with capitalism like Uncle Milton. Of Chicago, Milton Friedman or Milton Singer 1983.

That was a brainstorm for the Chinese, initiated by Deng. It proved Milton Friedman's theory was right if you give people capitalism then ever so slightly they will justify your Nobel Prize winning theory, they will get political freedom. The Chinese, now, have the best economy in the world. Tibet would not play ball. I learned from Vincent to like the Chinese. They were key to his story.

An Ute moved in. And with the People. After the NCA A National Championship, it seemed like the entire football team move in to Vincent's duplex. Because of Lorenzo. And yes he was first a native of Italy. Then he became an American. And no he was not with the Italian mafia.

My honey, Sherry, was not with me at the time in that this was 2004. And it was no racist Cheech and Chong joke? Not that they were racist. But I am sure that there are people around the Americas who would take this to be a redneck joke. One day an Ute and a Latino and a Chinese moved in as roommates. They all pass around a beer and refuse giving it to a football player, 33. New hip.

This is what Lorenzo plead, on the turf. On the playing field with Michigan. There was a nose tackle on the defense, who later moved in with an offensive guard and a defensive down lineman, DL. Their numbers were 81, 54 and 85. They all made it into the NFL, like Homer's suitors. Where Odysseus is still <u>The Stranger</u>.

Now, this was so fantastic I could hardly stand it. The amazing thing was they were all from Vincent's apartment complex. Teams go 7 years and would be considered lucky to get 3, if that, players into the NFL. Like California during the early 1950's. Way after the CCC?

Let me go over the story again. One day Vincent got two letters from the city Los Angeles. The zoning department charged Vincent with two crimes? It was like saying that he was un-American? Thank you, he said. Being a good Republican? In the PE?

Eventually, a flood of football players came in. One was a linebacker, 55. His name was Ogden. That's how Vincent learned to play ball. Like Justice White on the United States Supreme Court. No mean trick. And I noticed how it was like the name of the case *Ogden*. Which I distinguished.

Stranger than fiction, there were two players on the team, Darcy and Pops. They were down linemen. They didn't live with Vincent's People. I met them one day, They seemed like nice guys. Everyone on the team liked them. They were sons who did not make it with the NFL. Like Lorenzo, <u>The Stranger</u>.

Vincent's lawyer did not know jack about civil rights. He was very old. He could remember the Atomic test—Mike. Which I hated.

Vincent's Lawyer had never heard of Art. I Sec. 10 of the National United States Constitution. Vincent's situation was like a "Mike" pleading. As to due process. Like Osysseus Irony rules. It was that same lawyer that was his attorney for his commitment hearing. Vincent paid the $50,000 to take up the lawn and tar the parking spaces. He was a good Republican and he kept saying to himself, it can't happen here. He paid. As we are led to believe should be the case. The American dream. That down lineman, Reynolds, 34, was jailed for various charges.

The writer Milton Friedman was basically wrong about capitalism giving freedom, as was noted by Professor Reich in his book of worth *Supercapitalism*. He taught at the University of California.

Vincent at this stage started to be mad? He figured that free capitalism was just that, free? Check it out. I can't recommend enough Professor Reich's book. It was published in 2007. And is a snap shot of the world gone wrong. Right before the crashes of the stock market and the housing industry, in 2008. Us in the PM? Late Capitalism.

Vincent's dad, our Dada, could not afford the $50,000. So he let the Land Sale Contract revert back to the people who sold us the Houses. It was here that Vincent lost his mind. He started running through the streets of Los Angeles howling. Like a wolf. Don't worry about the Song. Given LA it could have been over $150,000, if they needed more Property, buy it from the people next door. Or, would it be more?

He wanted the Tea Bag Party, before they were formed, to take his republican case, the National Constitution Contract clause that stated "No state shall impair the obligation of contract". I say National, because Federal Judges won't hear the case because of *Ogden*. And it's a Federal case.

That was Vincent's case, like *Exxon*. It was their Odyssey. I have my own Odyssey but it reminds me of the old Indian proverb, if you help someone take their boat across the river, you find that you have taken your own boat across the river. The Ute that stayed, Vincent's place, was Mr. Red. Nobody is laughing. It's a tragedy. Like Justin.

Finally the police came and took him away. To the funny farm. As for Vincent he was bipolar. That is shrink talk for Manic-Depressive. When he wrongly ran through the streets of LA, he was manic. On recognizing his mistake, he got depressed.

This is not a *Lochner* case, the courts protecting workers from a 18 Hour day. It's an attack on Capitalism, of win-win contracts. As for me, I watched mimes. They mimed me. Because I made it and looked around, something you don't do in LA, with my "The Cherry".

Cities can moon people. They think most contracts are illegal like the case of *Lochner*. Not the mask of comedy of Republicans? There were two reasons our Vincent, like Vincent Van Gogh, went mad? First, it was Capitalism, he couldn't make a sale. Second, and I am speculating about Van Gogh, he couldn't stand the signs that the peasants were giving him? In come a renter, Joe Marx.

Signs are words, they can be hearsay or gossip. That's what they said about our Vincent. And Transnational capitalism is on the brink, now, let's all go out and paint pretty pictures. Of PMS? Are you cracking the code? Of Reality?

-5-

UCLA was where I went to preschool, in a special program they have to the north of the University, off Sunset Blvd, where the stars live.

Lorenzo told me about the big game between UCLA against Michigan. And how he did it. Yes, Lorenzo has a last name but I am protecting his privacy. For, you see, this is a true story here. With a few name changes. And the year. Lorenzo continued what they call in the NFL—Trash Talking. This is telling jokes or ranking the opposing side's players.

He would run with the ball, he was a running back. Then right before he got hit, he would say just loud enough for the blocker to hear, but soft enough so the refs would not hear, his trashing. He figured he had free speech. And he was an expert on signs, his professor father taught semiotics, the study of signs. Like PMS? Signs of later Capitalism. He played the fool sometimes like putting his finger to his lips and then say, do you hear me? That gave him consciousness. And running room. They Lost consciousness or they would smile. And that gave our Lorenzo 10 more yards. I don't need to tell you how unique Lorenzo was. But he never made it into the NFL. Just his friends.

Of course, the refs would catch him. Oh I'll tell you he was Lorenzo Amos. When they would catch him, they would make the appropriate penalty like grabbing one wrist with the other hand and make a downward movement. That was Shaw. Remember that name. He comes to me in my next dream?

That would Tick off Lorenzo.

Then on the next play he would talk to the <u>black</u> offensive tackle and tell him that he needed a block. On the next play, Andy, the offensive lineman who later moved into Vincent's apartments, would give him a 10 yard block. It was the most fantastic thing to see Andy and Amos play ball. They were telling jokes and having fun, like a couple of small kids. Sports is the opium of the people.

Then when it was UCLA's turn on the defense, Cheech, the defensive guard that later moved into Vincent's apartments, would get a sack. During the Michigan game he got 5 sacks, a UCLA record.

This was not funny. The nose guard, which their entire defense revolved around, and who moved into Vincent's place, would slowly push and push against the center.

The nose guard was so important because when Michigan would pass, and they were a passing team, the quarterbacks pocket would go all wrong. Michigan had just one nose tackle. Lorenzo was the running back and made yard after yard backing up Andy. Naturally. This is stuff they get in the real NFL and most people watching the game get.

Actually, Andy the key to UCLLLLLLLLLLLLLLLLLA's offensive yardage, was the most amazing tackle I've ever seen. He with Cheech made it into the NFL. There was only one problem with Andy, he was always holding. A trait he stopped once he turned pro. He was a giant and weighed about 320 pounds, and he knew where to throw around his weight. This was the Amos and Andy punch.

Chong wasn't there. But Lorenzo was right there. He would go on to get an MBA from Harvard. Naturally, Lorenzo was a materialist. He was 6 feet tall and weighed in at 200 pounds. None of it was fat. And off the field he was the nicest guy in the world he always smiled and liked business. His close Relations with Andy made Lorenzo an All-American. They were both freshmen. It was like going fishing.

Lorenzo would bulk up with spoonfuls of Ice cream. Then he would go to the gym and turn his fat into weight. He could spend 4 hours in the gym with the weights then he would turn to a friend and smile which he always did and make a nice remark about the person? Off the field, he was the nicest guy in the world. On the field he meant business.

Lorenzo lived at the apartments of Vincent. And he came by once in a Yellow truck and talked to Vincent, which he loved. This was 2004. Lorenzo was a heavy weight. He was married to a wife named Mini. By 2011, he had a computer business next to Disneyland. He sold software to corporations. The business of Lorenzo was very tricky to talk about, he did work with the Department of Defense.

Back on the Michigan game. Remember they were #1 in the nation in NCA A Football rankings. But that didn't stop our Lorenzo. With a 5 yard block from our favorite lineman, he would clear 15 yards, that down. Andy was great. And he made it big. Andy made it into the NFL. Amos and Andy, no joke. Both were not sellouts.

Lorenzo was humble too. He always gave credit to their undefeated season, that year, to the offensive and defensive linemen. Nobody ever noticed how many yards he made, and it was quite a sum. And especially nobody would tell him. Because he would always say it was

Cheech and Andy. And the other NFL Future player who made it. We never mentioned their names. Very humble.

Our Vincent was anything but humble. He was a proud Republican. It's just that the NFL signs people gave him, he supposed, drove him bonkers. I told him about the signs people made, but this was after he went bonkers. My <u>study of signs</u> said that it was basic, universal in the world. Of course, it was the city and zoning Department that made him mad? Where could they gotten them from?

So you see you don't need to be afraid of signs. Theeeeeeeeey are so universal I can hardly stand it. But let us go back to the Michigan game. With Lorenzo. What he did was fantastic. He ran for 400 yards or so. Don't worry it was Andy. In the CCC? Andy ran 10 foot blocks and Lorenzo would run around the free space.

I say don't be afraid of signs, because they are like baseball signs that belong to like a club and people steal those signs and that is because those signs are secret not scary and everyone uses those sign complex signals because they want to be in. Anyway I am disabled, and I liked signs because they told me when I was out.

Like I hope people who read this book for it is realism, will write their congress person to make a law that will distinguish *Ogden*? Not overturn it. Thaaaaaaat will free Federal Judges to allow them to use the original intent of the United States Constitution. And will allow the free market to work. With Congressional oversight.

That's my big game. But back to the Michigan game. And did I ever cheer for UCLA. It was so fantastic I could hardly stand it. Lorenzo made the first score. It was 6 to 0. We missed the point after touch-Down. My head went dizzy like a cosmos in my head. I threw up my hands which was the sign for touchdown.

He stole their play book. You see Lorenzo was a mime too. He was starting to read *The Great Books Of The Western World*. Published by the University of Chicago. Lorenzo's favorite was the classic Aristotle. He got from him the idea of—Imitation. He would get ideas from like Aristotle and translate them into Ref language.

Lorenzo would imitate every move of Michigan. So that he was More Michigan than Michigan. They scored next. It was 6 to 7. But Lorenzo was a Republican and Michigan was mainly Democrat. He learned how to be a Democrat. In the CCC. When they were winning, Lorenzo would translate everything into coded Democrat language, like <u>race</u>.

Vincent saw the game on national TV. And did he ever see Lorenzo. UCLA's helmets like the rest of the PAC—12 had no intention. And did Lorenzo ever make fun of Michigan helmets, Not that players of the opposition have the intention to lie. It's just that their motions are blinding. Their PE? They had beer.

Next was the most amazing thing I personally have ever seen. Lorenzo made a zig-zag motion with his helmet and with a 14 yard block from Andy, Lorenzo ran for 80 yards. And he was my friend. The score was 12 to 7. The score stayed like that for the rest of the game. It was a big defensive battle and dozens of penalties for our side.

It was all defense and did Lorenzo ever get penalties for his trash talking. He must have run for 600 yards. But it was funny the refs took back 200 yards. The coach argued with the refs about all of the penalties and I think that they did not like someone using ref signs to move people around the field, as they ran the ball.

-6-

Penalty after penalty racked-up against our Lorenzo. He started to give Michigan the peace sign. And they mimed him. He then said to their Linebacker, I give you a Republican peace sign so that you'll give me my Con law contract clause. Not the right trash to Michigan. They were alive again.

Penalties came left and right to us. They were the government too. If You will remember our times in the National courts, we lost. But not on Fraud. Just on the obligation of contract and was Michigan ever *Ogden*. We were too, it's just that Lorenzo a freshman got excited, he wanted it. He was like an instructor in sign language, because his father taught that as a pro, at Cal's Bolt Hall. Legal semiotics.

Lorenzo that year ran for about 2,000 yards. As a freshman. What he did was unheard of. Back to the game for it wasn't over till its over. And he was on National TV. He was brave. He took the charges they threw aaaaaaaat him. He played to the TV with his sign language of his, as if he were talking to a jury on non-verbal behavior, dad.

It was so charged, it must have been like that at D-day. His eyes nearly went blind and his body felt like he was a vet during his time in Army. Lorenzo went to the coach, I can't take it. The coach said, don't worry you're the Federal contract clause, just remember that, you have Zen on your side, I know you are ideological. The coach was not.

Lorenzo was quick and he knew that they were ahead so he started Pleading Michigan's side in his trash talking, so, he thought, protected free speech, it wasn't but he freely spoke any way, he was changing the way the game was played. In the PE. Especially, his use of Ref signs that was his way of trash talking.

And it came to pass, the UCLA quarterback did not know jack. So when it came to pass, he did not. So it was all Lorenzo's game. He considered himself a type, with non-verbal signs, to be together stating the State's case, and even pleading *Ogden*. He ran 5 yards and as he stopped he said, I believe in regulations. And even the sky showed forth light. They were playing at Michigan. This was Lorenzo's ideology. It drove Michigan nuts. Their quarterback's name was Cooley.

He saw signs, even his knees began to tremble. And he wondered if the other side thought he was deaf, even the sign language of the deaf. He was a good listener. He thought, that's why they dropped the charges, which were a pain in the head. Even did he vomit blood, the pain was so terrible. He surrendered at the right time. Because they started to ask if he was mad. He wasn't of course. Sarcastically.

He knew he was nuke waste. If he did not change his ways. He tried it again, I believe in regulations, and the waters did part, even his making 20 more yards. It worked and they were ahead so he kept it up, he finally communicated with them. Lorenzo cleared every Michigan defender off the field. He wondered why Vincent almost cut off his ear, even to it bleeding. Vincent only got a glimmer of what was going down on the field. Both of them were like hobos.

Vincent was not deaf, it was just that he got the neighbors charges directed towards Lorenzo. This made him very sorry. Even to the making him make 10 more yards. The other side could feel his vibes. He said, Republican. And the charges started back up again and the coach could not even hear him so much was his agony. The coach of UCLA was ticked off because his school wasn't private, like Stanford or USC. And even they did mime him after he had imitated them, Michigan being quick and good code breakers themselves. He dare not utter the word, oppressive, so exceedingly bright was his glory. Now it was time for the defense and the nose tackle got a hurry. At the next play even did the waters part and the right guard got a sack, for UCLA. The moral was, if you plead that you were a Republican, Michigan would be strong.

No words oppression or equal rights, passed his lips. And the pain did stop. They weren't deaf either. The United States Supreme Court held certain signs were against the law, like the dragging ones finger across the ankle and it came to pass that the people followed suit. Like in PMS? Signs of later Capitalism, strangers.

Lorenzo dominated because he could plead Michigan's case, and he got the full 9 Yards. Lorenzo was <u>black</u>. He heard Vincent and the government. He looked at the Refs and wondered about the other signs and he did not want to know those signs for they were a penalty and that meant loss of yards. The defense came on. Lorenzo's girl friend signed to him to, have a heart. It worked The nose tackle was white as a cloudy day. He made it past the center and got a sack as their quarterback was trying to pass they were on UCLA's 20 yard line. 3 downs and their defense held. Michigan tried a field goal and it missed. Michigan Fans did not lie. They hated their team. They turned against their own team. And all they did was to defend the government. Equal protection.

They tried sign language for the deaf. UCLA wasn't fooled for it was a gross violation of protection. Lorenzo made the whole 9 yards, By this time it was halftime. UCLA was winning and it was a giant of a game. What a show they put on at halftime. The teams came back. Michigan used all its firepower. Signs refer. So do refs who didn't like trash talking. Yes sign language can be like trash talking too, and get you a penalty, if you use it too much.

Then, Michigan started using baseball signs. They weren't on the same club. Lorenzo acted as if he were a Pro Wrestler. He fell back in horror so bad was his parody. He did not even mention about problems of referring. He didn't want to give ammo to the other side. He stuck with his parody. You can't believe what a whale of a game this was for both sides.

Lorenzo finally spoke, I like baseball signs. The Michigan team almost split a gut. So bad was Lorenzo's parody. He took the Supreme Court's holding as real, he was a rebel. He dragged his finger across his ankle. So exceedingly great was the anguish of the running back of Amos, Lorenzo faked a heart attack.

They were communicating. Lorenzo wanted more if you know what I mean. Signs refer, he kept on saying to himself, Why did the ref stop giving him a penalty. Capitalism in a general case is like being Vincent, Lorenzo thought. Why did all capitalists draw their finger across their ankle. He thought that there must be a meaning here. But nobody would explain it, he thought it might mean, somebody was knighted, but he wasn't sure. Vincent got the letter from the city early fall, that year, weeks before the Michigan game. Like Odysseus, <u>The Strangers</u>.

Lorenzo remembered the script. It was his game. He did quake. And he did not even mention the word Republican. Then he remembered hitting your ankle had such a bad meaning it was like to bite your thumb. Lorenzo could count the cash if and when he made it to the NFL. He made the sign for, holding. This stopped them in their tracks. For some reason it was a government sign, and stopped Michigan, unless it was some tactic. The above sign was in Shakespeare.

But the troops wondered, why did he make that sign. To refer was a sin. He had to have an excuse. It was necessity, his wrist hurt. That was a relief. He thought, I ain't got to show you no stinking badges, he was deaf no more. And the quake let up a little bit. The sign of Vincent's failure was a sign that America was no longer defending capitalism. If you get anything from this is that Lorenzo knew about Art. I Contracts and he took Vincent's case onto the field, with sign language from the NFL.

Lorenzo knew that the above drove Vincent nuts. First it was the charges from the city then it was the charges from the local police. And they were electric charges making any normal Joe-6pack buckle, and the ankles tremble. For the first time he said out loud, Art. I Sec. 10 of the American Federal Constitution is true. The war was over. The waters did part. He had become the defense. Which was great for a freshman Offensive player. His defense was that a friend was mad.

Lorenzo fell to his knees and looked at the coach, who was signing like mad. The coach said, you are like Justice White, we're keeping you in, until you get 2,000 yards, as a fantastic thing, Lorenzo maintained.

Okay, he said. Lorenzo connected in his mind the bite of ones thumb as being like a refs penalty. It was in one of William Shakespeare's plays and started up a fight.

They give you a sign to penalize for a mistake. It was an evolution.

I thought of Milton Singer, one of the world authorities on signs at Chicago, and finally knew what he meant, Holmes, about C S Pierce and indexing. Lorenzo was a type who was crucified for his beliefs. The capitalism of Vincent. Milton was my Prof. at my orals at Chicago. And Victor Turner. And so it goes.

So where did the charges come from? It wasn't the National. It wasn't the President of the people. It was Federal Judges who are enslaved by *Ogden*? It was a tragedy for all parties. They are innocent of the blood of this generation? Then who were those guys? The ones with the charges.

Lorenzo dropped the ball and it turned into a Rugby Match.

After the mayhem, the game returned back to normal. Please, go to a college football Game and buy a program and inside it should be a list of the NCA A ref penalty types. Memorize it and be on the jury and see if they don't use ref penalties every day. It's tradition. Don't stomp on the penalties or smash it, respect history for what it is. Just let it be.

The co-op was in a <u>trance</u> at my explanation of how Lorenzo Shaw got 400 against the #1 team in the nation, Michigan. Stay tuned there is much more to come. Of course, it's the ref's mime. It's the law. That's the reason for Legal Semiotics, the analysis of signs in the courtroom.

Mr. Shaw taught Legal Semiotics at Bolt Hall, of the University of California. Mr. Amos was Lorenzo's father. He was a lawyer. You might have noticed both Lorenzo and I have a handicap, of different sorts.

When you make a mistake they penalize you. You don't know it, but they are football signs. Just look at a professional baseball game and see the signs the coach gives. Blame it on the NFL? Lorenzo made 5 yards UCLA was grinding down the clock. He already had 380 yards. Both our teams were on the side of the government, so they wouldn't hear any of Vincent's pleas. He had been charged 3 weeks earlier.

He mimed or imitated what everybody else was doing. And he made capitalist yardage. Semiotics is a new field, its been around 100 years. It's the s in PMS? Postmodernism was the coolest thing going around. They are getting a workout. Milton did it, it's the study of signs and it's American. Spread all over the place. Now you are King Tut.

-7-

The study of signs is history. Especially in a courtroom. It's nonverbal comments. Milton Singer was an anthropologist. At Chicago. He is dead now. Chicago is the best anthropology department in the world. Suddenly the light came through the window. This was no ref sign you can call it what you want. But be careful, judges hate it when you pander with non-verbal signs.

Ideology was studied by Chicago's Mircea Eliade. You judge. Lorenzo kept on grinding out yards. Paul had PE? He was my judge. Are you into my sign, gallows humor yet? How about my <u>black</u> comedy Espionage yet? Don't blame it on Europe. Don't blame it on Russia or China. Now, they are our friends. I am giving you enough clues, I want you to be like a spy, there is a correlation, I believe, between the social world and the material world.

CCC is a perfect PE tool to decipher the spies that come in from the cold? Relax it's almost PM? They have written up Legal Semiotics in academic law journals for some 20 years. But they weren't as good as Milton. Lawyers use it to analyze evidence in a open courtroom. As the co-op is my judge. They could take my "Song of Songs" and I saw I was protected by the 1st Amendment. Semiotics is the science of the study of signs. That's the do of don't ask and don't tell.

Pablo doesn't like it because the sun's setting light keeps shining past him. Naughty Boy. Don't tear it apart, flow with it. They make a sign and you run a correlation. Like next year and its birth from the water in the belly. The ref just gave a penalty like crossed wrists. I don't know what it meant, to me it was like the sign of a slave. You can judge it any way you want. Like the signs from dead Zeus.

In an open courtroom, the judge can use Legal Semiotics to analyze nonverbal behavior. Oops, the Santa Ana winds just started up. The sun is going down. It's no signs at all for I am deaf to them. No longer the zen, it's the sound of one hand clapping. I rubbed both my eyes with both my hands and the winds started up. Now I can hear the barking dog. Like in I.B. Singer. Just from the perspective of someone from the Church of Pride. Sherry was very pregnant as ever.

I did not see visions. Nor did I hear voices. Rather, I felt a burning in the bosom, when I needed a message from Zen. Rather like Mitt Romney, I presume. <u>The Noble Koran</u> in Chapter 3, tells of the family of Jesus, Isa, peace be upon him, the Muslim Jesus. They believe that such a Jesus is their Messiah, who was not crucified. This is a point of treaty. See the above, at verse 45. The Orient, Oxford talk for the mid-East, is not easy place to treaty. There was treaty- recognition and enforcement. But in the Koran, chapter 2, "The Cow", it shows the love of Muslims to Jewish prophets. Congress needs to get a many sided treaty between Israel, and all the Muslim countries near them. Not a bad SiNN, or sin. It's the Islamic treaty of Badr.

The above is like a Statute and that Treaty is valid law for treaties between America and Islamic States.

Chapter 19

ESPIONAGE SIGNS

-1-

It had soul, said Mr. Salt. It had the basic City after artistic Nation after city goes for Opera like this. What of the politics of the Greeks? The Spanish? The French? The Chilean? Do the tea baggers want their revolution to spread to these countries, I don't. Our nation is enough. This is the irony of PS. This is the way a DA wants to lead a jury. I thought of my Sherry. The group met at Mr. Salt's as if it were a Tea Bag Party meeting. It was entrapment, by the FBI.

Do we want to adopt their politics?, said Salt. How many Egypt revolts will we see? What about Portugal? What about Hungary where their government bonds were rated as worthless? How many Communists are there in Hungary? What will we do? Surely not go to war. Is Hungary the new Italy of W W II? Right wing take over to cool the National Cure Duty of Congress, Art. I Sec. 7.

Mr. Redneck started to see with his Dodge truck and a 6-pack, unopened, on the floor. You see why I say that this chapter is not for the faint of heart. It's the reality of the world as we know it and wish it to be. What will we do? Go after every Communist on the block? What of peaceful assembly, not of the anarchists, like in the Oakland Occupy Movement, where press covered it. This has turned into a real detective story, with the FBI and CIA collecting information from the <u>signs of behavior</u>. Kafka rules this world. Not all Marxists are terrorists. Noon said, yea. I'm not through with you yet, Said Mr. Salt. I know you spent some time in jail for your use of a weapon at a tea party real rally. I think you, Noon, are like the Teabaggers and you need a good excuse for your use of a weapon? Seen in the context of history and the CCC. Do you believe in the 2nd Amendment? The Constitution?

At Davis, they pepper sprayed the peaceful assembly, of the First Amendment. They are more educated than you or I, said Redneck, are you surprised that I know their defense, I have memorized the Bill of Rights, and I can tell you that some day people will take away those rights. In the PS. And that time is not far off, they will take your Constitutional rights in the name of Hungary, Mitt Romney?

Will it be a revolt? Or an impeachment? Lautsky nodded yes out of sympathy, people not knowing that he was into anarchy. Americans don't have revolutions. One was enough. And you see what the police at one of the finest schools on planet earth thinks of protests like The Greeks, said Salt. In the CCC. The culture of the world was such that it produced these protesters. That's the CCC ideology that I want to be made public, here. The protesters were from the ground root up, hips slowly moving slouching towards Jerusalem, is there some thing to be born? Who will make the right connections?

Maria Latina, into politics as an undergraduate, agreed with Redneck and Salt. This is people's progress. Like Newt, she wanted a United States of America free from race tokens. Latinos are a type of black. They both want status. Like President Obama, did you think he would roll over and die, said Salt. He walks the fine line. He wants economic equality, as a way to stop a class war. Maria was with the FBI. We are FBI agents, said Mr. Salt, and you are all arrested. Especially you Mr. Nautsky. Then the agents that were in the back room came in and handcuffed them and took them down to the Los Angeles County Jail. They were not given their rights this was National Security. Very PS. The Miranda rights did not apply to Communists and terrorists? They all started smoking. Post-Structuralist? Anarchy is loosed on the world? What about National Security? January 6, 2021.

In time they were given a lawyer. But not as a defense as someone who they could confess to. <u>Just like in "State Police", as if it saw the future. And we released the sarcastic and parody album and it was another hit. It hit # 1 on the charts of America. And Europe again.</u>

People got the sarcasm and the reality. Was Newt right that there would be civil war? Newt was a Republican Candidate for President.

"Confession" and "Compulsory" went # 1 in the world. It not only talked of the protests it could be seen as a remedy in mass arrests, like the above. We took the state's position, like the police at Davis. Of course we backed the police our lines were on the line-up. Very PS? It's a play on words, it's a <u>post script</u> to protesters and it takes PS self-criticism of one own assumptions to get the entire story right?

<u>Noon Chuck went first</u>. Have you ever been or are you now a Communist? What did you think of the Occupy Oakland movement? Were you there? What do you think of Communist or Marxist reading inspired anarchy?, asked his government lawyer. Why did you have a gun? What else have you done? Seen in light of the Asian post-capitalism, PC? And this was his defense attorney, more like a firing squad.

How many witnesses can you produce to give you an excuse for saying you aren't a Communist? How many Communists are there in Seoul? <u>You came from the North can you defend them, if not, you are not Lil' Kim</u>? The United States secretly is in the process of making a treaty with North Korea? The old leader died last week? It is popular in the US to be against North Korea, so the treaty had to be on the down low? He married a communist.

They let him go back to his cell. Then came Butch Lautsky. The lawyer for the state asked him some pointed questions. Why are you in jail? Do you know anything about the United States Constitution? How much do you know? Have you read the book 1984? Seen in the context of PMS? Butch could have been a girl with his timid response, or like a man hiding the <u>Lautsky Arch Liberation Soldiers</u>. LALS is one of those communist punk, Marxist groups that is like a snake against large government, and for a land war. LALs is a 5,000 member clan.

They aren't for Revolution, per se, their goal is to create as much anarchy as the Roman Empire can stop. <u>Put with Nautsky</u> they are like a 5,000 person army, hips moving on to Jerusalem, 5,000 hips moving to defend a land-locked city. Do you have a wife? Perhaps she is your Communist?

It went on. Where were you when the President of the United States, Mr. Obama, was almost shot? Why did you go to the meeting with Mr. Salt? What did you confess? Can you defend *The Koran*? It can defend you, under the first amendment, do you defend Islam? He plead the first. They kept him. <u>Lautsky was truly an international Marxist</u>. Like the head of Syria blamed the civil war on outside protesters? Like <u>LALS</u>?

They had outside information on Butch Lautsky, that he belonged to Terrorist group LALS.

Then came Christian Nautsky. The government lawyer had it video taped. Are you now or have you ever been a Communist? Have you done your Geneology? Why did you go to Mr. Salt's place? How much do you know about the Teabaggers? Weren't you their principal? Why do you mention Jesus? Why do you say that Jesus is the revolution?

I plead the First Amendment, said Nautsky. His lawyer laughed. Donnnnn't give me the Constitution crud. What did you do for the Tea Bag party? Do you Know that they are going to put you in another jail and Divert You? Would you start a civil war? In the name of Jesus? <u>Areyou saying again Jesus Is the revolution</u>? They had a ton of witnesses to convict Nautsky. Kautsky was put on the line-up.

Why did you know to bow your head when they pepper sprayed you? To get some air? How many demonstrations have you been in? Do you even know what a principal is? Why do you keep mentioning Jesus in light of politics? Don't you know that there is a wall between church and state? Are you trying to give us that George Washington Crud? You believe in church and state combined, like Jesus is the revolution? Slouching towards Jerusalem, hips gently moving. Noon Chuck's silent friend, with him all this time, suddenly had a stroke. The FBI went on as if nothing had happened.

How do we know that you are a Communist? Don't you know we can read your e-mail? You are beyond belief? Where is your faith? Did I just breach the wall? How much do you know about Islam? Don't you know they think you are a roach? Out of the PS. Didn't you know that Osama Bin Laden was a Communist? Muslims like Jesus, are you telling us that therefore they are Communists? This was a major point that the public hadn't been told yet. That some Muslim terrorists are Marxists.

What's your belief in Jesus? Will he come again? On your side? What are the rest of us supposed to do? <u>Don't you think we know that you say Jesus is the revolution</u>? Don't you know how many years that will get you? Are you better than Jesus? Do you know how this will play internationally? Seen in light of the CCC? How many people internationally, besides the Arab spring, will buy that Jesus is the revolution? A nurse came in and took Noon Chuck's friend away, wagging his finger. Noon had converted to Christianity, when he escaped North Korea and went into Seoul. In came Lautsky. With Nautsky. Lenin said Kautsky was toast.

Would you use it with *The Koran*? Do you know about Isa, peace be upon him. Are you him? Don't you liken the scriptures to yourself? Don't you know that he, not you, are the Messiah, Jesus? According to their book? Haven't you read the book? How stupid do you think we are? We are shutting you down. What about the protesters in Russia who are religious? All across Europe? Like in Italy? Hips slowly move, as the body moves towards Jerusalem? Is there something that will be Born? Shoulders slouching towards the new Jerusalem inside you? Kautsky said, Jesus is the revolution.

<u>Nautsky left.</u> <u>He went to the cell with the North Korean.</u> A Mr. Street came to his cell. See how well we treat you? What's the matter haven't you had your dose of "State Police" the new # 1 best selling album by "The Cherry"? Why aren't you up today? Street talked to both of them. About "State Police"?

I told you about living in the United States of America, do you think you two are immune? What's the matter do you think I'm the devil? You believe in Jesus don't you? Why do you think we put you together? <u>Because you both are communists</u>. That's right you can talk that international Communist talk to each other. Be good friends. We'll get each of you testifying for the state against the other guy, don't you think?

Who's the cherry now? Do you think that it's the government? It's not what you think it is? Do you question our jurisdiction? Of course we have our power over law and order Jurisdiction. We are law and order. Didn't you see the protesters at the University of California at Davis, how they were gassed? Very PS? Someone came in and said that the man who had a stroke had died. Mere anarchy is loosed upon the streets. Karl Kautsky was Nautsky's Great Great Grand Father.

-3-

<u>Street stayed with Mr. Christian and Mr. Noon. Mr. Ox came in. So did Lautsky</u>. Along with Mr. Fast, who was an undercover agent for the FBI. He posed as a Teabagger. They got something to eat and Fast went on and on about the Tea Bag Movement. Very CCC? You are almost like the hero in *Faust*, having sold your self to the Devil? By mentioning Nautsky's claim that Jesus was the revolution? <u>These 4 terrorists were linked to International Marxism</u>? Through a special hole in the Communist bucket? Have you read Goethe?

Fast said, have you ever read Thoreau? Nobody had. Mr. Fast read them from a copy of a book of Thoreau. He told them, with the idea of trapping them, that Thoreau said that "a government that governs least is best". They had never heard of this reality. He went on about Thoreau. Who can't be understood without a type of CCC? Remember, Lautsky went into the Tea Bag party because they both use the word— Revolution. Nautsky was a speaker at the Tea Bag party meeting. Ox and Noon were there too. Want to get violent?

He said, Thoreau then said "Government is best that governs not at all". This was beyond belief. Beyond that, it did not register. The University of Chicago business and economics school through two writers, in a book named *Nudge*, was of the opinion you Should be a type of Paternalistic Libertarianism. This made everybody. It was an argument like that of Milton Freidman. Defended because he is a good friend of Capitalism. The 4 terrorists weren't linked to Libertarianism. By especially Mr. Street. But not Mr. Fast. Who explained that Thoreau was the first Libertarian. And that such was the belief of the <u>Tea Bag Party, which took Congress like a storm in 2010. But that they were somewhat disorganized and needed a leader and that such was the meaning of the 2012 Presidential election</u>. There was a Libertarian Candidate who wanted to do away with all foreign wars. And foreign aid. This is a mine field. Just, get me out of here, said Noon. But there were no people left to protest? Nautsky was the principal religious Christian Marxist? Noon was linked to him? The other 2 were Muslim.

Islam believed in Jesus, therefore, the argument went, The 2 Muslims could be linked to Christian Nautsky? Hated by Lenin?

One said that Latinos, some of them, were treated as if they weren't a citizen. This was especially true in Alabama, which was talked about on PBS last night. He said that the key to the election, among other issues, was <u>Immigration</u>. Fast said that if only the Teabaggers could organize they might get the Latino vote. Only Nautsky really knew about the Tea Bag party, he being the Southern California principal.

Fast said, in the name of the lord all mighty, if only the Teabaggers could get the under 30 vote, like those who listened to "State Police", and the over 65 vote, like Social Security, not welfare, which they generally called it, they could elect a person, a Republican, who shared their beliefs, for President of the United States. Running on a platform of equality, before Obama starts in on it? Noon smiled.

Then Mr. Fast said that the Teabaggers should suck-up to the Democrats, and be like more bipartisan instead of so libertarian like in their failure to cut the Trillion in dollars from the National Note, which was the reason people all over Europe were protesting, the cuts. In their own country. Very CCC in the PS? They protested first, because it meant a cut in pension and second, a cut in welfare. At first, they were peaceful demonstrations, then it turned into like Greece.

And nobody was left to defend the peaceful assembly. The falcon can't hear the falconer, things fall apart.

Fast said, that the Tea Bag Libertarian movement, of the Republican Party, could appeal to more people than the rednecks of the South. Then he told of his friend Frank and his brother Vincent, like in a Vincent Van Gogh, and how they wanted to enforce, like a police man, the original Intention of Con Law? The Libertarians were all over the place, radical right, for starters?

Somebody was in a Federal Court and argued for like Art. I Sec. 10 of the National Constitution which said "No state shall impair the obligation of contracts". And other contradictions. Chuck said, What's a contradiction? And Mr. Fast replied, that's what you see in "White-Collar Crime"? And hear in "Busted"? Noon and Ox and Lautsky didn't have a question. <u>Nautsky knew exactly what was being said, he intentionally infiltrated the Tea Bag party to bring them to Communism.</u> Hips arch and slouch towards the new Jerusalem of the mind, that divided city?

North Korea, Chuck's original home, didn't have an Art. I Sec. 10. In fact, they did not even have enough food to put food an the table.

Chuck heard of a hero American by the name of Dean who saved the war for the South. He stood off, with some friends, 50,000 North Koreans for just long enough until new US troops could come and save Pusan, which was the gateway to what was left of South Korea. In the PMS? An excuse? For <u>Amerika</u>?

Chuck said, starting to cry, What happened to our Dean? He was captured. And then he made history. The North Korean who was cross-examining him talked with our Dean, just like I am talking to you. After some time, the North Korean said that in slouching towards the new Bethlehem of the mind, Dean was an example of what they had in America, then give me Democracy.

That's it, said Mr. Fast, and everyone was in tears. What's going to happen to us? The North Koreans will come and get you for your espionage? <u>Why don't we sign a Treaty? That's the song I'd love?</u> How do we get the country going again? Said Chuck. They all talked about their own special beliefs and started to rap about Marx. They did this for a week. And felt they had come home. Remember, I said that this chapter is hard to read. This is because the characters try to seduce you with honey. Surely, some ideology. is at hand. The FBI had enough information on Ox, Lautsky, Noon, and Nautsky that they could throw them in jail for life. They were like babies throwing their food back at their mother, with a spoon. <u>Ox was wanted by China for espionage as was Noon wanted by North Korea</u>. LALS was like a snake, but had not yet committed any violent acts of anarchy. Nautsky, the person who betrayed the Tea Bag movement, was a self-proclaimed international communist. <u>Ox was a Chinese Muslim</u> and more of a terrorist threat to China than Tibet. The north wanted to get Noon for escaping from the country. <u>Lautsky was a Bosnian Muslim Marxist</u>. This hit all the papers.

-4-

They all got out of jail on a writ of habeas corpus. Sprung by a <u>black</u> friend. You see they put their story on national news and it made the world papers. And that black, or African American, if you will, heard the deadly news and sprung him. Only in America. I came to Nautsky's party. There is more deadly news, European nations are falling like lies. The Euro hangs in the balance. It's the Greek. They are protesting in the streets with signs and rocks.

Where was Sherry.

Hungary government bonds just became rated as junk. It doesn't look good for the Europeans. That's us. Fortunately, Spain and Italy are solid? They have new governments. Greece still has problems. All the guys went to a bar to share the good news. This looked liked the PS in CCC and the PC? That's academic spy talk on how graduate students and readers of this book and they are post-modern they do espionage? PC is Post-capitalist, like in Russia and China?

They all look like Berkeley, where I went to school. And did I ever see some riots. Dean went to Cal, Berkeley, I said going down with Noon. I heard the news too and it broke my heart. That's just what they do there. They call it—Free Speech. Noon and me and Nautsky and a little red hen went into The Crown bar. We joked. The sarcasm of the Commies was real, though nobody these days admits being a commie, just that they have read Marx. But who's left to defend them when the issue is criminal intent in criminal Marxism? <u>Attempted planned anarchy against the state? This was the FBI's case in chief. They heard "State Police" and got me to go undercover for them.</u>

Christian said, why does China hate me so much? He had a drink of Vodka. It's not China, they are some of the most "Christian" people in the world, can't you read? <u>It's the Russians that hate Nautsky. For saying that Jesus was the revolution,</u> that's just the Roman line. Cal is Pilate. So if you want to make friends with a Russian, you go to Cal? Cal Beuerbach, FBI agent.

I just made over a Billion enemies, Mr. Nautsky, because I said you are my friend. Can't we sign a treaty? Said Noon. It's always high noon between the US and the Russians? Not always but they don't like Beuerbach, said Noon. There were a lot of charges but no actual crimes. I am innocent. Attempts without action is no crime. Chinese don't like Marx. They think that he's worthless to read. That's why I like the Capitalist Chinese. To call them communist, is to misread their intention. Not innocent? Relative to Mr. Ox, who liked <u>Isa</u>?

I am. I rode a tank held a generals rank, when the fighters stank. Because you went to Cal? Heck yea. What about the Chinese? They hate the Russians. But both of them are post-capitalist, PC? That's an espionage code. Oh, and know you are a party, I said downing a shot of Vodka. CCC explains PC? They all got good and drunk, as if that were an excuse for talking about politics. And it was an excuse. How I got to the party? I was moving my hips to the new Jerusalem?

I said, for me everything is like a computer, I go to save everything. But there are some things I won't save. And no matter what I have said in the past, I won't save Nautsky. He is *The Idiot*, saying he is Jesus and turning into the idiot. This goes against all that I have recently stood for, almost. <u>Not that all Christians are idiots, but a prince who talks like Jesus is the revolution is obviously out.</u> With a voodoo economics, that is left out. I won't be crucified like Ox, a Jesus is not the Christ. If people take my Church of Pride to be that I am a type, of profane, I won't be nailed to a cross for it. This should not be taken as racist, many Latinos name their son Jesus. It's just that I don't fall for everyone that comes to my door saying he is of my faith and is Jesus. This is key and the link to the <u>4 terrorist Marxist Anarchists</u>. Dostoevsky's <u>The Idiot.</u>

The Idiot is a classic Russian novel with a great deal of wisdom. Both the Russians and the Chinese hate Nautsky. I am a good American. But I draw the line between thinking I am Jesus and knowing I am on the Pride. I am materialist, but I'll let some other person die for me. I am not a type of Pride. See CCC? <u>It's the culture of the Russians that didn't want to mix revolution with Jesus.</u>

That Russian novel is very Oriental. And the Muslims already have a Messiah the Christ, Isa, peace be unto him. Even naming a boy Isa is nothing, like a Latino naming his son Jesus, like naming a child Mohammad, which is very common. They are not supposed to think that they are the original. And they don't. <u>But the Russians are protective of the start of their country, and don't want people protesting in the name of Jesus.</u> This is party line of the KGB.

I had a friend who was named Mohammad. In mistake, I almost said to him the salute to a prophet, peace be upon you. I have never seen a more upset person in my life, almost. It's the sin of pride, known so well to one of Homer's other classic beside *The Odyssey*. He knew he was not the idiot, and he didn't want me confusing The issue. Maybe we should think this out again.

The Church of Pride, I know, takes the name of Pride and says that they will be Proud. I will let them do that. The Church of Pride has become my new ideology. If one of them accuses me of not going along with The Church of Pride, I am no moron. I accuse them of not going along with their own belief. Suddenly I am the issue? It is excluded-middle reasoning, I like Jesus, Nautsky likes Jesus therefore I am Nautsky? The Tea Bag party is smarter?

For they have a special book, that is meant just for them. In it, one of the lessons is not to have the sin of pride. If it be that I am a type of Pride, I am prepared to say I have the sin of pride. I don't know anyone in my church who has acted like a type of Pride, to me. And didn't threaten me or my family. Attempt to be Zen-like? What's the matter with that? What of Mitt Romney?

I am human. But for Nautsky to say that Jesus is the revolution, is too freaking much. I am a type of another Pride. A peaceful one who gives the "Speech" on the mount. Not the one that was crucified by the Romans. If this is a "song" to them, I hope they learn their lessons too. Talk here is legal. I deny any connection with the 4.

They say we are to be a Fool on mount Zen? Some would take issue with my Quibble? Say I am a Fool type to my people? I tell them to read their own book. I am Proud. And my faith is that there is but one Pride. And no I am not in denial. There is nothing to deny, except the <u>SiNN</u> of pride. <u>So where is my treaty with Iran?</u>

The Russian novel is right. The prince felt guilty and called himself Zen. I am neither an idiot nor a fool. I am a type of Pride? I would like to save you from the sin of pride if you think like a fool and an idiot that you are God right now. They used CCC and PS and PMS codes of espionage. My culture says that I am like Proud, it's postmodern to admit and deny these codes. We talked at the party, it was like in the Halls of Congress. What of Mitt Romney? <u>Homo</u> <u>Dei</u>?

Nautsky made my hands tremble. He liked Russia. Treaties with that nation, were the key. But the historical Russia did not like him. He was caught in a contradiction. Offend Russia, by not liking *The Idiot*, a crown jewel in the crown of Russian lit and self-critically offend China, who does not like Jesus Christ, who I just say is Proud-like with the Republican revolution, the Tea Bag party? That's a big sentence, but I know international law.

This is a stark change in my thinking. But I like things that are logical and I like Russia's *The Idiot*. I admit I am no idiot. Nautsky and *The Idiot* are both substantially Universal in their appeal. That is you can be an idiot thinking that you are Jesus but not an idiot in thinking you are a type of person who is Proud-like? Just don't be an idiot. Slouching towards the new Bethlehem of the mind, that divided city of David. I don't know how my beliefs were the issue. Perhaps too much Vodka.

And still I am not a fool. I am not an idiot. And I am not a "Proud" fanatic. Like Kautsky.

Mohammad, a friend of mine, gave me their sacred book. And he was Proud-like to me. He didn't think that he was the Mohammad. Republican revolution aside, it is tough for an American to plead to a Egypt audience. President Obama did. None of the above are idiots.

-5-

They then went to Nautsky's home, which was rightly bugged by the FBI. Christian told of his work with the Tea Bag Party, slipping in the National polls. I got this conversation from the FBI. <u>Christian told the party at his home, that he aided the radically conservative movement</u>, don't tread on me or the Teabaggers in their revolution. Which was before the Arab Spring. They were not, contrary to idiotic thinking, International Communists revolutionaries? <u>That's what they called them 150 years ago</u>. Now, it's anarchists and terrorists, in a country. Understand? <u>Iran youth in 2009?</u>

First came the national sweep in November 2010 then came the start of the revolts in Arab nations in February of 2011. This made Nautsky the Principal in the revolts. <u>That's why I left Nautsky. I did not want to be in complicity</u>. All literature aside. Christian told Lautsky that he mirrored him, which was wrong, it was the other way around. Their connectedness is seen in the closeness of their names. Some Muslims Mirror Communists.

A Christian kept on how, wrongly, he could get the Chinese vote, if he were their candidate, he would misread China.

Christian would cite Deng Xiao Ping's—Two Whatever Philosophies. <u>The Chinese are totally against the Lautsky Arch Liberation Soldiers.</u>The new President was Xi Jin Ping from China, rare and clean, is PC. They said that China, and Deng was the President at the time, would *not* buy members of the Communist Party of Russia or their key writers. Nautsky wrongly reasoned that this meant that the Chinese would buy Nautsky, which they would not, the way that Tea Bag Party members would drop their support of him like a dead fish. I can't over-Emphasize how their principal betrayed the teabaggers, like Judas against a Jesus.

Omar Isa came in. Christian was a good friend. Let me tell my story here that goes from tragedy to comedy. Christian said, Jesus is the evolution. Christian told this to The Tea Bag Party. Who's vote I have now lost. This is code of how self-criticism can help your own tragedy? Seen in the PMS in light of the CCC?

Isa said, Jesus is the Christ. Translating from the Arabic to English. It's just that nobody there had read *The Koran*. Mistakes happen. Nautsky was the principal and the key to the party and was the mistake of the Tea Bag Party. They permitted him to mix religion and state, against the Constitution. I am not Nautsky. Not unlike Moses is a type of Jesus. Just don't hurt yourself with this philosophy, soon comes lunch. What does Romney believe?

Isa found common ground with Mr. Ox. Who was an outcast from China because he was Muslim too. Like the Chinese tactic of going against Taiwan. Everybody was against Christian for being in constant revolution in all countries. Nautsky thinks he's a real Jesus Christ. Ox, was a Muslim, and was against Mainland China, like Tibet and Taiwan and student protesters. I went back to work. Like <u>The Stranger</u>.

Lautsky said he had the blues. We did not know why he was talking. They figured that it was his girl, Miss America. Everybody laughed. Lautsky had a strange sense of humor. He said that America gave him the blues. The light came out more in my room. <u>Christian said, Jesus is the revolution</u>. The light came out a little bit, although coming from a scientific background, I learned to doubt everything, this is the key to me none of these 4 terrorists really <u>did</u> anything wrong? But it was their <u>intent</u>, that bothered the FBI?

The Teabaggers were loosing ground in the National polls. The light remained constant. Isa was a CIA plant. He said, he was speechless. He did not want to be in agreement with anybody. The subtle thing was that they all had the Americana Blues. They called it plastic America. <u>They betray the Tea Bag Party</u>. Just as much as a liberal would betray a conservative. That's international politics.

Nobody knew where Christian was from but they were not rooting for him. He majored in foreign relations at college. This should have kept him out of Asia and the Arab States. He wasn't a good student. He did not really know about Transnational Ties. Which was his problem. His curse. They all were busted that's why they had the Blues. Understood mainly in light of PMS and CCC? <u>Fortunately, I was a FBI plant and just entrapped the 4 international religious Marxists. With bad praxis</u>. Christian said it again, Jesus was the evolution. Isa had no idea what this meant to him or to his Pakistani people. To a good Muslim, not Lautsky or Ox, Jesus was the Messiah. They told of this in *The Koran*, a book neither of the other Muslims could read. If you caught it, Christian changed from saying Jesus was the revolution to Jesus is the evolution? That's why I think he is so dangerous. They all stayed away from "Occupy Wall street" protests. They knew that they would be caught.

Christian gave everybody the blues, he said, Down with Americana Kitsch. Noon Laughed, he was from South Korea, where they wanted their families to unite with The North, in need of treaty attempts. Noon said, one thing I can't stand are symbols, like fire. I can't understand them. Like a new galaxy. Like The Big Bang.

<u>Down with American kitsch, said Lautsky, repeating</u>. They all got warm at the thought that he was suggesting. I hate art, I hate American art, he said. Then he made an economic and ideological and a political statement, America was <u>Kitsch</u>. He meant all the people that could not understand that he wanted a civil war in America? Yes there are international people in the United States who want a class war, and they will bring it about, by eventually uniting with protests like the Occupy Movement? Like anarchists?

- - -

It was his ideology to mirror everybody around and this meant the Tea Bag Party. Christian got worse, Down with kitsch Americana art. Isa acted like he could not understand. He knew darn well. He was saying that America was Plastic. They all pretended to act like they didn't know what Lautsky was saying. But he meant that American art was plastic. Then he said that this was like the 1960's *The Graduate*, that blamed the Berkeley riots on outside agitators. Here are your agitators. <u>Lautsky explained about his group LALS, Lautsky Arch Liberation Soldiers</u>. They all loved him? But not Isa. He was getting evidence to pin them. He said that he was the same as Al Qaeda, which America thought they had done away with? Isa knew better and finally got the proof. No breaking CCC heart? LALS was one of the most dangerous groups in the world. It was from the Lautsky clan, out of Bosnia, about 1-5,000 people world wide? When the President of Syria said the international had caused the riots, he meant groups like LALS. And they were Muslim. <u>Isa religious Marxist a contradiction?</u>

I at once knew that this was evidence of his complicity and Marx had not kidnapped his ideas. I felt just like the FBI, justifying our last album. Nautsky was from the Christian right which I denounced now, the Evolutionary Republicans. Like the old Tea Bag party but more secure, giving them a mirror The term Republican Revolution was the way someone in High School would talk, or someone who wanted to set up the Republicans, like our Christian Nautsky? It isn't.

I repudiate Nautsky, but I hate the Tea Bag party and the Republicans. Who get my vote? It's just that we are an international band. And even Spain has turned conservative, riding the wave of the planet, anybody's guess where it will end up. It's all our National Notes, and production, that downgrades countries like ours, making it hard to get credit and putting countries like Spain on a Cross. And inflation?

Lautsky, who's Jesus was on a cross? Said that they organized LALS because America did not recognize the genocide in Bosnia, against Muslims, groups like his would add to revolution internationally, even in Mexico. And they would make the US government spend time and energy on them instead of solving our problems. This is the new Al Qaeda, now that Osama Bin Laden is dead. Lautsky was an Osama Bin Laden in waiting? Still, where's the proof?

<u>We have caught international terrorists?</u> No matter what their excuse? Apparently they haven't acted yet. But the FBI knew. They had caught a conspiracy and <u>anyone that agreed with Lautsky would be part of the conspiracy.</u> He got up and said that he had to go. He left. The FBI followed him and eventually arrested him again.

It was at this point the FBI came and raided Christian's place. Here is where the reader's espionage skills will be tested. It was the radical right in Nautsky and the radical left in Lautsky who were helping each other. Nautsky had insight into The National problem, way long ago? The FBI rearrested him and put him inside a jail. Nautsky had duped the Tea Bag Party, he was their type of Judas.

The FBI needed some comic relief. They kept the group at Nautsky place and <u>cross-examined</u> them. Nobody knew anything about football, the topic, but Christian, so they knew that he was a good American, almost? We are ready to play ball with Congress, only if they know football, said agent Mr. Yick Wo.

Football?, said our Ox. He said that they were not friends of Nautsky. And he blamed Lautsky! It was the Chinese against the Arabs. That's how the FBI looked at it. The whole room was under arrest. They kept on. It's like we have just climbed The Grand Teton and only enough room to huddle, said agent Mr. Yick Wo, finally getting serious. We play ball and we don't want you to say you don't? Equal protection did Not extend to these people, there was a rational basis behind National Security. The <u>truth was that Lautsky and Nautsky were united in</u> <u>purpose, Muslim and Christian Anarchists</u>. Again, none of these people actually did anything wrong. They just were a threat to the FBI.

-6-

Yick Wo, the leader, told the group that he wanted their <u>confessions, under International Law</u>. And to FBI policy. He used CCC to get their character's intention? Not my PMS Time, which was for a Democrat evolution? They confessed to everything. All except Nautsky who asked for his Miranda rights. They took him right to jail for he was too much of a risk. He was a con man.

"State Police" is what came to mind especially the song "Confessions". You might look back at that chapter and read the repeal of The Bill of Rights. But this was National Security. The sun is going down slowly, as my hands tremble slowly. All of this is so confusing, adding in the Occupy Wall street anarchists, my head is swimming like I just saw a Supernova in a Different galaxy, swirling around and around.

Yick Wo came in with an Indian agent, Dog Yellow. He wanted their true confessions as to their agreement. The FBI was heavily armed, as my heart is heavy going over the agency's transcript and deposition. Ox claimed that he was a terrorist and that he was a *mujahedeen* against China. Yick Wo breathed easier. Not all people with foreign sounding name are alike, and not all believers in Jesus are the same, <u>not with standing Christian's con of the Tea Bag party</u>. His hips grind shut.

Christian was a novice when it came to terrorism. He had no idea. The people left were Chuck Noon and Chang Ox. They both turned states' evidence. One of them remembered Christian saying, Isa is the revolution. Yick Wo said, words like that, start civil wars. Dog Yellow, a Ute Indian, agreed. Isa had caught our Christian, it being so confused you needed an expert in logic to make the differences. And tell of the contradictions. Slouching towards the inner new Bethlehem. their hips grind to a shut.

Noon waived his Miranda rights. He said that it was rough to get to know this Christian. Ox admitted that this was especially true.

<u>Ox was wanted by China</u>. <u>Chuck Noon was wanted by North Korea</u>. America wanted them both. That's because both Noon and Ox were international Criminals. It's hard for an American to think of terrorism against China or North Korea, but we, like them, were victims. Then there was LALS.

- - -

They were being treated like Islam victims. Though they were forced to confess that they hated Isa, who was still undercover. CCC told the story of these two, not me? They had their own PM? I was wondering what was to become of the republic? Nobody would be able to follow this international espionage?

Ox taunted the agents, an unwise move. He mentioned about Kitsch Americana on TV sit-coms. They had tea and everybody woke up. To a world that only the FBI and me knew existed. Seen in light of

PS? I knew about it because of my work at the University of Chicago. Ox got with Lautsky and threatened to lead an attack against China. Lautsky nodded, yes. They got Nautsky to agree in the plan? By iphone. The guards heard them, and came in and out of revenge, said that they would never get out of jail or its hospital. Noon had agreed to the plan after the fact? Not all people who hate Kitsch are crazy.

-7-

I wonder what kind of Democracy we have left. China's old President, Deng Xiao Ping, came up with—The Two Whatever Philosophy, which stated that they won't buy Whatever was Lenin or Whatever was left of Marxism. This, not Reagan, opened up China to capitalism. Now the entire world is at Cal. On an economic icon. Like the withdrawing of troops from Iraq, we need a peace treaty with the North Koreans, with their new leader. In late 2014, a movie came out. It was The Interiew, about killing that new leader? Free speech is great. But such mistakes should be checked, treaty with Korea. Like the new pope said. As he helped get good US relations with Cuba. China admits that they are slowly getting rid of the "Two whatever philosophy". <u>And that they will be socialist by the year 2050.</u> The 4 terrorists, here, are like in Homer's The Odyssey. They are like suitors for Odysseus wife and she doesn't want to have anything to do with them. Meanwhile, Odysseus is still acting <u>the stranger</u>. With something brewing in the mind of Odysseus. This 2017. Where are the Democrat talk show Radio programs? It's like <u>1984</u>.

Chapter 20

FIRE DREAM

-1-

The next night, bipartisan, wide awake, I closed my eyes and saw a big pair of lips facing me, like at the start of the underground movie, of the underground culture of the 1970's "The Rocky Horror Picture Show". Then I saw a tall building that was moving every which way, like a picture in New York's Museum of Modern Art, and I so wanted to be modern, like Paul giving up on his PE, I gave up my pretense of my PMS? This is my Chinese self-criticism? This dream, in fact, is ill and become my nightmare.

The building went up at all angles, first right then left, it was one of the first to me modern paintings, I was in horror at calling myself with PMS, that's why Ricoeur did not call his trilogy anything, I call his work there PE which was PMS, but he could not call it that, such would be his SiNN of pride like in Homer's other book? Then sometimes I viewed this novel as even modern. Candidate Romney came out and denounced the term "revolution" and called in "evolution".

I dreamed Ricoeur wrote another last book on Death, which meant he had the Chinese self-criticism, which because of my Achilles' heel of hubris, I failed to see, Homer's *The Iliad*, where the hero pronounced his own fate as a character, like a <u>prometheus</u> giving fire from the Zens to humanity, an Achilles' heel. Now I am M. Now I reach in vain to call my novel Modern, with my self-commenting narrative, being such a relic. Please accept my book, at least as Modern.

Then my dream turned to a Mid East market, where they were selling grapes and figs, one grape fell and someone was there to catch it, and tender it, more grapes were trucked in, the reader must decide if this book is modern or something more, like our Paul Ricoeur, a 21st century Einstein of Philosophy, PMS, oriental? Pastiche.

With me it's a question if my near materialism is even Modern, not having read Einstein totally, but knowing enough that he had self-criticism of his theory, and that he believed, something that Modernists would like to claim is pure ideology, that's why I personally hang on to Paul's PE, which I named because he was too humble of a man to put a name on his work? Like he's got PMS? Ricoeur was like an Einstein because he put down his whole idea of PE, in my dreams, self-critical, as sign of PMS? It's not all propaganda.

More and more figs were trucked in with grapes were selling, as people took them home, in Adam Smith's trade, which I turned on his head, this was being recorded in my dream as an interactive movie, like some video game, nonviolent, people in the movie threw toast at the movie. As if on fire, I knew I was no Adam Smith, but then I wondered what wrong road I would send the reader on, like Smith's imports? This is my self-criticism, sign of PE? Not "false consciousness" in my dream. At Democratic wedding, people threw rice at the movie, it was quite the show, me knowing to my horror that I did not want to be a <u>spark</u> to the American new civil war. My dream kept going on and on, a rusty old train went past Stanford University, from San Francisco. To my horror the groom took a new job at Wendy's. He was a Stanford new graduate. That's what jobs were like now, new grads lucky to get a job flipping burgers? At any place the 1 in 100 job offer there is, CCC? The peoples' <u>omen</u>, they all wanted to barter goods in a square, like Adam Smith. The end of the line was in Kenya, where President Obama's lineage, not himself, came from. In the square, in my dream, they traded grapes for cheeseburgers. Like Isa Smith would have done, my CD for a dozen bananas? Zen doesn't run the economy. It's bad enough and you want to blame Zen for the mess up? How can we be like Smith, and <u>truck and barter and exchange</u>?

Then a man came up in my dream and said, Standard fire he wanted to catch a ride on the train to Libya, where there was oil, this was after the revolution, where the oil wells were damaged by the new government, due to the fighting. The man from standard oil, was upset that there was no obligation of contract for the oil. We got on the train and we went past burned out buildings. It was savage econ.

England defended us, in that they had oil of their own to the north. When Mr. Standard looked around in Libya, he saw the result of the civil war or revolution which ever your heart can take, Gaddafi having been disposed of, unlike our United States where we have <u>elections</u>. United States doesn't have revolutions, it votes. And if it were, there are state National Guard troops, loyal to the Federal government. Reality. Not even Mr. Standard could defend Gaddafi, he being when alive a war criminal. Given the revolution or civil war was 15 of the Tarot, Mr. Standard Oil tried to be careful, in his knowledge of other Arab states, which in my dream were mostly following the Teabagger's revolution and heart break of the Arab spring? It's not a gang it's a club. We backed the revolution in Libya, what a bold move at such a dangerous Nation. <u>From England's point of view Mr. Jefferson was a war criminal</u> in out heart break for the Revolutionary war. Mr. Standard, was like an internationalist in that he was siding with Canada and England on the fourth of July, which to them was a mistake, from the view of a professor at Oxford. We would quake in our boots if we saw our image from the view of Oxford. As if Americans were from Frankfurt.

In my dream, I saw a next US civil war as evidenced by the gridlock in the US Congress, reflected by the several nations in Europe, like first by The Greeks, who were an <u>omen</u>, then reflected in Italy and Spain and Portugal and England? Civil wars start over the smallest of things like taking as serious the "State Police". You thought I was right on? You just did take me seriously? Cultural "illusion".

Having heard our Republican Candidate Newt, I like him wanted to stay off a future <u>civil</u> <u>war</u> first by law and order then by a history lesson, so that we did not repeat the mistakes of the past that lead to the historical American war, I having gone to a University that was like an Oxford. Chicago tipped almost every picture of the world upside down. Republicans all aboard, have a reputation of defending, but in my dream I saw Mr. Standard going in areas of such was looking for peace, not for political reasons, but for the heart breaking issues of economics, the trading of grapes for figs in an open market place? Permitted in various US cities. Like the trading of figs for oil. That was Adam Smith.

Founding Morals, on imports.

Mr. Standard, in my dream, was in Libya to look for oil, permitted by the government. Mr. Standard was even going into alternative fuels, but this heartbraking issue is in the future, and covered up? He found an oil well that had been ruined, in the heartbreak. We sided with Standard Oil. We saw oil rigs on fire, <u>sign of terror</u>. It was the stranger. He went to work putting out the fire that the oil well had become.

It took him several months to put out all the fires. Like in the first war against Iraq which was won by the American troops. That in my dream included me, as I looked for new oil. As the CCC hires? The customs of Libya ruled what type of economics we could go into.

Mr. Republican in my dream went into Tunisia and Egypt on that Stanford train, past a revolution that ended in a vote, like the Tea Bag party and their take over of half of Congress last year? The oath war cry was the heartbreak "Drink gas so you can spit out fire", a trope, a non-literal symbol. I wondered what happened to water in the belly, the non-literal metaphor for tomorrow's world, of social birth.

This was typical American, the heartbreak, live free or die. Or don't tread on me, like a mantra of the Tea Bag party, who won the House, in 2010. You could call it like a heartbreak cry to unfreeze commerce, a big idea in the next Presidential election. No I do not know who will win.

As is typical of me, if I were a judge, I'd be like Solomon in the issue of who was the mother of a type of the baby. I know the real mother would catch me in my mistake and defend me by taking the choice baby of the heartbreak. Who will save Social Security? Baby of F.D.R. And Medicaid?

In my dream, Mr. Standard made it to Syria where some on PBS TV said that they were civil, and he made it safe to Mr. Asad? They talked about the heartbreak and found the entire Arab nations against him. Especially Turkey. Standard, wanting peace, thought of defending the war. Syria had against it all the Arab nations against the civil war. Who would Treaty with Syria? And not bomb it? Or, let it continue to kill 7,000 people in a year? How many by 2016?

There was no fire in Syria, so our Standard made it to Mosul, in Iraq. There he found the oil that he needed. In Syria they had a poor and breaking heart about the economy, Standard being an expert in world political economy. Especially war, economics and revolution. In Iraq, we left in our wake a bad civil war. Would we create one over Social Security, here? Different from city bankruptcy? Sec of State?

Standard Oil, being Transnational. They made the most of it, siding like they did in the heartbreak Mexican government, with the ethnic people who were part of the government. For it was past Thanksgiving and I was ready for a Mexican new years.

The President of the United States, Mr. Obama, was pulling the last of the troops out of the heartbreak that was Iraq. Standard Oil kept on drilling, they helping the ethnic <u>Kurd</u> tribes to extract the Mosul oil. It was torture. Which some Republican Candidates tried to defend. They were the first to drop out. Help, I heard a Kurd say.

There was a wall of purple in my dream, don't ask me symbolic of whatever, this being a modern dream. It went back and forth putting me more into a deep sleep? It made me forget about Syria, it being their own territory? There were 5,000 dead citizens and all the Arabs were against them? Who would Treaty with the contradictions? Sec of State?

I dreamed Justin wanted to go to Syria, not knowing the Politics of the area. I got the message that he got married and was living a happy life undercover, he wanting protection from any government that would give it. By this stage of Sherry's pregnancy, and my change in ethics, to a social materialist, I took the Fifth Amendment.

-2-

I kept dreaming, as if time were not of "the essence." Mr. Republican made it to Kashmir, he went there with the president of Standard Oil. Who knew the road map to where pockets of oil were? This being a war zone. There was oil in the ground? It was <u>class not religion</u> that the people were really fighting for. It was 80% Muslim. What would Mitt Romney do? Treaty? No? Bomb Iran? In this nightmare.

The Indians and the Pakistanis had been fighting over the oil fields and Mr. Standard got the President of the United States to take his mind off the US National zero, to sign a treaty with these warring nations, it being in the interests of justice to keep Standard Oil in business? By Multilateral Treaty?

Eros of birth met Mr. Republican, as the US economy was in a slump, due in part to the non-enforcement of constitutional political economics, like the constitutional contract clause of the United States of America. The clause I went to National Court for? All this time and nobody saw what I was trying to say, no matter which words I choose to express myself? What would Mitt Romney say?

Then it was all in Kashmir, there she blows? Standard Oil had struck oil and it gave half the profits to the ethnic Indians and ethnic Muslims. The Secretary of State, rooting for Standard Oil, like Chevron in Angola, where it was a war zone in that African country? I heard Justin screaming in my ear. Keep cool, Alice? Like South Sudan.

Mr. Standard was the proximate cause of finding Oil in Kashmir and of stopping the over 50 year old war? It was like a three way treaty, between the two ethnic tribes and the United States. We made sure that it wasn't like the Indian treaties which we glossed over. Still, not giving anything back. We were proud with our treaty? Was Jesus the revolution? Like the espionage of Christian Nautsky? Isis?

Homer's Penelope, meanwhile, was fighting off all suitors. It was like, drill baby drill, in Kashmir? And like Angola, it was equitable for the tribal people? Not being able to distinguish one country, the Republicans took this as a cry for war, typical of the 1880's wars between the ethnic tribes and the Americas? And we made peace? And what would Republican Candidate Mitt say? Double the army?

Next we were in a pool of blood, that was on fire, like the Sufis, dancing to ethnic tunes, but this was kind of like Kashmir, where Mr. Standard Oil kept on pumping past the blood? There were no city regulations just the economics of oil, which hired a ton of Americans? That was part of the accord or treaty. There even was a clause there about the environment. What would Mitt say? Oil in his dreams.

There was no talk of a yellow dog contract like *Lochner* over a 100 years ago you see not all treaties are all contracts, as the United States Supreme Court sometimes supposes? It was a foreign country. And they could care less about the fallacy of the excluded middle reasoning about lumping all contracts and treaties as all the same. But that's legal justice for you. I saw Commander Cody.

In my dream, we signed a treaty with the whole country of Pakistan. We were prepared to use non-uniforms so as not to offend the Pakistani people, we with a target on our back? Mr. Standard flipped the President of Pakistan the peace sign as out of necessity, we had to defend Pakistani nukes. This seemed to be lost on the Defense Department. Would it be lost on Romney to forget about a treaty with Pakistan? Down Rose.

We stomped around the oil rig, in a bog this time, in a gusher, in joy at the thought that we finally had a job? There was no EPA or a city regulation to enjoin our oil find? Economics can be a gushy business, as Standard Oil kept on pumping. Chevron was the first to show up in a day, straight from Angola, learning from anthropology. Angola was a <u>class war</u> some 20 years ago. Stone Age Economics.

Exxon, an expert in material economic anthropology, came in a week? With all the right equipment. By the end of the week they found dozen upon dozens of oil pots? Exxon had all the trucks to keep on pumping, with thousands upon thousands of Americans employed, as per the treaty? It was a brilliant treaty, the tribes split the profits, we employed Americans. And it was the environment.

Chevron did carry the oil to be bartered. But not to a foreign nation it was like a domestic oil find and the oil went directly into the United States of America? Bartered fire. Like from the belly of the beast, a foreign term to me for I prefer the Joe 6-pack term from the water of the belly, the birth of the next years. Whatever term you used, it would be misinterpreted by the locals. Mobil? Transnational.

In my dream, economics trumped the politics of the region. They got their share and we got ours. If you can imagine all the domestic jobs such a foreign find would create. Would Romney Treaty with Kashmir? The environment?

We built a tin shed, tin being the Arabic term for a chapter in *Al Koran*. The meaning is for sure clear. It puts in symbolic terms, that there should be peace between Jews and Christians and Muslims, put in such symbolic beautiful terms that it was like grandfather to father to son peace. Such is my interpretation of their holy book of "Al Tin" .

-3-

Every once in a while, the fire would leak out. I don't need to tell you how careful we need to be. But mostly it was pure oil? Transnational treaties over the environment were needed. The sun just went down. I like live for moments like that, it's my 1st Amendment Right. I'll let Candidate Mitt have his ideology?

Trucking and bartering and carrying was Standard Oil's intention. In my dream, It was not to import the gas into Europe? Rather it was to keep it for America, in my dream? Vincent showed up and opened up a coffee shop. He sold it to the Hindus and Pakistanis who worked shoulder to shoulder with the Americans? We were still in North Pakistan. Which was next to Kashmir. How many treaty terms could Candidate Mitt come up with in a multilateral Treaty? Oil meat war.

Vincent, in my dream, talked with workers of Chevron and Exxon-Mobil, they might use the Federal Constitution's obligation of contract clause? Exxon still hurting from a loss at the US Supreme Court as to that clause. Taxing being a power of government, not an impairment. Standard Oil kept up pumping oil through the rigs.

That's why this is pure eros, Vincent working away at his tin shack, selling coffee. Mr. Standard played ball with our Vincent. He woke up, at least. This was a war zone, familiar to Chevron. And they didn't make fun of the name Vincent or try to call him crazy. They could deal with people's past without bias. It's a sign and I don't like <u>omens</u>.

This kept Vincent, once like a Vincent Van Gogh, pumping out his coffee for the troops, some of which had a broken heart on hearing his name. Nobody had beer, in that it was not allowed to the Muslims by their code. He wondered about the Hindu fire, and sold them coffee in this war zone. The oil kept the tribes and clans occupied so they did not worry about the <u>class war?</u> Would Mitt give mercy? Treaty?

I explained to the Hindus and Muslims, working together, about Homer's book *The Odyssey*. And how we were in chapter 20 and how it was near the homecoming of Odysseus. To Ithaca. Strangely enough the name of my home, which I longed for in New York. For you see, I am like Odysseus. I will make it home. In this zoo.

Vincent explained in my dream, an interpretation of the Cabala, but only to the Hindus, for it was as forbidden as pork to the Muslims. Notwithstanding anything I might have said, the book that I read about the Cabala was not for the Jews in a treaty with the Muslims. I had a conversion to the Church of Pride. And the civil Democrat party, anything to be redeemed. Would Mitt give me mercy with my Treaty? Likewise the Cabala was for the Hindus, with their many idols.

Look to Shiva and Krishna. A bone of contention with the Muslims, whom we shared the oil field in this foreign land. But it was like the many Zens of Homer. It's funny how wars are started regarding one's belief in Zen. You don't really mention how many Zens there would be, if we all are Zen in embryo, with Rosa due in two months. Or one. In my dream, a born again Democrat, who I understood, showed up and started to talk about the end. And how would it relate to Israel. A Sufi Muslim said that the Christian should keep his mouth shut in that someone might take him for *Tommy*, of The Who. I am not Tommy and I am not your sailor. Who will try to be a believer in Islam, to seal a Treaty? We should use diplomatic non-indexicality.

I thought of the many Zens of Homer. And Paul the Apostle in his talking to the Greeks. They even had space for the unknown Zen. Paul was not impressed. That's what the man from Israel felt about the born again Democrat. It was all like Greek to me. I like believed in the unknown Zen, my Sherry. It's "interpretation of texts".

Neither the Israeli nor the Muslim wanted to talk to the born again Democrat. I figured that they could agree to disagree about the end and that peace in the Middle-east was more important. I can't go on about this topic in that it is So sensitive a topic. Limping towards Jerusalem, something great will be reborn. That's what I used to call it, so dangerous as not to be able to put a name on it? Social birth.

The Shiites, however, talked to the born again Democrat about the end times and the 5th Imam, as some have called him. But civil wars, like in Kashmir like where my dream is, have been fought over such things. There I name it like a bunch of cats fighting as a dog barks, it, they are sliding towards Jerusalem, waiting to be born. Born out of psychoanalysis.

Sunnis can't stand the idea generally in the Arab nations. And from my understanding of anthropology, the study of ethnic peoples, there is only a type of understanding of a type of Jesus that could make the heavens part like it did for Mohammad, over 1500 years ago. And now they are not happy for a type of *Tommy* to come again. What words can we use in a treaty? A Sunni doesn't believe in living prophets, unlike in Iran. Would Mitt try a multilateral treaty on that one?

I am a writer of poetry, not a seer. But I believe in two things. The Church of Pride view of types and the belief in treaties. So we have two or many beliefs. Let the world see and then let there be peace, even in Jerusalem. A treaty though we can't find the words to make the terms of the treaty. With the EPA, in 2017. And beyond.

-4-

Giving birth all day long as a birth mother, creates new worlds to open up, it does not carry a gun, the male metaphorical trope, the non-literal symbol, this thing for that thing. Fire is what the 2nd coming gets. I awoke and I could not get out from my mind the outrageous

<u>LALS</u>, who come as a type of Judas. They had, it was said, Napalm and were ready to use it if the troops come. There go those dogs and cats again outside my window. That's the fire that the FBI arrests. But what if it were like Palestinian? Would a future Mitt Treaty with that? For peace in the middle-east? What about the two nation state and the Camp David Accord. Did we all of a sudden drop out a term? Could we add in Iran? Who will talk to its prophets? Because they are Shiites? The dogs and cats stopped making so much noise. Laustsky is like Kautsky, I dreamed.

LALS needs to be policed by national security, which in turn needs to be adapted to the Israel. And to the two nation state, breached by security. I went to sleep, and I saw a nation of fear. It's by treaty with states like Syria and Palestine that we can give birth to a type of new world.

I saw East Jerusalem, and the fear of the Israelis in confronting the Dome of The Rock. The holy site of Muslims. Closed down out of fear of arm and the possession of property. Give it up for peace. That is the message of Zen. Who wants the Muslims to move into The East Section, of Jerusalem? And there are those Palestinians who were displaced for the last half of a century?

A few brave Israelis connected to their Zen Elohim went up to the Dome and talked about the one Zen Allah, the compassionate and the merciful. 2,500 year too late for the obscure reading of the Cabala, that Family was Jehovah. Like the ancient Greeks and their many Fates. I am not even a shadow for Homer. That's the one Zen I give it up for. Where will our Mitt play ball here?

The Sufis and the Shiites have common ground in that they believe in the one Zen too. Elohim is the key for the Israelis. They can disagree about the name, like Paul to the Greeks, had the tribute to the unknown Zen. I think Israelis think a 2nd Coming is like LALS to them. There is a reason for their National Security and their fear of war talks. It is a horror. One that I share a common cause with Pres Obama.

Sunnis won't hear a profit. Treaties of commerce and trade fit in with *The Koran*. The Chinese are in fear of the terror of Islam and westerner. Prophets like in Iran, need to make peace. This is solving the paradox of the Middle-East. Drop your arms. By treaty. All of Asia follows what might go down in Jerusalem. Can you follow my espionage? Is it just espionage? Is it positive? Justice Holmes?

People give birth to each other and to their freedom from slavery to property, the territory that they believe their one true Zen gave them? What about the Palestine people? We can give back meaningful property to such displaced people? We can give Palestinians work in the Israel co-op that they are so good at? Mitt?

Nautsky, that type of Judas, is hated by the Russians. That's the fear of the Orientals that Jesus will "come back" and start a revolution. The Sufi in Iraq, disarmed by the US, is left talking in Arabic. The Sunnis did not like it. For them, there is no prophet besides Mohammad, peace be upon him. Who would follow a Sufi? To East Africa?

The 5th Imam, according to some experts, is to be the new Prophet, like in Iran. This scares the US. The Sunnis are asked if they believe in the Arabic *ayat*, or sign from now, as is so common in Islam. Spoken of many times in their holy book. Yet, the Shiite Imam gets inspiration all the time? When is a prophet not recognized in his own home?

I dreamed on of colors and rainbows. Jerusalem has never claimed to be a city of perfection, as its founding King David, recognized by Jew and Christian and Muslim, made a mistake as to his wife. Some say that he is not forgiven, but I do believe that. What was it he wrote, Lord my Zen why have you forsaken me? A familiar phrase to westerners, the last words spoken by the believed in Jesus Christ. I ask Mitt Romney what does that mean to him?

Jesus is not LALS, but according to Muslim tradition he is Jesus, the Messiah. Jews aren't so positive. And with good reason. The Muslim Isa, translated as Jesus, was never crucified. Something is lost in translation. And the Jews feel the same as per the 2nd Coming of Jesus, allegedly to bring horror and terror to the earth? That's the line up's view.

Pension social security? That's a lot of votes for the Democrats. President Obama, in my dream, is by no means yet voted out of office. The fire Mosque is the key. They believe in Jew and Christian and Muslim, it's in their *Noble Koran*. Despite practice.

Moses is a type of Zen as are the people on government Social Security. I would not want to be the Presidential Candidate of the Republicans who was against that. Lorenzo Shaw starts to talk of bipartisanism. Hindus are not in the equation in Jerusalem. It's the cube that they would give a Peace prize to the President who attempted to make right the Treaty Postmodern philosophy, unlike postmodernism which is said to have died, is Ricoeur and others, who have taken to task the hermeneutics and ideology of Heidegger.

- - -

Like with South Sudan and the Neur and The Dinka tribes, fighting over oil.

More fire filled the Mosque, a target of civil war. Predicted by Presidential Candidate Newt for the US. What if the Saudi's Sunnis made a treaty, in their book, with Shiite Iran? Its not beyond the area of hope. The reading Muslim grasps this very Muslim notion of a treaty. My mind went back in this dream, the galaxy swimming in my head. What would Mitt say? The Treaty of Bader?

Speaking of treaties, the US could form a treaty with the right information. Like the attempt to talk with our historic enemy of choice and our ignorance of Islam. This fire dream went on and on and on.

Stopped by the fact that I just woke up. I awoke all sweating from the <u>terror of the dream I had been dreaming. You can awake too. Treaty.</u>

-5-

The Gaza strip could treaty with Syria. When will the Israelis give up the property in the Golan area? Like a Mexican Christmas. The Sufis danced in Jerusalem, that city of contradictions. I wish that I could relay my vision, but nobody likes the messenger of good news. Especially the Jews. Someone's Coming is another person's nightmare.

The contradictions of David, the star of David being the Israeli icon, could mark a starting point, given all 3 major religions of the area believed in him. A fire haze overtook my dream, stopping all talks. All they need is a 50 ethnic and national treaty, recognized and enforced. David that tainted name, and they had to name the city after him. Will you treat the city of David the way his name is sometimes treated? Mitt? Camp David, how many years ago was it, could be a start with each of the 50 sides reading the other sides books. Democrats write it down, it's your candidates' Nobel Peace prize. Better than a prediction of downing Jerusalem in fire and brimstone. No you don't have a preemptive strike on Iran over some Nuclear fuel, as one RepublicanCandidate said he'd do. Know the alleged enemy.

Don't get me wrong. I wrote a play called *Reality*. Now, I am a realist. But with the future of Islam and Christianity and Jew in the balance we should make an attempt. It is all centered in on Jerusalem, that territory that nobody is willing to give up, in my dream. Which turned all green and white? All in my dream, thank goodness it's a dream.

Multiple treaties using the sacred books of the above, with a little give and take, could be helped by the United Nations, if we could keep from walking out of speeches we don't agree with, I was in a dream? It's better than ending up like Vincent. In search of a valid obligation of contract. Impossible? There is a way to dream this so we are not mad. Some way, I plea don't be mad, okay?

Amos goes on still about civil rights. Not unlike the present President of the United States of America. Oh you of little memory. Republicans I have told you about how your business contracts are a civil right? It's trade and commerce at the Israel commune that brings jobs.

-6-

I dreamed, when my father and I finally got down and talked about racism against blacks in this world. He reminded me of events in my early life memories where I was discriminated because of the effects of slavery.

He reminded of my early life in Selma. It was Martin Luther King Jr. Day and we were walking on the Selma bridge to the west of the city. My father reminded me that some white boys were driving past us, and one of them yelled, Hey young Nigger. It was right after that, that we moved to Los Angeles. In Alabama, we were the only members of the Church of Pride. Like the Greeks with their Zeus and the rest of the Olympus Gods, of the country of old.

At times, I felt like <u>the</u> <u>stranger</u>.

We moved to West Los Angeles, near UCLA, where my father got a residency in psychiatry. He later drove to the Sepulveda Veterans Administration Hospital. To work.

As I was growing up we went to a park. Where I took a knife to work on wood. There was a police officer who saw me and stopped. I was relatively young. He came over and said, what was a colored boy playing with a knife. The incident ended and he did not give me a criminal record. It was because I was with my father. Later, I was busted once and that's why I am so submissive. Really. Especially with Article I Contracts. I wanted to look "Capitalist".

Later we drove to Compton, where my cousin moved to. I remember all the police cars. I remembered how one police man stopped a young black man and frisked him, near my cousin's house. He told me that they do that all the time. My cousin wasn't a gang member, but they stopped him all the time. There was no probable cause or charges, just a stop and frisk, to let the blacks in Compton know that the police ruled the streets. Later he was arrested, without charges, and taken to the police station. They hold him for as long as they could. He wasn't given his Bill of rights. It was then that I became interested in US constitutional law.

Vincent lived with us in the West Los Angeles. He was my only brother. I had no sisters. He once took a bus into downtown Los Angeles. Where there were a lot of latinos. The latinos didn't like the blacks. And he found that the local whites played "Got ya" with both races.

It's very scary. In my dreams.

That's why I have suppressed my memories. At Berkeley they treated me like every other student Before I transferred there, I majored in Constitutional studies. Then, I at Cal wanted the down low of African American major. I was raised, with Vincent, like a white boy. So I was taught what it was like in Africa, like Zambia the country of my mother. She was a Ndembu. She came into the country of the U.S, and settled in Ithaca, New York where she met my father who was getting a M.D degree, at Cornell.

Back at my high school years, I went to University High School. Somewhat near the UCLA area. Eros was my thing. There were a lot of Hollywood stars children who went there. I first had a reefer there. The police were all around. It made me feel like "Basketball Jones". I took a class on police science, there, and our text was the California Police Code. I had a friend who was black and he had a run-in with the law over marijuana. There were other white students there, but the police busted him. He was not given his <u>Miranda</u> <u>rights</u>. And he threw away the roach before the police came to him. He kept his mouth shut. The police did not like this, so he was charged with—intoxication in public. The problem was a proof. The police had no physical evidence.

Just what they had witnessed. And he wasn't that stoned. They took him down and booked him at the local police station. He stayed the night there. The next morning the judge let him go. This was not in Compton.

But that was close enough. Since that time, I swore not to get in any situation like that. He was my best friend. In Compton, they would have got a group of police and they all would swear to the same facts. It would have given someone like that 30 days in Jail. I was aware of how the streets worked. And the united front of the police. I got busted, later, at a civil rights protest.

When I saw the police, from then I went to Chicago, I always was afraid of getting arrested and getting framed.

By the time I hit Cal, I was weary of "street people", the homeless who gathered in on student petitions in Sproul plaza. The crowd could be easily framed, the mentality of those who used their <u>Free</u> <u>Speech</u>.

Looking back on it, it was this dream that was a sign or an Omen, like in <u>The Odyssey</u>. I decided that I could no longer be on a wall politically. I would become an Independent. Mitt had become the Republican Candidate for president. And I just did not agree. But I did agree with the president of the USA.

I wanted my wife, who was a Republican, to unite with me, an Independent, and give birth to the future of the Democrats, Rosa, the future. This would be a coming together of ideologues and towards "The Center." A token of this was Art I Contracts, controlled by the Federal Congress. It was all I could conceive.

So I made the theme of <u>Water In The Belly</u>. The above dreams were more in line with my personality as an African American. Protecting the Bill of Rights. I could think of Vincent as a slave, without me becoming a member of his party. I would remain for the rest of my time as—The Other. I made my money with rock and roll and I wasn't going to give up my memory, not to mention my <u>blackness</u>. Even Reich's ironic, monumental <u>Saving Capitalism</u>.

I responded to my father, that it was not only race but <u>class</u>. We were raised middle class. In my dream my father was my master, as if I were in slavery. And he treated all his clients as slaves, as is mentioned in this book.

On class, its postcolonial and post-imperialist, like in Viet Nam. And once you have reached international imperialism, you have found <u>late</u> capitalism. We as an <u>elite</u> were destroying capitalism, which is exactly my point in this anti-novel. I kept petitioning my father, the psychiatrist. And, His siding with Nixon, during the late 1960's, was aiding and abetting the demise of Capitalism.

This is CCC. A cultural, or political economic, analysis of America in the world. Dominating and degrading the native peoples of the world, not caring about the health of our nation, as a cultural whole, by trying to force democracy down the throats of Nations around the world. That's postcolonialist criticism.

In my dream, I was on the living room sofa, on an all-white sofa, with my father sitting on a chair, smoking a pipe like Freud. Bu in my dream, I was talking back to the cultural machine. This was PM. PM critique and cultural criticism, like a token of <u>the</u> <u>Limits</u> <u>of</u> <u>Critique</u>.

I was on the chopping block, tied to the whipping-post to my father's psychoanalysis.

I told him of my contradictions. An MBA and a punk band writer. The words of my songs were like those of Maya's <u>I know why the caged Bird</u> <u>sings</u>. My Sherry was like my father's pipe, absent racism. It was the class of my father, that kept the African American, any American, in the chains of slavery.

Psychiatry in the early 1950's, said it was a psychosis to be LGBT. Today they still cage them, just in different chains. The chains of the color of custom. The lesbians are chained, as I wrote. And in solidarity with them all, I told my father that I was glad for the 2017 Grammy awards mix-up, confusing <u>La</u> <u>La</u> <u>Land</u> for the real best picture of the year, dealing with class, gender and race-<u>moonlight</u>.

My father's jazz was caught up in a type of tropical, <u>LA</u> <u>LA</u> <u>Land</u> when he should have been taking the case of me and Justin. Who knows?

<u>Moonlight</u>, like an underdog, came shining through. They were all slaves to the customs of the world. But America should, honestly, have known better. It's difficult to write good black realism like that. Now, I told my father, smoking his pipe like Freud, that he should turn his psychoanalysis onto western Civilization.

At that my father got up, in my fire dream, and walked on the zebra-hide rug we had in the Hall way. And he went over to his bookshelf and got a copy of Freud's <u>Civilization</u> <u>and</u> <u>its</u> <u>Discontents</u> and started to read it for himself. It was CCC.

I had finally contacted my father with his anti-animal, totem-loving heart. He worked with the government so he wouldn't hear any black from an African American. But he heard me. This time he did, in my dream. He heard me and my California major in anthropology of the African American, a token of all resistance.

It was then and there that I got back in touch with the "American", in me. I realized how I was like the mask of a white man. Trying to please all the "master" in the country.

I decided, then, that I should keep a journal and write down all I could of my experiences. And I had a good memory, too. It was then that I wrote the first draft of <u>Water In the Belly</u>. How people can be given a new "Social birth", through many ways. I then used that trope, and took a tropical metaphor, of psychoanalysis as like real birth, that I remembered in a play I had seen during my time at Cal, it was a play by Saul Bellow. Like one of Bellow's book's, Chicago's <u>The Author Withhis foot In His Mouth</u>. I woke up.

It was difficult to maintain my distance from <u>The Odyssey</u>, for me like a journey down a whole other world. And I went to read as many book's as I could find of Ishmael Reed. <u>Mumbo Jumbo</u> was my favorite from this U.C. Berkeley prof.

Odysseus is still undercover, but soon there will be terror. It's crazy, demented, mythic. Like the coming home of Odysseus. Why did he have to be <u>The Stranger</u>? Why didn't he warn the Suitors? Why not make pacts of peace? Before the killing? How <u>wasn't</u> this like the 400,000 dead in Syria? In the last 6 years?

Paul Ricoeur, in his translated version <u>Oneself as Another</u>, argued in his postmodern philosophy that the self, in the world is an-"other". So Odysseus coming home as if he were a stranger, grabbed the modern essence of one's self as alienated. As if we all were immigrants or refugees, with our Being in the world. <u>The Stranger</u>.

Mr. Kautsky was the founder of the 1917 German Social Democrat Party. His theories of economics for socialism did not exist. Now, Socialist governments rely of the economics of capitalism, as Russia and China showed.

VANS
Ventura
CVS pharmacy

Chapter 21

INDEPENDENT PARTY

-1-

Democrats were for regulations, not for homeless anarchy. The Democratic Party tried to separate themselves from the street anarchy, that followed, The Poor so-called intention to have Constitutional peaceful assembly and redress of complaints against The Government? Most of the world is not Communist, a fish from the 1950's. No matter they were, the opposite of the "Song of Songs" and I didn't need communion. I changed back to the Independent Party.

Republicans, in 2009, went mad too. There were the so-called Birthers, who had the complaint that President Obama was not born in the US. Obama produced a birth marker from Hawaii I think. And the Birthers for a good year kept claiming he was not born in the United States. In the end, I think it hurt their cause to be so irrational, eventually they dropped the issue?

Now it's time for my commitment. I am a fiscal and material liberal. I back the status quo. Thus I am for Constitutional law and contracts. And a trillion drop in the national cure. I am now for President Obama. Though on my own terms. Like I could see me being Police Chief of my home town, Ithaca.

If that's confusing, you don't know me. I am also a scientist and did work in law and see the need for doubt when it comes time for proof. Call me an Independent for I am for the status quo. I am right too. <u>The Republicans would sell out the poor and the old</u>. I am simply and absolutely with and for the 1st amendment and would love to police their protests. I am bipartisan. They do it on the backs of the poor.

Constitutional contracts must bow to safety and health regulations I mention just two because I am no expert and can't think of any other stipulations I would put on such contracts. Of especial importance is fiscal democracy in that we must bring down the fever of the national eros, so we don't go down like so many countries of the Euro. Like France, who was downgraded last week, to the level of the United States. Will it happen to us again, like so many other countries in Europe?

I might contradict my self, for it is a big wish list. I am for entitlements. Let the rich feel the weight of the tax code, which could in a bipartisan way go back to the 1981 Tax Code, the Bush tax cuts would end and they would go back to higher tax brackets and an estate tax. It would go back to a Republican tax code era. This would bring in revenue and it would be a higher capital gains tax like for the Republican Romney. Tax credits for hiring.

Personally, I make millions and wouldn't mind paying my fair share of the tax load. I just want the national eros to drop by 1 trillion or so. I am also a realist. I want the balance of power in Washington, and it looks like the Republicans will take the Senate. I couldn't stand a Republican president that would rubber stamp cuts to the poor and the old. Bipartisan politics says take it from the rich. The corporate tax level would be 1981. But The House is ill. Somebody is giving birth to a 7 pound giant Turning and turning towards Jerusalem, of the here. It is not bipartisan, in 2017.

Republicans, in 2009, made a move to the right uniting with the teabaggers in their revolution. If one candidate that is a Republican is right we are looking at a civil war. The Tea Bag party with their cuts to the poor and the old would only add fuel to that class war. I can't help it if Nautsky was a type of Judas to their party. They followed him. In violation of the separation of church and state. And I am no George Washington. Why couldn't post-2017 be the Democrat's turn.

As for my own water, Sherry is at term and is about to give birth to a girl. We hope to be in Ithaca when the event happens. It is the birth of the future? I can Bellow and say that the birth of my girl will be the political birth of my beliefs. It is December 1, 2011. By new years we should have a new baby girl. This is so symbolic to me, the metaphor of a new life and civil redemption, Water in the Belly.

Democrat birth?

As of now, Congress has failed to bring down the national Note. It was their baby. And they failed. Their motive was to see their man elected president. I am a poor politician, but bipartisan politics on both sides would have solved the problem. If you are a Democrat forgive me. I had to be redeemed in my own way of the pilgrims' progress start of this novel. Or, I wouldn't be having you read about the birth of my baby. Contrary forces.

As to pilgrims' progress I have got married, found pride and distanced myself from the free protests that we did not know would get ugly due to anarchy. I call this change, along with constitutional contracts and lowering the national Note, becoming a status quo liberal. I call this civil redemption because it is like a feeling of religion but it is totally political. The feeling behind the trope of Zen is my redemption as a liberal Independent.

The one thing that distinguishes me, Independent, is that I don't think Zen regulates the economy. The Adam Smith notion that there is a Marshall self-regulating Republican and Conservatism Economy with Darwinian Capitalism, is false. This has been proved by many economists and I don't think Zen caused the 2008 stock market crash or the present real property failure. It's difficult thing to imagine a Zen like that. George W. Bush wll not be remembered as a great President. Not only was he like Nixon, in 2003, his tax cuts started the increase in the Federal debt. See generally, Reich <u>The</u> <u>system</u>: <u>Who</u> <u>Rigged</u> <u>it</u>, <u>How</u> <u>We</u> <u>Fix</u> <u>it</u>. Unions.

As of now, I have offended just about everyone, but I am not running for President and I shall work for what I think is good for the US. With a lowering of the Note, there could be a class war. I saw the start of the ugly thing with the Birthers and European political economics. And, of course, the anarchy of Oakland, and the burning of the US flag? I am not dreaming and this is no joke. And I am here like a cop. <u>Lowering the debt could cause a class war.</u>

10th Amendment claims of the Republicans are the direction of the future and it breaks my heart? I learned in moot Court the weakness of pleading State Constitutions and have learned from my mistakes of law? Mistakes of fact could result by the failure of the giant United States Supreme Court case on health, in June 2012. What about after 2017? Teabaggers with their revolutionary intent could cause a class war in America against the poor and the old. But you don't predict. England, as of this writing, has done a strike of 2,000,0000 people over the issue. Not to mention other Europeans. The Euro was nearly cut in half due to the national Note problems? It's winter so the protests have cooled down a bit? The answer isn't what I hear, it's a Republic, working.

Privatizing Social Security would be terrible and failed in Chile. Imagine people investing in the 2007 stock market, all those people would have lost their Social Security. President Obama raised the stock market from around 6,000 to its present rise out of the grass roots to 12,000. What scares me is that I am a fiscal materialist, and he wants to raise the National Note level, the issue that has lowered the worth of European countries. All I care about, now, is our economy.

If some political party could tell their true feelings about the poor and the old, it could incite a riot. Bringing to pass what happened to the Greeks. With my home in Ithaca. This happened before in London and in Spain and in Portugal. We are waiting on reason from Ireland. They don't protest they are good Catholics? The rest I don't know about for sure? They are in a Democracy? And the Democrats?

-2-

Sherry was a Republican I am Independent, the baby will be Democrat. Of contrast, the Teabaggers want libertarian paternalism. This is the belief that mine is mine, and yours is yours and let the government keep out of it. Ironically it is also the maintaining of troops in foreign wars, contradicting original libertarianism. I am not running for anything and I have no platform. I just am telling you about my politics and its changes. Like the birth of a small child, not a monster, to be born, without a heart?

This recent type of libertarianism is the type that could cause domestic class wars at home? Because of the forgetting of the poor and the old, with their Social Security. The beliefs that have been enforced since right after President Kennedy and the Great Depression. Every true American wants liberty. But practically it is not a party that will reverse President Obama's 50% approval, to take the White House?

Pluralism is like bipartisanism or like using the will of all—We the People. Rainy Isa, Audrey Isa, Harold Isa, Jefferson Isa, Washington Isa, Jackson Isa, Grant Isa, Wilson Isa, Truman Isa, Ike Isa, Johnson Isa. A common name like naming someone Mohammad. It is part of *The Noble Koran* that Jesus is the Chapter 3 verse 45. Independent.

- - -

Republicans want to take the next election and their answer is a paternalistic, no, to Pluralism. President Obama wants jobs, and private independent contractors building schools. Birth. I can't again say who will win the election, but if the wrong party wins it will mean a class war from the right to the poor and the old. I am no fraud, but I can see that. Help me draw this portrait. It's all changing so fast.

Knuckles on top of my head again like in pro Basketball, in the trade cycle if we make the wrong economic decisions, we could go back to the Great Depression. If we don't embrace pluralism. And stop Washington politics as usual, a bickering over points to get your candidate elected in the next election. That's the need of a bipartisan material political economics. Because I cannot predict the future.

Treaties with Islam and its evolution by turns and twists like the start of Homer, are the way to get a President the Nobel Peace Prize. Let's play our big games of the Pac—12 and play ball. The Euro was held hostage to the Greek vote, which never came to pass and the rest of the Euro states are right on with their dealing with their banks. We need a bipartisan President, who is not afraid to treaty with Islam, like Obama did with Iraq. Know the enemy. The Frankfurt school, lile Adorno, helps in who we will be making a treaty with. Or, We can't stick our head in the sand, and pretend that we can't see the world. Don't print money. graded as junk, because of the national cure. It was like Oakland and the California budget dealt with by the Gov. Jerry Brown. Facing domestic strife because of Government debt. There were gassed protesters as UC Davis and Mass eviction of Oakland's striking protesters. Europe is a good mirror for the fiscal fate of California and the USA? What I care about is who will pay to feed the baby to be born? Slouching towards the Bethlehem of the mind. The House failed by trillions. Not Obama. Elect Democrats to Congress.

It can't happen here, the mantra of the right, was disproved by the above linking of European failure of cure and Depression-like restraints on protesters in California, a Mantra that was proven false? This is my entire point of the possibility of a <u>class</u> <u>war</u>, over the old and the poor. Like The Greeks. You go give birth to this baby. Proven Science.

In Oakland, prior to the above, the Mayor called off the police, which tear-gassed the movement the week prior to that. Fire and Time and Birth. These movements pass and fail but they are nothing to a Federal arrest of the old and the poor, one can imagine the nation-wide and the world-wide response and the reply of the Stock Market to the strife? This nightmare, is not a poem. It's difficult to read, because it's the irony of history. Tropes of history, this book.

I am against that strife. I learned with the anarchists and the homeless that hung on to the Occupy Oakland movement? But what of National eros Pressures and subsequent arrests of the old, petitioning the government about their Social Security? There are 50 Million on Social Security. And they aren't all singing patriotic songs? What is to be born, if the right ones were sung? Where is Pres. Obama? Unlike "state police"?

It's like the vision of Scrooge? It's an example of one possible future? Of like death? The death of a peaceful assembly and the 1st Amendment, which can and usually does end ugly, time after time, as were the fall endings of the Nation-wide Occupy Wall Street movement? They did not know law and order and how to obey the police? In light of outside agitators? Slouching towards Jerusalem, a baby will be born. I was jailed for my civil rights protest.

-3-

Independent contractors such as building trades and trucking contractors, as well as state and Federal OSHA regulations should view health and safety as a bar to State and Federal Constitutional Obligation of Contract claims. FDR Christ, Washington Christ, Jefferson Christ, Ike Christ

- - -

"State Police", my true intent in light of the Occupy Movement, was a world-wide hit, the realism and the <u>sarcasm</u> hit every facet of the diamond's light? Our baby will be born, I plead, to a world of law and order, not class warfare, where brother is against brother, parent is against child? As is one candidate's vision. On the right. Am I an Ahab? Like Melville.

I am on the left. I'm dead on in the center, I am a material Independent. And a fiscal Independent for the lowering of the National Note, and the taxing of the rich, like myself to pay for it. It's just I am not for the class warfare that would result if it came on the backs of the old and the poor. Give birth to America, who wants the baby?

The "White-Collar Crime" album was right, I just did see the 99% movement, it would start or the homeless and the anarchists, what would happen if there were taxations of the poor and the old, in a takeover of Constitutional protests, or excess as in UC Davis, where they pepper-gassed the protesters right in the face, at 6 inches?

Portugal, with their strong unions, had a strike over cuts to worker pay. Portugal Pleaded its bonds were worthless. Europe agreed. The world Stock Markets dropped. "State Police" was the aftermath. It was like an America where the 1% rich directed the police state, to stop a right-wing provoked <u>civil</u> <u>war</u>? They are voting in California, in cities like San Jose, to lower city worker pensions by half? It did.

This is not my baby, my yet to be born little girl. I hope the class war I have already talked about doesn't happen. But like with the Occupy Movement it spreads to Europe, like it did to France, and The Greeks, not Homer's Greeks, but today's Greeks, spread their strikes all over the world, a small place when it comes to protests and Stock Market responses? What if Europe spreads back to the US? I am not giving birth to the joker. Are we giving birth to America? Are we a Republican Ahab? Are the Democrats, the fools? or, Ahab. Catcher in the rye.

The French protested the G-20 meeting of the world's top 20 nations. At Cannes, France. There being the new Portugal we saw them protesting too. It made our "State Police" album relevant and World War II Italy. That album was meaningful to most protests, needing law and order and not the anarchy of The Greeks. <u>Catch-22.</u>

I say anarchy of the Greeks because their fire bombs, like London and Oakland, In the United States, were the response of a few anarchists to the natural plea of the Greek Police for law and order when their protests were in deed out of order, so these type of anarchy protests spread all over the world? This is starting up again in Europe and US now that the winter is getting over? They will probably keep it up? We can't reverse it, that's why I became a poet? I am not for fascism either. Neither is Bipartisan Democrat Gov. Brown either. I haven't given up on California. And what will be born? Not cultural kitsch.

"State Police" was meaningful for many protests, where there were confrontations between protesters and the police, justified by National Security, the doing away with the bill of rights? I have already made my point, for now, as to which party could cause this near civil war? And it would spread to the world and the planet's Stock Markets? Being a fiscal material Democrat is the way out? And don't shoot at protesters. My wife had become the party I hated, to be ready for when they take over all 3 branches of Government?

But let me continue, it was the ironic plea for Democracy by The Greek President that started the World Stock Markets dropping. His not accepting the 50% bail-out of Greek National Note, seemed mad? The irony was that Greece, after Homer, was the birth-mother of Western Civilization's Democracy? Who can critique that?

This paternalism in the name of the Republic was the cause of world economic loss? This is the 1950's belief that father knows best, the name of a well-known sit-com? But it was this Paternalistic Libertarianism that was the ironic cause of near anarchy? What will the next Presidential election bring? In the United States of America? In any year?

The Greek President, not of Homer, had a wrong reading of History.

The way that the President of Italy, for different reasons, in World War II was on the wrong side of History. Stability of the Euro, in the former situation, was more important than a blind Following of history. In Hungary, they turned to the radical right, too fiscally blind? At the expense of what? Why hasn't world poetry been born in you yet?

The Greek situation is chilling. For a blind looking for a vote, because of the past, of a Democracy, destabilized World Stock Markets for a moment in time. What would our ironic blindness do? Except in the Greek case the vote idea was taken back in a day? What would years of blindness do at a key moment of time?

California is a good cauldron for the world. And the Occupy Oakland movement is a good lesson for the world. Now California buckles at its 3 billion dollar debt crisis and the students are radicalized the way Europe is with Greece, Italy, Spain, Portugal, England and Ireland? As the middle classes are taking it in the end in higher than 34% property losses. What will be born in 2020 as we go towards birth? Inserted the key and aiming straight and true, Shot back the Bolts. As Mr. Knox united the Odyssey by Homer with <u>Ulysses</u> by James Joyce.

-4-

The fall of France's Wall street movement was a multinational fall. An international portent of the doom of United States' Occupy Movement. Except as I recall there was no anarchy in the streets of Paris? They had learned from 1968. The lessons of what protests can turn into. And France is an European giant. And it fell to the level of the US. Are we crawling, looking at our selves, go to Bethlehem? The sarcastic parody is not madness, it's the world nightmare.

Something is fishy here. The answer I believe is in our California, where the Occupy Movements have faded like the streets in Russia, Where organizers were given 15 days. The State's gridlocked over its billion dollar deficit. How are they doing it to keep from radicalizing the laid-off city workers and state teachers? I don't know. And international organizers of the left are waiting off stage?

Of course they are. My hands tremble at how long a history Gov. Brown has with the state. And he was a Mayor of Oakland. He must know something. And he is by no means done with his work. Banks have historically needed money to fend off a Depression or a fascist, like Hungary. Romney would not bail out GM out of the recession. But the students in France wanted the money for themselves? And France fell. As if they were poor. The future of Europe and United States and World hangs in the balance. And then there is Social Security, pensions. We know what happened to the Greeks. And France and Germany have just dictated terms of the Euro, whether there would be 27 nations or 17 nations. Regulations of Banks in 1999 caused the 2008 stockmarket crash, which caused all markets around the world of the west to crash. Frankfurt is the German Wall Street. Can't we talk with these people. With crazy immigration. Green Industry.

Where is the United States? Like California? What are the differences? What of the upcoming election? Would we dictate terms like the Northern European nations did to the Southern nations? What is the difference between Europe and the United States? Aren't these the questions that the next President will need to solve? What about a bipartisan Treaty policy with all our enemies of the world? After 2020. Police states were something that the rest of the people of the world could relate to and the youth even got the sarcasm of our #1 world-wide hit "State Police". The middle-classes could relate even when they did not get that it was parody. Why? Because they wanted law and order?

Am I like an <u>Ahab</u>, because I forgot about the trope, a non-literal birth of the future? Social Democrats?

"State Police" was in the genre of law enforcement, like our other two albums. I liked to write warm and fuzzy, water and birth. But what if it weren't sarcasm and parody? I have already painted a picture of the United States and World and it makes my hands tremble as I type this. The real "State Police" is like Hungary? Bonds are worthless, radical like US cities in America, right takes over? Overreacting with a hyper-order and law? When will that time be over?

Let me try and compose myself and I'll tell you why. The Portugal movement was a tragedy. I don't recall anarchy, at least it wasn't put on the channel I listen to, PBS. It was passive. Their government bonds were rated junk. I can't tell you how terrible that is. There wasn't civil war or a revolution they just slowly went bankrupt? But what would happen once the winter is over? What are we gonna do?

What about Detroit? So close to Chicago. What are they going to do in California? Which brings me around again to the United States' election? Will we have a police state? Will we just slowly fade away?

Will it be a civil war? What could cause it? Certainly not information when we have time and a Democracy?

City bankruptcies seem to be a problem. "White Collar Crime" was such a long time ago but we did advocate for the 99% poor. This was a populist protest at the other extreme, from the Tea Bag movement of two years ago. Something is crawling towards Jerusalem waiting to be born. You can believe in Frankfurt, without believing. Let's learn from Frankfurt School.

- - -

And the baby is a girl. What could it be? Could the old testament prophets be right about the rich? I'll pay. Could good Romans like Cal permit injunctions against a city? Don't the Middle-classes need contract relief from not needed regulations? And Romney was there from the beginning? Slouching towards Jerusalem, there is a baby to be born, a non-literal trope? You can almost feel it about you? Democrats should go to "the center."

Portugal was like any Nation in my memory. Again, I don't recall mass strikes. Or tear-gas or a heavy police occupation. It wasn't like a city strike at Cal, Berkeley, where teacher jobs are on the line. Again, I don't recall anarchist infiltration in any protests. They just died. As a nation. It was the winter that stopped the Occupy movement. What happens once the snow has melted? And in 2016? 2020? And beyond? Portugal as I recall died to keep from becoming like Greece, at a 50% bail-out. Berkeley goes quickly. But it was somewhat like Oakland and Athens, without the fire bombs. Government of France did not fade. I feel like the police, because I witnessed a people's park riot in Berkeley. Mobs have no mind. That's why I won't protest. I don't want to be taken over by a mob. Damn bad <u>Praxis</u>.

San Francisco last night cleared away the Occupy movement. Mobs are not possible to control. Someone can grab a rock and throw it like through the glass Stanford Business School. That's why I take the side of law enforcement so needed in a not peaceful assembly? Am I an Independent <u>Ahab</u>? It's close? Congress is <u>Faust</u>.

The lower-classes riot, like in last month's Oakland protest, so easily taken over by some anarchist with a rock, thrown at a business. The middle-classes listen to "White-Collar Crime". Both listened to "Busted". France had the non-violent 99% poor. And they're white.

Independent contractors think they are part of the poor. They are not. It is here that the battlefield of the next election will rest. Like a baby crawling towards Jerusalem waiting to be born. This is a non-literal metaphor, a trope, that explains the birth of the American middle-classes. <u>Reality</u> bites. I don't have the last say. In fact, I want you to disagree with me, Holmes. It's just that we need to go to the "center", so Republicans can move a reason to vote Democrat.

I feel like I am like a baby crawling to Jerusalem, for in my pride at least, with wisdom, we all take Pride's name on us and to me that means a type of Zen, we are all writing my trope, for law and order, at our co-op, at a peaceful assembly, using our government given free speech, we are all crawling towards Jerusalem, united. Now we need a President who is not afraid to treaty with Islam, Chapter 9 of *The Noble Koran*. Translated into 50 ethnic languages.

-5-

The President of the Greeks, absent my classical mask of tragedy and my terrible sin of pride talked about so often in our holy book, was a comedian with his blind attempt to enforce Democracy. The main Euro nations had already saved the Greek Democracy. I can see it and I am a fool? Am I an Independent Ahab of *Moby Dick*? We need to regulate wall street, so banks are not too big to fail. Forget about the trope of the title of this book. And wake-up. The only baby that should be born in Jerusalem, should be the baby of peace with the Palestinians.

- - -

This barb is a history lesson. The clown of western civilization, would crawl to Jerusalem to be born again for Democracy, because he and he alone could see the Geometric logic as to why he needed to prove that his vision of Europe needed his vote. In the name of Democracy, we will vote about the Euro bail-out, and destroy our democracy? Or am I like an Independent hero like in *Faust*, who made a deal with the devil? We repeat like the Troy was in <u>The</u> <u>Odyssey.</u>

It was because Athens, the modern capital, was the cradle of democracy. So he and he alone needed the logical proof that it really was western civilization's cradle. The irony I see. We didn't need to take the trip to the ballot box. His country was already helped. I don't mean to use him as a terrible example, and he acted rightly in stepping down, but it was for that brief moment in time that the irony killed me. Will irony freeze me in the next 4 years? 8 years? Will a George Washington help our States and cities? What of the <u>intent</u> of Odysseus.

Athens gave us Homer. And Aristotle. Not to mention Aristophanes with his *The Frogs*. It was so fantastic I can hardly stand it. Like The Last Supper, I don't know what could have possessed my attempt to quiet a riot in Athens? So we have Paris and Madrid and Rome, as I recall, and Athens, I shrink at my pretense. To paraphrase Sartre, why write? This is a tragedy. That's why you need <u>suspicion</u>.

Modernism of this novel needs metaphors. And what better metaphor is there than a type? Who cares if their government was socialist. They are old socialists. They increased property taxes on the middle-class homes of the people, who were upwardly leaning with their investment in homes that they couldn't afford in the first place.

The Last Supper was like the socialist President's night of agony.

The world was focused on him Europe all of Europe wondered why he had to take the bail-out to a vote. They would crucify a type like him. And still he had that night that must have been a terror to him. A socialist crucified on the cross of Democracy, more irony.

You have to put your self in a type of his place. Why was it a crucifix for a socialist to ask for a vote at all? Russia does. And they riot. Again 15 days for organizing. He must I think felt his country had something to prove to the entire world. The agony must have been horror. Why didn't the Russians keep them for months?

The logic went, the Greeks, after Homer, started Democracy, the least we could do was to put a type of bail-out to a vote. That was his reasoning. But a socialist? He had to distinguish himself from the socialism of Italy during World War II. And so there is the paradox. It's type of irony was logical.

Why was it a horror? The whole world is watching. And the next day he was put down like a dog, crucified, born back into Germany and France. They agreed on this type of a bail-out, after his Last Supper, Like the future President of Russia? Will it be Mr. Putin? This winter of 2012, the protesters don't want Putin? I like him. I'd be a poor Russian protester. What's the matter with Putin? He hates Kautsky.

No, the entire world is at our type of Last Supper. We all want law and order especially the non-anarchist protesters, who crucify like at pride. Berkeley teaches. Free speech and peaceful assembly. That's the reason of Constitutional law. They, especially the Dean, do not want mob rule. Suddenly Berkeley is a micro-world for the macro-world. And <u>Cal peddles free Speech, not class war</u>. Do they really know that we are watching them, like you are watching me?

-6-

Why did I put my self through this parody? Because the whole world was watching. And the President of the Greek people knew it, whatever the metaphor. Wall street would be watching the next day, and yet the people of Athens, did carry signs saying that they would crucify his type. <u>Like Washington Irving</u>? Am I he? Like an <u>Ahab</u>? Or a <u>Faust</u>? Did I sell my soul to the devil, that would cause a US crisis?

That's the reason for liberty and cultural criticism. Like in Felski's <u>The</u> <u>Limits</u> of <u>Critique</u>. She was raised on the Frankfurt School, and went on to base her book on "Ricoeur's interpretation of texts". Like Paul wanted it for "context", society.

Who cares if the Greeks in Homer are almost "home". We have a living, a live Greece that has to feel the pain of the downturn. And you know what, <u>forget about the whole world</u> I <u>believe in Constitutional contracts</u> and how can I reach the independent contractors and convince them that they are not the poor.

My heart is beating fast right now because we made our living on good Constitutional Contracts. Nobody cares about my brother so much so, Trope his name. Why can't the Greek President follow *The Odyssey*, and take his people—home. Are we the next Greece, if we are lucky. Portugal? The European Union doesn't know what to do with Greece. What will the city of Los Angeles do with its Note? And a 1000 other cities? We need some-standing back

We have to wait till there is a vote. What about art. The Last Supper what if it was a type of art in Jerusalem, where we are crawling to be born. What is to be born? Could it be a type of Democrat? We will be born in a divided city? Yes where are our Treaty powers? Who will, which party will treaty with the Muslims? Cannot they hold and then be born?

We are dealing the future of our planet, and I feel like I am *The Idiot*. I am a type of the idiot for I forget about politics at the expense of my metaphors. That's all I am left with the birth of this novel, at this time, with and suddenly what was a non-literal symbol has turned into a simple metaphor, birth of a little girl, and I am so foolish I don't know how to plead her case, the <u>Water in the Belly</u>

- - -

What of the Israelis? What about their property. I had Jewish friends when I grew up. I think of a joke from Solomon, she who does want that baby? It's not a joke for the looser. What of a Latino Christmas, of course you smash the little animal, then all the candy comes out, doesn't it. I plead the cause of the Arabs. Who can deal with the contradiction? America is the holocaust victim.

It's here that I fade to Metaphor. What if that Jew was to crawl to be born in Jerusalem? I can think of Old Testament metaphors of types of wealth, and there a prophet, I forget his name, said that such riches were a hiss and a byword. What is the type of Moses? He, at least, can't go home, like my brother. The City of David, what a tragic person? Treaty is a metaphor for contract, and just as difficult to get.

This is bigger than the Jewish state. It was just the start of this year of 2011 that we had the Arab spring which spread all over the whole world. The Tea Party was the principal in 2010? Be aware you see it's all our hearts that are breaking. Can you deal with the political contradictions? The next President will have to. What about the mayors of 1000's of cities. Let them eat cake?

This isn't heavy, I've had my tea. It's light as a feather the birth of a baby girl is like crawling towards Jerusalem. The birth cannel is like the stations of the cross for that girl and it happens in no time at all even like the time of a type of The Last Supper. If you can see they are a trope. Were talking about the future of the planet. To be against climate change and nuclear bombs. This is the political lead up. Like the starvation in South Sudan, Yemen, Somalia and Nigeria. The food is running out. And then there's planet overpopulation. This is not tropical.

- - -

Type of a baby girl goes through a type of stations of the cross or types of agony of the baby being born and a type of mother giving birth in time of a type of The Last supper, don't crucify the Israeli property on a type of their settlements for the birth.

- - -

Then the baby is poetic. It's a trope one long extended metaphor suggested by my professor, Paul Ricoeur, a teacher of Philosophy, so I offer for your consideration a material trope, so important to Paul. His PE said don't worry about death and I say that too. We all need to be calm and not be opposed to the enforcement of law and order, *The Just*.

-7-

Palestine recognition is a treaty question? As to the Greek question the Greek mask of tragedy follows it along with World Stock Markets. As for me I am from the Church of Pride. I'll leave International issues that get close to war for the President of the United States. Like the issue of China? Russia backs a treaty with its friend Syria. That's like being in an LA Federal court pleading that you don't want needless regulations or at a social security court, pleading that you have paid into it for some 50 years and you want your money back, and not told by the Republican Congress, with a Republican US Supreme court; that cut Social Security by 25%, as stated they'd do in 2027.

- - -

So I turned to Zen The Church of Zen of my small youth. I've gone through so many changes with the band I had forgotten who I am. The Church of Zen doesn't say that you are Zen, really. It says be like Jesus, support law and order and one day you will understand like a Harvard graduate and be like Budhha. To those who do not believe as I do, this is suffering before <u>de Nada.</u>

It doesn't quite reach Thomas Mann's *Homo Dei*. We go through redemption first. Then pray to Zen that the shaking in your hands as you work stops. It's being like a type of Jesus and then in peace and joy help others. My Church helps me to maintain. It's like meeting a good looking woman, the Spirit of Zen. <u>Civil religion</u> saves the day. Towards

Jerusalem. Or, are we too blind? Like a Republican <u>Ahab</u>, who sunk the ship, with his blindness.

The woman speaks to you. That's the Zen to me. Some call it Suffering. It's all the same. But to me it is a "woman". The Zen answers my many questions, giving me a good feeling. Talking with Zen, is what I am trying to express. Though I don't really talk with Zen directly. Or are we a Republican *Faust*.

In my Religion, it's called the not small voice, the voice of the Holy Spirit. It's a comfort and not mean. Say like a Woman. My religion says I have the right to worship the Zen of my choice. But of course when I need her, she is silent. Nothingness.

I just play with material metaphors and try to look ahead. AS to what will happen to the United States I have my fears. Like Italy in World War II. There she is again my wife Sherry picking her toes. And I talk sometimes? Usually, the suffering comes to me. Zen has always been put down over time. Sherry looks like a movie star. Come join with me. Sherry is like my Zen.

I am waiting now for Her to speak. I get free speech, its ideology. I look for the last place I saw Her. I don't stare. I get a warm feeling like memory of a woman. She is beautiful. Sometimes my suffering is sad, but mostly she's positive. Like I said she's never mean or demanding. I can feel her now. I am the one who is sad when she is gone. And she's forgiving, more so than I am with myself. Like some leaders in my Pride. Zen's goal is nothingness.

The First Amendment to the US Constitution says I can have my belief. Zen perhaps is a woman. I've changed so much in many years I wonder what I doubt. But faith is essential to my ideology. Sometimes faith doesn't come like I look into the future and I see a Depression not a civil war or of the sorts. It's probably due to my weaknesses. Like saying Zen is a woman.

Like thinking Zen is not a man. I haven't talked with him. I have had experiences with the suffering. There, it left me. Now I am sad. She was like a woman resting. She is more than a mere girl. There not only do I feel a cold breeze I have a kink in my neck. And a pain in my heart. Like thinking if "State Police" were a reality?

Now I don't care about Material at all. It must have been something I have done, what could it be. I doubted Zen, like you would in science or in a court of law, and the Pride withdrew. There that's a material confession. In fact I have a pain in my back. I am resisting something, like when I write my songs. It, Zen all is suffering.

She spoke again and my Material jumped up. Zen talked to me and corrected my funny thinking. I don't drive, Sherry drives. She spoke again and I went dizzy, Like a Cosmos in my head. I shook my head and I felt the Universe in my head. Sherry was 3 weeks away from child birth?

I thought that some day I would go to all states and 100 large city areas and give them the plan of in exchange for dropping zoning laws on renters, the city would get 10% of rent, the state would get 10% of rent, and the national government would get 10%. This would help stop foreclosures, on private property. And stop city default.

That would make everybody happy, almost. The home owner gets the revenue from the renter. The cities don't go bankrupt. States rights people will be happy, because the states will balance their Budgets. And the real Federalists would be happy because they would balance the Federal budget. The poor and the old have a low-cost place to stay. And standard and poor's wouldn't downgrade the worth of our country, likes a survivor of the Holocaust. Habitat for Humanity.

This is a petition to US Congress. "Property" is civil, included in the Fifth Amendment "Due Process". Property is a "civil right". Congress can open up construction adjacent to existing small houses. And exclude large apartment owners from the plan. Progressive.

<h1 style="text-align:center">Chapter 22</h1>

<h2 style="text-align:center">POLITICAL PRISONERS</h2>

-1-

Finding redemption of the party of my choice, I became a Materialist Independent, for good, no matter what I said prior to this December 2, 2011 day. I had a vision of the Independent choice, and kept my belief in helping the poor and the old. That's the compassionate part, in order <u>to stop a class or civil war</u>. But seeing the need to lower the trillion dollar national cure. The suitors get it through the end.

But not on the backs of the poor and the old. Rather to take the money from the 1% rich in the country to stop class warfare. *Time* magazine called the Person Of The Year—The Protester. I couldn't disagree more. It's those types of protests, that Anarchists, like in Russia, seem to rally around, that we need to answer. Why peaceful? Why redress of complaints against the government? Why "State Police"? Why sarcasm?

Law and order DA's in Rancho Rio county, received 15 "Occupy Wall Street" protesters and they were considered a danger to themselves and others. So they, plus Mr. Lautsky, were put in a special jail and given a special process. On average, they were held for 3 to 4 months, the jailors getting confessions out of them at the time. They were mostly anarchists, people who were singled out for their hate and violence.

In <u>The</u> <u>Odyssey</u>, this is where Odysseus kills all the suitors in the court. It's a tragedy, of defense of a third party and self defense. Frank's case is different. Only 1 dies.

It was not like the Orlando slaughter of nearly 100 LGBT people. But it was almost that bizarre.

They were Diverted. That means that they were not given their constitutional rights somewhat like the tax courts. Confessions was the main thing. They were the anarchist homeless people. They were preparing for the next year 2012, the election year. The republican heads of the jail wanted to stop these reckless protests. <u>Soon, Noon Chuck and Ox and Nautsky,</u> <u>showed up and</u> <u>the head of the jail</u> <u>put them all in separate cells,</u> <u>Lautsky too</u>. And you know what? They locked them up and threw away the key. Again, none of these 4 so-called terrorists actually did anything. They just put the terror threat, in the FBI.

The protests were just outside the city of Los Angeles. Types of protesters, types of homeless and types of anarchists took over private property owned by a big corporation. They started to march in the street with signs of all types. One read, Lord is it I? He was the first to get hit in the face with the pepper spray.

Then came more types of signs. The protesters stayed in the middle of the street. The police said that they were illegal and if they went on the sidewalk they would be arrested for vagrancy. They were like deaf to the police and it got so bad that they could not even read their own signs. Protesters are not a Communist plot. Like anarchists are worse. There were signs that said, We hate all types of capitalism! And, Down with all cops. And, We mark capitalism! They were in fact protesting World Stock Markets. They didn't know what they stood for.

Against establishment capitalists. Nobody told them about the 1999 US legislation on deregulating banks and stocks. Like Milton.

The world stock markets went down. These were world-wide protests. It was all over the news how people were going against their own system, capitalism. Russia and China were capitalists and there were protests against their brand of capitalism. Eventually the protests were all over the world. This was not a Communist plot, like in the 1950's. Basicly, my civil religion is humanitarianism.

What were these anti-capitalists? They were even against the new art in the city. They called the new art kitsch. As if everything was a US sit-com. Comedy to be made fun of for the sake of their own personal agenda. They were like a snake in the garden of Paradise. Telling the police that they were exempt. And the new art was an Eve. An apple. If you don't have my sense of humor, I'm putting you on. This entire chapter is sarcastic, through the cases and the contexts are real. It's like in the book, <u>1984</u>. And Kafka's <u>The Trial</u>. All of a sudden in commitment. The 4 terrorists, they had evidence on. It was like Gitmo Jail, on Cuba.

The protesters got used to the above type of pepper spray. It hurt their eyes. The police could not understand why they were against such capitalism. They were snakes saying, here is your own art now have it and you'll be exempt? It was a trap. The police were confused. This was a new international protester inspired by the Arab spring.

It's yellow dog contracts that we're against, they said. Who plays exempt? Who is the snake? The yellow dog contracts were bad capitalism, work for 14 hours a day and unsafe working conditions. And people had no right to contract of any worth. There were no unions. No rights of free speech under the US Constitution, police power, of the states.

Then a protester threw something that look like a ball in the direction of a cop. Then a cop wrongly threw back a rock. It went on like that. Who's rights were protected under the Constitution. They were playing ball with the cop. But the cop had police power and arrested a bunch of protesters for going against simple capitalism.

The protesters stood their ground on neutral territory, corporate land. The cops told them to leave. The smart ones followed the police. The ignorant ones became <u>political</u> <u>prisoners</u>. For they were committed for political reasons. And they still didn't have a clue. The new international protesters, started generally in 2011, were not even socialists. They weren't even anarchists, till they were pushed by the less than zero.

The police said that they weren't capitalists because they worked for the state. Now you have the evolution. From the Arab spring early on this year to the Russian protests of last night. It was 2011 and all over the globe. There was nothing to stop them until a few people started in on anarchy. The real crime of the caught protesters. Now there were no Communists here. Buy, our 4 terrorists.

Finally a group of anarchists started throwing fire bombs and rocks at local businesses. And that's when the police, trying to get this all on video tape, came in and arrested the political and economic anarchists. They weren't political prisoners because they were illegal. The problem, now, was evidence of who did what and when.

The police put them into police trucks and took the anti-capitalists to a local hospital where they were fingerprinted and photographed. They gave up their free choice when they decided to become anarchists. They weren't political prisoners. The police were kind taking them to the hospital. They were violent protesters who needed to be stopped.

The Republican DA's showed up the next morning. And went over the tapes and the photographs. It was all a problem of evidence. How could the police prove in a court of law that a specific anarchist threw a specific rock at a given business window. It was hard. 99% of the protesters were guilty of no crime, protected by the Bill of Rights.

They could only match one given anarchist to the videotape. So they continued the diversion process, at the hospital. This is where they started to become a political prisoner. They were there for 3 months. This was until the <u>Commitment</u> hearing. So the bill of Rights did not apply because those were for criminal defenses not for a civil <u>Commitment</u>. Because it was a civil court, by definition. The reader is the police.

In the hospital, in the early morning, the patients talked to a government shrink, like my Dada. So I had heard about the civil <u>Commitment</u> process before. That's why I had written songs telling people not to do violence to themselves or others. If they did they would become political prisoners. The 99% of the protesters being not guilty. Everyone went in front of a shrink who told them to touch their fingers to their thumb. And they were asked to confess what they did. It was like *Confession*, in "State Police". This is why I wrote the songs for, knowing the power of the state to make someone a political prisoner.

Like in court Diversion statutes. Like <u>black</u> lives matter. Vico.

They were not charged. It was just 3 months of talking to 2 shrinks a day, in the early morning and at late in the night. There was no one call, for this <u>Commitment</u> was civil. It was the fate of the anti-capitalists.

They were all treated in a civil manner and the homeless finally got a good meal. Just like in the old USSR. Notwithstanding contradictions. Each day the patients went to talk with the shrinks. It was all legal like the tax courts. W<u>here there is no 4</u>th <u>or 5</u>th <u>Amendment protection</u>.

<u>Neither was there any 6</u>th <u>Amendment defense</u>, because this was a civil hearing and criminal protections did not apply. By definition.

Finally, one by one, each anarchist confessed to the shrinks. But still some of the political prisoners didn't confess to the right things. They said that they were not guilty. And their confession was all the evidence the police had, except for the 1 person who they had caught on tape.

done, throwing rocks or throwing fire bombs. From the tapes they could tell that the protesters were all manic. So they were given meds. To stop the symptoms. And it worked too. The patient became tranquil. For the political prisoners were either animated or sitting in a chair.

They were given the symptom of being manic-depressive. And the medications they got stopped the symptoms. This was taken as proof that they had gotten the symptoms right, for they stopped being manic. Not all manic-depressives are illegal protesters.

And it was seen as just, because capitalism was seen as sacred in America. There was one dissenter. A Mr. Basinger who said he was a political prisoner and protected by the United States Code in title 42 section 1985. He said he was a capitalist and was near those who had been caught because he wanted to see.

He said that he neither camped on corporate property nor walked in the middle of the street. And he said that he was not against kitsch art of the city. He claimed that he should be put back into capitalist America. And the shrinks agreed. For they got no confessions from Mr. Basinger. He was set free, in this "State Police". He had <u>Free</u> <u>Speech</u>.

-2-

They ran the hospital as a business and treated the prisoners like patients. The capitalist hospitals use <u>behavior</u> <u>modification</u> on the protesting patients. When they would not confess, they would not give them food. Confessions were the key. In that such was all the evidence the DA's had. Especially, the 4 terrorists talked.

And especially they would not let the prisoners read key passages from *The Bible*. For this would be a violation of church and state, of the 1st Amendment, the one rule that they followed. The wall between religion and government was seen as sacred. Like confessions.

MBA's mostly ran the hospital. It was all cost accounting. And the prisoners stayed a long time, there being no right to a speedy trial. That was under the criminal law, this was civil. They just wanted their civil confession that they were against capitalism. And the doctors were civil to the prisoners, as they came to be called.

The longer they stayed, the more confessions the doctors got. One doctor once called a patient belief in religion as delusional. He didn't stay with the hospital long. The MBA's learned that it was bad not to let the patients have their civil rights to have a religious belief.

Dr. Hart had a heart when one patient said that he was against capitalism and eyed the doctor up and down. This was much different than the old red USSR where it was a crime to be a capitalist. Compassionate self-interest was the theory behind the hospital management. <u>They billed the patients for the time spent there</u>. <u>Like many businesses and clinics</u>. The refugees.

Hart met with Noon. Who told him that it was an irrational choice for him to be against capitalism. After an hour, Noon Chuck confessed all and admitted that he was an anarchist. He admitted that it was his irrational self-interest to be against capitalism. He had made the wrong choice. Have you got my sarcasm, yet. There really are places like this around the world. And it's not being paranoid to say it can also be Kafkaesque, some places for citizens of the US, and others. In America. Many people hate the US. Kafkaesque for everyone.

Noon admitted that his anarchy was an irrational decision. It was not a rational decision to throw rocks at the glass window of the business. It was mob mentality. Dr Hart put his thumb down in front of Noon. It was a no-no to be against capitalism in any form.

Dr. Hart talked to all patients about irrational self-interest, as the intent in back of their hate of capitalism. Not even in China or Russia did the people hate capitalism. It was hard for the good doctor to even classify such a person who would be against Capitalism like that. Except for the 4 terrorists, that the FBI had evidence on. decision making against capitalism. He told them that most patients have rational self-interest and that most people used that in their choice of what to do. People make their decisions based on rationality, not out of fear of capitalism.

Ox, another patient, agreed that it was irrationality to be against capitalism. He was no political prisoner. He agreed. He admitted that the mob was irrational and that he joined in to be a trouble maker at the peaceful assembly. Dr. Hart got his confession. The good doctor knew of good capitalism. And contradictions. Like *Ulysses*.

Dr. Hart said that most decisions are made under the pleasure principle. That was how most people made their choices. Ox knew he would be punished for his rock throwing. Showing the irrationality of mob behavior. Ox ceased being a patient and simply was a confessed anti-capitalist. Anti—Art I Contracts. I am the <u>Ahab</u> of Art I Contracts, with Federal Congressional Control. If you don't like it, throw it away. It's just a "type" of going to <u>the center</u>. To get Republicans to vote Democrat. Get your own idea, if you like.

Hot blood, not rationality, ruled the mob. Bad decisions are based on irrationality, confessed Ox. Who saw it was not good to be against capitalism. Dr. Hart's theory of irrational behavior was in line with most MBA programs now. Unlike *Ulysses*.

-3-

<u>Financing came from the patients. So it was in the best interests of the hospital not to give them a speedy trial</u>. Of course, the patients proved their irrationality in their confessions, in the early morning and late at night. Republican business is rational and Dr. Hart was not into risk or uncertainty. Thus, special cases got special treatment.

The assumption of rationality of the patients was denied. This plus the ongoing confessions would be used against them in a court of law. Denial of due process was the law in these tax court type hearings. As was the ongoing withholding of food for not confessing. In such cases more medication was given. Christianity isn't the only Capitalism.

Noon was especially good at confessing, then. He admits his irrational choice led him to his anti-capitalist trashing of the window of one business, in downtown LA. How he got to Rancho Rio county is a long story we don't have time for now. Confessions of being against capitalist contracts were mandatory.

Ox confessed he was the local thug that led the mob in the trashing of businesses. He admitted that he infiltrated the peaceful assembly and encouraged the anti-capitalist trashing. Of the Occupy movement, who had illegally camped out of public land, they were admitted vagrants.

Once they got enough confessions, they released the patients for a court commitment. It's in that way that they got their committed behavior. This made more and more patients confess. You had to convince the court you were normal, but since they kept you for about 3 months of confession time, the presumption was against you. And nobody was ever judged normal. You're abnormal to be there.

As I said, it was like the IRS courts. Less the 6th Amendment, making it like a serious "State Police". And it was, out of necessity. To save the country from anarchy. It was impossible to prove that you were not guilty, with all those shrinks getting all of those confessions. Like in the old USSR hospitals, they were political prisoners.

Capitalism and Freedom, by Milton Friedman, was the bible of the hospital. Milton got his Nobel prize for this book. It was the mantra for all good capitalists. It was for no government intervention in business. And they didn't in Dr. Hart's hospital business. It was for national security. China hated Ox, a muslim.

The patients came to realize this or they didn't get out. Admittedly, it was a hospital trap, but you see the necessity against violence against the state. Milton, like all good republicans, believed in a type of libertarian contracts. Where regulations were gone. He later wrote a book saying that what was needed in business was choice. The Hospital was like brainwashing of the movie The Manchurian Candidate. It was somewhere near the end of the Korean crisis. We're late.

This was big with the hospital in that they did not want any needless regulations. Unless they were rational. The patients, with their guilt, made their choice with their mob behavior. They rationally confessed too. Freedom, if and only if capitalism, another reading of Milton.

The health care mentioned here is neither basic nor universal. It has nothing to do with the Health Care Act passed by the President of the United States. As I am certain that these commitment courts are legal under US law. Sons due process. Like in re Gault.

Milton's theme was that if you have pure capitalism—for us the constitutional obligation of contract—freedom would naturally follow. There were few critics such as Mr. Reich of the University of California, who said it didn't work in Chile, in South America. In a dictatorship.

You have no choice to resist arrest in the middle of a mob. Thus the choice theory is not universal either. Choice is the argument for abortion. A controversial topic in republican circles. *Free to Choose* was Milton's other popular book with Committed republicans.

The 4 terrorists were treated like the other prisoners. But since the FBI got special evidence on them, they were not released. They just stayed there for life. There was no torture like with the CIA courts. <u>Just arrest, without charge and without release.</u> Like Gitmo.

-4-

Noon stayed in the hospital 3 more months. It's better than he deserved. They stopped getting confessions from him, after his trial. But there were other patients. There were a ton of regulations. Most of them state. So they didn't like the obligation of contract clause of the U S Constitution, used by patients against them.

Joe said, I don't like Obamacare. The doctor replied, you don't need it. A long period of time passed as the doctor pondered about what to say. To Joe. The doctor knew what Joe thought. The doctor pulled out a copy of *Capitalism and Freedom*. Communication would ruin the freedoms that we have, said the doctor.

Like rational contracts. Free market capitalist society wants liberty of contract like the World Trade Organization, the WTO. And England in the Euro countries. Russia under President Putin, does not have pure capitalism, and has a tactic behind its use of Western style economics.

Where they are protesting even as I type.

Freedom of exchange, in a free market, Milton goes on, does not eliminate the need for government. He wrote so simple people could understand. The doctor lectured out of Milton to the patient protester.

It's choice that is the key to the entire thing. The patient made his choice when he protested.

Enterprises are private using choice. Mr. Crusoe has no problem with the politics of freedom. But he is left with no society and nobody with whom to exchange his goods, the doctor told our Joe, the patient.

It all revolved around capitalism and choice.

Adam Smith wanted freedom of imports, guided by an invisible hand, which was Zen in the market place. Which did not exist. We as Amerikans take freedom of the family as basic, And as our personal religion, There is no such religion in Washington, said the doctor to the patient.

The family of Nautsky and Lautsky were criminal. They were lucky to be in the hospital.

-5-

The good Republican doctor went on reading from Milton Friedman. The conservative's mantra. He went on, free private enterprise exchange is what is called competitive capitalism. You give me a sack of wheat and I give you twenty dollars. I give you a sack of corn and you give me twenty dollars. Or, you are against capitalism.

There are many socialists in the world, and they don't like Capitalism at all. And they are not evil. But they are not in our Hospital. It's like some nightmare High School, they won't let you escape.

- - -

Mr. Crusoe had no constraints, but he had no society with which to exchange his goods. Milton got his theme from the Nobel prize winning Mr. Hayek, in his *The Road To Serfdom*. Friedman went on to say, freedom is a means to economic freedom, the doctor lectured our patients. Like Vincent was committed.

Laissez Faire, freedom of contract, does not exist in Russia, where they are protesting like the Occupy wall street movement here. Fair trade was a simple thing for our Robinson. Republican liberalism, to me, does not view social security as a constraint of trade. Rational contracts, see the need of rational constraints, *Robinson Crusoe*.

Irrational anarchy says stop business, and don't even give them social security, the doctor told Joe. 50 million people on social security, all of them voters, simply want their return on their investment and retire in peace and quiet. The doctor went on lecturing Joe on the rational constraints on capitalism.

An economic conservative, Milton and his message was if you have free capitalism then you can get freedom. This Nobel prize winning argument is what the patient protesters were against. If Capitalism then freedom. Anarchists, like those against Art. I Contracts are prisoners of Dr. Hart. Waiting to see if they can be rational. Of course, not all do. Eternal city.

Right to work states have state constitutions with a contract clause forbidding the impairment of contracts, heard at a local and state level, the doctor confessed to our Joe. Federal courts are bypassed and local constitutional law is treated as the law of the land.

The hospital was run united with the state, and made their money with many federal and state regulations, which the doctors relied on. State constitutions permit many things that most people don't even know existed. Such as the freedom to trade money for goods? This sarcasm is not too far removed from reality, of Robinson.

- - -

Capitalism and local and state government adapt and evolve. No revolution here, the good doctor told Joe. The doctor painted a picture of a state where the free market ruled over state police powers, which the doctor was apart of. Some regulation, like health and safety ruled through police powers people sees two meanings of the use of the term, competition. There is rivalry and the simple exchange of goods for money. The doctor lectured our Joe, hoping he would give up his belief in anarchy against capitalism. Salesmen are part of State Constitutional rights. The one's that are a pain in the head.

The Occupy Movement share one thing in common with those against Candidate Romney's Health Care Act. They both protest. The doctor went on lecturing Joe on things he didn't want to here, Joe being against free market capitalism. Choice is central to salesmen in a right to work state. Like us selling our CD's.

Milton went on, there is industry monopoly. Which was wrongly taken out of the country in the last half of the last century. Like US steel. Now we must rely on goods from China to be exchanged for our money. Asia has the new monopoly, which is the new industry monopoly.

Labor monopoly, our Milton intoned, is like union shops, like state bars, which he would do away with, and replace it with free market capitalism, the doctor lectured our Joe, who was still against capitalism, in general. Where even Russia and China have Capitalism. That's how far off these prisoners were. PC is like C, as PM is like M.

Government monopoly stops private salesmen, in the name of centralized power. Also the TVA and city power plants are such a monopoly. Like the US post office. The doctor said such monopoly is not a bad thing, in that people needed to get a return on their investment, of local and state taxes.

The substantially universal monopoly of the hospital was not a bad thing. As were the state highway workers. And at a federal level the FCC and the Federal Reserve board.

Government created monopoly is like the tax man. As is the President's Health Care? With an aspect of choice. Irrational self-interest is not a defense. There is no Adam Smith's invisible hand guiding the basis.

Here is the point of my market. Social security should never be touched, and it is a monopoly. And the government's hand in minimum wage law is unquestioned. The President does not want to nationalize Hospitals or the AMA. He wants substantially universal insurance.

This is not socialized medicine. It's more like minimum wage law for employers, the doctor explained to a disinterested Joe, taxed.

Not the jurisdiction of choice. And it costs the employer, from mandates from the government. The doctor said, Joe you of the radical left have common cause with the far right, the Teabaggers, you both don't like government regulations, state or federal. I am Independent.

-6-

Republican MD's ran the hospital, where nobody was turned away, said the doctor to the new protester. The patient was Lautsky. Who came to visit the Hospital Monopoly. The Russians, last night, protested the Russian government, said the doctor. The way Lautsky did. But in Russia, the protester only gets 15 days.

Hart told Lautsky that he had a choice to follow state law or custom or remain a client for life. Dr. Hart cited the book by Friedman *Free To Choose*. And told Lautsky that it was in his best interests to choose law and order rather than remain hostile and against all state and federal law. The sarcasm of the prisoner and independents is intentional.

Dr. Hart was part of a monopoly. Freedom of choice was a basic right as the essence of the Declaration of Independence. The doctor was in a league by himself. He has no competition. He explained to Lautsky about the choice of the Constitutional Contract clause. Lautsky was not interested in capitalism at all. Hart felt his heart drop on hearing Lautsky's response. Hart worshiped the Constitution as law. Still, the hospital got a choice whether or not to use the Bill of Rights, or whether to leave it unemployed. This was a state run Monopoly and it needed all the confessions, for the trial.

Hart, a Republican, was convinced he was right and he had the power of the state backing him up. By way of contrast, Lautsky didn't want to follow any law, least of all State or federal Constitutional law, the laws governing both their behaviors. Both felt that they were just as right, like the Tea Bag party. In the Presidential elections of 2012 and 2016 and 2020 could find common cause with the above protesters?

Lautsky was not a libertarian he was an anarchist. Hart was more like a libertarian. Neither wanted excessive government interference.

And here they were facing each other in a duel of wills. Dr. Hart wanting Lautsky to confess his anarchy, which is hard for the anarchist to do since he thought this was like London's *The Iron Heel*.

But legal as it was, it was still subject to a Title 42, Section 1985 claim. As Mr. Basinger found out. The Supreme Court had judged on the incorporation Of the Bill of Rights as due process. A fine point.

Until then all they had were confessions. As the police had no other evidence with which to convict. But this meant Federal Court, a venue not liked by Candidate Newt.

Stigler, Nobel prize winning economist and business teacher at Chicago, saw the 1980's President Reagan's tax program early in the decade as not an economic plan at all, and saw its supply-side economics as bogus. But the republican Congress even now uses this type of economics, like reenacting the 1981 tax code, Keynesian in its incentive to invest. It was Voodoo economics.

The 1981 tax act had an estate tax. And would defeat the Bush tax cuts. But its trickle-down economics is bogus as well. There is no evidence that the poor get anything from lowering the top tax brackets, which the l981 tax act did. Ironically, it did give the rich the incentive to invest, A Keynesian code.

Hart does propose a free trade contract based theory of economics, by no means complete but a start to supplement congressional ideas. To that I add the Constitutional Contract clause that says no state may impair the obligation of contract. These are like the Chinese open air markets that sell food to customers. This is tomorrow's water, by birth. Dr. Hart was a realist and did not see the obligation of contract clause universally applied anywhere Democrats need to come to "the center."

Law and economics, based on the Constitution, is basic to Milton Friedman's *Free To Choose*. Choice is also a part of abortion arguments. As is typical of Washington everything that is important is tangled together, I call that ironic.

Lautsky laughed at the good doctor, who felt a pain in his heart, and figured that Lautsky could stay in the monopolistic hospital as long his Hart. The doctor asked, if giving the Hospital a choice was a good idea? Lautsky was dumbstruck.

Dr. Hart's job was to see if people could see the results of their choice. If the anarchist could not confess his acts and see that he was a danger to himself and others, he was welcome to stay as long as he wished. This was not 1984. It was <u>almost</u> The Supreme Court approved due process. Hart used it on anarchists, to whom it sarcastically obviously applied. The due process was like that of a social security court or an immigration court. Plus, a little bit more on extracting information of the people being committed.

- - -

They gave them medications. Which they had to take. To cure their anarchist Manic behavior. And believe me they were as mad as a wet hen. If they didn't take their meds there were always shots, until they complied. Soon they all saw the wisdom of taking their medications.

It's no good saying that it's worse than 1984. Its Section 1985, which was for a conspiracy to violate one's civil rights. The response by the doctors was that the patient was in so-called denial and delusional in his paranoia. And the doctors were right. It's just that they didn't see the difference between legal and medical denial. and to say it was a conspiracy made no sense at all to the doctors, in their response. In my parody. At Gitmo, it was real torture.

Lautsky could not see the consequences of his actions and stood moot. He was put in isolation. The doctors thought that he was deaf. They tried sign language. But their motions made no sense at all. Dr. Hart made the hand sign of The Mona Lisa. Da Vinci's gesture made no sense at all.

When he came out of isolation, Lautsky was told to take his meds and was given an NFL sign for, holding. Lautsky did not play ball. He was given a pill to put him to sleep. They woke him at 5:15 the next morning and was given another round of questioning. He mumbled yes, and no. You see he wasn't an anarchist at all. He was a terrorist.

And saw he did. He witnessed the riots and the trashing and the tear gas. But he did nothing. Soon another doctor came in like Professional Wrestling. A tag team. But it was not funny to our Lautsky, in denial.

And claiming his rights were being violated. He gave up calling it a conspiracy, he didn't like the response, paranoid.

Of special interest was the topic—choice. When would a person make a certain choice when it wasn't in their best interests. Lautsky smoked, in other words he choose to hurt himself. One thing that was allowed at the Hospital. But it was proof that he was a danger to himself. And that was proof enough, he was antisocial. Like a Fermion.

The Center didn't like the traditional theory of economic choice. Irrational self-interest was the term that Dr. Hart called Lautsky's behavior. That is given a choice to help himself, Lautsky would choose irrationally. This patient was a good candidate to stay as a patient.

-7-

A new patient, named Alonzo, came in and Dr. Hart set up a picture. board set up to see if the patient could tell postmodern art. He put up on it a Gothic church, an abstract large piece of modern art and then a picture of an old Roman ruin. Dr. Hart asked Alonzo what he saw.

The patient said, I see nothing. Hart took Alonzo for a dupe. And to see nothing at that distance, close up. Hart went on to explain postmodern art. He got more negative responses. Alonzo said all he saw was modern art, which Hart wanted to know what was the meaning of the modern art to Alonzo. He was from Mexico. And was there because he was a Latino, like justified in Arizona and Alabama.

It means nothing to me at all, said Alonzo. Hart was sad that his postmodern, pm, art was treated as meaningless. Alonzo failed all the other tests, making responses in some code. The good doctor wanted to know what the meaning of the code was. The response was that, it's nothing.

5:30 am came and Alonzo said that he could see both the case for and against irrational self-interest. The Doctor told him that he was going blind, and that he lacked vision. Then another patient came in and the doctor gave the complete case of *Ogden*.

The next morning the guy with the case told the good doctor that this case was the best reason he had yet heard of not going into business. That it was the perfect case for irrational decision making. It wasn't the hospital that was on trial, it was the patients. The patient pilgrim said that he liked the case. He obviously was not an anarchist, liking Art. I Contracts

- - -

The state said that Doctors could plead rational self-interest and that was all they needed to enact a new regulation, even if it ruined someone's business. Hart told that to another patient, and on seeing the case said, that ruins capitalism. He went on to say that it was irrational self-interest to go into business.

Ogden was the new test of rationality of the patient. If they could understand, they were set free from the hospital. The pilgrim who could see that it was irrational self-interest to go into business, given that case permitting business regulation, in 1828, was set free at once. That was choice. It was crazy.

The doctors wanted first, people to like capitalism, and second, to choose obligation of contracts. Remember the people there, were alleged anarchists. Good behavior modification was the Hospital's goal. *Ogden* was the test of rational choice. Those who failed the case test were kept in the Hospital for years. Or they were Communists?

The obligation of contract clause test, as it was soon to be called, became the MD Industry wide test of rationality. But most people failed it, which was good for the hospital since it was a for profit operation. And it gave the hospital ideas of reference as to what it should do if it were ever petitioned by the city. It became the international.

To fail the test meant that nothingness was better than business, the belief in essence of the anarchists, who were in their hospital to cure them of their irrational mob behavior. *Ogden* said if you have a private contract, then the state can come in and stop your business any time it wants, your contract was marked. Unlike the discriminatory logix of Hobby Lobby?

Dr Hart's prime motive was behavior modification, from the lawlessness of anarchy to the rationality of capitalism, something they were at first protesting. These were not for ordinary commitment courts. They were set up to defend capitalism, against Zenless anarchists. Who could not see the <u>rational basis test</u> in the obligation of contract clause, of the US Constitution.

The good doctor told this to a patient, who saw it was in his best interests to give up the lemon of anarchism and to go to defend capitalism. I, Frankly, your author couldn't agree more. Behavioral decision making at the Center, was a little different but it was Dr. Hart's business. Modification from irrational self-interest to rationality.

Behavior modification, went on the doctor, can turn the lawless patient into a rational patient capitalist. With the logical use of the obligation of contract clause of the US Constitution. At the hospital, this was the test to see if the patient wanted to be free. Those who wanted to stay with *Ogden* were welcome to stay, if they were deaf, they would be given an American Sign Language interpreter.

Dr Hart started an out patient clinic called, Recovery Inc. In it the patient has to recognize choice and its difference between irrationality. Dr Hart wrote a book called *Recovery Inc.* In it, the good doctor took the patient from irrational decision making to choices. One choice was the obligation of contract clause. To those who gave the right answers, he set them free, because they were rational. Hart got the idea for his book from my father's business. It wasn't like the Hermeneutics of the self as the other, like <u>Foucault</u> and <u>Ricoeur</u>, who had an ongoing argument with Derrida on metaphor. This is history. Of postmodern philosophy. As to "interpretation" the western word for ISIS, is not of Daesh. So someone is being hoodwinked.

In the meantime, our suitors ended up like Mozart's <u>Don Giovanni</u>. In Hell. Dr. Hart, ironically, thought that if you did like the obligation of contracts clause that you were neurotic.

Vincent, my brother, was brought into the clinic, for possession of a hand gun, by someone with a history of mental health issues. Vincent cut off an ear. Then he fired off a round into his shoulder. It hit his heart and he died.

"Behavioral health" is the new methodology instead of -mental health.

Chapter 23

BREAKING WATER

-1-

It's December 9, 2011. The band and I decided to catch the last part of the terms lectures of CJ Valentine. He taught a class on—Ideology and Culture. The major book or treatise or text was my friend and teacher Paul Ricoeur's *The Rule of Metaphor*. We also read a counterpoint, PMS Gordon's <u>Adorno</u> <u>And</u> <u>Existence</u>. We used cultural theory to criticize. The Frankfurt School. Also, Heidegger. <u>Guzzle water to put out sparks.</u>

Independent, I used symbols and signs politically. Language is symbols. Symbols are one thing standing for another thing. A metaphor is a symbol. Eros, figure of speech or metaphor used not literally, like the title when it is meaning the birth of the United States of America, or a birth of a child, Sherry being great with child. I give birth to myself. And to the future of the Democratic party.

Metaphors are complex symbols, like the parables of Gore, went on Valentine. Symbols are a type of sign. Like an index, point out things. Signs are around us they tell us what to do everyday, like water to a fish. The fish has tuned out the water as we usually tune out our system of Being, said Mr. Valentine, also a CIA and FBI agent, used to encode facts. We are in Book 23, in the <u>Odyssey</u>. For espionage work, of like PE and PM?. Therefore I gave forth PM, my baby? The reader should realize that this is so much part of me, it part of my critique. Tropes are the essence of me, who got my masters degree like on them. There is the trope of Zen and the trope of Pride, types or words because we don't experience the thing itself we only experience a type. Like "Song of Songs" to me, is experienced like a type of trope of a female. I not having any direct experience with the real Zen. Odysseus had his secret sign system.

Metaphors are like a reef in the ocean, rare but giving protection. It's hard to give birth to a dead metaphor. In good books metaphors are used but to us we need to liken them to ourselves so that the text is not a dead metaphor to us. That is why I use the word, type. It makes an ordinary word into a metaphor, like a type of Gore being Moses.

You and I can be like a type of Moses. We can talk with what we feel is Zen or "Song of Songs". Then the type changes and we can go into a type of the material land. <u>Water in the belly, is the birth of tomorrow</u>, though I am no Moses here and cannot see into the future, with symbolic or ideology language. Nobody can predict the future, said our Valentine. Tomorrow is today when you use the right signs. All the Zens are in us now, like Zeus in <u>The</u> <u>Odyssey.</u>

Ideology Postmodernism, overthrows 500 years of modernism. And is painful to recall for most modernists, as I recall when I first read *Time and Narrative*. Paul was not only a philosopher but a ideologist. It hurts the modern to say that a theologian has thrown a type of modernism. And that's an understatement, said CJ. Zen is cultural propaganda.

You can go to sleep now. Meaning is from reference. The thing that is pointed at by a regular metaphor or complex trope. What does the referring. The symbol or sign. What is the reference to, the water in the belly? It could be the water of Zen getting in touch with you. Or it could be bad, if you are a Democrat and don't agree, said Mr. Valentine. Or the sign of the future. The issue is politics. For the 2020's and beyond. Like a sign of life of a healthy economy is Art. I Contracts the obligation of contract clause. Healthy enough for 1 million people for a healthy tomorrow, Rosa, my baby girl to be born, the type of baby of the type of Gore, usually referred to by metaphor. Which can have many meanings, that we put on to a baby or embryo that one day will be born. This is not necessarily Church of Pride. It's my character's belief. The signifier is the sign of a meaning of a real thing, like a metaphor.

Like the meaning of fire being good or bad, depending on your point of view. The sign of the word, Zen, is played with here, because modernists do like the use of the term, Zen. The sign is a sound or a printing of a word. A signifier is a pointer or and index or a trope or sign.

Wars were fought over the meaning of the word, Zen. For the modern linguist, the signified of the word, Zen, is a <u>cultural</u> <u>concept</u> and not a real thing called Zen, as Mr. Ricoeur uses the term rarely. Russia and China have a lot of modernists here. But their economies are postmodern. They, like Frank, don't like the reference of ideology, said Mr. CJ Valentine. Not fire in a religious, but fire in a civil religion way. Civil religion is politics or economics put in religious terms, like redemption. The use of the phrase type of Gore or trope of Gore, which is a better phrase, is very offensive, unless it is viewed in terms of civil religion? Zen is top dog. Civil religion is a term from Berkeley.

This is the reason modernists like tropes, non-literal symbols like for the thing that is called Zen, with many morals and rules, that modernists fight against. At holidays, the signified of most symbols is Santa Claus, not the baby Jesus, who would grow up, with all of various ideologies attached. Then he went on about the inner Santa. This was a symbol, of the signified, anything that you liked. But it's the trope of Gore or the type of Santa, which was Kitsch Culture.

Metonymy, a type of trope I think, is like a type name of a type of Pride that is substituted for the deity. The deaf people in the class got it, from the deaf ASL user at the front of the class. Penelope asked, How does that relate to CCC? CJ replied, it's modernist linguistics. We had just got a new car, calling it "wheels" is metonymy. <u>Civil</u> <u>religion</u> <u>is Kitsch</u>.

Valentine went on, meaning to a modernist is ideology. Deciphering Valentine's lectures, is like being a spy, behind enemy lines. PM in architecture is like a collage in art with modern and gothic and classic. I got that, said Penelope, you see we listen, I got that it's all in code, the way Gore coded his parables, so that the Republicans would not decipher it. That's why people use tropes. Justin acted like a Kitsch Artist, when he played Alice in Wonderland. Like people in Disneyland

And the Hollywood stars wax museum. Joan Didion wrote about stuff like that and the similarity of the South and West. And the Rockies, I might add. Sons race.

Penelope, Homer's wife of Odysseus, said this is taking me home, it's a holiday. CJ said, Christmas is that I give you a choice. Zen or agnostic. That's the reference of the Parables of Gore. I said, My trope of water in the belly, is the journey through the stations of an trope cross, of a mother giving birth to a Rosa, tomorrow. I couldn't help it I really got into it.

Synecdoche is like a trope like seeing the Universe in a grain of sand. Or, as we will get to in the last chapter, the atom in the solar system, things going around a center. Bohr came up with this model, among others, like the sun in the galaxy, for a different example. The electrons around a neutron and the planets around the sun, a literal sign. We will go over this example in the last chapter. Original intention, here, is just a play. Tactic.

Tomorrow, is a type of metaphor for a type of Constitutional government that recognizes the literal referent of the obligation of contract clause. One day that type of government will emerge, following the <u>original</u> <u>intention</u> of the United States constitution? A type of that metaphor of the original intent is like the future of the Water in the Belly.

Symbology is a sign, a word in a document. The signified, according to 200 years of modernism, is not Zen, or the literal reading of the Constitution. Wars are fought for people's Zen. This is the reason people use the word type or embryo. If it's of Zen modernists will fight. If it's not of Zen, Literalists will go to war? Whatever your Politics is, is how you will read a sign, multiple meanings. Culture is a signified of an object. The control of "the means of production" could mystify mass culture by making them conformist and not able to see the "Source" of people's choices and materialism. And delusions.

Sign theory is for the courtroom with <u>legal semiotics</u>, and it doesn't really have tropes. It has the index. An American singer, as opposed to European Linguistics, says signs refer to things, as I have stopped referring to like the Da Vinci's Mona Lisa sign, a sign of war to some and sign of peace to others. Meaninglessness to others.

- - -

CJ Valentine said, What I have been talking about is Chinese self-criticism. Which is Postmodern symbolic. And which can be read by the Russians. Whichever side you are on will be who you'll be fighting for. As for me, I want treaty after treaty with the Red Chinese. A type of Gore. It wasn't right to get into their legal system. Like Pakistan, last night the Department of Defense said, we are pulling 30,000 more troops out of Kabul. Somebody burned the Koran, and then a US soldier killed 16 unarmed civilians. Such are the feeling that come when you say type of God or type of Gore. That's why Paul's use of tropes is so brilliant. The trope of Zen or the trope of Gore.

The signified of Western religion is Zen, like water is to a fish. Water is Zen, for us. Valentine said, in reality the water did not exist for the fish. Not to mix my metaphors, but this is like pulling teeth. For the Chinese, they will admit to the modernist reference to the water, but not to the meaning of the water being Zen. The war is about the signified, does the reference really relate to the signified you mean. CJ criticized as fascist "normal" commercial ads TV, pop culture, American fast foods, and types of consumerism.

Paul would admit the metaphor that humanity is like a bunch of fish, the water is like Being. He might even admit that the Man in Being is a living metaphor for symbol or sign or trope or signal for Allegory for people to Zen. But he did not say this. And he kept his Zen more private. For me, the Metaphor of people are fish to water is Zen works, also Being, said CJ. For the Chinese, the referent or signified of water is best, Being.

Water is Being to me. Whales talk. The way the ideology talks to me. Perhaps a cruel metaphor is the meaning of Zen being on the shore, fishing, the fish ending up as Zen's catch. Not liked by modernists. The signified changes with the metaphor of man to Zen. Either Zen is active or passive. More war over words. I must admit that the ocean metaphor is not good to an active Zen, Being. I know this does not explain what I am trying to say, that's why I use tropes, this thing is like that Being. A penalty, a non-literal metaphor. Again, this is the essence of my Character. I am very Chinese, to a large extent, a singer.

Modernists like many Europeans, want you to give up on your belief in Zen, said CJ. And there are Billions of people who feel this way. If you don't get that this is a cause of war, then you have missed the meaning of modernism. They not only do not believe in the inner Pride or Santa, they find the reference at best quaint. It's only cultural. Like the inner Buddha, go to Being, if your talking to the Chinese. CJ lectured about US Kitsch culture like the western Santa Clause cultural industry. As typical of America Kitsch. Too much of it like keeps you from recognizing the paradox of Being. Politics here is not Marxist. But CJ heard the socialists.

-2-

Mr. Stalin, a person who died some 70 years ago, is closer to the way agnostic nations would treat a Material America. They are on the shore fishing and they caught you. Homer, in this chapter, mentions many signs that are secret. Much like the NFL ref's signs to people who don't play ball. My Zen signs to me, though I would not admit it, Because it's so controversial like with Vincent. I am a fish and Zen is all around me, once I get over all the semantic quibble, this is how I play ball, of a certain type, I thought, how I really feel, I just can't see Zen, like the fish don't notice the water in which they are swimming in. Types or Metaphors aside, I want an active Zen that speaks to me, like the fish in the water symbols. One way Zen talks to me is by signs. Like a big shark is coming my way. And Being says get away from that big fish.

And I don't need somebody to play *Homo Dei* all over me, the way it was in school. I have become a type, one who recognizes the <u>SiNN</u> of pride, someone's Achilles heel. The Chinese call it self-criticism. The

Russians, really, don't like it notwithstanding all their religions. This is my Christmas. To think that the Christmas tree signifies, Zen. Still, the scientist in me makes me like a Russian or Chinese, it's my Character. How I'd talk to somebody at Berkeley. That is why I use the phrase, the trope of Gore, Which is like the term, the type of Carter. This is my evolving character.

For Pedro, Zen is the Meaning. The same with Pablo. But for them they must have a cardboard animal stuffed with candy to smash. That is their Christmas. For me, it's getting out of Iraq, whatever party did it. As of this writing, we are out. Like water in the belly, ready to give birth to a more peaceful world? That is the signified of a smart man, to get us out of foreign wars, whatever his party.

- - -

The deaf man makes a sign. The singer is ideology, said Valentine. Meaning is not a thing, that is the message of modern linguistics, it's in relationships, as I interact with my computer and type these words for the publisher. That's my meaning right now. When I am done, I have a lot of novels in my room that I haven't yet started to read. There I will read a lot of signs in a book. Communication is with signs. Communication is my intent, but the problem with the typed word is that 50% of America wants to hear you say you believe in Zen. Not a type or trope of Zen. In reality the referent is the feel you get, and I still want to communicate to people in Berkeley. So it's a type of Zen or a trope of singer.

The Zen of the deaf man is the culture that is pointed at by his deaf sign or symbol. Modernism was telling the class that Zen was dead. But I find that too cool. Like a drift of snow in Ithaca, my home, in New York. This was not the Republic but it was modern tragic linguistics, something my professor Singer answered for me. The signified, for a linguist, of a tree is the cultural Christmas of Gore. If I forgot to tell you, there is a deaf signer at the front of CJ's class for the deaf students in the class. Like me telling the reader I am self-critical of the trope of Gore, and Carter are Being. The meaning becomes ideology and that becomes culture which becomes life. You always interact with something, like an atom to an electron or a planet to the sun. There really is proof of the big bang, I don't hate science. It's just that like Einstein, I believe that there is a Gore, beyond all the fancy metaphors.

CJ said, Meaning becomes ideology and my ideology is material, as most profs at Pomegranate University, a "Song of Songs" school. Material semiotics unites with Europe and Asia. Meaning, real meaning, is use not types. This is American Pragmatism. More Democrats say ideology is your Zen. To me Zen is the way I use Zen's signs. A zen picture is like recognizing the shock of Being.

This was like CIA torture, to be frank with you. To use another metaphor it's like a drunk man who just got out of the car and is asked by a cop to walk a straight line. I can now. But getting there was torture.

And that's against the 8th Amendment so I give my apology to you the reader. That's an ideology. But others who are not so tortured will read this. I am an Independent from Berkeley. I think.

CJ went on, about modern linguistics. I bit my lip. Postmodernism, something most modernists and postmodernists hate, includes material things and Saussure? I failed my doctoral orals on this point and I knew it was referring to Zen. Which I had not stopped hating myself about. This was Europe and Russia and I failed because I did not know the key. The referent to the trope of Zen is the water in a sea, people being the fish. I am a trope of Carter, others say that they are a type of Zen, that is not my evolved self. Like a peanut farm.

My orals were on rituals and symbolism. I missed so many classes it's a miracle I got that far. But I went far enough that I can understand the angst of a Harvard grad. Or, Yale. I get my 15 minutes of fame and there it goes, especially for a Chicago and California man. It doesn't hurt to say, with linguists, that the meaning of ideology lights is the holiday season. Of course its happy holidays but for me that's Christmas. That's A good metaphor for belief in Gore and Carter. I can't say it enough times. It's <u>all</u> political votes.

They could have said, you are so stupid, you are not even modern yet. And that still haunts me. I can get as corny as Kansas. <u>Water</u> in the <u>Belly</u> is a tortured trope. And I know that I have made it to the 21st Century. I have solved the Zen Paradox. Beyond all the tropes, which you probably don't have the faintest idea of what I'm talking about, I try not to mix too many metaphors. I know I mix church and state, like

George Washington. But this isn't a public High School graduation. It's like a political convention. On with the Zen of Being.

-3-

The next day, class met again. Pablo spoke for the class, we are so confused now it's worse than when we started. He didn't see. I said, I think Pierce was right, reference is to real things. We want a singer from Zen. Just then the baby in Sherry's belly bounced. I figured Being was talking to me. The class was confused because modern linguists say the meaning of Christmas lights is the <u>culture</u>

The Holy Bible. Mark and Mathew about the birth of the baby Jesus. The baby moves. I hold up a cross, said Pablo. And that's a type, I'm told. That is a sign. I said to my Sherry, the denotation is to his Zen. Muslims believe in Jesus, it's the blind ones that wage war on Christians in some nations. They like think the signified of an American is the devil. They don't hate Christians, they hate the 10 years of occupation of their land. Muslims are a great people. Their Zen is not a trope. The academics need to get out of College and visit an Arab country, and read their holy book, for an *ayat.*

Like a big fish in a little pond. Why doesn't the CIA deal with that. There Chevron looks for oil. And they don't rip off the natives. What's at stake is your faith in Zen, said CJ. He put his hand over his heart. I cry for my new party, out of the good that the CIA could do in countries like the above. To read *The Noble Koran* and know what it means to the Muslims. A new Democratic party. And I'm Black.

Just then Valentine reached down and put on a Santa Claus costume. CJ said, You thought that there wasn't any Santa, where is your zen? Modern linguistics says that the reference to Santa is our <u>culture</u>, that's easy to swallow. But they say the same with the reference to the real meaning of Christmas, Jesus worship is just a reference to our <u>culture</u>, and nothing more. My heart started to feel pain. It says that there is no Zen. This was the fighting of 500 years of Modernism. Actually it's not Zen they object to, it's like 1000 years of the Crusades, that many years of western imperialism. Look at the world, through the eyes of someone that doesn't believe like you, but who is your friend. That is the meaning of those words. And a Zen is a Berkeley trope.

I spoke up, Paul Ricoeur was a linguist and he followed the cross, as a type, like the post-expressionist "Yellow Christ", a modern painting that for him meant Jesus. That was not a mistake on Paul's part, he just bypassed Saussure, a fellow French man. Paul had faith in the cross, though a postmodern type. I follow Gore's faith and let him Defend me in his books, the meaning of ideology is like water to a fish. A Muslim *ayat*, sign. Paul taught at Chicago and followed the American school of reference, a sign can be an index to a real thing and not just a French reference to <u>culture</u>. It was the American CS Pierce that said that symbols can be an index to like Being in the world. This is an earthquake in the evolution of language and ideology, CJ added. It says that Eliade's Mysticism is real and the referent to a sign could be to Zen. This is the answer to the statement that there is a trope of Gore, or I am like a trope of Zen. To many, that is toxic. But my great, great grandfather, head of the Church of Pain at the time, said like we can be like a trope of an embryo of Zen. That's all like he said, but it was so controversial. He was like a mystic, like Mircea Eliade, from the University of Chicago. This is the debate that nobody is getting. You lead with your heart and let it tell you that you are a trope of a Zen in embryo. The reason that it is so controversial is that you have a largely agnostic Europe and Russia and China. And to the Muslims, their Zen is not a trope. But to modernists, colonial or imperialist or other, the belief in Zen was answered by Freud in his <u>Future</u> of <u>An Illusion</u>. ready for a revolution for the French Saussure. That was modernism taken to the field of linguistics. Professor Milton, of Chicago where he was my teacher, showed the difference between European linguistics and American <u>semiotics</u>, of CS Pierce. This can stop wars, to tell someone that we are not the Devil, it's not the trope.

I said, this earthquake in language study is going on even as we speak. Jesus is an index. To a theologian like Paul he was allowed to have American faith in a real index to a real Jesus. Something that Mason, European linguistics would not allow? This earthquake was as big as the Grand Canyon, and just as American. To the average person in Iowa or South Carolina, they don't get the issue. They just want you saved, or redeemed. It's the <u>politics</u> of civil religion.

Sherry started to cry and said, that's my baby, we are fish and Zen is the water, the fish just don't know that they are swimming in water because their life keeps them going, like we don't recognize Zen, because it's all around us. The air is like water to the fish. We couldn't survive without air. How much proof do we need, more whale talk? To the Chinese, against Tibet, any talk of Buddha is wrong. Just don't bring it up. But at Berkeley, I do talk to the Chinese. And they don't want to hear about my Zen Buddhism. It's too political.

Gore is a sign, said CJ. Santa's workshop couldn't pound out better toys than that. The problem with Modern Linguistics is that it ignores the reference to a real thing. It's like saying I have a brick and I throw it at Frank. If the <u>reference</u> is just to <u>culture</u> he doesn't need to catch it. But if he does not it will hit him in the head. That's Zen. Zen is the brick. The singer approach to semiotics, is not the way the religious Muslims think. There is a real Allah, the compassionate and the merciful. And he talks to them through signs, an ayat. This is like the born Christian, from the American South. That is why they don't fit in at Berkeley. It could be Yale. I use the phrase trope of Zen, to mean the inner Zen, the born again Zen, the trope of the Zen in embryo. This is a real fight. They say that I am not Christian. I say that I have been educated. Have faith, it's the 1st Amendment.

Ideologies could not give a better present to you, said Mr. Valentine. Say that it is a Valentine's Day present, or a skyrocket on the fourth of

July. It's so big a deal like The Grand Canyon, it can only be protected by the Federal government, as a National Park. Zen lives because of— <u>legal semiotics</u>, proof in a court of law. He signs to this, he indexes that. It's his Valentines present. Calm down.

The gates of Zen itself couldn't prevail against the Grand Canyon, said CJ. It's a great place you should work there some summer, on the south rim. It's natural, you get in with nature, get out of this smog, ride a mule, down into the Grand Canyon. Look at the air, as we are to it, a fish is to water, Being. He was referring to green, the Green party, the Enviornmentalists.

The reference of the cross is not just the cultural church, it's to a real Gore. Your fate takes over from that. I'm not a magician, I am Santa Claus. Mr. Valentine went on and gave out presents to the students in his class, in his Santa Clause costume. You have to get your Being yourself. And don't let anyone say to you that Zen is dead. This class turns modernism on its head, as if by Paul Ricoeur. But it is modern.

Denoting is like saying there is a real reference to the word Zen, said CJ. If you say that there is a referent to the word Zen, then you buy the complete works of our Paul Ricoeur. He told the modern Europeans and people at like Yale or Stanford that there is a Zen. That's like saying the real referent of Christmas is not to Santa Clause, but to Jesus. I have no problem with this, it's just that I am a poet as well, so I talk about the trope of Zen or the trope of the inner Jesus, and then I can talk to Harvard, someone in the theology department. And don't say that I am not a Christian. It's just my religious character. Like Candidate moderate Mitt Romney.

Denotation comes from American Semiotics, punch that word into the internet. At Google.com. To denote means to index, like the billion Christians have meaning in the cross, as a sign of Jesus, to be born on Christmas day. There is a reference, beyond belief. It's just we are like performance in Santa Claus and not Jesus being born.

Mr. Valentine said, let's go over it again. There is a cross and it is a type of meaning of the <u>historical</u> person of Jesus. Our different <u>denominations</u> give it special meaning. The signifier is a cross or *The Bible* or *The Koran* where Jesus is talked about. How much proof do you need? Jesus is the signified. <u>Interpreted through your Church. Which is your culture</u>. That's the reason for the 1st Amendment, for freedom of religion, I am not trying to make it a <u>state</u> religion. Just allow me my <u>personal</u> <u>belief</u>. It's big here, because it's part of the plot of this book, my character, Holmes. As Odysseus believed in Zeus. Dead.

We assume that we have already answered modern Philosophy and thought. So we take zen as a given. You get a flash of cold. Don't worry, it's just snow in the Grand Teton National Park. Where I climbed the Middle Teton in winter, said Mr. Valentine. When I say Zen you think it's like the air all around you there. You can feel the cold. So you know that your fate in Zen is there CJ talked of Kitsch Christmas.

What you need during the day is have an inner Santa or whatever sign you use to get in touch with that better power. You are roped up and you have plenty of wool, on your trip up the Middle Teton. I don't care what anybody else would call it, it's Zen and the 1st Amendment lets me have my belief and metaphors. The air is like Zen, at the top of the Middle Teton. That's a trope of Zen. Its like a parable in our zen book, symbols of this thing for that thing, and you are talking to Berkeley or like some undergraduate at Yale. Being is Zen.

Modernism and most of higher academics say Zen is Dead. That makes my heart drop. What if you were in a war. And the enemy could say your Zen no longer had any type of sense, it only had liberal meaning, it would freeze you in your tracks. And you would roll over and go to sleep. Or to "Song of Songs". That's how important this is. Belief in Being is a matter of life or death. And Eliade's signs aren't eating you alive. Half the earth hates Zen.

It would hit you in your heart, as if your soldier friend had just been shot. You can't go on. You grab on to Paul Ricoeur, Google.com him. Go to the University Library and read his works. All of them. He was a professor at the University of Paris and he was speaking for you and me against all the <u>acts</u> of philosophy. Don't give up the war. That's what modernism said, that Zen was dead. But I say that I am slouching towards the inner Bethlehem, waiting for my character to continue to evolve. This is it. It's how Federal judges think.

You can't see the water and its everywhere for the fish, the water is Being, or man on the shore. Don't believe when they say ideology is guilt and slavery. That is the type of modernism that Paul fought against.

Your heart fluctuates and you have made it to the top of the Middle Teton, and *Homo Dei* would put you on your bed. Just remember the Achilles' Heel, that's saying you are Zen now. That would cripple you.

It's freezing rain you get on the top of the mountain you are almost in shock, said a postmodern professor Valentine. You are not in a war. They have signed a peace treaty and your soldier friend did not get shot. Lay down you are in shock. You are replacing your disbelief with PM metaphors. And you reached the top. Of course, not <u>all</u> PMS is ideology, it's just Paul had a joint appointment in theology. And Philosophy. So he can talk to the Philosophy student at Harvard. <u>For him the referent of Modernism, is the biggest thing in his mind</u>. He is your friend. Like in an army and you are trying to keep each other alive. Your soldier friend did not die because of you. And you still get the old type bit and the new trope bit. The trope we used before, you remember it, Water in the belly. Your words are like water. Not "Satan."

Zen is not dead to Paul Ricoeur, our neutrino a particle faster than the speed of light at the Fermilab, where they first split the atom. Whatever metaphor you need, grab on tight, it's going to be a bumpy ride for the rest of your life, said our CJ Valentine. But remember the embers of the fire, of the inner Santa. That's Eliade's sign of Yoga, his mysticism. In the embers of the fire of religion comes heat to your body, also a 21st century discovery like tropes of fire, safe in the burning in your bosom. It's a tropic sign, from Zen. It's a bumpy ride, because this is just the start of the 21st century, and there is so far to go. Like a paraphrase of Robert Frost, the woods are lovely dank and deep, but I have promises to keep, and miles to go before I sleep. You are our neutrino. The problem is world education.

Mr. Holmes' semiotics said, the modernist Saussure was partial about his theory of reference? And how words did not refer to Zen. Zen the freezing rain isn't Zen it's just a memory now. You are going down the Middle Teton. Zen is signified in the books you read. Don't let them laugh at you for you have the memory of the top of the mountain. Just then, Rosa kicked inside Sherry's belly. I saw it. Well, she told me.

It's all about the fish and his meaning. Meaning comes from ones Zen or in inter-relationships. It's the relation of give and take from one thing to another. Or the in between one person and another or in a hope of a relationship or care and concern of one person to another, and there you need to step back, so its positive. CJ continued, that's just saying you are a fish and the water is just meaning, it's all around. Now you are reading my mature character, the purpose of this novel is its evolution. Chicago Cultural Critique, CCC, looks at the <u>water</u> of the fish.

As I look at the Pregnant Sherry. What is my CCC? What is yours? Generally, we don't critique the fishes. They are not in question. It's the <u>environment</u> of the fish that makes for a material Being. How did the fish survive? Is it too heavy for us? It's not the meaning of the author, it's the meaning of Prof. Valentine. There was the use of the term evolution, which there is so much proof for, it would spring you in a court of law. Beyond a reasonable doubt, its proof like the Big Bang. Sure there is doubt, but you are set free beyond that reasonable doubt. You are me. This is my character. I doubt.

Valentine doesn't realize he's a fish in the same CCC water where he looks at the fish through PM glasses. It's material. I want to know if my PE will be understood? Postmodern Semiotics, PMS, says that the water is real and that gravity keeps things together? I am the man on the bank of the river but I am not fishing. It's not about me it's about my Valentine.

- - -

And I am not your Zen. I get in the water and swim around too. It all depends on the season. Pretend you are in a feast. You have to say positive things to keep the party going. I am speaking in multiple, living metaphors. And its not easy. Those who would take away my metaphors don't understand communication. We all are like fish. It's just the meaning of the referent changes. To my kitsch tragedy. Justice Holmes.

The CCC can feed us all? It's cultural. We are a product of our culture. The questions are what was the <u>culture</u> of Frank? How does that differ from that of Valentine? I am a product of the band. And so is Sherry. We went through a bunch of change. We got married and then Sherry got pregnant. We take that as a sign, like becoming Independent. I have changed my party because I changed my ethics. We want just one child, like the Chinese. Zen is Being.

That's our <u>culture</u> now. And is the way that I would like to be judged. <u>My culture when I started this novel is different that the way I am now</u>. My religion changed from agnostic to the Church of Zen, a church I try to live for, though I now am a poor member. That's me. And the 3 monster, multimillion dollar selling albums. That's what you judge me by, how have I changed? I am not being sarcastic now?

My ideology now sees the need to follow my book where it talks about the sin of pride. This keeps my head on right. I am somewhat like a fisherman of Gore. I don't want the credit for my CCC I let my fish beat me? I am on the shore and I have a net, not to eat my fish, but to take them past the CCC? Just as I have changed? On the contrary, I have made my case for my <u>politics</u>, and am not trying to convert the reader, what's—Green redemption? The green party, the green of the <u>environment</u>, get out and look around, it's a holiday, now. It's cold.

I am with the fish I see and they are not my victim. I try to take the lead up the middle Teton. If you can imagine a fish with feet, I believe in evolution of the species and of my "Song of Songs". I am arrogant and my rock and roll made me that way. But Sherry, my sweet Sherry gave me her heart. <u>That is my most recent culture</u>. And PBS nightly news. I haven't been watching the news recently.

- - -

I have turned into the deaf signer and I eat my former hate? That is my metaphor and my CCC.? The rules of a novel almost made me become a CCC materialist. But a moderate one with a heart, a compassionate Independent, that's my <u>culture</u>. I have just changed. Because I did not want to be accused by the words I wrote for my songs. It makes me <u>sound</u> like an Independent, my words to my songs, heard by the world were so liberal. Everyone hates liberals, especially themselves? I wish I could trash the words of my songs? No let them be, just as the sign of a liberal. Just read them in context, evolving, to my present character.

Compassionate Independent person, is what I am becoming, <u>I change every chapter and the person of half way back in this novel, is not the man that I am now</u>. I have lived through too much. I with the future President of the United States all the luck in the world. It's congress. And I don't really like one Republican candidate. I am waiting for next summer, when my baby will be 6 months old.

I think I have stabilized about this holiday season. It's Jewish too. I have turned into a G rated movie, which are radical usually if you can read them right. I will be going back to Ithaca, New York. It's a college town. Homer's Odysseus went home to his Ithaca. But I had not Penelope to greet me. My wife came as part of the journey. To Ithaca and to Cornell.

I am human too. I want to go home. And I am most fond of the fish and the water metaphor for humanity and Being. That's all I can say. I haven't seen Zen. All I am left with are traces, which I call material. Odysseus goes home to Ithaca. I go there in New York, and Cornell. Home is where the reference is. Zen is the water, humanity is the fish It's eros of making it.

With one foot on the bank, and the other in the water, I am evolving. I'll let Odysseus stay with his secret signs, as Homer noted in his Chapter 23 of *The Odyssey*. For those of you who are following, I have added, at the end, an extra chapter, it's my new pet. Zen goes from being water to being like a planet going around the sun. That's Gore. Just duck if you see any dark energy, it falsifies my theory of the Solar system?

Back on planet earth, water is to a fish, as Being is to Zen. Zen is like an atom expanded into the cosmos. The deaf signer started up again. Odysseus and his friends knew each other by their secret signs. It's <u>political</u>, if you follow. I am material and hope to make a profit.

Such signs, then, are almost 3,000 years old and existed in Greece then. We learn that from Homer.

- - -

Being is to man as water is to a fish. There is always my dead brother. So he kept learning. Just like a man learning to meet Zen. Saussure said Zen did not exist, a word without reference, the way that modern paintings don't refer? A modernist painting has twisted and turning referent. That was modernism, twisted reference to Zen.

I am really modern. But I can't stand their theories of Zen and Death. So I grabbed on to Paul Ricoeur and rode him for all he was worth. And it was a good ride. I just called him Postmodern. He, at least, was humble. I will let the reader name this as what she or he will. I am in the 21st Century. There are other PMS, it's just that mine is tropes, like Paul. Postmodernism is my pastiche of Homer.

Valentine said, we want Ricoeur philosphy. Being at least. Remember the examples of the cross and the fish. And when you think of reference, think of me. View types of Paul's PMS. In light of American Semiotics. Which says, as it was evolving with modernism, that signs refer. Postmodern not only refers, it's multiple reference, to the Greeks to the Romans to Italy and to Modernism.

I hope you are still reading, despite my arrogance. Every word in the last paragraphs was specially crafted for you. It's like the ho, ho, ho of Santa. I make you a *Noble Koran* deal, a bet. Trust me if ever you are in a war you want Paul in your foxhole. And I don't want to hear their lower class racism. Back and forth.

When your buddy points in the direction of some gun fire, you want to follow. The above is what we were fighting in World War I. It's Gas. And I have given you a Gasmask. It will save your life, the way that I saved someone who fell off a raft, so many chapters ago. That's the point, to save someone else. That is the meaning of ideology to me. In using Critical Theory, it's good to know that Lukacs said that the Frankfurt School had no "praxis". <u>Saving Capitalism</u>.

We are like a type of the mother of Gore, standing near. You don't need to be afraid of this sort of postmodernism. Why? Because I like you. The first chapters were the Realism. This is the cure. We are at the base of capitalism and decoding it. Over the hill, are the Chinese, the nicest people I have ever met. But they will put you in one of jails of ideology or their jails for soldiers, if you can't give them some good self-criticism. I wrote the last 10 chapters with them in mind. And no response is not an option. Just keep reading and have a heart.

I'll say it again, we are at the base of the cross of capitalism and we are coding it. That was a baseball change up. If you can follow me, you are like the San Francisco Giants first baseman who put out someone at the plate who was running from third base, plus saving the Giants bat boy who was caught in the middle of the action. It was impossible. That's a true story. At Cal, they still recognized Being.

Why are we decoding Gore? We are in a stance with the Chinese as our enemy, we having troops in Australia. I can't tell you how much the Chinese hate Christianity. And yet since chapter 8, I've been decoding it. Hence the signs. I like the Darn Chinese. What are you going to do? The cold is not an option. Hopefully you have PMS? Dig it, if you can't you are that bat boy, and I'm that first baseman, Odysseus on the bed of Roots.

-5-

Professor Valentine said, I like types. They are like linguistic tokens. So don't get excited, some things are scary. But there are linguistic types and tokens. This was mother's milk to me a child of Zen. View a type of Paul's PMS, he hated death. I agree. Gore is a type as was Carter, a cipher. Something the CIA knows of. That's where language study and the CIA combine. Don't worry I wont torture you.

I know this is torture for you but try to get just a little bit. We are also at war with a Muslim nation, and have made a mistake with Pakistan. *The Koran*, a sacred Book I have read, could be read as a code for those nations. A Muslim wanted to like read people from the Frankfurt School. He was my friend but like Lukács, I think that they have no <u>Praxis</u>. And the Muslims, in some countries and sides, they have too much. Up and down.

- - -

The CIA is very professional. How can we work together with Kabul and China, in a professional way? You want to know the answer? We play ball with them? This is more than a trope, a cipher, it's something every nation can deal with, one baby girl born. We figure it should be born about New Years day. We play ball through treaties. Many treaties, one child. That's big with the Red Chinese. And they fight like the Muslim Asians, they turned <u>into</u> the enemy, with the—Two Whatever Philosophy too. They are Capitalist. With Deng Xaio Peng. They just don't like your religion. Explain your beliefs in a secular way, with tropes. They are postmodern, late capitalist.

A girl came into the room, dressed in a swimsuit, covered with a banner that read—Happy New Years. She told a few jokes and when the laughter had stopped, she said welcome to the future. <u>As somebody got access to the fire alarm. This going off, it triggered the breaking of water of Sherry, who was 8 and a half months pregnant.</u> She wasn't at full term. I was ready for the delivery. We called like 911 and they came and took my Sherry. I went with them and held my Sherry's hand. We both were scared. But we planned ahead what we would do when it came. I made it like meeting a Kabul enemy and I read from their book. Then I pretended I was meeting a Chinese friend. We were in culture shock. Just 1 child. By 2017 it's become 2.

-6-

That day she gave birth to a baby girl, at the Hospital, and we named the baby, Rosa. The next day Professor Valentine held class. And started out by saying, Free choice goes with fair trade. This was pure Chicago economics department. He said, Rockies and the South unite. I'm still a Daddy.

He got some laughs. But he was playing ball with us. I am a victim of Pride. Now, I worship people who are good to me. They are my type along with Being? Paul is someone I worship, because his Time works for me. I can play ball with PE? Physical education and political economics, we have already talked about it before.

Capitalism, the form of economics I was born with, is based on freedom of obligation of contract. Water in the belly means jobs and for us is China's—Two Baby Philosophy. It said no more Marx and should be given birth like the fire in the heart. I can see Rosa out of the corner of my eye, she is moving as I type into the computer. Christmas no more Lenin. That made them the best economy in the world. The above two thinkers, I can barely type their names, were against things like the US Constitution's obligation of Contract clause, in our Art. I Contracts. That's how they did it. It wasn't President Reagan.

Dizzy, I see the ideological here. And as I said I have the inner Santa in my heart. A Santa is being given choice. You have the liberty to choose. I am a type of Santa. I did not want to go to Professor Valentine's class any more. I have my Rosa. Postmodern economics is the Chinese—Two Baby Philosophy. They separated from Western Civilization and Russia and modern Europe. Now, the Chinese have the best economics in the world. Don't say, whatever. It's P.C.

I saw Rosa crawling to Bethlehem. To give birth to the next several years and I saw the birth of Rosa in me. Rosa has passed the trope.

Would we be like Europe? We just need bipartisan politics, not politics as usual, if we are going to solve the property and Wall street issues. I know so vote for me, and I'll set you free, for I am no <u>Faust</u>. Like a smart person love Muslims, Russia and China. Like many Democrats. We made it to the here and now city of divided Jerusalem. Our baby of capitalism. Compassionate independent was born in me. A type of National direction, like Italy. Anything but not Greece. The city of Jerusalem was named after David, that person with an Achilles' heel. The everywhere city. David had the mistake of pride and he had bad ethics, that's why he wrote so many psalms, to redeem himself. I don't comprehend the mind of David.

Water in the belly turned into crawling, through birth, to Bethlehem, the new Jerusalem, of everywhere. I could feel the water in the belly in me, and it was like the "Song of Songs" in me. It was a type of Zen giving birth to a type of Zen, Rosa. I could look around and see the material city of David. It was another peak experience. I have only got there once or twice before. Who will treaty with Syria and the middle-east? We can't betray our self? What's a type of Zen? Go learn Russian. Why treaty with Syria? They are good friends with the Palestinians and Iran. How would we not want to have a multiple treaty and not want to make friends with them? It was one of my peak experiences, for when you decide to have just one child, to be in line with the new international, how could it not be a peak? Now, like with a reconciliation committee.

I carried the trope like a pride, the non-literal symbol of the material coming in you? Zen forgave me. Water in the belly turned back into a literal symbol, Rosa was born. A symbol of the tomorrow of capitalism.

Symbol because it was a this for that. Now for the future. The Water in the belly was the Song of Songs and it knew where to reach me. The economy is going to be like China.

-7-

Sherry said that she felt a literal burning in her belly at the birth of our Rosa. This was not a trope for her, it was a literal symbol, the water in the belly. I view the little bit about being Zen in embryo as a good trope. It's not literal, in that we wouldn't really be in embryo again. Candidate Romney is relatively famous, whether or not he becomes President. I could go 1 on 1 with him treating him as if he were Chinese. I would try not to make the mistake of pride with it. I know they won't elect him.

I felt a dizzy feeling in my head, of a galaxy in my head, the Milky Way. They are symbols I use to explain the trope of the water in the belly. I got the poetry of the water in the belly as "Song of Songs" burning in the bosom. It's just to me it's a fire in the belly. To me it was symbolic.

It's like the whole Zen history happened to me all at once from pain to nothing. In the here and now all at once. The macrocosm of Zen history in the microcosm of me. It was a trope of Sherry giving birth to the trope in me. For me, call it a trope. It's not church belief, but it's the <u>feeling</u> I got. And what a rush.

I kept my vision and I was the same old Frank, just history in the trope of me. Through the birth of my Rosa, the trope birth of this book in me. It was a trope because it wasn't for real it was a feeling, and that is how I explain my vision. Of a real birth of a baby and a material rebirth in me. These were feelings not just tropes. But if you think of them like a trope you will grasp what to me was an Eliade's <u>ayat</u>. The trope was just language that I use to explain what I call a real experience. There was the experience on the boat and the experience in the park and the Last Supper. They were like the sign experience that I call human. It's a trope, because it was not literal. I was not again in my mother's womb. But I felt protected and it was if it was a sign. Almost like being born, except the trope was born in me. That was my Eliade sign. Eliade was real Genius.

I understood Rosa was the trope of a fish and we were the trope of water. These were images to explain the imagination in my mind, a class I took with the Chicago Mircea Eliade. The real water in the belly of my Sherry I felt as a Burning in my Bosom. Those are the words of my Pride. Am I too a Independent <u>Ahab</u>? I don't think so? I am like Paris? In <u>The Iliad</u>?

And the real pains of child birth, my Sherry felt in my belly, which I felt in trope in the galaxy in my head. Sherry fed the baby, as I contemplated in the memory of the burning in the bosom of me. The trope of water in the belly had two dozen meanings. And the literal pain in the belly of my Sherry giving birth.

Tropes, non-literal metaphors or symbols or signs, came to me this Holiday in signs. My Sherry said, what is a trope? I told her it was the symbols that I put on the pains of childbirth. Like the trope of ecstasy. It was a figure of speech, I said, not a theology of the Church of Carter. That said we really take the name of Gore, a type on us at time of election. Like the Parables of Gore we take on us as our law.

That was a trope of a type that we take on us, to have his spirit to be with us. That's my politics, what can I say, it was my <u>belief</u>. That's a close as I can get in explaining the key contract, among many, that I make with Zen. Those tropes were holiday signs. Material independent was what I was and I was getting tropes for me and my Sherry. You could not go against the poor and the old in total war, it would be like a civil war, like the Greeks, protests as if it were a trope of the end? That's the reason for my new conversion to Bipartisan politics, a turn away from the Democrat Ahab, and not sinking the ship, to the moderate?

Sherry is the Christmas tree, she told me. It's a capitalist sign. Only 1/4 of the world recognizes it. A tea bag is a sign. Of the constitutional obligation of contract clause. It was the morning of Christmas. Rosa was a little over 2 weeks old. And the above tropes are the Christmas presents we gave each other. How beautiful a trope, a vision without father telling me what to believe.

The lights of Christmas were all over our land last night. Now, we were planning the move back to Ithaca, New York. The way that Homer's Odysseus went back to Greece, His Ithaca. Christmas was for taking care of the poor and the old. The Christmas lights reminded me of Homer's tale. And the horrible journey that got us to this point. That is the message of Homer's *The Odyssey*.

To now in my heart, right now. That was the Ithaca of my dreams. It was the burning in the bosom of me and my Sherry. This was a keeper. The prodigal son comes home, figuratively the here and now, wherever you are, is your Homeric Ithaca. That's the issue of this novel. It's a portrait of good character? My very being is at issue? Am I a reverse read, from the back forward, like many languages, then a 21st century fraud? Did I kick my ethic flaw? Judged by my own ideology? Am I, not guilty? Like in a court room, can they rehabilitate my character? Does "State Police" stand as evidence that I am a horrible sarcastic, liberal parody? Is this a terrible parody of itself. Do my songs speak too loudly that I am a <u>radical</u>? Or did I change enough for you? Does the mere mention of birth control, guilt and lover allow a mature rating? One honest word of character in this fiction? Did I succeed in putting my character up as a mirror of Odysseus? Was that the intent? Was that my plot? Is my CHARACTER, now, innocent beyond a reasonable doubt? Did I acquit myself? How is the birth of Rosa like Democrat? Why is going through all that I did not render me a crippled character? Like my songs? Why do I feel such guilt, now, that I seek forgiveness from the reader? Have you noticed that over the last dozen chapters is 1st person narrative? As if a confession? Did I confess my character change? Was it enough? Was it a trope of the political 2020? Was it sensual? Would that take away from it, as if to call child birth that? Why do I almost have that feeling now as I type? Am I really not a <u>Faust</u>? Or, not an <u>Ahab</u>?

One thing America needs is affordable "assisted living" for the old. See the end of Chapter 21. Democrats have failed the old.

PART III

Trump in the 2020 election to betray and Deny!

Mr. Holmes likes Zen, but hates Tibet, politically.
<u>Historical materialism</u> and it's twists and turns is used in the
final chapter to see the orient, the Oxford term for middle- east.
After the Muslim *Tin*, the Fig, Jew and Jesus,
After the analysis and meaning, Art I Contracts
clause is a criminal defense,
This is our last stage of the ritual of
Odysseus, Homer's Hero. This is Frank's coming home,
Both physically and emotionally, Recognizing his
Weaknesses.
The last chapter is his redemption
From history.
And a vision of how to be a tropic scientist, Following the evidence.
Which ideology will help to Stabilize.
The National Defense.
In physics metaphor, we find redemption.
And rules to live by.
In light of President Barack Obama, who saw
the need for regulations, like OSHA.
And the extinction of 100's
Of species,
Including our own through nuclear bombs.
And climate change.
"Economics " is the base of "Legal Semiotics"

Chapter 24

BEING'S THREAT

-1-

Red contracts, we moved to Ithaca, New York. A few years have passed. It's like at Homer's Ithaca, the home of Odysseus. Rosa is healthy and is typical of a small child of 5. We live near Cornell University, where I have been taking a class on Political Philosophy. I am still an independent. I don't want to trip on someone just because of my ethical stance in life and my ethical change and ethics play my social drama of my water in the belly trope, though I still liked eros with my ethics, that's some change to lead a bunch of people, that's some Change. But years <u>are</u> a long time and I am no longer a famous Rock star, I have become a human being, who has been forgiven by Zen. I am not a type of <u>Ahab</u> or <u>Faust</u>?

There is a problem with the recognition of Being Consciousness. It could be such a shock to you you might think and freak out. You might think that you have total freedom and liberty and class. Which we don't. but Heidegger is right, we just don't recognize it.

We are going on a trip to New York City. It's the day before New Years eve. And we are driving there to the Thoreau Hotel. On 2016.

We would spend our new years day, 2017, at the Thoreau Hotel.

Like the Independent party for contracts. Civilations' eros.

Democrat is what the local and state government is. I fit right in. Remembering what I used to be and how I related to the people of California. I have redeemed my character, in literature and in eros of my soul, both at law and in this novel? The key change is in ethics. If people want to know my politics I say that I am a Independent conservative. That's New England. What of the note of eros for loving my wife Sherry. Like the philosophy of Habermas.

Of the political change, if one is asleep for 20 years, as seen by Washington Irving. Which politics will awake and take us to an Ahab or Faust? In the next 20 years? Not me, it's as if I haven't changed, I still like Eros, the sensual, it came to me in a dream, I needed to be more human. It also came from Sherry, I hadn't turned a swift. Trump. Paradoxical Conservatism has taken over the Nation, which is an abrupt change from the Obama years? The Senate was taken over by Republicans? The 3 branches of government have been taken over by Conservatives? The main concern is to trim the large national Note, by trillion dollars. There I am a fiscal liberal. By 1 trillion that a bipartisan Congress could pass. We don't have enough time to become like some Greece or Hungary. These are two sides of the political spectrum. Socialist or Fascist. The way it's been in Washington DC for too long.

We need a new Independent & Democrat party.

I personally have gotten interested in state and local politics. I have redeemed myself by self-consciousness, of eros. That is I now judge local politics by the recent trend to the conservative right, which is the right, as if local politics is out of touch with mainstream America. See how he confuses fantasy and reality. He won't admit it when he is wrong. We have trouble believing what he is saying. There are always leaks. And the protests. What will he be like when he becomes President Trump. I feel like I am still America, and the Jew has returned home. I have taken, still, the mask of tragedy as my motto. It's employment and Art I Contracts. It's the eve of New Year's eve. Eros, is my mistake of pride,

I have found with my talk with the students of Cornell. I know how they feel, just don't teach to me about your Kafka.

Rosa, some say, will live to the turn of 2100. And the costs of sending her to Cornell, have gone up so that it will cost a half a million. We plan on feeding her on *The Great Books of the Western World*, a collection of classics out of the University of Chicago. It's the ethics of Aristotle and Spinoza that will be my guide in this chapter and bipartisan Independent Mr. Thoreau. It's not Democrat, but it is from New England, like Emerson.

I talked to Sherry and she said it would be nice to see the ball drop in Times Square at the turn of the new year, of 2017. We are going to drive to New York City, and stay at the Thoreau Hotel. Within a mile of Times Square. This chapter is an account of our talk in the turning and twisting eros, slouching our way to Jerusalem, the material now, on the way from Cornell to near the Thoreau Hotel. <u>Don't be caught sleeping, like Washington Irving's hero</u>. Like a teen on weed.

We got in the car, the 3 of us, and headed for New York City. We talked on the way there. Ethos Independent and for law and order of traditional values, except when it comes to civil rights, where I am Independent. The Thoreau of the right plus the liking of the environment, the green party. This is not a Presidential platform, it's how I have seen my history progress and how I have seen the US and The Euro Evolve and how I feel, me Frank you might say that I am challenge in certain areas. I make up for it. In that I can read. One article said Trump was German.

- - -

We talk of the past, of the revolutions across Arabia and the counterrevolutions at home on the economy. Thoreau, in *Walden*, wanted liking of the environment by getting back to nature. That was my Democracy, plus boycott foreign wars, like Iraq, you don't need to be afraid, I am against war like Presidential Candidate Bernie Sanders. Some might say I have turned <u>into</u> a <u>Faust</u>, with my eros.

From Tunisia to Egypt, we suppose a religious revolution occurred, of class, as predicted. Years ago was the year of—The Protester. I was only impressed when it wasn't in our back yard. For the Arabs it was great, not for Occupy the eros of our home or Oakland. Let them be represented by equality of the classes. That sounds like eros and Independent, doesn't it? It was a class revolution.

Then to the Saudis who at first crushed it then embraced it. Then a bloody one happened in Libya. The counterrevolutions came in Yemen, Syria and Bahrain. The one in Syria. Redeem a people and redeem a future generation. They can't stand the word class. Let them stand eros. Sure I got helped. But deal ethics to the Democracy, so we talked. It's Kautsky.

You want revolution, you take your chances. The 2016's must have got their idea to revolt from the Tea Bag revolution of 2010. Both staged an overthrow of the status Quo from the right side of the equation, contrary to 150 years of history that said that it was from class, and religion, the revolution springs. For the Republic, don't use the term revolution, use evolution. Like Egypt turned on itself, in vote.

Conservatives are generally for a Republic, rule by an elected minority. Revolutions are against conservatives. The terms are confusing. When I called myself the <u>Ahab</u> and <u>Faust</u> of eros of the Culture Revolution, it was a right use of terms.

Liberals were on the left. It's a historic term, that Milton Friedman used on himself. Now nobody wants to be called a liberal, President Obama hated the term. It's a slang word you throw at someone when you hate them. Liberals are hated by the radical left because Liberals are not for revolution. Which gets us back to the American Republican Revolution. Confusing isn't it? Now were in Germany.

- - -

<u>Homo Erectus</u> is in all of our lines. The cabala, an interpretation of Hebrew, furthers our evolution. Sherry runs our home. Her time is my zen, as I use a figurative expression. I gave Rosas to our Sherry, she being for the Republic. Even now she has the ethics of Aristotle you can read it, eros but with one child, Rosas next to her, with Rosa. They took off the police. In New England, evolution is not a controversial issue, like at California. Like Karl Popper.

Tradition is Capital Independence, mine. To conserve Cornell and the wildlife. Tradition is the best way of explaining my meaning. Like the Halls of Cornell. Like at our home, with my Sherry and eros. We have a hopefully just Democrat mayor. I will have to be Bipartisan. With my tradition of contracts. I want to talk to the mayor about Art. I Contracts, not do battle with sublimated eros with him. To give birth to Capital Democrats.

But I am still Independent, the way I was when I wrote our last album, so full of sarcasm. That's still me. I don't mind saying, I defend capitalism. Like a President who taught Constitutional law. Bipartisan accepted. I can't now tell the world what to do. I just want Con Law enforced, like a police man. And eros at home with my Sherry. Democrats should go to "the center".

I am not for fascist invasions, I am for the Republic. With the same economic plan that I had from the start, use the tax system to encourage factories and things of the GDP, and the obligation of contract. And tax the 1% rich and reduce the National Note starting with the Department of Defense. I am a Moderate Independent. This is my Bipartisan politics. And I'll talk with you no matter where you are.

Authors from Chicago, wrote a book called *Nudge*. In it they were for Libertarian Paternalism. It was not a primitive Thoreau. They were not for neo-conservatism, of the early part of this century. We destroyed the Iraqi people in our non-egalitarian Quest to control an un-wanted dictator. We don't want a dictator in America, no matter what his eros or which party, that's why I use bipartisan tropes Germany.

Civil religion is the democrat on stump.

Conservative revolution or libertarian conservatism or eros of the <u>Faust</u> Republicans, it's all the same. Just don't go back. There is an irony here in that Paternalistic Libertarians bought and sold us through the 1999 Banking Act, which still had control of the Stock Market crash of 2008. The point is we live in a Democracy, be Bipartisan, work it out.

That's what I learned from being around Cornell students. Like the University of Chicago, to an extent. Do we have cold feet about the Cosmos? We are talking for the eros, the dusted? From Washington, the intellectuals like me get it like the old and the poor. They wrongly get the dusting from politicians. That's bipartisan common ground, on a local level and at a National level. I sold my soul to Faust.

I am not anybody's type of help. And I'll try not to mention ethics again. It's as offensive to some in Ithaca as was my ad for common law marriage, legal in California. But I have changed, though I am still a returned prodigal son. A prodigal is like a type of eros, of mistake in the eyes of conservatives, that curve their spine. But that's my historical portrait in this novel. The character of an eros, old rock and roller, with his Sherry.

Full of the mistake of pride, Title 42 curves the spine of the city, like arrest with not appropriate rigor. And still there is state law, state constitutions and the state non-impairment of contract obligation clause. I fought for bipartisanism, for capitalists like my dead brother. They'll never get my <u>Faust</u> eros. The eros self-interest of my mind. It's me. A typical American stance. With my Sherry.

Apocalyptic Conservatism is now, where there is a trial of our Capitalism. Not some time off in the future, for example. We all are judged. We need to help the old, who's health in Medicare is on line. Not recognize it, then help to bring about a social apocalypse. We don't have the heart to go through the revolutions of Europe, or the money to bail-out every business in the world, I said.

The prodigal son, I hope my <u>tragedy</u> to independence can be read as a story to help with eros people. What am I saying? I go from old

liberal to the material postmodern. There you have it. Defence of a 3rd party as a defense to the globe. Don't judge me by my songs, it's them that I am up from the dust.

Though bipartisan, I believe in Federal green and Social Security, for example. I am a bipartisan Independent, I like to get out and about, in the environment, green. And the apocalypse, politically happened in 1776. I traded driving with Sherry and I held Rosa and it's there that

I had my parable of the tooth. Like a Pluto, what was downgraded as a planet, but its space still is in our solar system. The tooth was the Democrats.

Have you heard the one about the Irishman on a drunk, he like me can't tell the difference between religion and politics. What of a Independent coming, not forgetting eros, up from his roots, up from the bottom? Like our band. The roots of the tooth of the economy were left, after they pulled out the bloody tooth that needed a root job. No money. <u>They pulled out those flare roots of Medicaid and you could feel the</u> <u>constant pain</u> from the tooth that wasn't there. Like the usual contract dissatisfaction. The ghost of the Middle-east still hurt our body politic, the way it seemed that there was a "not" of a tooth that still hurts you, you could feel the pain of something that wasn't there. It's strange but true, I said. Democrats adopting "The center" could stop tragedy.

The way they say you can feel the ghost of Social Security, in an arm that was taken off at war. The pain of a nothing is felt even though it's not there. There are things like that everyday in Kabul, now. Limbs are cut off and the soldier still feels his foot. Like a tragic, Bohr who sees Pluto in our solar system, and in it sees the eros of the atom.

Vote.

Civil religion is Independent on the stump. Like me, forgetting about the wall between Church and State. The nerve of the extracted tooth is where the pain is coming from, like I got a flash in my memory of Dick Clark, who brought down the New Year's eve ball. Justice can be like an extracted, political tooth, the way they cut off aid to the old and disabled in the USA.

Likewise, the pain of US colonialism in Iraq can haunt us, years later, knowing what the cause was. And what caused the rotting of capitalism. This is strange but true Libertarian stance on war of the Senator Mr. Paul. Like the extracted tooth of Medicare. Did I say that they also took out your front tooth? I am thinking of the Thoreau Hotel. Is that the marker we all are to be judged by? Wasn't this place ethical? For my eros? And Constitutional contract? Compromise.

-3-

I forgive anyone I have offended with the above. It was a necessity, you see my politics are just that much of a paradox. Independent carter is mixed here with the eros of a born baby, the old water in the belly. The real political redemption, as if I were a blind man, attempting to wave my banner of Bipartisanism. But in the last 5 years in California and National congress, the Non-Bipartisanism as a remedy is no longer business as usual. We all are like <u>Faust?</u> I hope people that I have offended forgive me, I said. I want to go to "the center" to win.

It's <u>civil religion</u>. That is it's political remedied with religious words. There you go. You really got my game. I was remedied and I am going to try to politically remedy you. You say, what about ideology? That's what I am talking about. Didn't I just tell you. Civil religion was taken from a class on the Sociology of religion, and it meant that that's what politicians, in fact do, when they are running for election. Like <u>Faust</u>, who made a contract with the devil. It's a trope.

Conservative, used as a put down by liberal media, Independent bipartisanism is my tactic. It puts down the right with their own laws. I am not for keeping people down, the eros of my soul, sold out to <u>Faust</u>, in the name of supporting some. But that's the way the liberal press seems to use the terms. Democrats need Mr. Blair's "center". And beyond 2020. That the point.

Civil rights can be like practice, and I don't mean a real one, of a tooth. That has been pulled, the way that the Capitalist Chinese don't like, like with a contract. See my brother for starters. The nerve that is left causes the pain. It's like you feel the pain of a <u>Faustian</u> tooth of eros, a tooth that has been extracted. Why don't we get some Chinese and have them help us, with their #1 economy in the world. It would be great for Treaty protection. I am like Chinese. Just *don't* try to sell me any Russian Lenin or Marx. That was the key extraction.

Redemption of the prodigal son is a thing to learn from, like from Mr. Rogers. I looked like a lonely pilgrim, in need of a change. But to go back to our metaphor, eros in the belly, there is no getting back the lost tooth of Medicaid, judging from California all medicaid help for teeth will soon be gone, as before. Gov. Brown, who I like, is slowly taking apart that safety-net. The problem is Non-partisan politics, I could deal with him, George Washington.

People, a mouth that has false teeth, if they get extracted. Take out all the teeth, in our metaphor and its there is no Democracy. Who is to know what that must feel like, but I have faith in our Federal leaders that they won't let our economy get that bad, if there is no infection. Like Tolstoy.

That's why I became an independent. The remedy was a root job and a crown. But you can't afford that. So, the extraction. Then, don't blame capitalism. It's the whole world that is capitalist, and yes Greece it is still protesting, as are other countries in the world. Are we slouching towards an everywhen?

The crown was, if you're paying attention, Title 42, sorry you missed it. There are bad consequences to you if you go to that civil rights remedy. Like a Treaty with Pakistan, a country you have so much in common with, we both have nukes. Why treaty? Because we like you. It's by no means Mickey Mouse. Though we are in a Faustian, eros Bipartisan club. 42 is an important number.

Thoreau, like in the Thoreau Hotel, was against foreign war. He boycotted a foreign war. The best politics I have ever seen. The government is best at the international level that governs least. Don't go take your eros to some foreign country. Like Title 42 and Ferguson. Speaking about Capitalism, it was a bridge. But you can't afford that either, sorry to confuse you. And all because your filling fell out. The extraction was the obligation of contract clause of the US Constitution. The Chinese do it. You can too. Or did you want a civil war, like Republican Newt saw coming. This is a theme of this bipartisan novel.

Why don't you take a stand, then they can judge you?

Then there's Section 1988 that pays for the lawyer's fees for your civil right. It depends on what the weather looks like, but it doesn't look good for the plaintiff. It's not okay with the mayor of Ithaca, or the company of Cornell. So why mention it? It is Newt. It's a dire remedy when people are not communicating and civil talk has broken down. They've confused you and your character. Or me and my eros. I have <u>the politics of a monkey. I am a self-interested primate</u>. I want to help the world, and I can't even help my self, I said.

Civil redemption is needed for my character. I bleed too much. But it could be like eros. Contract clause. And I don't mean slavery.

There used to be so many teeth which one was the obligation of contract clause, the one says that the government can't impair your contract rights. Trust me its "the center". You don't need to fight City Hall. Just get an appointment with the right person, and talk, like George Washington.

I can taste the blood of that extraction in my mouth. It's also the University of Chicago method, according to one. No, it's not Title 42. It's Art. I Sec.10, of Rosa, of The United States Contracts Constitution.

Famous for *The Ritual Process*, Professor Victor Turner developed what he called the social dramas. The start of the novel starts off with a crisis and goes towards redemption. An anthropologist on my Doctorate Orals. For this novel, what was the ethic breach? And when did I know it? When was it remedied? There has to be certain things? Why? Because every society has it's traditions, and when there is a breach, there has to be a redemption, or it won't be the same society for long. That is the reason for my novel, because this is a character portrait, the novel. So why eros? Why <u>Faust</u>? If I was ethical, why isn't eros a revision? Isn't eros like the trope? That you contracted with? Like <u>Faust</u>?Who said that sex with your wife Sherry was the trope?

You look in the mirror. You have a puffy face. I can't sue worth a darn, but I know my social dramas. I had to redeem my character. With Capitalist econ, of my brother, you have gauze stuffed in your mouth. Don't try Title 42. We are fighting the obligation of contracts battle. Forget about the crown. You aren't the ACLU. It's my empathy with the people. This is the view of life, from the poor. Win the votes.

What was my breach? When did I recognize it? Oh, it was the nerve <u>of tragedy. And it was a duel plot. Personal and Capitalist. Tragedy</u> redemption, it's not just Victorian. It's in the courts of law every day. When did I change? Why? The extraction left blood on your sheets?

The tooth is symbolic of Democracy, and some property deals can't be sold.

-4-

Civil social drama crisis is the sin of hubris or mistake of tragedy. In need of civil redemption. I am driving the car into New York. Then we arrived. We parked and went into the Thoreau Hotel. I had a vision of ideology when we went in the Hotel. It was that I wasn't running for President of the US. Let the President help capitalism from slavery. So what if I like eros? That doesn't make me like <u>Faust</u>. My duty stops at this point of the novel, I'll let the reader contemplate the remedy. I am not the <u>Ahab</u> of constitutional contracts, bringing down all on board into the sea? Get your own "center".

Full of the mistake of pride, I can't tell you all about the remedy for all the people. I refuse to solicit any more about the two things that the United States needs, protection for obligation of contracts and civil rights. Of course, I am protected by the first amendment of the US Constitution. But its too much. It generates more heat than light. We need bipartisanism to generate more eros light and votes.

The pills you have say, take one every 6 hours. And there is your pain. From the nerve. You should have gotten a bipartisan crown. But it was too much. We can see, oddly enough, the bridge from our room, at the Thoreau. The bridge that was too costly. So you had an extraction. You had the tooth pulled. It was using the legal system to remedy a Title 42 claim. Make it all Democrat, in the 2020's and beyond.

Don't go to sleep on me. I had and have the 1st Amendment. There is tragedy in everyone's life. The question is when did you learn what you needed to learn? Right on eros, now, I learned that I am all right. I can write songs, but people don't expect to find the meaning of life in a Novel. And that's exactly what I am trying to stop. I cant help others when, self-interested, I can't help my self, round and round my eros self, we talked. Am I <u>Faust</u> or <u>Ahab</u>?

You see the cost, and the bloody sheets, the nudge of your wild love. And you can almost feel the nerve. Civil rights gets you bloody sheets, and as for contracts while I could write a book about contracts and the

government, what do you think the state of New York would think of such a book? Now, they'd hate it. Consciousness needs to change.

When this book is sold in California, what would that state say about my novel? I know, it would rely on the 1st Amendment, Freedom of Speech, Freedom of the Press, Freedom of Assembly and Redress of Grievances In a Petition to the Government. These are real defenses and allow this novel. But such are the changes. Learn from my mistakes, <u>don't</u> use Section 1983.

-5-

<u>When did you see the problem</u>? <u>What did I do to withdraw the attempt, to exercise your 1ˢᵗ Amendment rights</u>? Your puffy face shows you that something is not right? Did you withdraw the attempt? And the blood on the sheets? You take an Ibuprofen. The blood clot needed to form. You want to put in a gauze pad to stop the bleeding. This complex trope is an non-Literal metaphor. It wasn't a real tooth, it's a symbol of the obligation of contract clauses.

We need the ethics of Mr. Gore and the Business of Mr. Carter, to find the electable "center."

- - -

You need Political imagination, subject to the sin of pride. But there are so many ideologies and the one in North Carolina, the main one doesn't recognize your need. What if the novel is sold there? Why aren't you communicating? You can't plea that you are Left. That religion is different than yours, and they are in the majority, there? And you are not into crucifixion. They think you aren't starting your own religion. With the Church of Zen and eros. And we want only 1 child, to be like under the quota.

Now, I have a long way to go yet. I learned that at the right time. You see I am a <u>handicapped</u> person. You now see. Why was I trying to help Capitalism? From a Civil War? You have the nerve! You don't have the 99% helping you now? A voice, still and small says that you need to be redeemed. And for that you use the Constitutions, of the Federal government and the states. Without a Title 42 civil rights statute?

That's like going into the city with a megaphone or a gun, pleading the 2nd Amendment, They hate it. Go vote.

<u>Civil religion says the tragic flaw is the sin of civil rights pride.</u> They have found a new tooth. That has infection. It's on your front tooth. If you can't afford it, why extract your front tooth? Do you know what I am talking about? Can you read about me being like Faust and the contradiction of my eros? What about <u>Ahab</u> and what I wrote before? Not about civil rights. That's the infection? Go into the Senate and explain the nature of your business and the relevant constitutional clauses. That should keep you from suing, with a section 1983 claim? Are you mad?

It is now a trope or complex metaphor of bipartisanism of contracts as an <u>infection</u>, because the state won't hear your claim. All you can do is withdraw the attempt, that is the only way to redemption. Fire now is birth to a world of bipartisanism, your state is like Alabama. And they don't like civil rights. You could be in the South. It's civil rights for racial violations, not for capitalism. All you can feel, then, is Eros.

Don't worry. Go inside, its your own personal tragedy. It's your teeth again, a token. The tradition, the status quo needs to be maintained? The right side of your tooth hurts, like little pins are making an impression. It's your lost tooth of capitalism, not a stroke? Now they say, Defend Capitalism? It's too much? Think of a business you could run from your home? On the world wide web? Then keep thinking.

In the world of "State Police", you are told you can't do it. It is too much. In the real world you can, but this is not the real world. Arguing multiple tropes, you remember your civil religion. You are about to say a prayer at your High School thanksgiving party. It's pretty bad. That's the reason for Constitutional law, to help us to communicate, the intent behind this novel. Can't I be a sarcastic parody?

Liberal Independent, I try to comply. If you plead the Constitution Contract clause, they will think it's CCC? And they will be confused? Like you are now? Writers too can ask for forgiveness? That's all I am doing? My CCC is for judging novels? I pray too that you will forgive me and my vision. They are just tropes, non-literal symbols or signs or metaphors. They are taking you literally. I'm <u>Ahab.</u>

Where is Hoover? I am J. Edgar? I worry that bold capitalism is not enough to save the economy? You need the state on your side. Notwithstanding my independent bias.

Liberals will want to read it backwards, as if in Arabic language. Boy is liberated by girlfriend. But in Arabia, they wouldn't lie to you. Your reversal sucks and isn't universal. New York City is like Chicago, and they want your ethics? Why marry your girlfriend? That's what the 80% religious people in the US want? And still they won't give you with your eros and your Sherry a voting remedy? There is still one more chapter. Maybe you can find non-selfish remedy there?

There is the city and State power. Only Cal will recognize your free speech, freedom of the press and your desire, redress grievances against the state. Or a State school that defends the 1st Amendment. Rare among judges and the like. In my vision, I can't even mention the civil rights laws, and yes it is like "State Police". Welcome to the City. Don't forget your eros. You love her.

- - -

And you can't even mention Rosa'sParty. They have never seen bipartisanism. This is the new year. And a new vision. We can't wait to see the ball drop in Times Square. Rosa can't stay still. Rosa is on a trope. Can't we be civil? We have to. It started with tradition, and living with you lover was its breach? You needed to remedy the breach. That's the late half of this novel? And my Sherry's eros. This book is world wide.

You can't even plea the old case of the fire of Tunisia. You might solicit the 1st Amendment. Or, the Constitution of the United States, you know the place where you were born with the eros of the belly, and where Rosa And I were born. The Arabs would not like it if you mention that Egypt went in to civil war. This goes on the internet and goes world wide. And the world is more conservative than you think, people even flee New York City.

Don't mention Zen, you are Jewish and the city is Muslim, where this is being read. They don't recognize the US Constitution. Look, I am not pulling your leg. You just got arrested for mentioning sex. They don't recognize the US Federal government. They don't have US common law. They want to off you, I said.

It's your baby, Rosa, and she's Miss America. But you are in China. Where they are reading this. They had the—Two Whatever Philosophy, which said that they can have PC. They are more capitalist than the police, who say you sound like "Police State". America is on a trope. And they could care less. Your story said you married a girl young enough to be your lover. They want you in New York City.

- - -

Constitutional law says that you are home, but not like a barking dog, which was the complaint. Evidence and proof don't matter, they have the papers and you just have yourself as a witness. We went down into the streets of New York. It's 9 pm. And it's new years eve. There are firecrackers going off everywhere. And they got your speech. It's Eros. They misunderstood your liberal sarcasm. It's a parody of the conservatives talking to each other. They think you are serious.

Of course, you have no right to religion. What's that literature you are passing out? The city is on lock-down. They even allow peaceful assembly on private property, but not you. You keep walking. That's why Conservatives want rule by an elite, in a Republic. I say of bipartisan Constitutional law. They call it free speech, that's your eros.

That's New York City on new year's eve. Forget about a Democracy, rule by the people. Including the poor. This is 21st Century New York City, on news years eve. You are pleading eros to a teenager. You can't have remedies of the contract clause, it's in your face. At this stage, the people start coming in to see what the noise is all about. It's the age of your wife. How could this happen? Where could you go? It's a mob.

Don't get on the News. You are already on the line up. You say it's a mistake of fact and one of the people says, you have got to be kidding me. YOU could be in downtown Bei Jing. You remember Judge Posner, of Chicago, and his last book, on the down-turn in the economy and the collapse of Western Civilization. They are blaming the sliding down on your ethics. They think their government is like China, I said.

-6-

<u>Conflict of laws says the police have jurisdiction and you have the mistake of fact</u>. And you have a common law claim. They just laugh at you. Police protection lets you Plead Federal Constitutional Law. They will hear you at least. Your ego is elated. The obligation of contract clause is your free market, be bipartisan? But it hits them in the heart. They don't buy your remedies by eros claim. They claim that your breach of social ethics has only turned into your remedies, therefore there was nothingness.

Out of necessity, they let you use free speech, like a voice out of the dust. You were ready for it, since you saw the videos of "State Police". You look all around and its like, rule by Zen, Why did you forsake me? The City has been on lock-down since 9/11. Where have you been sleeping for the past 16 years? They are mobbing you?

Liberal Independent, I observe. This was The City. On new year's eve. On the turn to 2017. Half the City has no free speech, so be careful of pleading the sin of Pride, they will believe you. Back to tropes, non-literal metaphors, someone is on the cross. You did not know that it was a mistake to be a Capitalist. It is, if you let it. Why did you move, isn't it furtive? Of course, I am joking. The world is not like on a lock-down, I said. Is it?

They just like gave you a denial of a factory permit. It's no longer birth, the Water in The Belly is the terrible Fives. Rosa does the opposite of what you want her to do, and that is frustrating. Like dealing with the City on economics, and I don't know why they do that, perhaps it's just that they want to maintain their power, at any cost. And you with your "daughter" smacks everyone in the face. Sherry is too much.

Economics of the Law is your plea, like the University of Chicago. At the law school. Linked to the economics department where they got Nobel Prizes in just over some 35 years or a quarter century. I distinguish Mr. Marshall, in that unlike the city, there are no self-regulating markets. There is the fair market, and I self-regulate it? You are on your eros and they think you are like <u>Faust</u>, and on your <u>Ahab</u> own. And the attorney's say you have no cause? Zen doesn't run the economy? Why blame that trope of Zen on the fall of wall street back in 2008? The free market? Why do you seem to want to redeem people, they don't know you. Leave them with their own material culture.

Fair market economics you can talk about. About the give and take of free speech and the <u>choice</u> to buy your product. Don't overkill. You are running a business not running from the law. It's not that constitutional economics is a sin, in fact the disallowance of it is a sin of pride. The Chicago think tank of econ will direct you but don't over do it about your will or they will think you are <u>Faust</u>, like in <u>Ahab's</u> ship somewhere, like the ethics Department? And they haven't yet forgiven you about your vision of the Church of Zen?, I said.

Every 50 years or so there is a new revelation about constitutional law. The 1983 was for *2060*. Have a heart. So there is a time and place for everything. So there you have it, root work and a new crown. All for the bipartisan constitutional law, just for about a half of century from now. And remember to keep your mouth shut. You are one of the crowd. Go with the flow who are following the police, duck and you'll be lucky. That's the bottom line. There's your remedy.

But free speech says you can talk about it. Just don't tell me. I know about how the city feels when its agents are working. I did the extraction and you have a lot of rotten teeth, like an old man. Free speech says you can defend capitalism. But it's when, and where. This is your vacation.

You have your Federal 1st Amendment. If it's the right jurisdiction, they will want to read more. Just defend the political economics of capitalism, that's like mom, apple pie and the trope. If they don't let you just move on, Let them read on. Capitalism is how you let eros and <u>Faust</u> feed your family. It's still rated character, It's New York City, read your book. <u>They want to read it backwards, from family to common law.</u> With your wife, you even have a child, nice family touch. They read it backwards, you left your wife and baby for another woman, too young, and then you go into a rock and roll band, to fulfill your fantasies. Now it's not remedies, it's eros realism. The people in New York City like to read your novel backwards. Like some languages. It's the Odyssey.

The extraction went poorly. There weren't any exposed nerves. We used pain killers. But the excuse of the root of the tooth was flared. So

I broke it and had to pick out the roots in pieces. That's poetry talk for I used the constitution to use the fair market. But that's eros and with it you have turned into a Faust. It was a job and it worked.

-7-

The eternal city contradiction is that you enter "Song of Songs" tempted into thinking that you are Zen, in irony. And then you become Gore. Just hope that there is a Carter out there somewhere. The US almost believes you with your mistake your constitution, like Rosa, she needs people to hold her up. Don't go to sleep. I was pleading backwards. Of course, it would not make it in Iowa or Southern Carolina. But you remembered you are not running for President, on a platform. It's your eros. It's a shock. But that's a way to look at your painting.

Every Sunday is Palm Sunday, the entrance into the faked city. The next Sunday is the ideology. In poetry, a type. Forgive Rosa, America. It's just like the Myth of the Eternal Return, by Eliade. My teacher at Chicago. One and one more child, we gave birth to our Rosa. Don't worry it will play well in China. Just not in South America, where they don't like birth control.

to mankind, as he stole it from the Gods. It's not you or me we don't steal. The poor say, Where is the job? When do I start? There is no reply? The people are dumb? We are bipartisan? There are plenty of people who will read it backwards, in New York? They like to read that they are Zen, so they love the Church of Zen, like Feuerbach, modern. Vico.

We gave birth to a fire, our Rosa. Don't mention peace treaties anymore. The President will not get a Nobel Peace Prize. What did he do? In this capitalist parody, the irony is that you can no more defend <u>capitalism</u>. Why are there so many things you can't say, with the Supremacy clause of the constitution, Bill of Rights rules? But there is the color of custom in The City? There are a lot of people from Poland, like Chicago? Or from the old country of Italy? They are good Catholics? And they don't like you mentioning Eros or that because of it, confessing that you are <u>Faust</u>, I said.

Marriage of Heaven and Hell, the extremes, is like the ideology of William Blake, like the last chapter of this novel. Finding no Zen, America declared itself Zen, in Iraq. President Obama got us out? <u>Have another Thoreau treaty, like with Mexico?</u> <u>Or Arab States?</u> Don't mention Palestine or Iran, the Department of Defense isn't talking to them anyway treaties are part of the supremacy clause of the Constitution, so you see why there were so many broken treaties with the <u>Indians</u>.

Perfectionism is the trap of Western Civilization, thinking they're Zen. Because they are Modern. So the state will win in most state impairment of contract claims. The myth of the Eternal Zen Now, is that they are a tragedy in need of remedies. It's their Homer Achilles' Heel like eros or <u>Faust</u> or <u>Ahab</u> there is always the Sin of pride. I'm from the Chicago School, so I follow the ethics of Homer, don't worry you made it home. It's fate.

Zen was mankind in embryo. That is the trap that you get remedied from only by Gore. What is your Carter? Circe and the lotus-eaters are strangling our free speech. Contrary to Adam Smith, Zen doesn't run the economy. A type of Gore redeems you from Eros and from *Homo Dei*. The sin of pride. Yes literary criticism is probably against my behavior. Bad characters in the 19th century committed suicide. In the 21st Century they still have to follow the law. And rehabilitate their character. Like we almost did by selling our <u>Faustian</u> soul to lit.

I learned from my mistakes. I don't repeat them. Therefore I am not tragic. The child of the Union, Rosa, is our baby Jesús. I'll tell her later about the sin of pride. We finally recognized our many contradictions and got to Times Square. We took it with us. Now its our <u>black</u> comedy.

It was new year's Eve. The ball dropped. We made it back to the Thoreau Hotel. You know my politics, ethos Independent. But what you didn't know is who I voted for in the 2016 election.

- - -

It was for Bernie Sanders, Senator. One that believes in real socialism. That is the biggest put-down I could think of calling someone. That they have the Achilles' Heel of Ahab, of *Moby-Dick*. Like having the selling one's soul to the trope of Eros to become a <u>Faust</u>, but I directed the ship, U S Constitution. And we went whale hunting, all in the name of capitalism, in our trope. It got complicated for when we got the Whale of capitalism, it was rougher than I thought it would be. It in fact rammed our ship, this dual trope, non-literal analogy of us being like <u>Faust</u> and <u>Ahab</u>, not bad, I got a hit and made it to 2nd base. And brought down our ship. The Whale of capitalism is a monster, and I tried to bring down *Ogden*. The case was so strong it's the sin of pride to plead it and think you got away with a good one following capitalism.

It destroyed the person who was trying to kill it.

Part of my remedies, was maintaining my wisdom. I brought down the ship of all those who were following me. That's some Achilles' Heel. So unlike "State Police", which was sarcastic, I just say when I come to the US Constitution don't sell your soul to the type and be like the literary <u>Faust</u>? So make sure to be aware? Or you too will be like an <u>Ahab</u>. Then you'll see that I'm saying that the key symbol of America, is like a survivor of the Holocaust. Unlike, but connected to a Kafka.

-8-

As to Ricoeur's "interpretation of suspicion", I might add that my view of Constitutional law could be informed by Ricoeur. I have <u>doubt</u> that so called "original intent" of the United States constitution is the primary key in its interpretation.

There are areas that deal with "privacy" in the traces of the Bill of Rights, that have agreed with-choice. And I agree. There are things in the 21st century that were inconceivable to the framers of the document. Therefore, we need a "living and breathing" constitution.

And the totem, or sign, I used there was "original" pleading the case of The Federalist.

Again Asia; Russia & China, don't believe in nonverbal semiotics.

America recognizes it. That is the "Poverty of Economics" paradox.

The solution can be seen in part in Van Overtveldt, The Chicago School. Signaling theory is an alternative Chicago view, id p120. Compare with the work of Mr. Stiglitz and Mr. Arrow. see Human Capital.

Also see Nobel Prize winner Stiglitz, People Power, and Profits: Progressive Capitalism For an Age of Discontent.

The above places the "economy" at the base of "Legal Semiotics". This is a major theme. Also See Ginsburg and Huk's How to Save a Constitutional Democracy . I said to Sherry, with her hand on her hip of the silk, golden dress she was wearing.

My wife then got two cold beers for us, and talked about Progressive Taxation.

Chapter 25

THE PLAGUE

-1-

We jump up to May 21, 2020. Rosa is 9 and is asleep in her bed. I have just finished a term, where I took two Physics classes at Cornell. One of the micro-universe and one of the macro-universe. It blew my mind. So the following is the start of a continuous poem on my class, last term. Of course, it's more than a poem, but I am in Ithaca, New York, meditating on why I am a <u>Faust</u> or <u>Ahab</u>, the end of the last chapter haunted me for years. I'm a penitent person who no longer thinks the world revolves around me as if I were the sun, fully awake. I am a Professional song writer, not a grad student of Physics. Ideology is seeing, like Blake, like a Bohr, fantastic, like the atom and its electron and the sun and the earth going around it. That ideology is so fantastic I can hardly stand it, as you have probably guessed that's the line I use when I think I have found something that's good. And a good Zen. See both of them. In this sight of the bipartisan this is it, world at peace. If you want your character remedied at law, as if in a court, don't read the book backwards. It is not the Victorian ethic that I plead. It is the reality of law. This is a modern novel. The world doesn't go around us. With both feet on postmodern planet earth, we revolve around the sun. That's the right order of our solar system, like reading this book from front to back, the proper order and right reading of this novel. Reading the book backwards, you miss the tradition, breach and humanism of the universal social drama of our Victor Turner. The rite that excusesour <u>behavior</u>. It's a test to see if your mind is in fantasy or reality. If you think that this novel is a fantasy, you are tragic. It's 21st century realism. Electrons go around what used to be called the atom, in the rapidly changing world of spin, Physics, of the micro-universe, the creation. Playing poetry, of the universe, like the paradigm of our superstar Rosa. Round and round go what used to be called electrons, watch quick there they go. And the moon goes around the rule bringing earth. <u>The key isthat the universe doesn't go around me. I am with my Sherry on planetearth, and we revolve around the sun</u>. The sun is a trope for my Zen. I go around my Zen. And Sherry and I go around Zen, as we remain on planet earth. This is the right order. So I am not an <u>egoistic LiteraryFaust, having the world go around me</u>. If I can maintain it, that's my remedy. This is another election year. Rather revolving around the people. The people revolving around it. Reading it backwards, you are on the barren moon, lost in space. And not with your feet on planet earth. It is barren to go from a good economy to a recession, like being on the 2020 mar's explorer.

The yin of quantum physics and yang of astrophysics of the macro-universe unite in Quantum Mechanics, the photoelectric effect of light, in our galaxy, so I interpreted Einstein. This I could barely see, in my poem but I knew It was there. Because I could see the light jump the space between two spaces—of course it's paradigm, just like the rules of astrophysics, We on earth, Sherry and I and Rosa holding hands, as we revolve around the sun, object of what is in my head, and the eros between Sherry and me, on earth, with our gravity field, of time and space, in my head, in the cosmos. That is my teacher's, one of them, theory besides the belief in Zen.

What we have been calling the particle atom, is like the sun, with electron-like planets revolving around it, in my head, in the cosmos. The curve of relativity made me speechless, and left me flat, in my head, you got me my head was swirling around with my pillow acting like a rule bringing Bohr-like vision. This is mind blowing and makes me say again, I am a scientific we got of course like electrons, going around Washington DC, with it still in the same universe as the rest of the world. I am Ahab because I have the fetish of Zen, and thus, pride.

The Plague, Coronavirus, Trump, Racism, economic Depression hit the US. We needed light. Not anarchy against the vote.

- - -

Philosophy of the atom, evolved the way scientific theories do, the way we measure the sun's gravity, matter relating to light. I saw all these things evolve, in time, the light rays coming off the sun, reflected on the moon. Matter relating to light. We had lecture after lecture on dark matter and dark energy, in outer space. What's in the space electrons revolve around? All I know that I am on earth, with Sherry and Rosa, and a good father, as we revolve around. Like revolving around Zen, in my Carter Universe, like Einstein's cosmos, earth revolving around the sun of the solar system, as we get a tropic charge, Sherry and me. Around the sun takes us a year. Two Impeachments.

Particle physics seeing the smaller world, and astrophysics seeing the larger worlds, if you can see this scene then you see the yin and yang of Physics, first seen around the Time of Bohr. If you can grasp this so fantastic I can hardly stand it, then you are one of the initiates of the Universe grasped by Einstein. We are home, in Ithaca, near Cornell. With pacts of peace. For Public Policy.

The general theory of relativity, which explains gravity, as the curve of time and space unites the macro-world to the micro-world, hence multiple universes, or worlds, deflecting starlight, over my head, as I held my Sherry. Even the explaining of this scene, I feel light as a cloud.

I have my head in the sun and my feet in the center of the gravity of the center of the our planet, with levels of light coming in a tropic order to our earth, and is it ever hot. To see both of them. Then work in that position. Economics goes in cycles, as my belief in the Church of Pride, best seen reflected in *The Tin*. This parables of the Universe. Waves of matter hit waves of light, on planet earth, uncertain in energy and time. I kept on writing uncertain when it would end, matter turning into energy and energy turning into light, making it look like a video game of the cosmos, as I held my Sherry ever so tight? On went my mind. And my poem, the one that questioned why the colors were named <u>dark</u> matter and <u>dark</u> energy? They were so important and made up most of the cosmos. I hated dark energy. I say this is my <u>parody</u> of Joe 6-Pack, right-wing populism, hostility of migrants and multicultural racism. And a debunking of their intellectual authority.

- - -

This thought experiment kept me fixed in time and space, though I knew that the laws of thermodynamics would govern my energy transfers, in the cosmos in my head, coached by Sherry touching me, as I slept. The heat of our bodies like the light between electron and proton, we both revolving around the other, in another galaxy, two supernovas, or black body radiation? Bohr names it <u>black</u>. Don't get confused there is black body radiation and dark matter and dark energy. It thanks Zen for both levels. <u>Federal law is like on the sun, for our solar system, in our model, we revolving around them, not the other way around like a literary Faust</u>. That's the trope I use to explain in my humanism, tolerant of all.

The poetry of my simple theory of the universe and the atom, was just that, poetry. But I was right on the connection between the macro and micro worlds. The relative Independent family and nation being symbolic of Physics, a trope a non-literal sign in <u>waves</u>, though I can't see a year into the future, except my Rosa, who is like a new galaxy they have just seen, round and round. If you can relate Quantum Mechanics to micro and macro physics of super theory, you are with a prize or in the world of 2050? Some say none of them are right.

In my poem, I saw the interaction between waves of light and electrons, an almost impossible thing to think, but so beautiful in my poetry. Between light and electrons, between Zen and Sherry and me, sharing with Rosa. I <u>proved</u> my William Blake theory of seeing the universe in a grain of sand, Physics Being the realm of the tropic, particle physics? What became of the Chicago Fermi's Quantum Mechanics? It was Einstein's too, and he was self critical of his own theory? Was he critical of his own Zen?

- - -

The Great Books Of The Western World were my help in understanding the history of Philosophy and science, of light and particle waves, so mystic, in my poem, that I put my hand up to a wall as I saw the light hit it and go through it. The evading Photon of light, in the universe and the atom. These theories change so quickly, like neutrinos, the things that were proved to go faster than the speed of light, which Einstein said there was nothing faster, but Einstein was substantially correct, because a fraction of a fraction of a second is the same as Einstein. Could we have a different model of <u>dark</u> energy? This is my "Hermeneutics of suspicion" or interpretation of doubt. The Fig is a call for unity.

-2-

Symbols kept banging around in my head. Motion electrodynamics, as we have seen, deals with the classic power of motion and force, and links the three forces of electricity in Quantum Mechanics theory, in my presumption, and electrons and light, or so I would presume, in my poetry, of the galaxy? This is a vision of the mechanics of the universe. And why Mechanics? For the Milky Way or any other way my poems are written talk with Zen? With the galaxy? For the Universe? Like two adults on the floor at the Prado Hotel? Like Sherry, Now, explaining to me why she is Zen? Like the reporters revolving around us after our show trial? And the members of the band that are still of the Church of Zen? I am no orthodox Church of Pride.

The Greeks, after Homer, saw the difference between the poetry of the atom and the poetry of the wave, at first. This was the start of particle physics, seeing in a wall the particles it is made up of, and the wrong thought to revolve around earth like skates. Forgive them for their many mistakes about the Solar system. They got enough right for 2,000 years? They got the moon going around the planet earth, like my theory of <u>Ahab</u> and <u>Faust</u>, where Eros was in and for itself, not like revolving around The Sun or Zen, in our trope? It's not false to call it a trope, it's just a paradigm like Zen is on the Sun, we don't know where Zen is, but suffering, we go around Zen with Our Eros. Not the Sun going around our Eros? Why poem?

Soon, in my tropic poem, I saw light's colors, in waves. I saw this happen and, in my tropic poem, I saw a rainbow, my head peeping through the bottom of the rainbow as if I were discovering a new world, on the other side of the rainbow. The new world was symbolic of the William Blake ideology. *The Marriage of Heaven and Hell.* My view of treaties. Circling the a square at the end of Dante's *Devine Comedy* like a new theory of <u>dark</u> energy? Civil religion like 2017 and beyond. While still having a separation of Church and state, breached by <u>Hobby Lobby</u>. I marry the right and left. Know thy enemy.

The creation of the world, thus, prepares us for the growth of a child, a universal quest like the marriage of atom and electron, tropical in a cipher. Both types in a marriage like a treaty with Islam, like Iraq, that yields the creation of a consciousness, like almost the creation of a rainbow Supernova. Signs of tradition, the answer I got right in my doctoral orals, like Victor Turner's *The Ritual Process.* Like Novel Theory? How much of this don't we know? How much of dark energy is positive? It's like Turner's anti-structure? Rites of Econ.

Flags of all nations came into my tropic poem of the rainbow supernova, where evolutionary universal types were resolved in my poem. Our atom, revolved around the sun or tope. Rosa just came up on our bed, wanting to sleep with Mummy and Dada. Why, is all she asks. A rainbow for <u>dark</u> energy? Then why rainbow energy? Why light refracting in energy that is <u>dark</u>? Why name it dark? Are they from India and that's the only color that they see, Dada? Or, was it just that it gives off no light, and reflects none, hence <u>dark</u> energy, in my poem. Out of Africa. Cycles of depression.

The child born from tropes. If I call your name, would you see me in Paradise? These are our names for the traditional next of kin. The sun is in our solar system in our galaxy, the names we use are historic, contingent, all depending on space and time. <u>So why do we keep calling dark energy, furtive?</u> We respect a relative position so we treat it like the Sun. Like I treat Sherry as like Zen, so I talk to her, or I talk to Rosa, so she is for the moment like Zen, the Sun. Not the Church of Zeus.

Let the heavens shine on him, on a type, the future of life, light give me light, was the cry of my poor blind body, another tropic, poetic type. We are like on a spaceship which is on practice of a treaty with Asia? Journey, to the promised land, a spaceship earth, we are with a Russian crew, so I have to translate my poem from that language. They don't believe in Zen and they don't buy the metaphor? They aren't color blind and would they call the energy <u>dark</u>? 70% of the Universe? the tropic Rosa. Her head swimming in dreams, I dream of her in my universe, swimming in my head. Seen by her father as she sleeps, ops she moved again. I see her as my sun and I read her every move hoping for a sign, from my tropical. Rosa revolves around me.

I dreamed our spaceship turned into a Phoenix, and rising out of the ashes of the ship, Rosa continues on in her journey? Life is born out of death, the phoenix born out of it's own death? That is my belief. The spaceship landed on earth, with only Rosa surviving the timeless trip to a moon of Saturn. Like our old car, a Saturn. 30% of the Universe like gravity? Dark matter. Poetry is our humanism.

Tradition gives us light in a atom of light. Why? The atom is dark and a photon of light lights up the atom. We have made it back to the micro—world. <u>Back from the photons of light from the sun</u>. We find an old Bohr. We have found the microcosm in the microscopic world of the atom and the electron, excuse me, the Fermion to the solar system. This is a mind blowing thing of the University of Chicago, understood by a Nobel winner. And in the macrocosm. I relate the universe to Rosa, and she thinks it's fun play. Yes, since Einstein we have the world of quantum Mechanics or Universe? And his self-criticism?

This is our journey home, that is the back and forth goal, from our birth. I explain to my Rosa the meaning of the microcosm and the macrocosm of the Universe and we make up a game, seeing the supernova we ran from, in the spaceship. We learn to walk, keep practicing, to do many things, By the act of belief. Let's not loose it. Please let me play? With my world of Treaties? With Asia? With Orient? We follow the route of the spaceship from those who had gone before. It's everyday that we begin our journey again. By tradition, what do they call me, atom. <u>With the electron of Rosa swirling around me. I</u>

swirl around the sun of Sherry. No, we can't afford any more electrons, one is enough. Would 70% of the <u>dark</u> energy destroy the Universe?

Crossing over from tradition to tradition, we start to communicate. The child is growing up. It was one of my family who said, everyday is a birth. And people revolved around us, in our orbit, as we revolve around others, like my wife. Down is where I am having my tropic poem, on my bed, so warm. Like on the light side of the moon. I revolve around the laws and strange customs of mother earth. The Blues.

Let's go back to our original symbols of the cosmos, inside and outside. Einstein had many theories and his theory of the relativity of time I can understand. <u>Time is not universal</u> between different galaxies. Time coming from the rays of our sun, different planets in different galaxies have different time? In my play, is there mistake room? President Asad of Syria wanted the people to revolve around him?

Einstein had more theories of universals, like the speed of the light from our sun. Though disproved in some models, he held that he questioned his own quantum Physics almost to say to me, my models of the universe don't answer the question of Zen, who he believed in. Am I allowed my Zen? In the Solar System? You can have your Zen. Is 30% of dark matter gravity like a <u>black</u> hole and would help to stabilize our Universe?

- - -

<u>Time is relative</u>, because it is not consistent between one galaxy another. One wonders what Einstein's and Zen is like. The earth's light is contingent on the rays of the sun. In another galaxy, the planets have another sun, <u>hence the relativity of time</u>. Their light and time different than planet earth, our orientalism.

Going from the macrocosm to the microcosm, of atoms, electrons and light and atoms give us pause as to what is the field of physics. Symbols, like a type of sun and math, are like tropic poetry? As are Suns, a paradigm? Are they electric or magnetic? I wondered in my poem. Einstein was a founder of a branch of quantum mechanics. As Marshall Sahlins' materialism, <u>Stone Age Economics.</u>

The Universe is made up of bunches of dark energy. This causes the universe to expand. Beyond the cosmic inflation at the theory of the big bang. I can't explain beyond this point, the space between stars? Dark matter is like a black hole, in that they have gravity? This is so fantastic I can hardly stand it, the gravity that will let our Universe stay in peace, like planets and sun in our solar system? I will let the dark energy remain, just not part of my meditation of our Solar System. We are not threatened by dark matter 30% of the cosmos what is a threat to the Universe is the 70% dark energy, it is just that it is not our metaphor, trope, of a stable state. It's billions and billions of light years away from us? Dark energy and dark matter of the Universe is not a threat to our Solar System, for some reason? Perhaps it's the gravity of the solar system greater than dark energy? Dark energy is like the slopes of the world. This is my <u>Ahab</u>? At the end?

The basic theory in physics, which is swirling around in my brain, like a child Rosa, going through every day, a creation, is constant in matter. It changes in time when a new paradigm starts up. Explained in *The Structure of Scientific Revolutions*. The sun is constant, whether we revolve around it or other wise as was the paradigm shift some 500 years ago? Who is to say what will become of the theory of dark energy in 500 years from now? Can you see the rainbow? Or, at least the Solar System orient is a college term used not for China, but for the mid east. All the tribes and *The Noble Koran*, oriental treaties. <u>The Qu'ran</u>.

Particle physics is new as of about 100 years ago, about the time of Einstein. New is the theory of waves, and astrophysics talks of the space, in outer space. Where is gravity energy in dark matter? Again, Enrico Fermi went through a paradigm shift, when he split, on the way to Winning World War II, the atom, in Chicago, in 1942. It must have blown his mind. He called the new particles of the atom, fermions. This is so fantastic I can hardly stand it. Fermions totally blew me away, in their Quantum theory. What would dark matter do to dark energy in a billion years from now? How would that effect the Solar System?

Probability is seen in the math of physics, as tropes and symbols are used in this novel. What will my child be like after the water in the belly? What will the future bring? We grasp it through metaphor or signs or signals, I am turning 40. Will I hate my rock and roll? Will I love my Rosa? Will I still love my Sherry? What of my Zen? And the Russians? Can I speak Chinese? We need a basic and universal language that will let us talk through time? Hence, the Solar System model is greater than the models of <u>Faust</u> and <u>Ahab</u>. Historical materialism takes chapter 9 on treaties from *The Noble Koran*? I am against totalitarian states, whether in the middle east or Franco's Spain. Math doesn't come out of nature, it's our paradigm.

A bipartisan Independent, is how I call my politics. And no, no civil war has happened yet. But there were a lot of protests. It was over food and Medicare and Social Security. And Medicaid. A civil rights republican is like the Republicans after the 1860 Civil war. An old republican. Give people their Bill of Rights, and take money, Treaties. Standard and Poor's kept down-grading European countries like, Spain and Italy and Portugal? This caused world stock markets to go down? It had to do with the National Note and the countries' Gross Domestic Product. For a while, it looked like Athens. The production of this book was in the US and helped boost the US GDP. France, just a Fraction of a second ago, was downgraded to the level of a United States of America? We both were in the Milky Way and were hit by <u>dark energy</u>? <u>How can we create a stable state like our old Solar System?</u> So our eros is not selfish like a <u>Ahab</u> or a <u>Faust</u>? Can we permit dark energy70% of the Universe to peacefully co-exist? It doesn't threaten our Solar system? Let's explore our Solar system, and let the rest of the Galaxy take care of itself? Dark energy is not a threat to our sun? There seems to be an energy outside of our solar system, just let it be? More poetry.

-3-

The solar system theory of the atom, says the sun is like the atom with electrons or planets going around the center, like the Euro. This old theory was the theory of Mr. Rutherford, spinning in my head. Atoms take in light, like the sun gives off lights. I can't really grasp this tropic poetry, But it is so fantastic I can hardly stand it. <u>The people of earth are like 70% dark energy, like a world democracy, formed already at the United Nations.</u> Let the United Nations have more power to deal with the 70% people of the world to take command of them. It's a fallacy of analogy. If it isn't, let the UN take care of them.

Unlike electrons in atoms, why don't planets jump down an orbit? The answer is gravity, like with dark matter and black holes. To be talked about later. <u>This we all take for granted, like the continued existence of the United States of America and it's Bill of Rights. Like the gravity of the Constitution that unites The states into one Union, states going round and round Washington, the original intent of the Founding Fathers. Playing with the meaning of Federalism?</u> We all being like a type of galaxy? How will dark matter help? What is it?

Light hits atomic matter. Like in the solar system theory. Uncertainty or doubt is essential to science as it is to law. This goes against the grain of most ideology belief in Zen, where the assumption is taken for granted. But doubt that a defendant is guilty, sets him free. The state has the burden to prove the defendant is guilty.

- - -

Uncertainty, or doubt that a law was broken, is like physics in prediction the position of an electron. We just don't know, That said of a defendant, sets him or her free. That is the essence of Physics. Like the knowledge of a Doctor of laws. The defendant is innocent, beyond a reasonable doubt, thus he goes free. This is bigger than my tropic poem. It's Zen. What words can you offer to talk with Asia? What is our dark matter? Is it helping our solar system? Do black holes help our Solar System model? Doubt? is there Answer, denial.

Doubt that energy will go right or left, is the realm of the physicist. Likewise, doubt that the charge, or paradigm, is related to the facts of mistake of fact, sets the defendant free. The ideological mind, on the jury, for example, almost can't grasp this concept, having spent all their adult life knowing absolutely that Zen exists? What is doubt? How can I find the defendant not guilty beyond a reasonable doubt? What is the connection between Zen and Law and Science? To hunt the Red in the mid East, you need a cover, the orient.

- - -

I doubt. I got my masters degree from the school that split the atom which allowed the US to win World War II. Electrons, of an atom, are dealt with on such a theory of doubt. That's universal. It's uncertainty, with atoms and state law, that ironically lead to gravity linked stable states. So fantastic I can hardly stand it. Art IV of the US con law.

<u>Photons, proved as waves of light, can't be doubted</u>? An expert witness can be called to set up a scientific experiment proving their existence? I take the fifth amendment.

Like the right to drive a car or the right to fly a plane? Some things in science and law should not be doubted. Photons hit the atom.

Who can <u>doubt</u> the existence of self-regulating economic systems? I do. I am not your Adam Smith. That was the basic assumption of the market economy as seen by a conservative. With the Treaty in my mind? Who is the next President? And beyond 2020?

It is impossible to predict elections. All I could do was be a bipartisan Independent, and vote my conscience. To stop the class war that would result if fiscal conservatives at a federal resolve of the revolution level got their way? That's my status, and I know it's confusing as all heck, but that's the way it went down. With civil rights.

Protest against wrongs in interpretation of doubt at law is in my state constitution.

Heisenberg's indeterminacy principle kept coming.

Science like law has doubt written in it blueprints? I thought about ideology and the politics of law as to the doubt beyond a reasonable doubt that my client is guilty? I doubt that the charges are valid? Can you say, I doubt therefore I am?

There is a difference between a paradigm, or charge, and the facts as witnessed. The paradigm is the Heisenberg. Rotation exists in electrons and planets. With so much spin. Ideological juries rotate around states and don't know doubt exists. I am instructing the jury? It's all backwards, you don't have to prove you are innocent at all? It's all on the state? And still all I hear is Rosa saying, Dada!

In one State's Constitution, it says that the people have the power to alter or reform government, like the police, because of mistakes of law. That is just as much now law as is magnetism or gravity. I come to see home, where I don't know, I thought in my poem. So fantastic I can hardly stand it. I rotate with a spin around that document. Yes, its in the Solar system and our Milky way It's just a different rotation and rule's the Universe. It's the rule of uncertainty and doubt? And the justice.

<u>Particles of light hit atoms the way the sun's light hits earth, or moon in the night.</u> In the politics of law, we want as much light as possible, just to show the doubt that in one or another case you didn't do it?

Like in one State's Constitution, I have been giving you my ideology for over 10 chapters, and the above states that nobody shall be held incompetent because of his ideological belief. Like a microcosm of life is in a tree swaying in the wind and the macrocosm is like a comet going past the earth. It's my ideological poetry. So fantastic I can hardly stand it. It states in one state constitution that you are protected if you believe in Zen, or don't.

-4-

Too many photons of light, can leave an atom in an agitated state. And in our poetry of the Solar System, we want stable states as much as possible. Blessed are they that have rotation for they shall find it. Have spin on me, Zen. According to your trope. Stable states are they that have enough photons. This poem is so fantastic I can hardly stand it?

A type of the sun of Rosa. Be not afraid, be of good cheer, oh bipartisan. Arise and take your bed, and go unto your place. He that is without mistake among you. Cast the first stone. Our band was the atom of the Galaxy? The general laws of the cosmos say that light is a relative absolute wave. <u>But time is relative, the sun hitting the moon, making time relative to other galaxies.</u>

Hence Einstein's theory of the relativity of time is proved, in our solar system, spinning around in my head, next to my Sherry, like a Rosa. Believing, you might have life in her name. Some photons make an electron leap down a shell, and cause an atomic unstable state. Fortunately see the solar system, and you are a scientist. <u>Just don't be afraid of doubt, it will spring you if ever you are a defendant and are</u>

charged, <u>the state needs to prove you are not guilty beyond a reasonable</u> <u>doubt</u>? Remember our talk such a long time ago in the second chapter about guilt, this is similar? For all the world.

In my next poem, the next night was simple. Of electrons leaping down a shell, as they rotate around the center of the atom. Either political party with its light, could create an stable state, like Social Security, as the status quo. An atom left, to go into the flatland, do not cast off the widow or the poor. I am Independent because I can talk to the leader on the other side, a Democrat, and get a dialogue, of poetry. Give to Rome what is its due, but don't hunt the handicapped. The cripple and the lame are electrons too. And seek a stable state. The status quo. Dire economic systems should not be allowed to remain unstable, to jump like an electron to an unstable state. Why would dark energy come to mind? Bertolt Brecht, like Lukas, put down the world Critical Theory of the German Frankfurt School. No Praxis. Civilization's Cultural Critique is wrong, in the minds of some, because it refuses "bad" practice.

- - -

The poor are not Buddha and the US is not China. They should not be allowed to leave the game. Ideological cripples, are those who would say that Zen does direct the world economy. Consider the lilies, we cannot eat them. Let the field keep them. <u>Like a Faust or an Ahab</u>. I still am a man of poor songs. Do I still believe in the "Song of Songs"? Like eros of Sherry and me on earth, revolving around the Sun, not around ourselves. Like Ahab. I just collect the evidence of States Right

Uncertainty in National economic debt, does not justify putting the weight on the old, Social Security being just a breakeven affair. George Washington would unite church and state, but George was not on the US Supreme Court. George would use the trope as a base to measure the poor and the old. So fantastic I can hardly stand it.

National health care is a cross for both parties? We found that you can't force down that electron, making an unstable state. The one with the loss having cause against the other. <u>It's the leap down of the electron,</u> <u>caused by a photon</u>. That gave a cause to the one party to make unstable

states. Like the nuclear bomb test, Mike. We began in the black dirt of South Africa? Where's the Evolution? Lucy?

We began in dirt, and after that it was photon after photon. Can the Euro stay together? Can Europe stay together? If not it will effect our own atom. Europe is presently like a falling electron? Because it knows Zen doesn't direct the economy? The alternative causes an unstable state? Like when Syria used chemical weapons.

- - -

They are on the eve of our atom. I pray we don't all turn into a wolf in the battle. Ideologists with your string theory, Zen help us, in the Cosmos, in the Universe. We move on into our wilderness of dark energy, in my tropic poem. We are moving towards Jerusalem, surely something was born. We will vote.

It's the ongoing republic. Europe, now not in the news, is slowly falling, France with US? Why did we not wait till spring, now we are all frozen up? Captain, oh my Captain, can't you see the wilderness child. Are we dead yet?

How is the company doing? We are starving. Wait the red cross of the Republic has come. Strings attached, the microcosm of the atom is like the macrocosm Zen. Order has returned, I can see through it now, or no I can't humanity makes itself yes. So fantastic I can hardly stand it.

The macrocosm of the company is like the microcosm of the Adam, I mean atom, will we fall into group homes? How will we feed ourselves? We must keep up the performance. Will there be another Revolution? Who will be its type of Gore? Why have we forgotten civil rights? Why can't I practice my tropes? What happened to my political economics? When? Are we like in outer space? What's the rainbow people of dark energy doing to us? Are we like Greece? Hungary? When?

Black body radiation today is a question still in light of motion physics? Light particles finally reached the revolution. Of electrons around the National Debt. Einstein's theory of photon reaction with atoms, remains with us still. It's the center or the Atom that is the problem? And we don't want a nuclear reaction, of protests. Vote.

We need excited atoms, to build a laser, the help to the going blind. Fermions are protons and neutrons. This is the center of the atom, an exact number of nucleons make for a stable nuclei, or society in our trope? Electrons are Fermions too? This was a major breakthrough in physics, as discovered when they split the atom, like high National note and protestors, neither party understanding, like Hungary's right wing state We need the "interpretation of context", live Ricoeur in suspicion of Civilization's Cultural critique, CCC. Like his "Hermeneutics of text". So that we will learn from the tropes of history, so as not to repeat the mistakes of the past. That's why we read. Erich Fromm and Walter Benjamin, with his cultural and literacy theory of Kafka, Baudelaire and Proust, point to the good aspects of our German School.

We want a stable state of economics, microeconomics and macroeconomics. Fermions were named by Enrico Fermi. Who split the atom in 1942. At the University of Chicago. The school that got 11 Nobel prizes in economics in the last part of last century. Economics and Physics being our Trope. The Harvard, as it were, of *The Just*.

<u>Electrons have rotation around the national note of the inside of the atom, just as planets, in our solar system, go around the sun. The sun is the national note. Giving us too much light putting us in an excited state?</u> The planets and electrons have spin, like subatomic particles, I come. So fantastic I can hardly stand it?

This is not history and I am not trying to falsify particle physics. Newton did that some 300 years ago? Mine is poetry from my <u>dream</u>, making tropes, non-literal metaphors, of time and space. In Chicago we swapped state for state, much the way you would exchange cultures in a scientific experiment, Mayan for Muslim?

An electron, like the people, is the sign of a stable state. Something Mayans did not have for a long time, as an archeology of their pyramid building will show. Earth, too, is like that electron. If a type of electron jumps down a shell, it could be like an atomic explosion, violent protests. Far from a stable state. Or in outer space, in a billion years from now, our solar system is on its last legs? This is like billions and billions of years from now. Don't worry.

<u>Nuclear structure is like the revolution of the earth's revolution around the sun</u>. If a comet, the Euro going bust, should hit the earth, it would be like an electron, of a special type, dropping down a shell, treaties unmade or broken, causing a nuclear reaction like an atomic bomb, or all out class war or protest for protest. What would make us like the Mayans? The people of the world. Bohr

Comets, with life on them, can change earth's nature. Enrico Fermi, of Chicago, determined the atomic structure to such an extent, he split the atom, like rebuilding factories in the US, so we would be like at least Japan, with no growth, but <u>exporting our goods</u>. Mr. Fermi's work led to the end of WW II, one wonders what the Chicago Economics department would do to such materialism? Of Sahlins, a Fermion?

Fermi was like an Einstein. Both saw the earth rotate from state to state, the comparison between the Chinese economy and the United States. As if hit by violent protests. Einstein made many contributions to Mechanical Physics, including the Impeachment of his own theories, which I will attempt. Coming home.

- - -

<u>Comets, violent protests, are like earthquakes. And they say that Comets killed off several species</u>. The way that Fermi's work led to the atomic bomb. He was not a Native American, but his work was like with hand in hand with the US Defense Department. So fantastic I can hardly stand it. California and Chicago.

<u>Rotation from state to state is what we are seeing in Europe, first Hungary went Fascist right wing then Spain went conservative, all because of the center of the atom, The National Note. It's like a small comet hit the Greeks. One wrong rotation, and the country goes split.</u>

<u>Like the US civil war</u>. The sign of Zen is the reverse of the Swastika, to the left angles, taken from Korean Buddhism. The Japanese made Korea a colony of it, before and during World War II. Also see Geach, Galaxy: Mapping the Cosmos on the universe beyond our Milky Way.

Rotation of subatomic particles could be a metaphor for the European system. Rotate of electron or planet, in a world that needs spin, and you create an unstable Euro, which in turn hits Wall street, and the world stock markets. Some time ago England split off from the Euro. Then, there was Brexit.

Neutrons, protons and electrons are now called Fermions. The understanding of which would probably give you a Prize in Physics? In our trope, a non-literal metaphor could be like different countries in Asia, the deciphering of which would give you India or China and you a prize in economics. It's way beyond me.

Electrons of the US are no longer just revolving around Europe. There are the Arab States, which need to be stable. Qatar, the richest country in the world, needs to be brought in to the US orbit, for example. They control the means of communication to the rest of the Arab states. So fantastic I can hardly stand it. Where is the Russian? Where is President Putin of Russia? Thinking about Ukraine?

It's Wall street, for sure. But not greed. It is just one more electron, with other world stock markets. That rotate and spin around the center of the atom, of Arab oil. And Arabia had its Arab spring revolution. Key to a stable state is keeping world atoms Stable. <u>This means not jerky movements towards Hungary. Or, at Iran. Or North Korea. We wantthem in the Solar System model of the United Nations that works.</u>

Rotation of states around other states, places too much pressure on certain states like Greece and Hungary. They are like in a pressure cooker. The whole system is like a complex atom tropes. Electrons around a complex atom. <u>These are the ones that form nuclear fusion or fission?</u> Pick your heart attack. Mayans or Syrians or Iranians or North Koreans or the refusal to talk in this place?

Magnetic fields are like US politics for us. We need a compassionate right to be bipartisan so as not to agitate the old, with Social Security, and the poor, like the old medicaid. It is out of necessity, so as not to create an unstable electron. Rotation of world stock markets spin from world state to state. And you'll never go hungry again. Wheat lots and lots or wheat, you can eat them like cereal or potatoes for dinner. Or staying in our own solar system, not worried about dark energy, billions of years from now.

Entanglement is like one atom combining with another, in the same space, that is the way I explain it. It's like world stock markets, not just Wall street, rising and falling in union. That's stock entanglement. My constitutional spin is good politics, bipartisan, for the Cosmos and Universe. The issue is how can we create a stable state.

- - -

<u>Bipartisan entanglement could create electrons that don't jump down from shell 7 to Shell 6, for example</u>? What could best stabilize them? What is to be done seriously with protests? Berkeley? We have a Republic with aspects of a democracy, entanglement. World Civilization is one big entanglement, ideological. How is an election like an above electron? How is that unwanted like dark energy in our solar system? What of the next election? In 2024 and beyond.

Even simple states, like in the South Pacific and Africa, have past entanglement with Europe, and are no longer simple states. Some have called this colonialism, which Africa had its Arab spring in the early 1960's. What we do on Wall street trickles down to them. Imperialism? Like electron leaps? Towards late capitalism? PC?

World entanglement is more the norm. Wall street is London's stock market. US stocks are the Japanese stock market. The global reach is so great it is in the best interests of the world to stop violent protests and keep our ears open, because we also are in a Democracy. How can we help Europe from being like the sun, and the planets like an Arab Spring? Will the next atom at a world level be color or otherwise blind? As if it were billions and billions, like dollars, of years from now? The Blues.

Science of doubt, says I shouldn't get involved in the heartbreaking business of political prediction. What will the last 4 years bring to the year 2020? It's an election year. I see a Muslim rotation and a China spin, neither predictive of that years election as of now? Bohr and Rutherford, we presume, meant the regular atom is like the solar system. Poetic, the Milky Way's dark energy can be assumed to be like the Arab Spring?

What Einstein, head swimming in the Universe, saw was that some things are not predictable. He called that Zen? How would you like to think the way he looked? He wrote a paper, falsifiable, where he said, in effect, the same. But he used math. That's so fantastic I can hardly stand it. To state again, to read the opposition critique of Frankfurt Critical theory and the like, means that the realist Lukacs, we can see in them their lack of praxis. There are two types. Illegal militant out of control protest. And other, know your enemy.

- - -

Einstein said the speed of light was basic and universal. And they are substantially so. Neutrinos named by Enrico Fermi, of Chicago, went a fraction of a fraction of a second faster than the speed of light. It was substantially the same. I always liked Einstein and the fact that he believed in Zen. And, this will kill you, he questioned his own theory the speed of light is basic and universally still the fastest thing round. Substantially so. Self-criticism is simple, see the Keynesian problem of cycles, and reread the first 12 chapters. That's the case of the Democrats.

-6-

The next night, I had the following mystic poem about the cosmos. An expanding supernova, in an expanding universe did not, I saw in my poem, falsify basic evolution, necessarily. In trillions of years, the Universe could end up in outer space filled with dark matter? Or, a universe filled with dark energy? What of South Africa? A democracy? Dark energy is like a South African reversal? Color represents the majority of the world and it could be an Achilles' Heel of our civilization, in event of a Mayan culture?

Light is an electromagnetic wave. In an expanding universe, we could expand into Nothingness. Caused, in part, by cosmic inflation, as a result of a big bang. They measure the light waves from a supernova, and from that conclude the universe is expanding, beyond the clouds of light? Zen started suffering and ended in "nothingness."

There were problems in my tropic poem. If there is no intention to the evolutionary-like universe, we can't say that there is an end that our universe is evolving to. We use the evolutionary model because that is closest to our creation, as seen by scientists, I reasoned in my tropic poem. I am like Wilson.

Science is safe with materialism. Universal evolutionary theory is a model that is not easily falsified, to be logical. I saw comets hitting the earth killing off large species. And the comets brought with them organic matter, that helped create more species? A comet hitting earth is like a supernova exploding from the big bang, I felt thinking of my wife next to me, in the cosmos? So fantastic I can hardly stand it?

Microcosm of atoms, matter. Is like the macro supernova? All filtered through in our brain, seeing solar energy and colors in the mind or brain, pulsating back and forth micro to macro then macro to micro. The electrons went around the atoms. And we went around and round the sun. Round and round in my trope. That's Blake and Bohr on the macrocosm in the microcosm, the selfish gene. Sociobiology?

Back to the macro, picture a cluster of stars, with a tail like a fuzzy dog. That's like my dream. That's a supernova, all in several colors. Except there is data like the data of third world people and their dreams, collected by linguistic anthropologists? Our mind is the filter between the macro-world and the micro-world? Like Peru?

This space between the micro and the macro universe, is the jurisdiction of the poet? Science is made up of oppositions. Resistance to contrary forces. Like the US celebrates on Jul 4th, sometimes you need to resist. Against a Franco. It's a contradictory paradigm, but one that gets me through my dreams, I thought almost waking up? Scientific paradigms evolve, why can't there be evolution at an organic level on some planet or comet? Life on other planets. Like dark energy going to the universe in a trillion years from now? Or, Zen knows what happened to the Mayan civilization?

If we go bankrupt in our micro universe, of the USA, like countries in Europe, the Saudis would love to take over. The same with China, though that is not their intent in holding 2 trillion in US debt. We all, in the long run, rotate around the sun, like we all rotate around the center of the atom, the people; dark energy, like anti-gravity, dark energy? So the Arab spring is not like an ideology metaphor? They being relatively <u>dark</u>? Like Nuer and Dinka over oil in Sudan.

And we have forgotten the gravity of the earth, and the moon's pull on the tides. Is that proof enough for some "intention" in the Universe? What I call Zen. Einstein called Zen something else. And its intention that most scientists say does not exist, I thought as me and my wife kissed. Was all of the Frankfurt school <u>all</u> wrong.

In that kiss, I was seeing swirls of supernova and black holes and the big bang, being drawn under by gravity, in space by dark mater and black holes, from some unknown source? But drawing some dark energy, of one of the big bangs? Dark matter keeps this expanding energy in check? Why call dark energy, dark energy? For the parody people. We want to read, so that we don't become part of illegal practice, praxis. So that if we do follow the constitution's solicitation to peaceful assembly and to petition the government for a redress of grievances, we don't become idiots or fools. That's why I write this tragedy.

- - -

I dreamed, the "intention" of black holes and dark matter, gravity, should keep the planets of the stars from expanding to nothingness? This was my metaphor, of a micro stable state, both in physics and tropics on earth? But dark energy, anti-gravity, is like anti-structure, the will of the people? That's why we are in a Democracy? In the long run, the classics say that's the best. Biden won the election.

<u>The next poem was that the material force of gravity should be relative between one galaxy and another</u>? That's the relativity of gravity? Dark energy, over 70% of outer space, will determine the fate of the Universe? Notwithstanding the poetry of my dream, it's we the people

in order to form a perfect union and the poetry of paradigms? Like the relatively peaceful Egypt? Hopefully we can reach a stable state and dark energy is understood better? And there is a fallacy of analogy with political states and states in physics? Yes.

My poem continued, the tides and gravity are so "intentional", people have been set free on less evidence than that. Like with the *Fiddler On The Roof.* Gravity is no match to cosmic inflation. Notwithstanding my hope in my metaphor? Plus dark energy? There being a colorful Metaphor for dark energy? In the wild one, Brando was asked - what are you rebelling against? His response reflects modern thought when he said, what have you got???? Not The Articles of Confederation, I hope?

The moons of Mars or Saturn probably have a different relative gravity, I dreamed in my poetry? That is like Europe? Things get worse now than in 2008? And the will of the gravity of the people there could be like for them, black energy, anti-gravity that causes the Galaxy to expand at an non-sustainable speed? Or the United States of America? I don't want to project the gravity and tides of our situation onto Saturn? The Galaxy of Europe is not like the Universe of the rest of the earth? Our solar system is safe? It's just that in the long run, we hope that the 30% Dark matter, Republics, will stop a Libya in the bud? So fantastic I can hardly stand it? Syria's Homs? US?

<u>The universal evolution of colors discovered at Cal, lead one to speculate on the way a scientist's cultures make them view, the moving colors of a Supernova, exploding.</u> Some scientist, in India for example, might see black where others do not, from the US. As to the naming of dark energy? It's the people in South Africa?

While evolution is grounded and different from cosmos expansion, the tropic poetry of my dreaming went on? It's the 70% of the people that could cause dark energy to throw a Greece into an Egypt? The 30% of the National Guard, in the US, that is like dark matter may not be able to stop the dark energy, symbolic of the people of the world? This is a poem theory of a stable state, like the Solar system? Politics not going on to dark energy? There are two state systems of poetic physics and politics. The solar system which is a stable state? And the Universe as an unstable dark energy mass?

Though I am not the same as The Limits of Critique, I agree we need to get to a "post critical" interpretation of suspicion that looks for reorientation, energetic participation and refressed perception through defamiliarization, in this anti-novel. A Professional group of astronomers on Earth just claimed to have taken a photo of the "blackhole" in the center of the milky way galaxy. What would Hawkings say?

-7-

<u>If scientists could falsify the dark energy theory, we could draw comfort from the micro level stability of states</u>? Dark energy is on a macro level, in outer space. We see our signs or metaphors and want our poetry to help in our tropes of <u>physics</u> and economic <u>politics</u>. We can draw comfort that dark matter will help in the like cosmic inflation of dark energy. <u>Or can we forget the dark energy of the Universe, as a poetic model of a unstable state</u>? And just concentrate on our Solar system? As enough?

The relativity of time, as seen in the light of our moon, and the light of a moon of Mars, is a sign of peace, in my poetry, I thought, the cosmos swimming in my head. Time is relative, a no-brainer? Light hits us as different from the planet Mars, and the effect of its moons sheds light at a different wave? What is my neurosis.

<u>The relative absolute speed of light, is not really falsified by neutrinos? Fractions of a fraction faster than Einstein's theory of the speed of light, he is relatively correct</u>. The new neutrino could be like a discovery of the slower speed of dark energy, the present paradigm proved incorrect? This I say, from a Republic? The Democracy being the people? Is there dark energy between Earth and the Sun? If so, then why isn't the solar system doing out of control? Gravity.

Contradictions exist, for example, between my tropic poetry of evolution, in the cosmos, and the ever expanding universe theory? All of these theories are rather new and changing all the time? Like on planets in or outside of the galaxy. *The Structure Of Scientific Revolutions* shows us how scientific paradigms change, now in 50 years or so, in

Physics? Of Bohr and Rutherford. Can't we exclude the dark energy in the Universe, for poetic sake of stability of the microcosm? And think of the Solar System the yang to the yin of the Atom, that ever changing mod? The above is the Limits of Critique.

We kissed and I said, and if comets bring organic matter to planetsin our or other galaxy, evolutionary life should be found on other planets. We kissed, the galaxy swimming in our heads. My theorem is that there is evolution in the in the cosmos or life in other places in the universe, not everywhere but in parts.

Due to Dark matter and black holes, the theory of an ever expanding universe is questioned, if there is something wrong with the dark energy model, which is possible? The point is that we want a poetry of physics that says we have a stable Universe. I assume this, whatever, in my dream and poetry? Like the poetry of the solar system. Or, am I totally wrong? And we don't need to negate the dark energy model, because the macrocosm of the Solar system, and not the irrational universe, is enough? Hawking, of Cambridge, sees that dark another way.

This has nothing to do with Einstein or Zen? It's poetry and we need a stable model so the micro model of electrons dropping from shell #7 to shell #6, which caused Mike, isn't a model we have to take as normal? Nuclear explosions are not the norm of the macro universe? And we don't need their theory messing up tropic poetry?

The ever expanding universe, rule by the people, is questioned as a paradigm? I no Physicist, I am a poet waking up out of a dream? And the universal nature of 70% of outer space making up dark energy is too much like the 10% cosmic inflation, caused by the big bang? What caused the dark energy?, I asked, as my head went into the cosmos. Or, in the William Blake model of the macrocosm is the Solar tropic, and not the Universe? The same with the Bohr and Rutherford theory of the Yang system to the Yin electrons and planets go round and round and round like system of the atom? So given the stability of our Solar system, we Don't need to worry about dark energy in the Universe, as to what will happen, in 1 trillion years from now, with the takeover of the people, in our poetic model? Making western civilization like the Mayan ruins?

Totally awake, I said color perception among peoples of the world is evolutionary and universal. I held the hand of my Sherry. It came out of Berkeley. Think of it as the opposite of the relativity of time and space.

Part of that universal, is exceptions, like the people in Hong Kong. What if there are exceptions to dark energy?

We need to remember my tropic poem of a stable solar system. Not worry that in a trillion years, the universe will expand to nothingness. Now we are safe with our vision of Solar system. Back to a human level, what if a people can't see the color red, for example? Like the people found by the Berlin and Kay theory, at Cal, Berkeley? Like Hawking?

Different people looking through a telescope can be like color blind? Like to the color red? Certain people can fail to see certain colors because their language did not encode the color like red? This bias would not be universal. We should not be so color blind so as to fail to make treaties with all the Arabs? Perhaps a certain people can't see a red people? Maybe for Western Civilization, we can't see dark? Rosa. With the paradigm of Berlin and Kay, Einstein's work is also poetic, like with the photoelectric effect of the sun at a macro level. Does it also work at the Micro level? Fiat Lux.

This book is a "Cultural critique" of american and european civilization. We side with professor REICH that we shall solve the "crisis" through democratic history instead of idealogical OLIGARCHY. there is hope in symbolism of US consitutional law.

The Voting Rights Acts   has passed the House, but not the Senate, as of now. No Nation-wide mail-in votes. No extended time for voting. No National day off for voting, perhaps on Saturday.

An Electors Reform Act needs to be passed. So state Republican, State Congresses should be stopped by 2024 from changing electors for electors of their choice.

A truth in Elections Act to keep candidates and internet companies from passing misinformation. This would be a Universal Federal Act, too.

A Universal Immigration Act with limits should be passed. Regulate the Federal Reserved and Banks.

The last 40 years has made the bottom 90% poor with no unionization.

Regulation Acts at the federal level like the Glass -Steagall Act, past in the 1930's depression was destroyed by the top. 10% of the population and led to 2008 crash.

During a strike like the COVID-19 plague, never should power be taken away from Federal Jurisdiction; and given to states rights. The US had the highest death rate in the world by now-almost 1 million.

The way that things got so screwed, among other structural and constitutional reasons, was that Trump during the 2020 election politicized the wearing of masks and the taking of vaccines. As of now, there was a correlation in some states between Republicans and those who would not get a vaccine, or those who hated masks that helped the- Big Denial! America is at the crossroads in 2024 and beyond.

It is crazy. Facts are brought by one party, as seen as lies by the other party, with the change of power in who controls the House. With the question at issues, who betrayed the US and who can bring charges. Black colors are called the color white with public figures like Trump, taken as political prisoners. This has become the continuing business as usual, with evidence as clear as Cal's nuclear fusion been denied existence as if the darkest night were seen as if it were bright as the sun also rising.